“Do you

Alena look ... a long swallow of her coffee. “If he were alive. Maybe.” She shrugged. “But if he were alive, he’d be pretty much out of my age range.”

“What, hundreds of years old?”

“Nah, probably more like sixty-five or so.”

Deb’s eyes narrowed. “That’s not dead very long, then.”

“Nope, only, let’s see, 1968...about forty years. Does it make a difference?”

Deb leaned in, her eyes widened. “You mean he told you exactly when?”

“Yeah. I brought his record, here.” She unfolded the copy of Joe’s record from the Vietnam Wall site.

Deb pulled out her reading glasses and scanned it. “Holy shit.”

“You said the S word!”

“So sue me. Can I keep this?”

“Sure, I have other copies.” She’d made ten, just to be sure she wouldn’t forget. As if she would. Ever.

“I’ll take this to John, but Lena, be careful.”

“Careful of what?”

Deb shook her head, removing her glasses and nibbling on the end of one earpiece. “There’s something to what you told me; it reminds me of some case I’d read about, but I just can’t remember what it is.”

“It’s not a good something?”

“I don’t know, but it may be. Not good, that is. Anyway, just be careful, okay? Don’t spend all your time with this, ah...”

“Dead guy.”

“Is that what you call him?” At least the twinkle was back in Deb’s eyes.

“No,” she said, looking directly into Deb’s eyes. “I don’t.” She reached behind for her coat and purse. “I call him Joe.”

Praise for
Carolina Montague's *DOOR IN THE SKY*

"*DOOR IN THE SKY* is not the typical fare found in today's romance market. It is a complex romantic adventure laced with paranormal elements, richly populated and beautifully written."
~*Madeline Hunter*

"*DOOR IN THE SKY* is peopled by corrupt clergymen, witches both good and evil, and gallant knights for an intense, memorable reading experience. This richly detailed novel is filled with magic, tenderness, sensuality, and violence."
~*Romantic Times Magazine*

Sacred Guardian

by

Carolina Montague

This is a work of fiction. Names, characters, places, and incidents are either the product of the author's imagination or are used fictitiously, and any resemblance to actual persons living or dead, business establishments, events, or locales, is entirely coincidental.

Sacred Guardian

Contact Information: info@thewildrosepress.com

Cover Art by *Angela Anderson*

The Wild Rose Press
PO Box 708
Adams Basin, NY 14410-0708
Visit us at www.thewildrosepress.com

Publishing History
First Black Rose Edition, 2010
Print ISBN 1-60154-714-5

Published in the United States of America

Dedication

To the real Joe, killed in action in 1967,
who, through Divine Intervention, saved my life
and the life of my child

Author's Note

This is a work of fiction but is based on a miracle that really happened to me. Angels exist.

Prologue

Quang Tri Province, Vietnam, 1968

He shouldn't have stepped on the clear patch of ground. It was smooth, swept clean. That should have warned him.

Joe Littlehawk halted at the ragged edge of the clearing, held his hand up, fist curled, and waited while the others bunched behind him. A crumpled cigarette pack lay half buried next to the level patch of earth. Lucky Strike—he could just make out the label—but his men knew better than to leave anything behind, anything Charlie could use. He stared at the soiled red and white wrapper, glanced around the cleared space at long, sharp grasses still clinging to earth blasted by mortar and shell, by napalm. Jungle coiled around the clearing in a tight, blue-green embrace. Moisture rising from the ground joined sweat sliding from under his helmet and made a slick track down his forehead. He blinked salt from his eyes and crouched, scanning the ground around the discarded packet.

"Hey, Tracker Joe," Lucas whispered. "Why we stopping?" He shifted his M16, resting his elbow on his hip, pointing the rifle upward, and peered past Joe toward the jutting ridge, the last barrier between them and the base at Khe Sanh. "Something wrong?"

He looked up. "Maybe nothing." It was getting dark. The men behind him were nothing more than grimy shadows and gleaming, jittery eyes. "Maybe something." They were about a thousand meters from base. "I'll check it out." He was tired, all the way to his tailbone. You made mistakes when you were tired.

"Oh, man!" Lucas stepped past him into the clearing. "Cigarettes!"

"No!" He rose to his feet and lunged for Lucas, just missed his arm. "Get back here. It could be booby-trapped." Damn pothead was always diddy-bopping around.

Lucas grunted, but fell back when he entered the clearing. "Sure thing, Chief." The rifle swung down and he grasped it in a shooter's stance, one hand on the trigger grip, the other under the barrel. "You're the point man."

He moved toward the cigarette wrapper. If there were trip wires, he couldn't see them, though that didn't mean it was safe to pick the packet up. Sometimes Charlie left a little surprise inside stuff the GIs discarded. A closer look would tell him if a toe-popper slept beneath the crushed wrapper, waiting for an American hand or foot to set it off. He leaned toward it, gently nudged the edge with the tip of his rifle. Looked okay, but he couldn't leave it for the Vietcong to come along and use it to set a trap. Better to retrieve.

His left foot pressed into the red soil, through the soft, squishy yielding of swept ground. The toe of his boot met slick metal that gave when he shifted his weight forward. A dull, thumping click shivered the air and traveled from his foot to his teeth. Every muscle stiffened. Even his eyelids tightened.

His men were waiting. He swallowed. The click from his dry throat mingled with the rustle of flak jackets behind him.

"Listen up." His voice was low, but steady, thank God. "I want you all back fifty meters." The air in his throat curdled, but he squeezed the words out. "It's a pressure mine." Couldn't move. "I stepped on it." He couldn't even turn to see if they had obeyed him.

"What?"

"God!"

"Sheeeiiittt."

The last voice was Lucas, for sure.

He took in a breath. "Back. All of you. That's an order!"

A blend of voices murmured now, sounds of distress that melted into an uneven patter and clump of feet retreating. One voice whispered, "Hang on, Joe. We'll call for evac." The pop and sizzle of the radio flared with a statement of their position and faded as the radioman fled with the others.

He counted his breaths. The minute he lifted his foot, even shifted his weight, the mechanism would detonate, splattering him all over the clearing. Damn, his fingers were already sweating. Had to relax his grip on the rifle, but not too much. No telling what movement would set this mine from sleep to explode. He eased off on his hold, one finger at a time, until he had the rifle firm in his grasp, not in a death grip.

Red spots floated across his vision. Had to get himself under control. He closed his eyes and forced his lungs to pump in a steady rhythm. Stay still. Stay alive.

He puffed air through his teeth in slow spurts. His breathing smoothed.

Hold on.

Concentrate, he needed to concentrate. His eyes were still closed. Should be okay to open them now. He blinked once, twice, and focused on the ridge, a spiked, raw curve looming above the clearing. Indigo and emerald rain forest clung to the rise and crowned the top.

So many different kinds of green here in Vietnam. He'd written this to his sister after he'd arrived two years ago. Brilliant neon green young ferns nestled among tired old ochre and olive grasses and shiny deep emerald palms. You just don't find these kinds of green in South Dakota. Would he see home again? Hell, he'd give it his best. How long would it take for evac? Could they neutralize the mine under his foot?

Just don't move, be still. Stay alive. His mama would want him to stay alive. That was all she said when he left home: *Just keep breathing, Joe.*

Pray. He could pray.

"Hail Mary, full of grace, the Lord is with thee. Blessed art thou among women and blessed is the fruit of thy womb, Jesus." His lungs clutched. *Hiyá*! No hiccups, please. Slow down.

"Holy Mary, Mother of God, pray for us now and at the hour of our death." But life would be better, Mother Mary. Latin—he should say it in Latin. "*Ave Maria, gratia plena. Dominus...*" He faltered. The Latin—he used to know this! "*...benedicta.*" What was the rest?

Well, if he couldn't pray, he could breathe. He took in air, slow and careful. The fetid kiss of the jungle delivered the faint garlic and spice aroma of *n'oc mam* from Ta Cong village and the bite of kerosene-soaked dung from the base, not so very far away. Why couldn't he remember the Latin? His right hand went into spasm mode. He flexed the fingers one by one to loosen them. All those hours in front of the nuns, and he couldn't even remember the Ave Maria.

Well, he could become a tree, grow roots, like Grandfather Mato Ohanko, Quick Bear, had taught him. He stared at his toes and pictured woody tendrils sprouting, sinking into the soil. The tremor in his hands ceased. *Hópo*. Now what animal could freeze and remain perfectly still for a long time? Gopher? Weasel? Rabbit? He carefully lifted the medicine bag threaded through a leather thong around his neck. His grandfather had given it to him when Joe received his Lakota name.

"Better forget gopher and rabbit." Though he was still Joe to the outside world, among his people, he was Wambli Ska—White Eagle. "Eagles eat rabbits," he whispered into the medicine bag. Grandfather Swift Bear said the power objects inside the bag were supposed to keep him safe from bullets.

"We should have added safety from bombs to the protections in here, Grandfather." He let the bag gently drop to his chest.

With the flurry of powerful, blunt wings, a fishing owl took flight.

His thigh bunched; his leg listed to the right.

A crisp snap shot upward, sucking air in a greedy frenzy. Dazzling, white heat streaked out and threw the dense wall of jungle into screaming brightness. The medicine bag flew outward, ripped from his neck, and tumbled end over end, coming to rest at the edge of the clearing.

****

Flying, he was flying. Way above the ground. But no tangled jungle lay beneath him, just a rolling stretch of grasslands streaming in a golden ripple toward the horizon. Like the South Dakota prairie. What the hell was he doing here? Where was Khe Sanh? Must be dreaming, or maybe there was something special in the dope Lucas was smoking the other night. OJ, they called it—dope soaked in opium. He didn't smoke any, but he heard the fumes could get you. Might as well enjoy this dream, but Jesus, Joseph, and Mary! How the hell would he get down?

He floated in a slow circle and looked for a place to land, but air pushed up and buffeted his face. Someone was flying below him, climbing to his altitude with golden, blinding wings beating in a powerful surge. Oh, man, now a guy with wings! The other soldiers always said he must be *dinky dau*, really crazy, especially when he greeted the sun each morning with the song his grandfather had given him. But didn't this beat all? Cool dream.

He looked down at the grace and vigor of the man's flight. Now that he looked closer, the wings were more like fingers of light, four broad and sinuous strands that flowed from the middle of the guy's back and spread out into thinner strands, glowing fluorescent tubes that could bend and move in ways he'd never seen.

"Now isn't that the damnedest thing?" Tubular wings. He'd heard of some pretty weird experimental aircraft, but never anything like a birdman. He tipped his head and watched. The guy seemed to know how to use his flying gear. The gilded, glowing wings rose and fell in a perfect arc.

Maybe they were right; he was crazy for sure if this was not a dream, but he wasn't about to let some *wasicun*, some white guy, outdo him. No way! He pushed out, extended his arms all the way, then banked and came around.

The man flying up to him looked Greek, or maybe Italian. He had the chiseled face you saw in statues, and golden brown hair streaming in the wind. Come to think of it, Joe had been spitting out hair blowing into his mouth for a while now. He reached up and grabbed a hank, then stared at the strands of long coarse black hair in his hand. For the past two years, it had been short, marine regulation length. Now it flowed to his shoulders, as he had worn it before he enlisted. He slanted a glance at the guy flying next to him. Looked familiar, but he couldn't place him.

"Those are some wings you got there, bro."

The man turned his head and beamed a killer smile. His eyes were a riveting green, dark and intense, the kind of green you see in young pine trees, not the color you find in eyes.

"You *would* say that."

What the hell? Great. A guy with a bug up his ass.

"Sure, man. Right. You got any idea how much time I have till wake-up call?" He hoped it was a long time. He loved flying dreams.

The guy said nothing. Looked pained, though, like he'd swallowed a nail. The wings undulated and beat harder, sending Joe's hair swirling into his eyes.

Forget this. "*Incoming!* Dive, dive, dive!" He spun around and fell straight down, leading with his head and pulling up at very last moment before he hit the ground, skimming along the feathery tips of golden grain beneath his belly.

"Yeeeehaaw!" *Hiyà* this felt good!

"Joseph."

The name rang in his ears. "What the…" Even his CO didn't call him *Joseph*. He rolled, sank into the wheat, flattening it, and looked up. The winged guy had followed him all the way to the ground. Looked pissed off again.

"What's up, big guy?"

Big Wing took him by the hand and jerked him to his feet.

"Hey…" He pulled on his hand but the fingers that dug into his skin were stone hard.

"I see I have been remiss."

The wings no longer beat. They belled out from the guy's back and draped to the ground. Bundles of light formed each strand, and a humming pulsed toward Joe from their tips.

"What is this?" He glanced at the restless ends of the filaments, flashing indigo lights bleeding to red and sapphire. The humming increased in volume. There was something weird about the sound. He could *taste* it. But how could that be?

"What are you, anyway, the purple people-eater?" He chuckled but the sound of his own voice grated. "I mean…Uh, you said *remiss*?"

The man pinned him with his gaze and dropped his steel-trap grasp on Joe's arm. "Welcome to the afterlife, Joseph Littlehawk," he said, then stuck out his hand. "I'm Ramael. Your guide."

Chapter One

Present Day

Alena Morgan reached into her pocket and yanked out a crumpled bill, a wad of old AC Transit transfer tickets, a number two pencil, and a grungy stick of Juicy Fruit gum. She smoothed out the worn picture of George Washington. Her last dollar. Sorry-looking old thing. She'd just blown eight bucks on a Bay Area Rapid Transit return ticket for herself, and another four on one for her three-year-old son, Michael. He sat kicking the seat in front of him while the BART train slowed, bucked, and pulled into its smooth slide and teeth-wrenching jerk as it came to a stop at the Fremont station.

She scrunched her eyes against the headache gripping the base of her skull and jammed the dollar, pencil, and gum back into her jeans. She opened her eyes, wadded the old transfer tickets in her hand to throw away, and rose from her seat. Should give the dollar to Michael. Maybe he would be able to buy some crazy popcorn or something with it.

"End of the line, Michael-my-boy." She slung Michael's backpack over her shoulder and pulled him up from his seat, entering the throng of passengers disembarking. Baby-fine hair trickled over Michael's collar. She smoothed it back from his neck and blinked away a hot prickle in her eyes. Friday evening. She looked up and herded Michael through the doors before they sounded the warning bell and whooshed shut. End of the line. The early spring scent of wet cement and bus exhaust puffed into her face as she stood on the brick platform.

"Will Auntie Deb be here? Where is she?" Michael broke away from her hold on his shirt and barreled down the staircase, toward the street outside.

"Michael!" She sprinted in his wake. "Goddammit, get back here!" She spilled apologies to people she brushed past. A few drew back from her in alarm. She snorted and the ring in her right nostril shook. Probably should have worn something with sleeves. The long line of earrings studding her ears, the spiked hair, the nose ring, and the Greek caduceus tattoo, two snakes wound around a winged staff, that climbed up her left arm never failed to freak some people, even in California.

She leaped three steps to the bottom of the stairs, catching her breath when the headache jabbed at the back of her eyes when she landed, and raced after Michael. Her son never did anything by half measures. He was born at a dead run. She grabbed his arm just before he could slip under the turnstile and held him close.

"Remember the rules about riding trains, Michael?" She fed the machine first his ticket, then hers. "We've gone through this before. You gotta know the rules." She'd taught her baby all the rules she knew. "Gotta follow them too."

Just because she hadn't followed rules for most of her life didn't mean Michael couldn't. She wanted him to have a good life. A clean life. The life she never had. He wriggled against her as they slid through the turnstile.

"Okay, buddy, we're almost there."

Deb stood just beyond the station entrance, sending blue plumes of woodsy smoke from her stubby cigar into the air. Alena's feet stuttered to a halt as Michael tore out of her grasp and pelted toward her best friend in the whole world.

"Auntie!"

Deb crushed her cigar under her heel, dropped to her knees, and opened her arms wide. Her sea-foam green shirtwaist dress billowed out. Jet beads strung with silver moons and stars swung from her neck.

Her friend Deb was a large woman, ample and soft everywhere. Not pretty. She stared while Deb rocked Michael back and forth and made sloppy raspberry sounds against his neck.

No, Deb wasn't pretty. Pretty was too small a word for her. Deb was, well, splendid. Incredible. Shining with comfort.

She forced her feet to drag across the pavement to where Deb and her son crouched as pain crept from the base of her skull to behind her left eye. "Hey, Deb." She rearranged her face into a smile and knuckled moisture from her eye. Damn. Cinders from the goddamn tracks. Or maybe smoke from Deb's latest find. "Whatcha smokin' now?"

Deb's eyes sparkled up at her. "Astral Perfeccion." She rumpled Michael's hair. "Honduran." She scraped the remains off the cement, stood, and hobbled over to the sand-filled trashcan, with Michael attached to her left leg.

Of course. "That's cool, Deb." Only Deb would combine her passion for New Age spirituality with her love of tobacco. "Just don't smoke it in the house around Michael, okay? I mean, I stopped smoking when I had him." And the smoke was starting to elevate the migraine that still beat against the back of both her eyeballs now.

Shit. She'd just taken a shot of Zamatrex. It had to last until she got back home, it just *had* to.

"I never smoke around him." Deb tossed the cigar bits into the container and wrapped her arms around Michael, enveloping him. "I don't even burn incense around you, do I, Michael?"

"Are you sure you want to take him for the night?" The sight of Michael in Deb's arms seemed to ease the throbbing in her head. "You sure? All night?" Her smile slipped when Deb looked up at her. "He can be a fu...ah, well, a little maniac." She crinkled her eyes and showed her teeth in her best attempt at a grin. Great. She must look like a real moron now.

"Give me a break! Hey, Michael—you can be a triple maniac, you hear?" Deb squeezed Michael and smiled. "Where are his things?"

"Things." She peeled her fingers from his backpack. "Oh, yeah. Here. Pants, underwear, socks, shirts, an extra pair of shoes." She handed it to Deb. "And his stuffed dolphin, Chuckie." The headache started to thump against her teeth, thrum, thrum, thrum... "He never sleeps without Chuckie." *Damn*! She rubbed her temple.

Deb stared up at her. "Alena, you could come with us. I mean, we'll eat popcorn and watch *Shrek* or some old show on DVD. We wouldn't mind having your mom join us, would we?" She nudged Michael.

"Nope. She can come." He was fingering Deb's beads and didn't even look up. "Stay with us, Mommy."

"No. Sorry, baby." The lower lid of her right eye twitched. She looked away. "I have a lot to do. A bunch of job applications, you know." When she turned back, she had control of her face again. "It's too boring for you. You'll have more fun with Auntie Deb." At least she could do something productive if the headache decided to retreat. *Go away. Just a little. Please?*

Deb shrugged. "I still think you should try the university. After all..."

"Yeah, right. I will." If she could concentrate long enough to fill out the application.

Deb was staring at her again, brow crinkled.

Better be on her way. She extended her hand toward Michael. "Hey, how about a hug, huh?" She knelt down and took Michael from Deb, buried his face against her chest. "Be good, Michael." Mustn't let him see the way she gritted her teeth against the pain. His face still had a little baby-plumpness, a delicious, soft resilience that always brought a lump to her throat. "Mind your Auntie Deb." Now the goddamn lump threatened to choke her. "Eat your dinner," she managed to croak, then nuzzled the space beneath his chin and took a long breath of the warm, salty sweetness of her boy. "And, oh yeah, right. Brush your teeth."

She blinked hard and pulled herself away. One hand trailed up across his ear to the top of his head, then hung in the air when he bounced over to the outside ticket machine.

Deb took her hand. "Alena?"

"Huh?"

"Are you okay?" Deb's fingers squeezed and released her hand. "I mean, the headache isn't back, is it?"

"No, Deb." *The headache isn't back, it never left. It's always there, even when I sleep*. "I'm stylin'. I'm okay." Her mouth was dry; her lips caught on her teeth.

Deb wavered. "Well, if you're sure."

"I'm sure." If her goddamn smile got any wider, she would split. She needed this time to go through what should be done. She just *hated* asking for help. If she could only get through this, get a job, she wouldn't need to beg. She felt like such a wuss. It was only a headache, right? *Right, just a ten on the Richter scale for the past two years with puking my guts out as a daily event.* When Michael was around, it was so hard to mask the pain while she worked on trying to find a solution, trying to think through all her options. Once she had a chance to do this, she could talk to Deb.

Deb reached for Michael and tugged him away from the ticket line. "C'mon, Michael. Time to boogey."

"You have a good time, Michael. And don't torture your Auntie Deb."

Deb held Michael close. "Let's go, kiddo."

She gulped against the burning in her throat. "Take care of him, right?" Zamatrex always did that. It usually kicked back the pain, though. Usually.

"Oh, I will, Alena." Michael squirmed and Deb planted a kiss on his head. "I'm his designated auntie, aren't I?"

"Yeah, Deb." Her back started to tremble. She forced herself to slump, to release the tension that came from her rigid stance. "You are."

"Well, we should let your mom go back home to Berkeley." Deb stood and grabbed Michael's wiggling hand. "Let's wave together, now. Bye-bye."

She lifted her hand and watched the two traipse off into the parking lot. She held her eyes wide. Wide and dry. Her lower lip trembled. But she stood tall. Just like when she had her nose and tongue pierced. Like when she had the dragon tattoo etched deep into her right breast. Hurt like hell, but she hadn't even flinched when she had that done. This stupid headache would *not* defeat her.

She lowered her hand.

Aw, shit. She'd forgotten to give Michael the dollar.

****

The Zamatrex stopped working, *completely* stopped right about the time she slid her key into the door of her apartment. She stumbled headlong through the living room and into the kitchen.

"God. God. God." The pain never fucking stopped; it just faded a little, then roared out and swallowed her whole. Light from a bare bulb flooded the kitchen when she flicked the switch. She squinted against the spikes the light drove into her head.

"I need something to kill this before I get to the puking stage." The applications lay on her coffee table; many were complete, but what employer would hire a woman who lay shivering on her bed most of the day, struck down by pain that never ended?

"Only one more med to kick back the pain." She rested her hands on the counter. "This sucks."

She looked up and opened the cupboard. Two packages of macaroni and cheese stared her in the face. No other food. Nothing but ice cubes in the refrigerator. They'd used the last of the milk that morning. A bottle of vodka, the red and white seal unbroken, occupied the right corner of the middle shelf. A gift. She hadn't had any alcohol since she got pregnant with Michael, and after he was born, she found she'd lost her taste for it. The vodka had sat right there for, oh, maybe a year or so. The last of the Zamatrex lay hidden in back of the top shelf, out of reach of small hands. She stood on the tips of her toes, leaned in, and grabbed it.

The wrapper covering the nasal plunger went flying when her hand shook. She grabbed it and peered at the expiration date. Still had a few months to go. "When did I take the last dose?" She counted the hours, using her fingers. Had she already taken some that morning? She rubbed her forehead; why couldn't she remember? She stood and tried to breathe the pain out, taking healing air inside, as Deb had once showed her at a bullshit New Age conference.

A sigh passed through her clenched teeth. Breathing just made it worse. *So much for New Age crap.* With the migraine this fierce, she couldn't possibly have taken a morning dose as well as the dose she took just a few hours ago, and maybe a little booze might dull the pain a bit, allowing her to function; she was sure alcohol didn't interact with Zamatrex.

After welfare cut her off, she'd gone to a doctor at the clinic and he'd given her all the samples of the expensive migraine meds he could find. "Damn, he was such a good guy. Why can't they all be like him?" He couldn't give her any more, though. It might endanger his license, and his clinic needed to be paid; she could no longer pay.

She set the injection plunger on the counter and reached for the vodka. The vodka bottle slipped when she lifted it and nearly fell out of her hand. Her breath hitched and she slowly put the vodka down on the counter, wiped her palms on her shirt. So far the migraine hadn't made her nauseated. Yet. It just made her want to cut her head off. She knew each stage of it. Nausea came last; she'd better hurry so she could actually get something done tonight.

Zamatrex first. She pulled the package apart and snorted the injection carefully, not allowing any of it to drip out. "Jeez. All those times my folks wanted me to do coke with them and I wouldn't snort it. Shit, who'd have thought I could have used *that* skill." She tipped her head back a bit and let the drug soak into her nasal membranes and trickle down her throat. It burned a little, but already the light from the kitchen bulb was a bit more bearable. "Excellent!"

The top of the vodka twisted off easily, thank God. She reached for a glass, but lowered her shaking hand. Straight out of the bottle would have to do. As quivery as she was, she might drop a glass and her vacuum had died; she didn't even have a decent broom. She didn't want to chance glass bits on the floor that might hurt Michael's feet.

The light in the front room shuddered and blinked. “Goddammit.” Bulb must be going. “Thought I just put in a new one. Oh well.” She shrugged and sat on her sofa bed and lifted the bottle to her lips. Vodka scorched a trail down her throat. When she lowered the bottle, she was a little dizzy, but the headache faded until it was only a throbbing at the base of her skull. *Thank you, thank you, thank you, thank you!*

She set the vodka on the battered coffee table in front of her and took up the partially completed application that rested on it. *Okay then.* She filled in her social security number, address and phone number, the date of her GED and the two college courses she'd taken.

“Job experience.” She filled in the time she'd been a waitress at Larry Blake's before she met David. Her David. Michael's father. The pen slowed.

She wiped at the dampness under her eyes. Damn allergies, anyway. She sniffed and looked up at the picture on the wall. It showed David holding Michael on his lap. She'd taken it right before…well, before. She coughed and rubbed at a growing tight band that gripped her chest, a pain that radiated all the way down her left arm.

“What the fuck?” Her heart was racing and skipping. Was it the alcohol? Couldn't be! She stumbled to her feet and grabbed the medication instructions. Her eyes could barely track.

“Huh?” It wasn't the little swallow of vodka; she was right—it didn't say anything about alcohol. She blinked and focused on breathing slow, forcing her splintered memory back to that morning. Michael was pokey getting dressed and she was still in bed. It was already ten in the morning and they needed to get ready so she could take him to Deb. She saw herself in her nightgown, reaching for the medication, contracted with the pain that lived in her day after day. “Shit!” She’d just gone and taken way too much Zamatrex. Better call 9-1-1.

Her whole body was shivering now. Something frigid and damp ran along her arms and twisted around her neck. For a moment, her stomach twitched and her heart quivered with something that felt like fear.

Stupid, stupid! She should have remembered that she’d already taken a dose that morning. You had to make sure twenty-four hours had passed before taking a third dose. She drew in a trembling breath. Getting enough air into her lungs was really tough and it felt like her chest was on fire. She lifted her hand and tracked its movement. It looked like she had several hands, all of them drifting through the air, one after the other. Couldn’t even punch the right numbers on her phone. It took two times before she thought she actually got 9-1-1.

She slipped to the floor and clutched the receiver in her hand. “Help me,” she whispered. “Please.” All she could hear was the purring ring of a phone somewhere on the other end of her line. Had she really gotten the number right? Her chest hurt like hell, but she felt sleepy, so goddamn sleepy. And breathing was more and more difficult. It was…

****

Her mouth was sour, her gut ached, and some jerk kept whacking her on the back. She opened her eyes and stared into a porcelain bowl. It was her toilet, and it was full of stuff. *What the?* Weird goopy stuff that shimmered and glowed. What the fuck happened?

She reached out a shaky hand and depressed the lever, watched the crap whirl down. The headache had faded to a whisper. She savored the moment, to be able to see, to think, to feel like shit but without the spikes driving into her skull. Now, could she stand? She grabbed at the sink. At least whoever it was who'd been pounding her had stopped. Her stomach clutched again. She looked down at the floor to steady herself and saw...feet? Raised her gaze higher.

Knees, encased in worn khaki.

Muscled thighs.

An ivory T-shirt stretched across the broad expanse of a man's chest.

A face.

Her jaw creaked before her mouth dropped open. A man stood there scowling at her, but damn, what a face he had! Strong, straight black brows drew together in a frown, a long, slightly flared nose, cheekbones to die for, a broad mouth pressed into a thin line, and thickly lashed eyes of a brown so deep it was almost coal.

"Fuck!" Her heart jumped into her throat. She coughed real hard. Yep. There her heart was, beating a classic Ginger Baker right below her Adam's apple. But her chest—it felt okay now. No more tightness or pain.

"Who are you? How did you get in?" Oh man, if this guy was a paramedic and they'd busted in her door, she'd have the landlord on her back forever.

The guy startled, but he still stared at her. His frown grew more intense.

"I asked you—who are you!" She backed away and banged into the toilet. At the same time, the man's hands came up, palms toward her.

His eyes widened. "Oh, Christ!" he breathed.

Air slammed into her. She blinked against its fury and opened her eyes again.

She was alone in the bathroom.

Chapter Two

Joe Littlehawk crouched on the roof of the weary apartment building. Coarse gravel and flaking tar caught on his hands as he leaned forward. He looked at his palms. Shit! It had happened. Big Wing had warned him about this. It was one of the rare hazards of looking after people. When you got a little too close to the living, your form could become solid for a while.

"Double shit." He tried to float up, had to settle for standing. "Goddamn." Three rules, Ramael had said. Follow the three rules, and he could actually have an A-class job in the afterlife, instead of hanging out in Purgatory until he could be born again. Just three rules. Don't interfere. Don't ever let them see you.

And never, never touch.

He'd just gone and broken all three.

This had never happened in all the years he'd been on the job. He'd never gone solid before. Not one of his cases had ever seen him. Why had this happened now? Worse than that, would Ramael cut him loose and cast him into Purgatory?

"Christ!"

The in-between world of Purgatory was the pits. He'd seen people caught in the vortex that spun them back into rebirth. They just went around and around and around. It looked like some kind of toilet set at an endless flush cycle. Once in a while, someone would get to the bottom and pop back into dense matter, into the lifetime they were intended to have. The rest seemed unaware of this. In fact, they seemed unaware of anything but the spinning and an ongoing review of their prior lives.

He did not want to go there.

"Forget this." He had to return to Alena. What if he hadn't freed her of the overdose she'd taken? He'd poured his own essence into her to counteract the injection she'd taken. That usually worked. He made a fist and groaned. Still solid enough to actually make his etheric hand into a fist, but he needed to get back to her. He bent, pushed his hand into the layer of slate and tar, all the way to the thick beam, preparing to dive through, and halted.

"For Christ's sake!" He should be able to push on through with ease, no problem, but sticking his hand in there was like dipping it in Jell-O.

If he was still this solid, substantial enough to have a problem pushing through dense matter, Alena would be able to see him again and she'd completely freak out. She might even have the heart attack that the overdose would have caused if he hadn't intervened. He dragged his hand back up and sat on the roof. He didn't even know how to quickly make his form more transparent. Ramael hadn't covered that in the angel's version of *This Is Your Afterlife* for him. But then, he'd never expected to be dense enough to touch, either. Maybe the angel thought this would never happen.

A shiver gripped him and trembled inward. Alena's neck had been warm, so warm. Even the memory of carrying her into the bathroom made his thumbs ache. And how the hell could that be? His thumbs? He was dead, for Christ's sake. It had been years and years since warm or cold meant anything at all to him. The form he inhabited was exactly that, a shell to encase his awareness, his consciousness, so he could work. His job was to help people, not scare them.

What the hell could he do now? Surely there

were times when it was okay to go the extra mile to help someone. He hadn't intended to touch Alena. It just happened. He had to help her. She'd just made a mistake. Anyway, this was supposed to be an easy case. All Ramael had said was for him to watch Alena, keep an eye on her.

He'd had done just that, floated about like Casper the ghost and watched Alena spiral downward. All those months he'd followed the rules and held his hands behind his back while she shook on her bed, when all he wanted to do was draw her into his arms and rock her like a baby. He was a Sacred Guardian, a ghost assigned to watch over and guide people. He was supposed to assist Alena, not freak her out.

Help her. Not interfere.

Well, he didn't have much of a choice, did he? Until now, he'd been the perfect Sacred Guardian with Alena. For the past six months, he'd been whispering in her ear and sending gifts to her, the only things a Sacred Guardian was allowed to do.

That goddamned woman had ignored him.

Not that people truly heard anything he said; that is, they didn't exactly hear the words, but something always got through. But not Alena. She never noticed his guidance. She'd just flicked her hand by her ear whenever he tried to whisper to her, swatted him away as if he was a goddamn fly. She'd tripped over all the opportunities he cast her way. Just last week he'd managed to place a newspaper, open to the classified section's listing for the Free Clinic, on the seat Alena usually took on the bus.

The goddamn woman had *sat* on it! Even though he could tell Alena was hurting because the stuff she had for the pain didn't really work very well, she'd had gone and plunked her little butt down there, with Michael right beside her. She hadn't even looked at the paper, hadn't even picked it up.

Alena Morgan never noticed any of the gifts he sent.

Damn woman had gone and nearly got herself killed.

On *his* watch!

A breeze sent bits of dust over his nose. He drew in air molecules and blew the dust away in one irritated puff. Ramael had no problem swiftly creating a bright shield that held the physical world completely away from the angel's form, but he always had difficulty sealing his own form, keeping him separate from the elements.

There was only one thing he could do.

"Time to camouflage."

He opened his mouth wide, pulled a massive blob of air into his form, shaped it, bent it, and released it in a measured flow, sending bursts of translucent, gelid, half-dense matter, half-etheric vibration all around him.

Ramael had shown him how to mix the stuff of the third-dimensional world with the faster vibration where he existed. The mixing created a shield of some sort. Big Wing had spouted off a bunch of stuff sounding like mathematical equations when the angel had explained this, but to him it was an art, even though he wasn't as good at it as the angel.

To him, it was more like cooking than anything else, yet even that was weird. He was dead. How could he draw in air? How could he move, sometimes like the ghost he was, but other times like a man?

How could he have touched Alena?

He pulled at the ropy strands of etheric and dense atmosphere, weaving a flimsy barrier around his form. Ramael had explained death to him many times, told him of astral forms and different levels, but it had never made much sense. Big Wing always made it sound just like a lot of gibberish, talking in another language and never translating it. Whenever he'd asked for formal training from other angels, he got the "you're lucky the Eternal even allows me to do *this* much for you, soldier" speech from Ramael.

He tugged the last bits of atmosphere over his toes and poked at it until it settled on his form. He had a form; that was for sure. He could even stand on this roof. But all it took was the slightest flicker of intent, and boom! He could plunge right through a mountain.

Well, he could do that before he went solid, that is. What about now? He glanced out at fingers of mist creeping up from the bay. The distant cry of a foghorn met the dull grunt of an oil tanker. What time was it anyway?

He looked back at the roof and curled his hands into fists again. Time. Now, that had not troubled him for as long as he'd been dead. Why had he allowed that thought to enter his consciousness? What did it matter? He never needed to rest.

Don't worry about this now; just go back and see if she's okay.

His fisted hands grew misty. He tried wiggling his toes. Well, okay, he still moved a bit like a man, but the currents brushing across the roof slid right through him now. Good enough to hide him and he could sense Alena's pain. She wasn't out of the woods yet. Anyway, he had already broken the three rules. She had seen him, he had interfered, and he had touched her. If she died now, it would all be for nothing.

If she died now, he needed to be near her body to help her cross over.

That was his job, too.

****

Alena lay sprawled on the couch. He froze, but the gentle lift of her chest thawed him. A smile wreathed her mouth. She seemed okay, not even in much pain. His senses must have fooled him this time. How curious.

He floated over to her. The couch was now angled across the front door. Well, he'd frightened her, hadn't he? But she must be better. How else could she have dragged the couch over to block the front door? He glanced at the low table where the couch used to sit. What happened to the vodka? He drifted from the room, searching.

It sat next to the kitchen sink, empty. *Hiyá*! Did she drink all of this? How stupid was that! He eased his form back into the living room and peered at Alena's neck. The steady pulse in her throat proclaimed a strong heart. If she drank all that vodka, wouldn't her heart be irregular? She seemed fine, but he should check it out.

He returned to the kitchen and glared at the phone. Calling 9-1-1 was out. No one would be able to hear him. He had to be close to convey messages or influence people. Might as well contact Ramael and face the music.

"*Eco Iad.*" He intoned the first part of the chant, the words Ramael had taught him to bring the angel to his side, and started the second phrase, but a glint from the sink stopped him.

It was clean. The bottle was washed clean, empty. A film of soap that still covered the rim caught the light, sending its bright glimmer to him. Hey! She poured it all down the sink. Maybe he wasn't such a bad Sacred Guardian after all. The close call must have scared her. He didn't like to think of scaring Alena. Still, she really needed to be more careful.

But he ought to stay close to her; make sure the medicine was out of her system. He'd been too busy getting that overdose out of her to do a scan of her vitals. Better be thorough so his report to Ramael was complete. He eased back into the living room and glanced up at the picture of her husband and Michael when he was a baby. How had the guy died? For a moment there, he thought Alena was going to cry when she'd looked up at the picture before the medicine had nearly killed her.

As awful as her life had become, he'd never once seen Alena cry. He glanced over at the journal she kept on her dresser. He shouldn't, but maybe he could just take a peek. He kept track of Alena's breathing as he lifted the journal and allowed the pages to flutter past his gaze. Most of it was little things: Michael's progress in homeschooling, her delight at the coming of spring. Yet there were tons of pages where agony lived. Several pages had the word *Why* written hundreds of times, the pressure of the pen breaking the paper in several places. He glanced at the dates of the first entries. "Two years! Fuck! This has been going on for two years?"

He finished scanning the last pages and let the journal settle back in place on Alena's dresser. His form started to oscillate, to ripple like water in a kettle, near to boiling.

"Big Wing didn't fill me in. Goddamn Ram!" He fought for control, but his form dispersed and spread out; his essence filled the room. The light bulb in the living room flared into brilliance, then burst, sending glass fragments flying and smoke seeping out of the light's guts.

He slowly reassembled his form and floated over to chill the burning wires with his etheric breath, vaporizing all the slivers of glass on the floor as he unscrewed what was left of the bulb. After a moment, he dropped the guts of the bulb on the low table so Alena would see it when she woke. Her confusion over what had happened tonight would cover the state of her ceiling light fixture. At least, he hoped it would. He hovered close to the ceiling and looked back at Alena.

"Alena, I'm so sorry. I was never told that this had been going on for two years. My...superior never told me there had been an accident. I haven't been with you for that long. I just thought you had bad headaches." He let himself drift closer to Alena and glided above her. "You were in bad pain all that time and goddamn Ram didn't tell me." He leaned in, nearly touching her cheek. There was much more going on here, but Big Wing had kept it from him. Why was that? Ram had often toyed with him but was all business when it came to helping humans, at least, until now.

"I thought Ram had given me a simple case. He didn't lie, but he also didn't give me all the information on you. I don't know why, but I'll find out." He floated up from Alena; the shirt she wore billowed upward, toward his departing form.

What the hell? That had never happened before either. He made note of it and continued, "I'll make it up to you, Alena; I promise. I'll stay with you as long as I can."

She looked so fragile lying there. Every one of her nails was bitten down to the quick. "You should paint your nails. It would help you take care of yourself better. You won't want to bite them if they're painted."

She was way too thin. "You need to eat better. Bubble bath would be good for you too. Something with roses, some girly stuff. If you take care of yourself that will help you heal. And could you do something with your hair?" His fingertips passed through the short auburn spikes on top of her head. "Let it grow or something. Braid it, okay?"

He pulled his hand away from her head, but stayed close. She'd never do any of these things. If she hadn't been carrying the boulder of two years of constant pain on her shoulders, who knew? But if she hadn't, Ram never would have given him this assignment.

Alena's eyelids twitched and she moaned. He let his hand shimmer over her face. She needed to sleep, and her body might still be carrying the pain. Maybe he could soothe her. Alena hadn't slept much in the six months he'd been her Sacred Guardian. Perhaps he could help.

A sob shuddered through Alena, but stopped as her body went rigid, fighting the urge to cry, even in her sleep. Her eyes screwed shut and she curled into a ball, her chin against her knees.

How could he help her? He couldn't enter her dreams; the dream path was only available the moment a human fell asleep, and Ramael had to help him the first time he entered a human's dreams.

"Shit." Here he was, stuck in the afterlife with an angelic commanding officer who hadn't given him the essentials to do his job, to carry out his mission.

Alena needed to sleep. He ached to help her.

His hand was only an inch away from her face.

What if he touched her again?

He made his hand stop. Ram had said this was the most important rule. He could *maybe* explain interfering and letting Alena see him, but touching was the biggest rule of all. You never, never touch.

But why not?

His hand still hovered over her head. He let it dip even closer, half an inch, quarter of an inch.

Alena was muttering now, and her forehead creased.

"Why not?"

He'd already touched her once, slid his astral hands along the pliant roundness of her arms when he lifted her, ran his thumbs over the damp back of her neck as he held her in the bathroom. Her short hair had licked at his fingers.

Yes. She needed the sleep, and he could give this to her, stroke her, soothe her back to sleep. He had seen her do this for Michael. His own mother had done this when he was a child and couldn't sleep.

"Well, hell." What could it hurt?

He closed the distance, placed his misty fingers on her forehead and stroked. Each touch of his hand left liquid light in its wake. The crease between her brows smoothed and she uncurled; her hands went limp and fell to the side. Her mouth slackened and fell open. He stared at the moist pink sheen of her tongue. Moved down toward her.

She drew in a long breath.

He lifted, but couldn't wrest his fingers from her forehead. The breath she took filled him somehow, with sweet air and the faint taste of toothpaste laced with vodka. The tight salt streaks of her dried tears crackled her face. Her jeans were too loose; they sagged at her waist.

He wrenched his hand away, flew to the ceiling, then held the hand up and watched sparks fly around it in the shadows. What the hell was happening here? He looked back at Alena. She'd thrown up all the etheric essence mixed with the drug from her bloodstream. He'd seen to that and had given her a little Sacred Guardian gut-cleansing as well so her small intestine did not absorb the small amounts of the drug that had gone from her nasal tissues into her throat. Ram had taught him that much, thank God, for the extreme hospital cases where an accidental overdose had occurred and the Eternal allowed life rather than death. Surely he could leave Alena for just a little while.

He whirled and shut down his power of sight when he passed through the roof. Going through walls or roofs was always a chore. Joints and beams clutched at him, and all the goddamn *nails*! Once he reached the air, he cleared the dizzy tremor from what passed for his eyes. Stars spilled in a crazy tumble of silver-blue radiance. He sought the golden track, the shimmer of Ram. A flicker from across the bay tickled him. There. Big Wing was there. But he wouldn't say more than he needed to. He wouldn't tell Ram what he'd done, not yet, anyway. Let the angel make the first move. After all, it was Ram who had thrust him into a case without proper training or orders. Nothing more than "watch this woman," for Christ's sake.

He had a bone to pick with white-boy Big Wing. The angel might be able to best him in a fair fight; that was certainly a fact.

But he'd done two tours of duty. In-country. Where fights were seldom fair.

He coasted on the air and forced his etheric form into the sluice of particles that would hurtle him all the way to where the angel rested.

Chapter Three

Something pounded her again. Alena opened one gummy eye and closed it quick when the vise that gripped her head tightened. *God, the migraine already?* Hadn't she taken some Zamatrex?

"What day is it?" She lifted her head. This felt different. More like a...hangover? The surface she lay upon shook in time with the staccato rap that issued from just above her shoulder. What the fuck was that? She groaned and turned onto her back, then peered up at the front door. The chain rattled when the door bowed inward.

She rubbed grit out of her eyes. Right. It was just someone knocking on her door. She levered herself up on one elbow, then rose all the way and stood staring at her couch. How the hell did it get in front of the door? She leaned her full weight against it and set her teeth when it screeched across the floor to the wall where it usually rested.

What had happened last night? Her brain felt like cooked asparagus; thoughts slithered and danced just out of reach. She unlatched the chain and dropped to her knees just in time for Michael's launch. Deb stood behind him.

For a moment, she froze. She'd overdosed, hadn't she? Light stabbed her eyes; air stretched thin around her.

Aw, fuck! She'd screwed up. She really had. A thump-thump-thump hammered inside her skull, yet it wasn't her normal 100-decibel headache. "What happened?" If paramedics had come, wouldn't she remember? Wouldn't she be in a hospital right now?

Michael crashed into her, full force. He clutched her with his little boy hands. The scent of cinnamon toast and his baby shampoo hair hit her hard. She folded him into her arms and forgot how to breathe.

Solid, her baby was solid. *What happened*? She looked up. Light swam in a flurry around Deb's face, then the older woman's features sharpened into focus. Someone flushed a toilet upstairs. The gurgling rush of the pipes traveled the length of the back wall. Golden light crept around the window shades and sent a whole universe of dust spinning. She plowed her face into Michael's hair.

"Michael, Michael, Michael! Oh, baby." God! "Mama missed you." Alive. She hugged Michael close and pressed kisses all over his face and neck. Alive, alive. She was alive! Somebody must have heard her on the phone after all. But who?

"No, Mommy! It tickles." He giggled but batted her away and tore out of her grip. "I wanta watch Uncle Fart on *Space City*."

"Yeah, right." She blinked hard. "Watch Uncle Fart."

"Uncle Fart?" Deb raised a brow.

"Didn't he tell you?" She glanced over at her son. "*Space City* is his favorite show." The headache was still there, but it was bearable. "Anyway, what are you doing here now? I wasn't expecting you two until tomorrow."

Deb shook her head. "I don't know, Alena. I had this feeling about you." She moved over to the coffee table and lifted the guts of a light fixture sitting on it. "So what happened to this?"

She rubbed her hand over her head. "I dunno." She took the fried bulb in her hand and frowned at it. "Something…I just don't know."

The tall dude last night! Oh. My. God. Was that *real*? She swallowed.

"What took you so long to open the door?" Deb had her hands on her hips now and was giving her *the stare*. She ducked her head. She'd been leveled by that steely gaze before, when she did rehab in the clinic where Deb was working. Better come clean. She stepped back and looked over at Michael. "Deb, I have something to tell you." She motioned for Deb to follow her. "But not in front of Michael."

****

"A man, you say." Deb did a graceful pivot and backed away from the toilet, spreading her arms. "Right about here?" She was dressed in black today, with a trim white collar and mid-calf skirt, strawberry hair pulled back. A red-gold nun.

How the hell did Deb always manage to look as if she'd just stepped off the pages of the *New Age Journal*? "Well, yeah." The refrain from *Space City* drifted in from the living/bed room. "I guess." Last night was coming back in fragments.

"You're not sure a man was in your bathroom?"

"It was late." Hallucination. Had to be. "I dunno. Maybe I was dreaming." That's it—a dream born of the alcohol and Zamatrex. Maybe she was wrong and she hadn't accidentally taken an overdose. But if that was so, she'd just have been on the floor by the phone, wouldn't she? Not on the couch blocking the front door.

She sagged against the sink and stared at the bottle of Excedrin Migraine in her hand. Not much of it was left and this would bring her ulcer to life, but she needed it. It often did not work on her type of headache, but she'd take a chance. She reached into the cabinet for the little bit of liquid antacid still in its bottle.

"What did he look like?"

Like a god.

"Ah, yeah, well…Tall, real tall, with long, dark hair." She ran her hand up over her short auburn strands. "And a long nose too, but kind of Asian, you know?" Deb was nodding. "Dark eyes and brows." Why was Deb nodding? "Oh, and a broad mouth." Now Deb's whole face quivered. "Dude looked angry." Her voice trailed off as Deb bent at the waist. "God, Deb! Are you sick? Can I get you some water or something?"

Deb held her abdomen, leaned against the sink and looked up at the ceiling, laughing so hard that tears leaked out of her eyes and sluiced down her cheeks.

"What's so funny?"

Deb wiped her streaming eyes and her laughter subsided. "Does this guy have a brother? I love tall, dark, long-haired men. But Asian? You've got that wrong, Lena. Asians aren't tall."

"Goddammit, Deb. Cut it out. I get it. You don't believe me." Well, she wasn't sure she believed what she'd seen either. After the man had disappeared, she'd lunged into the living room looking for him. She was certain that Deb had sent a friend to check on her, or a neighbor had seen her through her kitchen window and called the paramedics for her. Yet the apartment had been empty and silent, except for the slow chug and hum of her old refrigerator. The door was locked, chain still in place. How had the guy gotten in? And how had he gotten back out?

The Excedrin Migraine rattled into her hand. She took two and popped them in her mouth.

"All I can say is he seemed real. I wasn't gonna take any chances." She drank three glasses of water to dilute the effect it would have on her gut, but it still burned a raw track all the way down her throat.

"Any chances?" Deb grabbed a length of toilet tissue and wiped her eyes. "What do you mean?"

"I put the couch across the front door." Dammit, she really *had* taken too much Zamatrex. The medication instructions must be bogus just to cover their asses. But if that was so, why did she only remember blanking out by the phone and coming to in the bathroom? Had she had crawled in there herself? "That's why it took me a while to open the door."

"You were afraid the man might come back." Deb nodded and chucked the tissue in the wastebasket. "This man who just up and disappeared."

"It must have been a dream." But why did she remember strong hands under her arms, a low, exasperated voice murmuring in her ear? Saying words she couldn't understand, words that sounded foreign and yet familiar. Something like, *Taktókanun han hwo* and *Léci uwo*. It was more than weird. When he spoke those words she could almost tell what he was saying. The meaning of the words had dangled just out of range; the pressure of his hands had warmed her all over.

She gave her head a firm shake and the headache beat against the back of her eyes. "Fuck." Ridiculous. She chased the pills with even more water and sagged against the sink. Must have been the booze that caused her to blank out. And either she was so very lucky, or well, something else was watching over her. Something she didn't believe in. *But hey, thanks, Whoever. Or Whatever.*

Deb reached for her arm. "Hey, watch it with the F word! Michael's in the next room, remember?"

"It's not like he doesn't hear it on the playground." She turned away. "But I know, Ms. Jenkins. I'm careful around Michael."

"Alena, I'm Deb to you now, not Ms. Jenkins anymore." Deb tugged at her arm. "Why don't you try 'frick.' "

"Frick?"

"Yeah, as in 'I hate this fricking place.' Just give

it a try." Deb nudged her arm.

"I was fricking scared." She snorted. "That sounds stupid, Deb. Really scanless."

"Hey. I know something more is going on here, Lena, and I want you to level with me."

"Yeah." She rubbed at her eyes. "I've got some more to tell you. Let's go in the kitchen." She strode out of the bathroom and flicked the switch on the radio atop the refrigerator, drawing Deb over to the sink. "Michael won't be able to hear us in here." Silken tones of her favorite Sigur Ros album, *With a Buzz in Our Ears We Play Endlessly*, spread into the kitchen from her old FM radio.

She leaned against the sink and breathed, in, out, in, out. Where to start? "I've been in pain, bad pain, for the past two years."

Deb just nodded. "I thought something was going on." She looked closely at Alena. "The headaches?"

"They're more than just headaches. The last doctor I went to see prescribed migraine stuff to take before the headaches get too bad."

"Aspirin doesn't work? Ibuprofen?"

"I used those too much and blew out my stomach."

Deb straightened. "But I just saw you…"

"I know, I ran out of the prescription stuff, since welfare doesn't cover me anymore. It's okay, I mean, I'll be all right if I take it just this once." She held her hands together so tight they went numb. "I, I've got to talk, Deb. Please don't say anything until I'm through."

Deb just looked at her, looked really close again.

God, it's her social worker look. But she had to enlist Deb's aid. Just like she had to do years ago. "It got so it sucked so much that I, well, I think I took too much of the migraine stuff. I forgot how much I'd taken yesterday and I needed to focus in order to fill out the job apps."

Deb moved toward her, but did not speak.

"I'm okay." She was, right? She must have been hallucinating all of it, the chest pain, trying to call 9-1-1. And the rest of it too.

"Are you in pain now?"

"Some." She unclasped her hands and wrapped her arms around her waist. "It never goes away. It just never stops, Deb. I wanted it to stop." Her hands started to shake. It was weird because only her hands shook, but they made her list to the side.

Deb took Alena in her arms. "All this time and you didn't tell me?" She felt Alena's forehead. "I should slap you upside the head, you know?"

"I've asked for so much from you, Deb. You've done so much for me."

"Well, you're one of my kids, aren't you?" Deb smoothed the hair across her forehead. "I remember you when you were fifteen, the knife you carried in your boot, the torn fishnet stockings, even the Goth makeup."

"Yeah." Why did the motion of Deb's fingers on her forehead send shivers through her? When Michael needed to sleep, she did this to him, but no one had ever done this to her, stroked her forehead, until now. So why did the motion of Deb's fingers vibrate all through her? She moved away so the stroking would stop, yet she held onto Deb's arms. "But you took me in."

"There were other kids in the group, too, Lena." Deb touched her cheek.

No shivers trembled through her when Deb touched her cheek. But her eyes were going all damp. "I remember them. Do they still visit?"

"Some do." Deb gave her the social worker look again. "But only a few were my real successes, my reason for taking kids in when I did."

She brushed at the dampness on her face. This

was not the time to go all gushy. "Do you still take in kids?"

Deb sighed. "The county bumped me upstairs." She shrugged. "It happens. More money, more paperwork. But I can help you, Alena. Please let me in. There's a doctor I want you to see, Dr. Ravi. I think he can help you."

"Deb, thanks." She stiffened. Time to ask for what she needed. The money, the help with social services, the health stuff. *Goddammit, it's hard to do this.* "Okay. Here's the deal." She opened the cupboard doors. "No food. No meds. No job."

Deb shook her head. "Is that all?"

"That's it."

"What about the phantom man?"

"Must have dreamed it."

Deb sighed, looking at the two boxes of macaroni. She opened the refrigerator and stared at the empty shelves. "Holy cow! You weren't kidding." She pushed it closed and yelled out to the living room. "Hey, Michael, you want to go to the ATM? You get to push the buttons."

Michael stomped into the kitchen. "Ro-bo-cop! Ro-bo-cop!" He swung stiff arms and stared straight ahead.

"Oh dear. Alena, I let Michael watch that old movie last night. Since then he just goes into this…robot dance." Deb slung her mirrored handbag over her shoulder and caught Michael's hand. "How about lunch, Mr. RoboCop?"

Alena took a deep breath and followed them out the door.

****

It was bright outside. She squinted against the light. The aroma of star jasmine sweetened the air. Deb and Michael skipped ahead down the sidewalk. Michael's head tipped from side to side, chestnut curls tumbling. She buried her face in the jasmine but stumbled back, sneezing and laughing. When had it bloomed? She looked up and down the street. Clumps of trees in full leaf stretched toward the sun; brown-shingle craftsman houses sat crammed against adobe bungalows; purple and blue wisteria ran riot over the wooden awning of a mottled yellow apartment building.

The very air around her lived. She trotted behind Deb and Michael, dodging boys on roller blades, all graceful leaning and raucous clatter. Farther down on Shattuck, weekend street vendors sat behind tables filled with Technicolor cotton tie-dye T-shirts, fluttering crystals, smoldering incense of pine and rose. Even the stoplights beamed a blessing, scarlet triumph and emerald hope.

Shit, now stoplights were making her gooey! "Oh, fu…frick! *I'm* going all New Age." Still, a grin crept across her mouth and widened.

The fragrance of rich espresso from the Coffee House and chilies from Zombie Burrito twisted her stomach into a hungry, roiling gurgle. And just last night she'd been so scared, on the floor with the receiver to her ear, gasping against the pain in her chest.

She stopped, put her hand against the plate glass of a storefront window and stared at the faded jeans and flowered shirts displayed there. All right, now. Something had happened; either the meds' instructions were wrong, or somehow, something had saved her. She looked down the street where Michael and Deb had slowed. Nothing had changed. She was still out of work, and now would owe Deb again. There was no guarantee that she would find a job anytime soon. The doctor Deb recommended may not be able to do much; other doctors hadn't.

Michael waved. They were waiting for her. She managed a weak flop of her hand and stepped after them. *Gotta just trust this.* One step at a time, same as always. Michael wound his arms around Deb's knees and gave her his best imp grin. One foot in front of the other. That was the best she could do.

They were first in line at the ATM. Deb lifted Michael to the ledge that fronted it, let him put in her card and punch the OK button. The machine delivered a smooth packet of twenties to his eager hands. Deb retrieved them and handed the packet to Alena.

She stared at the bills. Two hundred dollars. She could buy groceries and pay part of her rent. The landlord may or may not wait for the rest. But it was all she had. "This is a loan." Her voice cracked. "I'll draw up a, um, a contract or something when we get back to the apartment." She knuckled her right eye and stuffed the money into her wallet.

"No problemo, we'll sign a contract." Deb waved her hand and pulled Michael close. "But first, some lunch." Michael jittered up and down. "Where shall we go, eh? Will it be hamburgers or burritos?"

She looked up as Deb conferred with Michael. A man stood a few feet away. Waiting for the ATM? Deb had already finished there; Michael now had Deb's hand and was tugging her toward Burger World.

She moved aside, out of the man's way, but he just stood there, looking down at a slip of newsprint in his hands. He was tall, over six feet for sure. She tilted her head to see his face. Seemed like she knew him, but where had they met? He stared at the slip of paper in his hands, intent and focused. Maybe he was one of Deb's "kids." There were ten in the group with her. That's probably why he looked so familiar.

"Hey." She started toward him, hand stretched out in greeting. He ignored her hand. A line formed between black brows that twitched and drew together.

It was the frown that did it. The greeting died

on her lips. She froze while hot prickles danced up her arms and down her legs. The edges of her vision wavered and went gray. All sound receded except the frantic thump of her heart. She bunched her hands into tight lumps. Air rattled down her throat. Dammit! She would *not* pass out! She took another breath.

Just as her vision cleared, the man lifted his head. It was the same guy, the guy from last night, same broad mouth, same glorious, midnight eyes. She groped behind her for Deb's hand. "Shit. Deb-Deb-Deb," sputtered past her lips in tiny squeaks. She stumbled back a step. Was he a psycho? He didn't look dangerous, standing there as big as day in khaki jeans and an ivory T-shirt. His wondrous deep brown eyes were wary and resigned at the same time.

Damn, was the dude stalking her? And how the hell did he get out of her apartment so fast last night?

He just looked at her and opened his hand. The bit of newsprint he held fluttered to the ground. She startled, tracked the floating paper for an instant, blinked, and looked into the space where the man had stood. Her throat seized.

He wasn't there anymore. It could not have taken more than a second for her to look back up, but he just wasn't there.

"Mommy, Mommy!"

"Huh?" Michael was tugging at her arm.

"I said, Burger World or Zombie Burritos!" Michael's plaintive voice whined *I asked you this ten times, how come you never listen.*

"You choose, kiddo." When she turned her head, the bones in her neck crunched.

"Are you okay, Lena? Are you in pain again?" Deb had Michael's hand now. "You're pale." Her eyes radiated worry.

"Um. I'm okay, but didn't you see him?" She waved at the space where the man had stood.

"Who?"

"That guy by the ATM!"

"I didn't see anyone."

The bit of newsprint still lay on the ground where the man had dropped it. She squatted and picked it up. It was real. The ink smeared on her hands.

"Ah, okay, I just thought I knew him. He dropped this." Better not say more. If she told Deb she had just seen the phantom man, and he had disappeared again, her friend would be seriously worried. Her heart did a dip and extra thump as she glanced at Michael. Maybe worried enough to ask Child Protective Services to take Michael away from her. If Deb thought she was truly seeing things, well, Deb *was* a social worker, and one tough lady. Michael's safety would come first. As it should.

"Let me see." Deb took hold of the newsprint slip.

She forced her hands to release it, wiped her fingers on her shirt and shivered. How bizarre. She didn't want to let it go. Something seemed to whisper in her ear, "Read it, you dummy!" Was she hearing voices, now? Shit! Air puffed by her left cheek. She rubbed at it. Just for a moment, she thought she heard someone laughing.

"Lena!" Deb tugged her arm now. "You should apply for this!" Deb shoved the newsprint under her nose. "Look."

She took the slip of paper, backed up a bit, and stared around her. A group of young men walked by, dressed in adolescent finery—cut-off jeans several sizes too large that sagged at the seat, king-size muscle man tees and faded flannel shirts that flapped around their knees. When they passed, she looked up and down the street. Two businessmen in gray and navy suits carrying buttery-soft leather attaché cases stepped on the tall escalator that descended to BART. A clump of chattering Japanese tourists wandered past, cameras dangling. No tall, gorgeous Indian guy. She jumped and grabbed at the newsprint as it slipped out of her fingers, forced her eyes to focus on the minuscule print. Indian? So *not* politically correct. Where the hell had that come from? And where had he gone?

Read the ad.

She rubbed her ear. Damn, the print was so tiny. "Administrative Assistant II," she read. "Living Light Seminary." She scanned the rest, lifted her head. "Isn't that up the hill on the north side?"

"Bingo." Deb took it back. Her lower lip stuck out and she frowned. "Pretty minimal qualifications." She looked up. "The closing date is Friday—you'll have to get your butt in gear. I'll get you to Dr. Ravi before then so you won't be in pain."

She reached for the slip. "Hell, why not?" A stiff breeze from the Bay found its way up Center Street and pushed at her back. "I'll apply for this, give it a try." She turned and looked up when a shadow, a cloud, surely, passed across the sun.

Chapter Four

"Alena can still see me." He blinked away droplets forming on his astral lashes and moved closer to Ram. The angel sat on the crest of Mount Tamalpais, undulating light-wings outspread and eyes closed, facing the ocean. A curtain of fog slipped around his arms. The slate track of a bike trail snaked down the landward side of the mountain behind him.

He waited until the dance of quantum particles that made up his body steadied with a slippery tremor, settled upon the ground, and looked down to the shore, hundreds of feet below. Good thing he didn't mind heights; not that it would hurt him to fall, but Ram had told him early on that the dead brought all sorts of baggage from their lives with them. If you suffered from acrophobia when alive, you'd carry that with you into the afterlife, for a while, anyway.

The ridge the angel sat upon fell away in a smooth mound all the way to the ocean. Dark clumps of pine dotted the slope. Beyond the breakers, a whale breached, bursting into the air and slamming back into the swells.

He turned to the angel. "I just told you she can see me."

"Indeed." Ram's eyes were still closed.

When Ram shut his eyes, he looked like a statue. It was always weird to look at the angel when he spoke with his eyes shut, like seeing stone awakening and starting to breathe.

He looked away from Ram and focused on the

turquoise ripples of the Pacific Ocean, beyond the wall of fog that crept past him. The early afternoon sun was chasing fog from water to land in a drift of floating shadow and pallid light.

Usually, the fog bank retreated out to sea, but sometimes it flooded the land, dissipating as the earth heated it. He poked his fingers at tendrils of fog and watched the mist climb up his wrist. This was not good. It should pass right on through, or mingle with his etheric form.

"She saw me just now." He sneaked a peek at Ram and straightened when the angel's eyes opened. "In front of the bank."

Ram just looked at him.

He turned and gazed out at the ocean again. Last night, he'd only told Ram that Alena could see him, not that he'd touched her. If the angel didn't already know that, he sure as hell was not going to offer the information. But how would he ever find out what had happened to him when he touched Alena; how was it that he had felt as if he were inside her skin? Why had sparks flown from his hand when he pulled away from her?

Probably would never find out. He'd lied. For the first time, he was keeping things from the angel. He told Ram Alena had taken pills, not Zamatrex, and that she had got rid of them right after she had taken them. He didn't say that he'd poured his own essence into her to bind with the drug in her bloodstream and cleanse her. The really weird thing was that he'd expected a fight; he thought that Big Wing Ramjets could tell what had happened and could sniff out the lie. But the angel had accepted everything he said.

If Ram didn't have the power to read him, to know everything that happened, well that meant the angel had limits. Limits could be useful.

A liquid rustling shook the air beside him. He

looked back. The angel's wings were rippling again, but Ram said nothing and kept staring.

He stared right back. Last night when he'd told Ram Alena had seen him, the angel had just said, *Don't let that happen again.* So what now?

"Are you listening? I said I went solid again." He drifted closer, moving in on Ram. The angel hated to be crowded. He floated so close his own particles nearly blended with Ram's.

This time the angel didn't thrust him away. Ram just tipped his head. "Did you remember the barrier?"

He drifted back, but just an inch. "There wasn't any time to make the shield. I flew up and had to leave so she didn't go on seeing me." He'd managed to get her to look at the job listing, though. That was something.

"You're wet."

Beads of fog dripped off his fingers. "So I see." He drew air molecules through his nose, blew out a wash of clear oxygen-sacred-guardian-essence and bathed in it, shaking his hands. Silvery drops pattered upon the soil around him.

"Joseph..." The angel shook his head, but only asked, "How did all this happen?"

"All this?"

"Why didn't you call for me when Alena took the pills?"

Ram's gaze reached into him, all the way to his toes.

She didn't take pills. "I didn't see her take pills." That was God's honest truth. Maybe this was why Ramjets hadn't tossed him into Purgatory.

"I thought you said you were with her all the time."

The weight of Ram's stare pulled at him. He fought the impulse to look at the angel. Ram was his Commanding Officer, after all. He owed the angel this much. "There was only a moment, one moment, at the BART station." He focused on the angel's toes. "I looked away."

It was when Alena had been saying good-bye to her little boy in the train station. He'd stood and watched her hold herself away from Michael. This had taken him by surprise. Why hadn't she gone with Deb? The job applications could wait, couldn't they? He'd been whispering to Alena for months, telling her to go to Deb and ask for help.

"It was a personal moment. I left her alone."

Alena had just stood there, rigid, holding back tears. Her pain had pushed an ache through him, starting around the middle of his form and ending at his fingertips. It had stunned him, completely floored him. He couldn't even move. He goddamn froze up.

"When I looked back, she was gone. I thought she was still in the station, but she'd already gotten on the train. When I caught up with her, she'd already overdosed." Not on pills. This was the truth

"I see." Ram nodded. "How is she now?"

"She's okay." He looked out at the waves, but risked glancing back at the angel. "She needs me, though."

Ram raised one brow. "Does she?"

"She's not out of the woods yet. Hasn't found a job, still in pain."

Ram uttered something between a grunt and a snort. Fingers of the sun coaxed the fog into oblivion. Water vapor first roiled and then dissipated into clear dampness.

He looked at three people on mountain bikes huffing up the trail behind him. A slow wind brought the scent of brine and dolphins. The tortured breathing of the bike riders dissolved into watery echoes.

Ram was watching the bike riders, too. "Things

will change for Alena." He nodded. "How are you doing?"

"Huh?" Well, hell. Why did Ram ask him this? "Fine, just fine." What was his game?

Ram abruptly stretched and yawned. "We were worried about Alena." His long fingers scratched behind his ears. "None of us could reach her."

A brief glimmer of heavenly teeth dazzled his eyes.

"What are you doing?" God, he hated this.

Ram raised a brow again. "What did I do that disturbed you?"

"Scratching your head. You don't need to do that. You're an angel." Not a man, not a ghost. *You outrank me, but don't take this too far.*

"We take on human characteristics so the dead can feel more comfortable with us." Ram touched his arm. "But don't belittle yourself…Joe. We call in Sacred Guardians for the most difficult cases." Ram's wings shuddered, then stretched out full and started to beat in a lazy arc.

He removed his arm from Ram's touch. "Why?"

"Sacred Guardians have had lifetimes, and can better understand the problems people face."

"I see. And you would know this, how?" He folded his arms and faced Ram. "Have you ever had a lifetime?"

The gilded wings stilled. Ram looked away, now, silent.

Okay, be that way. "So if Sacred Guardians are better in these cases, I'll be staying with Alena."

Ram still looked away, staring at the Pacific. "You will stay with her." Each word was scrubbed clean, empty of any emotion. And yet, the very stillness of Ram threatened; it was the stillness of a predator before striking.

Well, well. Big Wing didn't appear to have a choice in this matter. How very interesting. "Sure.

First, I'll help Alena find a job."

"Joseph, Joseph." Ram finally turned to face Joe; the Greek statue smile of deep amusement graced his perfect face again. "We can't interfere. You must know that by now."

"My name is Joe." He'd like to show Ram *interfering.* "Not Joseph." Only his mother got to call him Joseph. And oh, how he missed the huge, sharp hunting knife he'd taken to Vietnam. *Wonder what effect that would have on those tentacle wings?*

Ram snorted and turned his head, staring out at the ocean.

He fell silent, studying the angel's face. Damn, he hated to admit this, but Ram's profile always caught him. Renaissance artists had painted such faces, the high brow, long, thin nose, clear wedge of cheekbones, deep-set, jewel eyes. Botticelli, Michelangelo, Raphael. He used to thumb through gigantic books of Renaissance art in the boarding school library when he was little, looking at the colored plates.

Not that he liked remembering school. Life at the mission school had been hell. He had to swallow white man's history, the endless, picky rules, and the beatings whenever he slipped up and spoke Lakota instead of English. He couldn't even see his sister, Sammie. The Bureau of Indian Affairs split them up. She went to Holy Names on Rosebud Reservation.

He'd run away three times. They'd dragged him back and he always swore he would escape again. But one priest took a shine to him and gave him a job in the library. When he saw the shimmering plates of Donatello and Da Vinci, he was lost. He spent hours poring over Tiepolo, Tintoretto, and Caravaggio. After that, the priest had shown him a way out, a way to escape the desolation and chaos, the utter hopelessness of life on the reservation.

Escape from a life lived in lockstep with the Bureau of Indian Affairs, or with alcohol holding him in its hand.

The way out. By way of the local tribal college, then boot camp in Louisiana. The few, the proud, and the brave. And a war that sucked the life out of all of them. But he'd held his own. Made rank, too, above a grunt soldier, anyway. And Renaissance art, well that made staying at the mission school worthwhile. Despite the way things turned out, he never regretted the time he spent studying the sculpture and the portraits.

His mother had loved the paintings when he'd shown the prints to her before he went overseas. He'd always planned to take her to France and Italy when he got out of the marines. They could both see the real paintings in a museum.

But he'd returned from in-country in a box.

A red-tailed hawk gave its high whistling cry before it dived. He watched as it plummeted to earth, talons in front. It had been years since he last thought of when he was alive. A thin squeal splintered into silence when the hawk pinned its prey. He looked at the mat of grass-covered earth underneath his form. Right after he died, he often checked in on his family. Now he only watched over his nephew from time to time. When had he stopped visiting his sister and his mom? His dad had died years ago.

"Why can't I see my dad?"

"He's out of our reach now."

"Exactly where is he?"

"I told you this when your father died." Ram still stared out at the ocean. "He passed to a different level where he can learn what he needs to learn before he takes on another lifetime."

"You don't have enough power to have us pop in on him?"

Ram just glanced at him, but the wings were buzzing in agitation again.

He shifted. An annoying itch started between the shoulder blades of his form. He stretched up his arms and tried to ease it. "So what is it then? Why can't we just go see him? What harm would there be in that?"

"I know it's hard to understand these things when you have just had a lifetime on earth."

"I died over forty years ago."

"A mere blink of the eye."

"For you. I still have family alive. In fact—" He leaned in toward Ram. "I've been meaning to pay a visit to my nephew JJ."

The angel was starting to seethe.

An intense particle dispersal flew off Ram and mingled with his own form. He stayed in Ram's face, staring at the angel's eyes, adding, "After I see how Alena is doing."

Ram stood his ground, but his wings began to make a high buzzing whine. "I already told you. Alena will be fine."

"Then I'll see her after I visit JJ."

Ramjets put his hands up and laced his fingers together, right in front of his face. "I need to talk to you about JJ."

The stony angelic joints cracked in little bursts when the angel stretched his hands in front of him, forcing him to move away.

He groaned. More humanlike characteristics from the angel. He was certain Ram was doing that just to annoy, though the angel's wings were still doing a buzzing dance. Something was going on.

"What has JJ done now?" Why couldn't he have been assigned to a more kindly angel, maybe one like the angel in *It's a Wonderful Life*? Any angel other than a pissy wasicun with a bug up his heavenly butt?

"JJ is back with the Travis Beekman crowd."

"I forget which one that is, booze or pot?"

"Alcohol."

Christ. JJ was a good guy, but he was taking a godawful time finding himself. "I guess he's due for another bad dream from his Uncle Joe, eh?"

Wait, that reminded him. "Hey! I could help Alena in her dreams too." Just the thought sent a spark right through him. *Hécetu!* He shook his hands. Bursts of opalescent flares streamed from his fingers. He needed Ram's help, though. Entering a living person's dreams for the first time seemed to require the intervention of an angel.

Ram looked at the sparkling embers and frowned. "Calm down."

"Sure." He chilled his emotions, went blank as he'd done when he needed to fire on the enemy in Vietnam. The flow of sparks dwindled.

Ram nodded. "You're getting better at that."

"What about going into Alena's dreams?" That way he could help her, he really could. It would be perfect. He could touch people in their dreams; he often grabbed JJ and hauled him up into the sky to make a point.

He could show Alena what it looked like above the clouds at night, the tremble of silvery blue that tipped the ocean of cottony mist with sapphire. Like a painting by Chagall he'd always loved. They could see paintings too. He could take her to the Louvre. Or even the Vatican. They could go anywhere in a dream. He just had to get the angel to agree. He couldn't do this on his own, at least the first time he couldn't.

He looked over at Ram. The angel's eyes had narrowed into slits. Ram had that Commanding Officer look about him, the hard-ass glare that preceded a reprimand.

The rumble of a jet pounded the air, pulling his

glance up to where the sun lived. Snowy puffs of the jet trail sparkled against the immaculate azure of the sky. When he looked back down, Ram was shaking his head.

"No dream visits to Alena, Joe." The angel's wings quivered in a wild dance of light and sound, then stilled. "And I'd better give you a stronger shield."

"I don't need it." He moved back.

Too late. The golden wings pulsed. Ram lifted and swirled into the sky, yanking him up by the arm. Air rushed past his ears, toward the angel's open mouth. The veil that divided the physical world from the etheric plane tore loose in a series of tiny pops. Colors that had no name, hues that had *never* had a name blinded him. A flood of deep indigo fading outward to pale violet in gradations that were impossible held him in thrall. The sound that always followed, the cry of adoration and joy, seized him through the rent in the veil between earth and the heavenly realms.

He shuddered. The first time Ram had done this to him, his astral ears had ached for days afterward. No way could he tear himself from Ram's grasp now; he knew this from all the times he'd tried. He held himself still while the angel pulled in the mantle of heaven and poured it over him.

"Close your eyes, Joe."

"Done." Even with his eyes shut, the longing sucked at his gut. But heaven was not for him. "Ramael?" Not yet, anyway.

The angel stopped the outward flow that trickled over him. "What now?"

"I'm dead."

"No kidding."

"How can I have eyes to shut?"

"Jos...Joe." The surge of particles faded to a whisper. "We've been over this before."

"So?" He risked a squint. The veil was closing in a sinuous fold. He could almost touch it. His hand rose by itself and reached toward the final glimmering splendor. But the colors now had names: magenta, purple, teal. The rip sealed with a hiss. "Tell me again."

The angel turned his face away. Ram paused; he seemed about to say something.

He waited. It had taken years for Ram to tell him that he was a Sacred Guardian. Before that, the angel had just ordered him around, telling him what to do. It was at a moment like this when Ram had revealed his status in the afterlife.

But now, the angel's silence stretched into several hours, into days. Night claimed the mountain six times while they hovered there. When the seventh morning came, the angel still hung in the air with him, looking away.

He stayed silent. If Ram thought to wait him out, the angel had another think coming. During one vision quest when he was alive, he'd kept silence for three months. He looked out to the ocean and watched the uneasy tossing of the waves. Storm coming in? April could be pretty or a real bitch here in Northern California. It was hard to tell.

The motion of the waves pulled at him. He liked to go out over the ocean in a storm. It couldn't hurt him and he loved diving through the roiling surf. Hell, he'd even surfed once in 'Nam. He...*Come on, Joe, focus.* He had to keep his thoughts anchored or he'd lose himself in the elements, and Ram would win this round. Many of his questions were never answered, not even indirectly.

Why couldn't Sacred Guardians interfere? Why couldn't they let their cases see them? It would make his job so much easier if he could communicate directly. Why couldn't Sacred Guardians touch people? Why had colors sparked all up his arm when he'd stroked Alena's forehead?

He glanced at Ram's profile. The angel was struggling with something; that was for sure. Ram's wings did a jitterbug, but the rest of his form was completely still. Such a simple question. Why must he have a form at all? He was dead. Why must he still have to look like a man, like he did when he was alive? Couldn't the angel answer that? Why the long wait?

Still, it was better to be quiet; let the angel deliver his message. The last time he asked too many questions, Ram had given him multiple hospital assignments. He shuddered. Hospitals were the worst thing about being a Sacred Guardian. Even the fleeting glimpses of other angels he'd seen within the hospitals had not made up for the cloud of depression and fear weighting the walls whenever he'd needed to help someone cross over.

"Aw, Christ!" Maybe Ram was communing with the other angels! Ram did that sometimes, going completely still and listening. Maybe they'd discovered he'd broken all the rules. He straightened and braced himself for what the angel would say.

In a sudden gesture, Ram loosened his hold. "Joseph, this body you have now—" The angel poked at his arm. "—is as real as the one you left behind."

"So?" When Ram didn't want to tell him something, the angel usually kept quiet. He looked down. At some point they had started a descent. The crest of Mount Tam was only a hundred feet below his toes. "You already told me that."

At least the other angels hadn't discovered his errors. Or maybe they discovered them and didn't care. Or maybe…Well, hell. It made him dizzy trying to figure out angels. It also made the place right between his shoulder blades itch like crazy again, which seemed stupid because he had an etheric form, not a dense matter body. Of course, this itch was smack dab in a place he couldn't scratch. Even if he *could* scratch it. Even if, even if...well, hell.

"This form of yours is simply subject to different laws." Ram reached over and lifted his hands. The angel nodded. "The shield should last you a while." He stopped and looked directly into Joe's eyes. "As long as you don't want Alena to see you."

"Believe me, I don't." He brushed the spot on his T-shirt where the angel had grabbed him. "Well. Thanks for the shield." At least the itch between his shoulder blades was fading now. That was something.

"Sergeant..." Ram bowed his head. "You will go and lecture your nephew, then you can visit Alena." He settled on the ground. "Keep me informed."

Sure. Just like that had been Ram's idea instead of his. Typical. "Lieutenant." He tipped his hand against his forehead in a salute. Ram hated that, too.

The angel stabbed him with a stare that reached all the way to his toes. "Just watch Alena. No dream work."

He backed away. "*Hópo.*" He wouldn't interfere, and he wouldn't let her see him. But he sure as hell would find out what was up with her. He floated higher from the ground and prepared for travel, focusing on JJ's essence.

His particles slid into the fluid stream that would take him where he wanted to go. All at once he became nothing, and everything. "Best way to fly real fast. Damn, but I love this." *Dead marine sergeant gets to be a flyboy.*

Right before he melted, the angel said something. He fought to keep his form from dissolving so he could hear, but it was too late. One moment he was there on the peak of Mount Tam, and the next he was floating over Pine Ridge, nearly a thousand miles away.

Had he really heard what he thought he had? He shook the sparks that always came when he traveled, off his fingertips. “Nah. Must have heard it wrong.”

He thought he’d heard the angel say, “Go with God, friend.”

He shrugged and coasted to the ground. The bit about God was pure Ram. But friend? Get real! No way would the angel be friends with a grunt like him. “Well, the sooner I take care of JJ, the sooner I can see Alena.” And test the limits of the angel’s powers. If he couldn’t ask the angels about what had happened when he touched Alena, he’d have to find the answer himself. Whatever it took, he would find that answer.

Chapter Five

"Goddammit. A church." Alena eyed cement steps climbing to large white double doors. "Another church."

It's just a church. One door stood open to the early spring air. *You don't have to go in.* Twin spires crowned by gold crosses poised above stone walls of faded peach and brown, with an undertone of gray. Across the street on the other side, a row of crisp apartments answered the peach tones of the church with warm apricot. Ferns spilled over the apartment balconies and the faint tinkle of wind chimes followed the gentle breeze. People must love this church. The walls were clean and unblemished, the grounds well tended.

What the fuck was she doing here? She glanced down at her watch. The interview had gone well. The guy interviewing her didn't even flinch when she told him she had a record. He'd asked some pretty pointed questions, though, showing he knew the score. And that was weird. He was the president of a seminary. A school for ministers. He shouldn't have known the real lowdown about soft time, hard time, time served, and shakedown plea bargain. She wasn't all that sure why she shared her history up-front. Hypocrisy sucked, but you were supposed to cover your shady past in a job interview, not lay it out on the table right away. She even told him about her neck injury and her health needs. He hadn't blinked. Maybe he was just being polite.

Still, he'd talked to her for over an hour. He could have just sent her on her way, but he hadn't.

She looked back up and shook her head. Why was she here in front of this church? It was way down the street from Living Light. Why had she come this way instead of the direct route to Michael's daycare down Hearst Street?

She had more time, but she really should go and get Michael. The drop-in daycare charged parents by the hour. She could save another five dollars if she went to get him now. Yet she stood rooted to the sidewalk, staring up at the golden crosses topping the spires.

She'd found herself standing outside of churches each day for the past week. First, she'd stopped outside the Buddhist Temple on Channing Way near her apartment. At least that one made sense. The only exposure she had ever had to any religion was a year in a commune in Taos her parents had joined when she was little. The leader had claimed to be Buddhist. She didn't know how closely he adhered to Buddhist tenets, but she'd liked being at the commune. Meals were regular, and everyone had a place.

She looked down at her feet and shrugged the stiffness out of her neck. It was too early for her to take the medicine Deb's Dr. Ravi had given her. Anyway, it had to last until next week, when she had an appointment with the pain clinic.

She'd never felt the need to go inside a church. When David died, she'd respected his wishes, taken a bus up the coast and spread his ashes at the base of a redwood tree near Mendocino. It was peaceful there and out in nature, as David wanted. She'd not felt the need for religion then. Yet now, every time she even came near a place of worship, her feet slowed and froze to the ground, forcing her to gaze at signs that proclaimed that the answers to every question lay just inside the doors.

Now here she was again, in front of another

church. She glanced at the letters etched in stone above the doors. St. Joseph's. Catholic. Her feet sucked at the pavement when she tried to lift them and go on her way. She stared up at the graceful arch leading inside. It pulled and ripped at some place near her core. She leaned back and tried to turn, to deny the lure of mortar and stone shaped to house something that couldn't be contained. Her tote bag slipped as she swung around and dropped from her shoulder to the ground. She reached for it and stood, hugging it to her chest. One step up, then another sliding lurch to the next step brought her a third of the way to the door.

"This is scanless." Why was she afraid? It was only a church. She could go in, look around and leave. Her feet tapped up the rest of the stairs until she was in the entrance.

Well, she might as well go inside. Something had saved her. Maybe even someone, though she hadn't seen the tall guy since the time he had appeared in front of the bank. The Zamatrex instructions had been really clear, once she read them after Deb had left. She truly *had* taken an overdose and should be under the ground right now, not standing here in front of this church. Maybe if she just went inside to see what was up and ran the rest of the way to Michael's daycare, she would make it in time. Five dollars wasn't much money to many people, but she'd sure like to hang on the extra funds Deb had given her until she got a job.

Still, she eased her feet through the doorway, until she stood just beyond the threshold. Chill shadows greeted her. She peered at the stone of the entryway and the shell-shaped font facing her on the wall to her right. Maybe whatever or whoever had saved her wanted some thanks. Yeah, okay. She could understand that.

"Here goes nothing." Her sandals squeaked all

the way across the wooden floor, down the center aisle.

Jeweled light from tall windows splashed across the ordered march of pews. She glanced across the expanse of the long wooden seats and counted three people. It wasn't the regular church service time, then. Damn! If she were among a whole bunch of people listening to the priest give a sermon, or whatever the Catholics did, everyone would be listening to the priest and wouldn't notice how out of place she was.

Her feet shuffled and stopped. The three people in the church didn't even look up. What should she do? Say a mantra? She'd never really prayed before and had forgotten all of the verses they taught at the commune. All she could remember were a few fragments of a Buddhist chant. Something seemed to murmur this to her from the walls of this church, speaking in the voice of the Tibetan master who had come to the commune when she was little.

No suffering.

Cobalt light from the windows blued the white hair of an old woman who knelt in the third row from the altar. Alena stepped toward the woman, the voice still chanting in her ear.

No end to suffering.

The old woman's head was bowed, and her fingers slipped across a necklace of brown beads she held close. Alena reached the pew where the woman sat.

No death.

She ducked into the row and shuffled sideways toward the woman.

No end to death.

There were padded ledges under the seats in front. She pulled one out and knelt next to the lady. "What the hell do I do now?"

She had only whispered, but the woman

swiveled her head.

"Where's your rosary beads?" Her rounded cheeks crinkled into gentle folds. Brown eyes glimmered behind dark framed glasses. A lace scarf covered the back of her head, but a soft cloud of hair made a blue-white halo surrounding her face.

"I'm not Catholic." *Swift, Alena, really swift. Try again.* "I came in to give thanks for...something that happened to me a couple of weeks ago." She lifted her hands and clasped them. "I've never prayed before." The ring in her nostril itched and she rubbed it. The poor woman would probably flee in horror. "I don't know what to do." And she didn't know why the hell she was here.

"I understand." The door behind the altar creaked open and a man in a janitor's uniform stepped out. "Well, then," the lady murmured, struggling to her feet.

She took the woman's hand and helped her rise.

"Aren't you kind, dear? Come with me, now." The woman beckoned, nodding toward the front door of the church.

She stared at the old lady. Aw, crap. Did this mean she should donate some money? She moistened her lips. Would they throw her out?

"I'm out of work and a single mother," she said. "I can't afford to give money, at least until I get a job."

The woman just shook her head and extended her hand. "Don't worry. I'll show you what you need to do." She took Alena's hand. "I'm Maddy." Papery fingers rasped against Alena's palm.

"I'm Alena."

Maddy's eyes glinted behind her glasses. "Pretty name." She still had Alena's hand. "Come along, now."

She rose and tramped behind Maddy in silence, all the way to the doors she had entered. Chest-high shelves spread across the wall to the left of the entry. Maddy released her hand and then searched through a stack of pamphlets sitting on top of the shelves.

"Ah! Here they are."

She looked down at the papers Maddy held. "The Hail Mary?" She wasn't sure she wanted this. "Aren't I supposed to be baptized or something to say these prayers?" Couldn't she just say her thanks and be on her way?

Maddy pressed the papers into her hands. "Just read them, dear." She nodded to a young man who ambled in and followed him, trotting back into the shadowed peace.

She moved out through the doors and stood blinking. The papers Maddy had given her rustled as a warm, damp gush of air brought a shower of blossoms from a plum tree across the street. She glanced at the sheets of paper. Well, okay. One way of saying thanks was as good as another.

"I guess." She pushed the papers into her bag and looked down the steps. A pale, watery shadow fell across her path. The beat of her heart slipped and pattered against her breastbone. Her own outline lay in crisp darkness to her left. She glanced up. No one stood near her, but the other shadow wavered and poured down the stairs. An airplane? She shaded her eyes and peered into the clear blue-gray arc above her. Empty. She rubbed at her eyes. Have to get to bed early. She descended to the street and settled into a slow trot, her bag thumping at her side. Michael was waiting.

Chapter Six

The shadow was there again.

Alena sat across from Deb in the sun-splashed courtyard just outside her office, sandwich in her lap, and peered at the concrete surrounding the bench. Yes. It was there, a wash of filmy darkness across the bright stretch of pavement, where no darkness should be. Deb sat next to her, smiling at the students sprawled on the grassy area that fronted the classrooms of Living Light.

She moved her hand back and forth across the shadow. The sharp edges of her own shadow pierced the other, paler shade that stretched out to her left.

"Shit."

"What?"

"Um. Nothing, Deb. You were saying?" This was not the first time the shadow had appeared. It wasn't the second or third, either. Truth was, no matter where she sat or walked, her shadow mingled with this other, taller splash of darkness.

"What are you eating?" Deb's upper lip curled a bit.

"Tuna and lettuce."

"Not even mayo?"

"Nah. Ran out."

"No wonder you're so thin. Here—have some onion chips."

"Okay." She moved so she was between Deb and the...whatever it was. "Lay on the carbs." She bit into a chip, eyes on her friend, avoiding the patch of darkness at her side. "Thanks."

For a time, she thought the shadow was an

optical illusion. But it persisted, through clouds and sunshine. She took a mouthful of her cherry cola and let the bite of the carbonated fizz draw her attention away from the wash of gloom tainting the dazzling whiteness of the pavement.

Thank God for Living Light health benefits. She'd already seen two doctors about her...problem. An ophthalmologist had judged her vision to be perfect. He had sent her to a neurologist, who poked and pricked her arms and hands, then had put her in a CAT scan machine and pronounced her brain perfectly sound.

Deb was leaning forward, talking to Janet, the Dean's secretary, who was also out in the sunshine, enjoying the lunch hour. Deb didn't seem to notice that anything was wrong.

She glanced at the space next to her on the bench and chewed her tuna and lettuce. Onion and salt from the chips coated her mouth with sharp bitterness; the iceberg leaves had wilted into mush. She swallowed and the lump made a slow descent to her belly. The shadow she saw was faint, but it took the form of a man. If someone sat beside her, he would throw such a shadow across the pavement, though a real person's shadow would be darker and more defined. Sometimes pieces of a form took shape. She could only see them from the corner of her eye—the line of a shoulder, long, dark hair, the curve of a cheek.

A shudder worked its way outward from the nape of her neck and traveled down through her arms, curling her hands into claws. She looked ahead of her, not gazing directly at the shadow and suddenly the form was there, right there, sitting beside her. Using her peripheral vision, she could see most of it. She breathed shallow and quiet, trying to slow her galloping heart. It did look like a tall man with long dark hair, but she couldn't quite make out the face.

Okay. Deb was beside her. All she had to do was to turn and confront the man. Her hands knotted into fists. "One. Two." Her utterance was so low even she couldn't hear it. She swung her head sharply around and stared directly at where the form sat.

There was nothing there. Just the shadow on the pavement. *Fuck.*

Deb paused in her comment on the ivy-covered walls of Living Light. "All through, Lena?" She laughed and pointed at Alena's lap.

She looked down at the mangled sandwich clutched in her hand. Cripes. This was all she had brought to eat. She mashed it into the brown bag and took a deep breath. "I'll bring some burritos next time."

"They have quesadillas at the minimart a few blocks away." Janet grinned at her. "You could use the calories. Lucky duck," she added, patting her own plump thigh.

"Sounds good. Let's walk, Deb."

She reached for her handbag on the seat next to her, where the invisible shadow man sat. A tingling pulsed along her arm, the same quiver that she felt whenever she placed herself anywhere close to the shadow person who stalked her.

Once when she was little and her mom had gotten it together enough for her to attend school like kids from normal families, a science teacher had let his class place their hands on a Van de Graf generator that made their hair stand out from their heads.

She clutched her handbag and turned away from the phantom shadow, back toward Deb. The electric prickle of her flesh when she touched the bench to get her bag was the same jittery pins-and-needles she had gotten from touching the generator.

The shadow was bad enough. She wadded the

paper bag and tossed it into a stone trashcan. If that were the only thing, she could deal with it. All she needed to do was to set it on "ignore." It was amazing what she could endure; the years she had spent with her nomadic hippie mom and drugged-out dad had taught her that.

But the voice was harder to overlook.

It was a male voice, a low, rumbling murmur with a cadence to it that she couldn't place, as if he were foreign. The voice whispered encouragement. Sometimes it teased, or chided. Like now.

Hey Alena—why do you look away?

She gulped, glancing at Deb. The older woman was checking her watch.

"We've still got half an hour left. It's not far, is it?"

"Nah. Just down the hill. You can just keep going down from there to catch BART." She stood, brushing breadcrumbs off her skirt. Fat pigeons lumbered toward her. She stumbled and skipped around them, ignoring the upward lurch in the phantom shadow.

"You've got a great situation here, Lena." Deb smiled at her. "I'm glad I had the time to spend your lunch hour with you."

"I'm happy you came to visit. Michael is gonna miss you." She linked arms with Deb and maneuvered the older woman away from the bench, shielding her from the faint stretch of darkness flowing across the brick pavement beside them.

"Tell that little boy his auntie will be visiting again in a month or so."

****

The page turned, tiny letters swam across its paper surface, and formed into words. She closed her eyes and shuddered. Crazy, that was what she was. Goddamn crazy. She forced her eyes open and stared at the words. Auditory and visual hallucinations.

Seeing and hearing things. Crazy.

She placed the book on the reference librarian's counter and grabbed her handbag, nodding at the clerk behind the desk. The Diagnostic and Statistical Manual of the American Psychiatric Association had a classification system for mental disorders. She broke into a trot, skipping down the steps of the library and making the right turn that led back to her office. The trouble was what she experienced didn't seem to fit any particular category very well.

She sent a quick smile to Janet as she slipped through the dark wooden doors to the tiny office that housed the secretarial staff. These people didn't know she was crazy. She'd better keep it that way. Make her face a mask. Go for happy and engaged with what she was doing, not worried and fucking scared. She let her mouth soften and eyes brighten.

Professor Pott's manuscript tottered in a stacked pile on her desk, yellow Post-its bristling from pages where he'd marked changes. She clicked on the word-processing icon on her computer and pulled up the latest draft of Professor Pott's biography of St. Dominic, then sighed at the red ink covering the first page on her desk. "Well, I'd better get going on this one."

"His deadline is months away." Jennifer Lewis, supervisor of clerical staff, patted Alena's shoulder.

Alena kept her bright eyes shining and smiled up at her boss. "I'll have it ready for him." She put her earphones on, cranked Live 105.3 just enough to rock out without bugging her office mates, and dived in to the manuscript. Ms. Lewis allowed the clerical staff to use headphones when they were working. Not only was Living Light the coolest job environment she'd ever known, the music always muffled her shadow's comments, allowing her to put in steady, good work. "Good thing I can still focus."

"What?"

"Ah. Nothing." She glanced over and winked at Ms. Lewis. "Just thinkin' aloud."

Crazy. That's what the book said.

Yeah, she did hear voices. One voice. It sounded like a man. She guessed she saw things, too, if you counted the shadow and the form as things.

But she didn't feel crazy. She finally had a good job. The pain treatment the clinic had prescribed was mostly working, if she didn't strain her neck too much. Michael was thrilled with the Living Light preschool. He already had two new friends. She'd paid off her debt to Deb, and had even scrimped and saved some money for the move to a larger space. If it weren't for the voice and the shadow, she'd have no doubts at all about her well-being.

So what should she do? If she were on the verge of a psychotic break, as the Psychiatric Manual seemed to warn, what would happen to Michael? His well-being was what mattered. Michael was everything to her.

She had to see another doctor. Somehow this experience could be explained. Post trauma something or other. Maybe the effects of accidental overdose...God, she did *not* want to go there.

The words on her computer screen fractured and ran together. Her fingertips made a cool pressure against her eyelids as she massaged her eyes, then she shook her head and typed out the last three sentences on the page. Better print it out page by page. It was easier to see errors on paper than on the computer screen. Not that Professor Pott wouldn't have more changes after she finished what he had given her. But he was a cool guy, all rumpled gray hair and spindly limbs, like a great heron. He'd look over her completed draft and hold his chin, then smile and draw out his red pen. She'd always have a job here at this rate.

Yeah, if she could avoid the psych ward.

While she waited for the printer to spit out the page, she looked at the business card that the neurologist had given her. John Henderson, MD, was the name, in plain black ink on fine white card stock. She squeezed her eyes shut, then opened them and stuck the card back in her wallet.

A psychiatrist.

Paper whispered out of the printer and into her hands. She should make an appointment. Yeah. She should.

She should. But she didn't want to.

She didn't want the voice to stop, and this scared the shit out of her. It was like having a friend, someone with her all the time. The voice suggested things. It even gave her good advice. She had followed its urging and tried some of the things it said. Like when it told her she should check in the East Bay Express for a new apartment. Right there, in the classified section, was her dream apartment, a two-bedroom on the north side of the Berkeley campus on upper Shattuck in a building for low income people.

The voice had told her to put a deposit on the apartment. They even had a special program for single mothers. She submitted her application and deposit, worrying all the while that they would never want to rent to her. After all, she had only been working full time for the past two months and there were so many people looking for apartments, she was sure it would never be hers.

She jumped when the printer light stopped blinking, then she held the page up to the light. It was fully recycled paper stock but gleamed in her hand. Looking good. Professor Pott would be pleased.

But not half as pleased as she'd been when her landlord had given her a glowing reference. Somehow, among all the applicants, the apartment manager had chosen her. She and Michael would move to their new apartment in six weeks.

The snowy sheet of the revised page slid with a smooth hiss into a new stack on her desk. She pulled out the next red-inked page and adjusted her chair. As she held her fingers over the keyboard, she glanced to one side, then the other, and released her breath in a wheezing sigh. No shadow now. Hell, maybe the voice was just an inner voice, her inner guide. As long as she didn't talk back to it, she wasn't crazy, was she? She could listen to it when she wasn't busy working and could consider what it said.

She fumbled with her headset to adjust it and the newest *Radiohead* track thumped in her ears. "Mmmm. Good band." Her fingers tapped in a steady rhythm across the keyboard.

****

Michael went down to sleep early. She allowed herself one last nuzzle right below his chin as his eyelids fluttered, then she straightened and picked up her new string of rosary beads hanging from the corner of her mirror, sat on the couch and glanced at the first sheet of paper Maddy had given her.

Time to practice. There may or may not be a God. All she knew was that *something* had helped her, and she fully respected that. Whatever had helped her deserved a bit of her time and effort in thanks, every day.

The beads slipped smoothly through her fingers as she read the verses on the page. Three Hail Marys. She recited the words silently, then turned the sheet of paper over and closed her eyes. "Hail Mary, full of grace, blessed art thou among people."

Among women.

"And blessed is the fruit of thy womb." She raised her head and shook her shoulders. The prickle was back. Little electric fingers danced across her neck and shimmied down her legs. She turned the page over and stared at the words. Hey, the voice was right. She closed her eyes.

"Hail Mary, full of love..."

Grace.

Her eyes blinked open. Right again. "Full of grace, blessed art thou among women and blessed is the fruit of, of..." Aw, shit! She'd gotten this right before—why couldn't she remember it now? She glanced down at the page. It wasn't a complicated prayer. Not as complicated as some of the mantras she'd learned as a kid in the commune.

The voice gave her the creeps. That must be it.

The word is "womb," Alena. A low-throated chuckle followed the words.

She squeezed her eyes shut. Screw this. She could listen, but she would *not* talk to it. As long as she didn't answer it, she wasn't crazy.

"Fruit of the loom."

Fuck! Alena raised her hands to her mouth. Did she really say that? She held her breath. Was that blasphemy or something? Would whatever had saved her undo the miracle? Would she lose her job? Would she find out she was actually dead from her stupid mistake?

God. Would something happen to Michael?

A deep belly laugh shook the walls.

Alena kept her head down and her eyes closed, but she had to keep her mouth covered against the giggles that bubbled past her lips, joining the bass chuckles of the voice. Fruit of the loom. Oh, man, that was *scanless*. She had to stop this!

If she just stayed quiet long enough, the voice usually went away. Both hands pressed against her mouth stilled her own laughter. "I am not crazy. I am not crazy. I am not crazy." Her fingers muffled her words, but the sound seemed to erase the male voice. She waited until the only thing she could hear was the slow tick and grumble of her refrigerator.

The beads rolled past her fingers again. "Hail Mary, full of grace, blessed art thou among women and blessed is the fruit of thy womb, Jesus Christ."

Amen.

She leaped to her feet. "Hey! Stop that!" She glared at the walls. "You never let me finish!"

Complete silence sucked at her ears. Even the complaint of the old refrigerator disappeared, though her heart thundered.

Shit! She'd really gone and done it now. The couch squeaked as she leaned her calves against the edge. She'd *talked* to it. Not just talked to it, she'd yelled at it. A quick glance around the room revealed nothing. No man stood there. She wrapped her arms around her waist and shivered. "I'm not crazy. I'm not; I'm not; I'm not."

A soft cry and whimper pulled her to Michael's side. "Oh, baby. Michael," she murmured. "Mama's sorry she made a big noise."

She drew her hand across Michael's forehead. Was he having a nightmare? His face was sweaty. She clucked softly and smoothed the hair back from his forehead in a steady rhythm. The women at the commune had taught her this. Babies and young children could be soothed back to sleep when you stroked their foreheads. Alena was just nine years old when they had shown her this trick. Every evening she'd watched the mothers in the women's common sleeping area, smoothing their babies' hair back.

Alena lifted her hand when Michael's face went lax again. When she was younger, she used to wish her mother would do this for her. Chase the nightmares away.

Sure. Right. She huffed and the ring in her nose quivered. Her parents were drug addicts. Who was to say she was any better? Just look at her, talking to shadows, hearing disembodied voices, and now her own crazy voice made her son cry out in his sleep.

Hey. I'm sorry.

She pulled a lump of blanket that had bunched under Michael's shoulder. "That's okay." Michael gave a long, slow sigh and turned over. "It wasn't your fault. I was the one who..." Her throat closed. She straightened, wincing at the crack of her tendons, and stared around the room. Still empty. Her shoulders slumped. Oh, now that was completely over the top! She was talking to it again. Well, she had gone this far. She'd broken her own rule. Might as well go all the way.

"Okay." She drew herself up to her full height, not much, she knew, only five foot five, but it was always better to face things with her head held high. She paused, searching for words. How should she address it? What could she call it?

"Just who the hell are you?" Her words rang against the walls and bare wooden floor, though she had barely whispered. But there was no answer. After several minutes, she relaxed her shoulders and gathered up the papers Maddy had given her. At least it hadn't answered back. She could throw away the psychiatrist's business card. It was her voice after all. She could control this. Now where was the sheet with the Hail Mary?

Joe.

The papers rustled in her hands. She still had several other prayers to learn, and the credo. The sheets were out of order; she ought to organize them before she started. "Uh, what did you say?"

My name, Alena. The voice had a fullness and timbre it never had before. It was low and rich, with an inflection she almost recognized; she just couldn't remember where she'd heard it before.

Her mouth went dry; her hands shook. The papers crumpled.

My name is Joe. Yes. It was a deep voice, dark and velvet smooth.

She jumped up, threw the couch pillows on the floor.

Wait!

The sofa bed extension screeched out of the couch when she yanked it. She covered her ears and stood shaking. "Stop!" Her throat rasped. "I am *so* not hearing this!"

What are you doing?

It didn't help. She could still hear it. "Go away!"

Aw, c'mon!

"I'm fucking not listening!" She dragged the blankets back and dove under them. "GO AWAY!"

Good God, Alena. Watch your mouth!

She pulled the blankets up over her head.

Chapter Seven

"You say you're seeing things?" The guy had wire-rimmed glasses. "Things that aren't really there?" Lots of junk on his desk, too—a little tray heaped with business cards, stacks of books, three coffee cups. A clump of rocks painted with petroglyphs crowded the speaker phone. Tiny wooden elephants marched across the surface of the desk, all the way to the edge.

Joe turned to diplomas hung on the wall. John Henderson, M.D. A psychiatrist. Board certified. Stanford graduate. Well, whoop-de-do.

The chair Alena sat in bulged with indigo velvet. She was lost in that chair, her green-gray eyes sunken, her vivid presence subdued. "Yeah." Her voice was low, but sure. A little husky, though, as if tears were close.

He started. If she broke down, what should he do? Would this shrink hospitalize her? "Don't tell him you hear me, okay? I won't talk to you anymore. I promise. Just don't tell him you hear me."

Alena scowled, holding her finger to her lips, looking right into the space where he floated. Dr. Henderson was focused on the file on his desk and didn't seem to see her motion.

He expanded, his essence spreading over the room. Could she *see* him now? Damn, he had to be careful.

Alena looked over at the doctor, straightened, and cleared her throat. "A shadow. I see a shadow."

He condensed his form, floated back, and glanced around to see if he was making a shadow.

The lighting in the office came from golden track lights recessed in the ceiling, not bright enough to throw a shadow off his form. Ram's shield must be holding up. *So how did Alena know exactly where he stood?*

The window behind John Henderson was covered with thin blinds, allowing soft, foggy, San Francisco light to seep inside. He peered through the slits of the blinds. The slate cornices and beveled windows of an elegant apartment building across the street glowed with pastel, sun-tipped fog. Still, not enough light came through to reveal a shadow from his form.

"You think you see, or you do see."

Alena looked down. "I see it." She pressed her lips together. Her nose ring quivered.

"And what does this shadow do?"

She spread her hands. "It's just—" She lifted her arms and let them drop. "—there." When Henderson didn't speak she continued, "It's there, it floats around, and then it's not there." She looked away. "Completely scanless, right?"

"Pardon?"

Alena sighed. "Scanless, like a scanner."

Henderson frowned and spread his hands. "Yes?"

"Scanners scan; scanless means it's bogus, it doesn't scan."

A little smile creased the face of the shrink into folds.

He snorted. Doc had to be at least forty. Too old for Lena.

"You had your eyes checked?" Henderson held his pen poised over a sheet of paper in the file folder.

She gave a single, definite nod. "They didn't find anything. My eyes are okay."

The shrink tapped his pen against the desk. "Why don't you tell me about yourself?"

Alena sunk into the plush depths of the chair and looked directly at the guy. “I’m a single mom. My son is three.” She clasped her hands together. “I got this job, a new job. Started two months ago. Hey, that’s not why I’m here,” she continued, when the shrink frowned. “My job is cool, I mean, I like it. I don’t understand why I’m seeing stuff.” She shifted in her seat. Her right leg lifted and draped across the other. She toyed with the fabric on the arms of the chair, thumbs nibbling the nap into a rough groove and smoothing it over.

“You say you’re a single mother?” At her nod, Henderson leaned forward. “How is your relationship with your son’s father?”

She looked up at the ceiling. “He’s dead.” Uncrossed her legs. “My son’s father is dead.”

“How did he die?”

Alena looked into her lap. Her hands went still. She coughed and cleared her throat again. One hand lifted. “Car accident. Um, that is—” She rubbed her eyes. “—a guy in a truck hit our car.”

“You were in the car.”

“Yeah.”

“Were you hurt?”

“Discs in my neck got all squished.”

Henderson flinched. “How long ago was this?”

“Going on two years now.”

“That must have been tough.”

“Well, life is tough, right?” She gripped the arms of the chair. Her foot twitched and rapped against its legs. “Shit.” She took her ankle in her hand and squeezed. “Give me a moment, okay? It’s been doing this recently.” Her foot shook harder. “It will stop in a minute.”

He put his hands behind his back. He wanted to comfort her. But not now. Not in front of Mr. Shrink dickhead.

“Have you had a neurological exam?” The

psychiatrist took his wire-rimmed glasses off.

"What?" She looked up and blinked. "Oh, yeah." Her foot chugged to a stop. "Yeah, I did." She pushed her hair back. "They aren't sure why this is happening, so they gave me your number."

"How long has your foot been doing this?"

She closed her eyes a moment. "About the past month or so. I had really bad headaches for two years, but they put a needle in my neck, a..."

"Cervical ESI under fluoro?"

"Yeah. That made the discs a bit better."

"So your headaches are gone?"

"Pretty much gone, yeah. I still get migraines if I'm not careful, but the constant headache went away."

"Can you tell me more about the accident?"

"We were at an intersection. The light, ah, went green, and David, my, my husband..."

"Take your time. Do you want some water?"

"I'm okay." Alena rubbed between her brows. "This guy coming the other way ran the red light."

"He broadsided you?"

"Fucker didn't even have a license. No insurance. Drunk." She sank back into the depths of the chair. "Bastard walked away from it."

"Alena, watch your mouth."

Alena glanced to where he floated and scowled again.

Oh, forget it. "I'll be quiet." He forced his molecules into slow mode. He might shimmer a little, due to the particle displacement, but at least this would keep him from reacting to everything she said.

"Didn't he go to jail?" The shrink must have noticed Alena's frown, but he didn't say anything about it.

"Damn straight he did. We didn't have any insurance, either. My husband, David, he wasn't good about keeping things current, you know?" A thin line of moisture tracked down her cheek. "But the District Attorney went after the fucker who hit us. He, he nailed the scumbag."

Joe stumbled against the wall. His molecular slowdown made him too dense. The diplomas rattled. He caught one before it slipped off its hook and he stood there vibrating, but neither Alena nor the shrink seemed to notice anything.

"I see." Henderson just looked at Alena. A motorcycle rumbled up the street, but inside the office, silence spun a tense wire through the air.

Finally, Alena spoke. "It was stupid, so senseless. My birthday."

"It was your birthday?"

She nodded. "He was taking me to the Aquarium. Our son was just a baby; we'd left him with a sitter, thank God." She blinked. "I liked seeing the fish."

"Do you remember anything about the accident?"

Her head dropped; her voice came out in a weary gust. "Not much. Just one moment we were fine and the next, well, it was weird."

"Yes?"

"All I remember is trying to get David's face out of the airbag." Her voice softened. "His face was mashed into the airbag. I thought, 'Oh, I have to get it out, so David can breathe.' Stupid, huh?" She pressed her face into her hands.

He glanced at Henderson. The shrink was oblivious. Why the hell do psych-doc types play these games, anyway? They think everyone is wacko, everyone but them? Couldn't the guy see Alena was beaten up inside over this? Just look at her! She was shaking. Why didn't the crap-head say something?

He moved closer to Alena. Not too close, though, not close enough so he spooked her again. He hovered just behind her, staring down at the sheen of her red-black hair. His mom would have called it "black fire." If he were still alive, well, he'd have brought Alena back to the prairie to meet his mom. Taste Mary Littlehawk's fried bread and *wasna*, pounded meat of buffalo or elk with chokecherries and bone marrow. Maybe go for walks along White Clay Creek.

He drifted up. Shit. He was *dead*; he was here to help, and that was all. Not to touch, not to interfere. But holy hell! Big Wing hadn't told him Alena's husband had been killed right in front of her. No wonder she forgot how much medicine she'd taken. She must have been holding on by a thread.

"There's a box of tissues right beside you." The shrink's voice made a harsh stab at the silence.

He jumped, but Alena only glanced up.

"Thanks." She pulled a couple of tissues out, and held them on her lap.

"Tell me about your marriage." The shrink tapped his pen against the desk.

She stared out the window. "Why?"

"Why not?"

The clock ticked. Alena sank back into the chair.

A bright spear of something sharp and hurting lanced his side. What the hell? He doubled over and held his arms across his heart. Well, where his heart would be if he had a physical body. Damn, this hurt. He hobbled toward the window and tried to straighten. A tug, like the pulling of stitches, sent another sluice of aching that grabbed somewhere between his belly and his throat. He glanced up. It seemed to emanate from Alena.

She sniffed once and looked all around the room. "He was steady. He worked. He didn't do drugs and he didn't screw around."

"What about you? Were you happy?"

The ache flared. He stumbled back and fell

through the wall. Aged wood and thick plaster sucked at his arms; granite and mortar of the outer walls forced his form through the magnetic resonance of stone as he punched through to the outside. He shook the buzz from his ears and looked down. Twelve stories below, an open-air market hummed with people. Crates filled with the bright glow of tangerines and the candy green of limes pulsed while something in this weird form of his vibrated with the agony pouring out from the window behind him. He turned toward the window and looked inside.

This was no good. He could hardly focus. What good would he be to Alena if every time she hurt he went into a meltdown? He lifted his arm, made a fist with his right hand, and followed it, barreling back through the wall into the office.

She was still sitting there. "I was happy. There was stuff, you know; he spent too much and liked to gamble some at Reno, but we were happy." Her face was blank and weary. "So, there you are. Am I nuts?"

Something flickered behind John Henderson's eyes. "Do you think you are?"

"I don't think so."

"What if you were?"

She gave him a long, assessing stare and looked down at her hands. "They'd lock me up and take my son away."

"Who is 'they'?"

A flash of smoky emerald blazed when she looked up. "I'm not stupid, doctor. Child Protective Services. Mother sees things and they take the kid away. I'd lose my job, too."

"I wonder that you are here, then."

"Huh?"

"Why wouldn't you try to hide it? You have so much to lose."

Alena leaned forward, nearly touching the shrink's desk. "It's my boy, see? My baby. I love my son. If there is any chance—" She clasped her hands and stared at them. "—any chance that I am nuts, he might be in danger." Her breath puffed out. "I don't want to lose him. But I'm seeing this shadow that nobody else sees." She nodded. "Look, doctor. It's like this. If something happens to me—" Her hands fluttered, face dropped. "I mean, if I'm..."

"Crazy?"

She nodded and raised her head. "I need to know. I've got a friend who will take my boy, but if I'm not crazy, well, I'm his mom. *I* want to raise him."

"Alena, from what you've told me so far, I don't think you're crazy."

Joe slumped forward. Alena would be all right. "Just don't tell him you can hear me," he whispered.

Alena's hand jerked. She turned her head toward him, but spoke to the shrink, "God, doctor. I mean, you just don't know...Nothing like this has ever happened to me before."

"What about your parents?"

"Dead."

"You'd better start at the beginning."

"Okay, okay." She shifted and looked away. "We moved around a lot. They didn't have much." She bent and scratched at her ankle. "When things got too bad, mom and I went into a shelter."

"Any foster homes?"

"Only two, when I was little."

"What happened?"

"I got picked up a couple of times for truancy. A few weeks later, my parents would get it together enough for the state to return me."

"Did you prefer to stay with your parents?"

She shrugged. "Don't get me wrong. I didn't want to live like that. I don't think any kid should have to live like that. But it was all I knew. They were my folks."

"How did they support you?"

She gave a hard-edged laugh. "They didn't."

Henderson just sat there.

"I did this little dance until I was, um, ten or so."

"A dance?"

"On the street."

"You stripped?"

She shook her head. "Nothing like that. Mom and Dad had a bucket and a sign, saying they were deaf." She tapped her fingers against her thigh. "I started dancing and smiling at people. They'd drop money in the bucket."

"Where?"

"Mostly near train stations, where a lot of people are in a rush to go to work and have bits of money to throw at you so they don't have to look."

Henderson leaned forward. "Where did you live?"

"Here and there." She sighed. "Wish I still smoked. I could use a cigarette now." Her fingers pinched the bridge of her nose. "After they died, I went on the streets. Until I got picked up and had a choice."

"A choice for what?"

"Juvenile Hall or Deb Jenkins' school for lost kids."

"I don't even have to guess which you picked," Henderson laughed. "I've heard of Ms. Jenkins."

"She's really something." Alena coughed.

"I'll get you some water." The shrink stepped from behind his desk and went out into the hallway where a water dispenser sat.

"Thanks."

Joe floated closer to Alena, landing right at her side. This didn't make sense. Any woman who had gone through all that Alena was describing was tough; she had to be tough. And yet she had overdosed. If he hadn't been there, she would have died. Maybe it was just too many things at once that sent her over the edge, made her forget how much she'd taken, but there was something here he just didn't understand. Something else Ram was keeping from him.

He couldn't help it. He had to say something. "They made you *dance*? Your parents made you dance for strangers?"

"Shhhh." Alena waved in his direction, her eyes wide.

"This should make you feel a bit better." Henderson handed the small paper cup to Alena, passing right through him.

He reeled, nearly bumping the parade of wooden elephants off the shrink's desk. Floating into the corner, he tried to keep his form from touching anything. He'd been so caught up in Alena, he hadn't noticed where the doctor had entered the room again.

"Kind of drafty in here, isn't it?" Henderson moved to the window. "Hmmm. Fog must be coming in." He turned to Alena.

"It seems fine to me."

"Well." Henderson moved to the chair behind his desk. "Why don't you tell me of a time when you were happy, when you were a child." The shrink leaned back in his chair and clasped his hands.

"Let me think." Alena closed her eyes. "Oh—right. We were at this commune. I can't even remember its name. Some Tibetan or East Indian place, I think it was in Arizona or New Mexico. It was cool. All the women and babies had a separate house and nobody got stressed about anything. They didn't allow any drugs." Her forehead smoothed. "The food was good, and there was always enough of it." She almost smiled.

If he had fists and Ram was here, the angel would be meat right about now. *Watch her, my ass.* Her best memory was of some cult commune? This woman needed help, more than many of the cases he'd ever been given. He started to drift toward Alena, but the shrink jerked his head and glanced at the clock on his desk.

"Mrs. Morgan, I'm so sorry—our time is nearly up, and I'm sure you have more to say." The shrink drew a card from the alabaster tray on his desk and handed it to her, then scribbled on a slim pad of paper.

"First, I want to assure you again that I don't believe you're crazy." Henderson leaned forward and took Alena's hand. "I think you've been under a lot of stress, for a very long time." The paper he had written upon made a sharp crackling as he tore it off the pad. "I do think you would benefit from therapy, though. This card has my intern's name and phone number. I'd like you to give her a call." Henderson's teeth flashed pearl. "She specializes in single mothers, and I think she could help you deal with the stresses you're experiencing."

Alena blinked and stared at the card. She moistened her lips.

He left the corner of the room and let the particles of his hands slide over the back of her chair. "Don't tell him you hear me."

Her hand jiggled and she glanced around the room. "Doctor." She looked down at the paper the shrink had handed her. "What is this?"

Henderson stood and moved around the desk. "I'm giving you a prescription for an anti-anxiety medication." The shrink opened the door. "This might help with your symptoms."

"Will it make the shadow go away?" She slipped it into her bag.

Henderson shrugged. "It can't hurt." The door

opened farther. "I think you'll find that this shadow you're worried about is really something natural." The shrink took Alena's arm and escorted her out. "Something you're misinterpreting because of the stress you're under."

He floated out behind them. The ache he'd felt before tugged at him again, not as sharp, but with a weight behind it. "Alena. Do you really want me to go away?"

Her head swiveled and her mouth twitched, but all she said was, "Okay." She reached out and shook Henderson's hand. "Thanks, doctor."

He glided behind her as she walked through the door. She stopped before the bank of elevators and pushed the button, then dug into her bag and pulled out the prescription. A mirror flanked by ferns faced her. She stared at the prescription, stroking it with her index finger. Her shoulders sagged.

"Okay, then." Her whisper was so faint he wondered if he had caught her thoughts.

"You don't need to take anything." He hadn't meant to say this—it just popped out.

Alena startled, looking up into the mirror. She blinked once, hard, and stuffed the prescription into her bag. The elevator door slid open.

She strode into the elevator.

Chapter Eight

Her eyes popped open. It was pitch black.

"Wake up!"

She turned over and squinted into the glow of the clock radio dial. Four AM. Shit! Probably wouldn't be able to get back to sleep. Stupid Voice wouldn't go away, wouldn't leave her alone. She shut her eyes and rolled onto her back. Ever since she had spoken to it, the Voice seemed to think she owed it something. It just wouldn't stop speaking to her. Well, she had ignored it ever since her visit to Dr. Henderson. She could just continue to pretend she didn't hear it.

The muted roar and clank of a garbage truck chugged somewhere down the street. Pulling her pillow against her ears didn't do any good, the rumbling of the truck and shouts of the men still came through. They just had to pick up the trash at four in the morning, didn't they? And she had a meeting at eight.

"Alena," the Voice barked. "Get up."

Get up yourself! She hadn't told Dr. Henderson she heard the Voice. They'd lock her up for sure. Throw away the key. Dammit! She rolled over again and punched her pillow. The world was full of widows, and there were lots of single mothers. They all seemed to manage. Why couldn't she? Other people didn't hear voices. Well, she wasn't going to give into this. The Voice wasn't real. It couldn't be. Dr. Henderson said the shadow wasn't real, so the Voice wasn't real either.

She buried her face in her pillow, squeezed her

eyes tight, and held her breath. The prescription Doctor Henderson had given her still sat on the bureau. She hadn't filled it yet, but if the Voice continued to pester, maybe she would give it a try.

A sharp plop sounded from her kitchen. Damn faucet must be leaking again. Underneath these sounds, something whistled, like a teakettle ready to scream. Now what was that? The heater wasn't on. Sometimes it came on even in the summer when the fog came in and made everything cold, but she hadn't heard the chug and whine that told her it was on.

The hissing changed to a hoarse gasp.

She rolled out of the sofa bed and hit the floor. "Michael?" She dragged her robe over her shoulders and slammed the light switch on.

Two scarlet spots marked his cheeks. His eyes were open and stared in glassy confusion at her.

"Baby?" She felt his cheeks. "It'll be okay, Michael." God, he was burning up!

She jumped up and went for the bathroom. How had he gotten sick so fast? He was fine at dinner. Cold water blasted into the tub. Just said his throat was a little scratchy. Was the water too cold? Two jerks of her hand twisted the faucet shut. She should take his temperature first.

"Alena—just go get him."

"Oh, shut the hell up!" She ripped open the medicine cabinet and pulled the thermometer out of its plastic jacket. "You're not helping." She strode into the bedroom, shaking the thermometer as she walked. "Here, baby." She kneeled at Michael's side. "I want you to hold this under your tongue."

"Mom?" The one word was too much for him. He gulped and exploded in a barking cough, ending the long spasm with a wheezing cry for air.

Oh, God. Oh, God. Oh, God. She spun around and grabbed the first thing her hands touched on the pile of clean laundry sitting on the table. Bronchiolitis again. She jammed her legs into the pair of jeans and hopped over to Michael's bureau sliding the zipper up and closing the snap. The last time Michael had bronchiolitis was a year ago. The doctor told her to watch for upper respiratory illnesses because Michael was the kind of kid who would become asthmatic when he got sick. She dug into his bureau and plucked a T-shirt with Spiderman emblazoned across the front and a pair of sweat pants and socks out of the drawer.

"It'll be okay, baby." He'd gone blue that time. Since then she'd given him baby cold medicine at the first sign of even a stuffy nose.

She peeled his soaked pajama top from his arms and tugged it over his head. When he had this before, they'd hospitalized him and puffed albuterol into his lungs. She wiped the hair back from his face. God, he was clammy. She knotted his pajamas in her hand. No children's cough and cold medicine would take care of this.

She had to take him to the doctor. Now. Where the hell were her car keys? She jumped and Michael's clothes dropped out of her hands, scattering on the floor. Jesus, what was she thinking? She didn't have a car anymore. Hadn't had a car for the past two years. She wrapped Michael's blankets around his shoulders.

"Just hang on, Michael."

"He needs to go to the hospital."

"I know, I know." The emergency number her health plan had given her was right by the phone. She should call. Yes, that's what she should do. She stumbled toward it. "Fuck me!" She'd talked to the Voice again.

"Watch the language!"

"Watch yours!" The receiver slipped out of her fingers and banged against the wall. "Piss-ass phone!" She would worry about the Voice later. The phone chilled her fingers. She punched the emergency number. The phone purred, one ring, then two, while Michael sucked air through his mouth.

"Calm down," the Voice barked.

"Yeah, right." One more ring, then a woman's voice. *You have reached Health Endurance. If you are calling from a touch-tone phone, press one now.* Her finger stabbed the one. Michael gasped and held his throat as he breathed in a rapid pant.

"Alena. Dress him warm and take him to the hospital." The Voice was firm. "That's an order!"

"You a cop or something?" The Voice was right. She swallowed and blinked. The taped message droned in her ear. *If this is hospital or medical staff, press one. If this is an emergency, please hang up and dial 9-1-1...*The receiver dropped to the floor. She would just take Michael to the hospital. Better calm down, first. If she flipped out, it would scare her baby.

She skidded into the main room picking up socks, T-shirt, and pants, then grabbed a flannel shirt from the stack of laundry. "Okay, Michael." Her voice rasped. Gotta do better. "We're going to the doctor." She couldn't seem to get the T-shirt over his head. He shuddered so much his arms got stuck. Once she had it in place, she pushed his hands into the flannel shirt; his fingers caught on the sleeve buttons.

"Stop." The Voice rang off the walls and startled her.

She shook. This was not good. How could she help Michael if she allowed herself to fall apart? "Okay, okay." She drew Michael into her arms and held him close, felt each struggling fight to draw in a breath. Oh why, why, why hadn't she taken that first aid and CPR class last year when she wasn't working?

"Just calm down. Breathe slow and easy yourself." The Voice was quieter now. "He'll follow your lead."

Her heart banged against her chest. She rocked back and forth, stroking Michael's sopping hair. "We'll be okay." God, what could she do now? Deb was too far away. Her next door neighbor Mrs. Ellison was out of town. Alena didn't know her neighbors on the other side, but she hadn't seen either of them all week. The new guy upstairs worked the night shift. He didn't get back until after six AM.

"All right." Now it was her voice that echoed in the room. "I don't know who or what you are." Her arms tightened around Michael. "I don't even believe you exist." She squeezed her eyes tight. "But if you are there, I could use some *real* help right now." The heat of Michael's body drew sweat from her arms.

Silence.

She snorted. Just listen to her. Talking to a Voice inside her head when her baby needed help. What an idiot! She should call 9-1-1. Should have from the start. What had gotten into her? She started to put Michael down, but he whimpered.

"I've got it covered." The Voice filled the room and curled around her with warm authority. "Wrap him in the blanket, tight, so it doesn't come undone."

She watched from someplace deep inside as her hands lifted Michael and she rolled him into his blanket mummy-tight, tucking the ends deep within the cocoon she had formed.

"Now lift him and go outside." The Voice had an edge to it, a ring of command.

She found herself standing, Michael held close, his little head tucked under her chin. "It's a mile to the hospital." Michael's face rested against her neck, furnace hot. But he was already breathing easier. "I need to call a cab."

"Just go outside," the Voice commanded. Then, when she didn't move, "Dammit, woman, get your butt out there!"

She stared at her hand pulling the door open. It was just like listening to her fifth grade teacher, the one who had actually given a hoot about her. When Mrs. Laughton said jump, her body always reacted before she could even think. She picked her way down the short flight of stairs to the front door and halted at the bottom. "I didn't lock up."

"Don't worry about that. Go outside. Now!"

"Okay, okay!" She staggered out into the soggy front steps of dawn. Stopped cold on the sidewalk.

A cab. Yellow and black. Engine running. Parked right in front of her apartment. As she stood there staring, a swarthy man, hair bound up in a turban, stepped out of the driver's seat and strode over to her.

"I can put the seat belt around both of you." He opened the passenger door and pulled her toward it.

Did she have any cash on her? "I..." Now she was the one who was shivering. She dug into her pocket, expecting only lint, but stared in shock at three ten-dollar bills crumpled in her hand when she drew it out. Stuck between the money was Michael's Health Endurance medical card. "But I just pulled these jeans out of the dryer after dinner." She hadn't even had time to put her clean laundry away last night. The pair of jeans had lain on top of the clean clothes.

"Let's worry about this later, okay?" The words fell across her ears in precise, softly accented English. She looked up. Who had spoken? The cabby gestured toward the passenger door. "Why don't you get in front with your little boy?"

She stumbled toward the cab. Michael had been still, but his chest was starting to labor again.

The cab driver ushered her into the seat and drew the belt across her shoulder, buckling both her and Michael securely. The door closed with a solid thud. The driver's door opened and damp night puffed inside.

"Mercy Hospital?" The soft accent teased her ears again.

"Please!" Michael was struggling to take a breath. "Hurry!"

The cab jolted away from the curve and roared around the corner.

****

"Miz Morgan?"

She started. "Yeah, yeah." She leaped out of the stool pulled up next to Michael's bed. Lighted machines blinked at her. Michael's eyes were closed. An IV snaked out from his left hand.

"The doctor will be in to talk to you soon." Nurses didn't wear starched caps anymore. This one had a blonde ponytail and dark-lashed blue eyes. A green lab coat opened at the front to reveal a black and red *Amnesiac* CD T-shirt. "Just going to check his vitals." This woman was tough. But a miniature teddy bear rode high in the top pocket of the lab coat. Her hands were gentle as she checked the IV and peered at the blinking lights of the machines.

"Radiohead rules." It had been ages since she'd attended a concert. "Did you get their latest CD?" She should stop chattering, but it seemed to soothe Michael. Whenever she went quiet, he wheezed. "They rock."

The nurse patted her arm. "Your boy is doing fine now." Her stethoscope caught the lights and flashed red and green. "It was good you brought him in when you did." She gave a little nod and moved back through the curtains drawn around Michael's cubicle.

She gave a long sigh and turned back to

Michael. His lashes flickered, but at least he'd stopped wheezing. Her own throat was sore from talking nonstop. Well, her chattering had drowned out the Voice. After an hour of steady speech from her, whatever it was that talked at her had stopped.

Michael was lost in that big bed, his hair plastered to his forehead and cheeks. She reached out and cupped his face with her palm. Still warm. But not burning. How had he gotten so sick so fast? The last time he had bronchiolitis he'd been hoarse for at least a day before he started having trouble breathing. Had she missed something? Had she been so focused on her job that she'd ignored the signs? Before she started working again, Michael had been her whole life. How could she have let this happen? "What did I do wrong?"

"Bull."

Oh, brother. "I might have known you'd be back." The Voice had talked at her, every moment, since the time she woke. Once the cab driver had gotten them to the emergency room door, she had thrust ten dollars at him and sprinted through the red-lined doors, Michael held so close that she might have smothered him if the nurses hadn't pried her fingers away. While the doctors worked over Michael, she'd talked a blue streak to keep from hearing the Voice and accidentally responding to it in front of other people. She was glad when it gave up and went away. Michael had her so worried that it had been hard to answer the doctor's questions. A Voice jabbering in her ear made it near impossible.

"Never left."

She blinked and stared all around the curtained space, at the IV pole, the gently humming silver machines. Couldn't see anyone. "So what's with the bull comment?" Just her and a disembodied Voice. Great.

"Kids get sick."

"I fucked up."

"For God's sake, Alena."

"Okay, I, I, um, *messed* up."

The Voice softened. "It's not your fault. You're doing fine."

"Glad you approve." She tried to sound sarcastic but her voice wouldn't cooperate; it went all quivery. Michael's little hand nestled in hers. She put her forehead against it and let her breath ride out. Ought to give the Voice a break. If it had really gotten that cab there for her…"Thanks for the help."

"That's what I'm here for."

She lifted her head. "What?"

"To help." This was mumbled, as if who or whatever it was felt embarrassed.

Oh, great. Now it was an *embarrassed* Voice in her head. Fine and dandy. Still, she did owe it some thanks. "Well, um, thank you." She'd figure out later how the cab had shown up when it did. "But I can't have a Voice telling me what to do all the time." The cab company would have the driver's name. She could call and ask them. Well, maybe ask the cab driver who had called him to her apartment at four in the morning. "Just don't talk at me around other people, okay?"

"Affirmative. But as I told you, my name is Joe, and I talk to you, not at you." The Voice sounded affronted, now. No. That's not right. *Joe* sounded affronted.

"Yeah." She stared across the bed, where the air had a thickness to it, sort of a translucent shimmer. "Thanks, Joe. But really, don't talk to me so much, okay?" God, here she was acting like it was real. Maybe she should tell Dr. Henderson's assistant about this when she saw the woman. Maybe they'd know what it was, have a drug or hypnosis or something to make it go away. Hearing things was worse than seeing things, wasn't it? Real psychotic stuff. She glanced at Michael's face, so still against the pillow.

Her jaw clenched tight. Michael needed her. She needed to hold it together for her baby.

"What am I going to do about you, Joe?" She shivered. "What am I going to do?"

Chapter Nine

He hovered over Michael. The boy breathed easier here at home, in his own bed, not strapped to a hospital gurney with tubes sticking into his skin.

Something about hospitals bugged him. He wasn't sure what it was; he'd seldom been in one when he was alive. Maybe it was the antiseptic, or the squeak of shoes on the tiles. Maybe it was the pain that filled those walls. He wasn't sure, but he knew he hated it.

He leaned in over Michael's chest and listened for the soft inhalation and steady sigh when the boy's breathing slid smoothly out. Michael's color was good, too, nice and pink everywhere.

He floated upward and glanced at the shelf next to the boy where a cool mist humidifier hummed, then over at Alena. She sat dozing in an overstuffed chair drawn up next to Michael's bed, head resting against a pillow she'd stuck between her neck and her chin, breathing in time with her son. Peaceful.

He pushed back and hovered near the ceiling, looking down at Alena and Michael. A mother and child asleep always touched his heart, made him wish he could draw or paint the curve and shadowed glow that shone from them. The picture of it dug right down deep inside him.

He liked watching Alena sleep. Rest was no longer necessary for him, but the sight of Alena asleep tugged him into a mellow doze. Almost drunk. Anyway, happy. He just half floated, half draped himself on the couch and looked at Alena.

She'd *talked* to him.

None of his cases had ever talked to him before. He'd never missed it. By the time he'd been called in to help the living, their lives were such a tangled mess of fury and despair that anything he did was like peeing into the wind. Their cries had been to God, not to a guy named Joe Littlehawk. He'd done what he could for them and then Ram would come in and make a suggestion or deem that the job was done. For the others, all he could do was to help them cross over, leave their bodies behind.

No one had ever really heard him. He wished Alena would wake up and talk to him some more. He knew it wouldn't be good for her to do this. She was already afraid she was crazy. If he kept talking to her, he wasn't sure what she would do, but it probably wouldn't be good.

Anyway, his time here was pretty much over, wasn't it? She had a doctor to heal her headaches and a job to support her and Michael. No doubt Ram would come by pretty soon and give him another case. But for the time being, he could enjoy just staying near her, watching her.

Alena slumped down some and was breathing shallowly. Her hands twitched a little. She seemed to be dreaming; her eyes darted underneath her lids. A slow, quivering light wavered, then flowed around her.

It was the amber road. The dream path. The way the living entered the Otherworld, the world of dreams where the living would work on the issues of their lives. Here they would go over the reasons they incarnated, the images and situations that would aid them in the journey they were taking here on earth, in the world of cause and effect, the realm of dense matter.

He watched Alena's spectral form break loose from her body and rise in a graceful slide. The silver cord that connected her astral form to her physical body snaked from her navel to her departing dream-body.

A dream for sure. He had seen this before with others he'd watched over. The golden dream path was the way he entered JJ's dreams, though Ram had told him not to follow Alena into her dreams.

He forced himself to look away. The gold-laced glow of the dream path drew him back. Where was Alena going? He slid forward and tried to catch a glimpse of the dream landscape forming around her. Some kind of forest. Lots of reddish broad-trunk trees soared into the sky all around her. Would she be okay there? Maybe he could just watch her, make sure she was safe without fully going into her dreams with her.

He rose and floated toward Alena until the edge of his form hit the golden light surrounding her and he felt the sticky tug of the amber dream road.

Hey! Wait a minute. How could this be happening? He shouldn't be able to enter her dream.

This would put Ram in a complete snit.

To top it all off, the sound of Ram's wings beating their whirring song filled the room.

A golden river settled around him, pulling him farther into Alena's dream. The whisper of Ram's slide through the roof shivered the air.

He did a quick backstroke and broke free of the honeyed dream path, shot over to the couch and draped his form in what he hoped resembled a comfortable, innocent sprawl.

The angel lighted and stood, head bent, looking at Alena and Michael.

What was this? If he didn't know better, he'd think Ram was sad. The strands of golden light that made up the angel's wings seemed to droop.

"Hey there, Ram." He rubbed the back of his neck. Damn, he hated pulling himself away from a dream path. "What's up?" It was making his astral neck stiff, and now the middle of his back was itchy and hot, too. He couldn't even ask Ram how he'd been almost able to enter Alena's dream without Ram's assistance. But if he could enter her dreams without Ram knowing...that was something to keep in mind.

The angel turned. Light spilled around his form. "JJ."

Hiyá! "I gave JJ a real talking-to just last month." What mess could the kid have gotten into now?

"You need to go to him again."

"Why?"

"He's in trouble. I'll stay with Alena." Ram stood staring at her.

"Michael is sick." He didn't want to leave. "Some kind of lung thing kids get." This was weird. Why didn't he want to leave her here with Ram? "Alena's been taking care of him." Alena'd be even safer with an angel than she would be with a Sacred Guardian. "She's pretty beat."

Ram favored him with a cool glance. "We know." He perched on the other chair in the room, allowing his oscillating wings to drape over the arms. "I'll stay with her while you're gone."

Damn! What if Alena tried to talk to him while Ram was with her? She hadn't initiated any conversations since the hospital, but that didn't mean she wouldn't. If she talked to him while he was gone, Ram would find out that he'd been, well, interfering.

He cleared his throat, but couldn't think of any objection. The angel didn't know Alena could hear him, didn't know Alena spoke to him. What would Ram do if he knew?

Well, right now he didn't have a choice. He spiraled up toward the ceiling. "I'll be right back." This had better not take long.

"Take your time."

He readied himself for travel. Molecules and atoms in his form started to disassemble. He focused real hard on his errant nephew. Quickest way he knew to get to JJ.

The room seemed to spin and wobble. He blinked.

****

A bar stretched across the back of a narrow storefront. Smoke and the pounding thump of a bass mingled with raucous, boozy laughter. He glided through a crowd of young people, looking for JJ. Found the kid slumped in front of a boatload of beer.

Hell in a basket! JJ had gone and had his nose pierced. A thin silver ring dangled from his nasal septum. Kid didn't even look Lakota anymore. A faded red plaid flannel shirt hung half tucked into skintight worn jeans. JJ's chest strained against the black T-shirt he wore like a second skin; the name of a local band spread across JJ's belly, topped by a dripping red skull. Grunge-punk clothes, for sure. Kid had messed up his hair too. The right side flowed in a straight river down to the middle of his back. The left side was cropped close in a buzz cut. A lightning bolt was shaved above his left ear.

Shit! JJ was forty. What the hell did he think he was doing with his life? He should be settled down with a job and a couple of kids. Right now he was smoking. A pitcher of beer stood by his elbow. He didn't look happy. A thin layer of smoky haze drifted chest high across the bar. JJ squinted into the curl of smoke flowing out of his mouth.

Beekman sat beside JJ, legs propped on the seat beside him, pimply face mottled with broken capillaries. "I am a loser" shone neon all over his bloated belly, right to the tips of his stubby fingers.

But JJ was smart. The kid hadn't had to work very hard to get by in school. Even graduated early and went to work in the motorcycle shop. What the hell was he still doing with this crowd?

He sighed and leaned against the wall. His nephew JJ knew engines and automotive speed. Speed, booze, and women. Used to be pills, too, but after the last few bad dreams from his Uncle Joe, the problem with pills had seemed to stop.

Still, at forty, the kid was going nowhere. He gazed at his nephew as JJ drew in another lungful of smoke and hissed it out through his teeth. Kid sure was handsome, though. Had Sammie's eyes, almost Asian.

Hell, JJ's eyes were like his own eyes. When he was based in Vietnam, many of the Vietnamese thought he must be part Chinese.

JJ lit another cigarette on the butt of his old one, frowning at it. The kid lurched to his feet and moved with the slow, over-careful posture of the truly drunk.

Itómni. Kid was wasted. His spirit was strong, though. Intense blue light shone all around JJ underneath the slick brown scum of intoxication.

"Where you goin', Parker?" Travis bellowed over the pulse of the band.

"Gotta open tomorrow." JJ swayed; then he steadied. "Dan asked me to open."

The bike shop. A real nothing job for a smart guy, working at a motorcycle shop, but at least the kid was trying to be responsible.

What time was it here? He glanced around for a clock and caught the glowing dial of a young woman's watch. Two in the morning. He looked back at JJ swaying beside Travis. Well, not very responsible after all. Shop opened at eight to clients needing their bikes repaired. If JJ was to open, he'd better get some rest and swallow a bunch of aspirin to kill the hangover he was working on.

"I'm outta here." JJ swung into a careful stride.

He had to hand it to the kid. JJ looked green but didn't stagger. Matter of pride, he guessed. He followed his nephew through the door out to the street, around the corner, and into the alley where JJ's bike stood. Hey—nice bike.

"Oh, man!" Wait a minute! He gulped and ran his etheric fingertips over the satin metal of the handlebars all the way up to the richly finished grips. *Hiyá*! Not just nice. Fantastic bike! A Harley XL4 883 Sportster. Must be one of Dan's bikes his nephew was using. He was certain JJ couldn't afford it.

He glanced back at the bar. So, who was going to take his nephew home? Travis hadn't gotten up when JJ left. Hell, Beekman wasn't in any shape to drive, either. It was twenty miles to JJ's apartment.

The kid hung his cigarette from his lips and fumbled with the ignition.

"Aw, hell." All the times Joe himself had pelted down the highway half wasted flashed before him. But he sure wasn't going to let his nephew drive without a helmet. And drunk as JJ was?

"Sorry, JJ. As your *leksí*, your mother's brother, I can't let you do this." He grabbed at the keys and felt the chill of the molecules of metal as his hand passed through them.

How could he fix this? He watched as JJ struggled to fit the key into the ignition. How had he gotten solid enough to touch Alena? How the hell had he done that? He hadn't even thought about it, just the need to help her had him…he stared at JJ. "I won't let you do this, John Joseph." He put all his attention into his own form, pushing past JJ in a quick lunge.

The keys went flying. *Yesss!*

"Goddammit," JJ muttered. The kid slid off his seat and peered into the shadows of the alley.

Now he focused on his own foot and, with a

grunt, condensed it enough to kick. He punted the keys all the way out of the alley, across the street, and into the storm drain.

"Wha?" JJ must have seen him do it. The kid's eyes widened until the whites showed all around. Then he pitched over and collapsed next to the bike, just like a marionette when the strings were released.

Well, now. He floated over his nephew. At least the kid was breathing, and he wouldn't be driving himself home tonight.

He drifted toward the bar. This was one time when being dead truly sucked. He really needed to get someone to help his nephew. Couldn't leave JJ out there like this. He'd see if he could whisper in the bar owner's ear. The guy was a good sort, and he might be able to influence him to have someone look for JJ, or maybe he could find someone sober enough to take JJ home. It was worth a try. But poor, poor Sammie. JJ was a real trial to his sister.

"Thank God you're not *my* son," he breathed.

****

Ram wasn't there. And Alena wasn't in the room, either.

He searched for the angel's essence and caught a whiff near the upper right corner of the room. He sighed. Ram must've just left. That was good, wasn't it? If Alena had spoken, talking to what she thought was him while the angel was here, Ram would be waiting for him, ready to nail him to the wall.

The bathroom door swung open. Alena strode into the room, wrapped in her bathrobe. She marched over to the small chest next to Michael's bed, bent, and pulled a squat white candle out of the drawer.

He backed away and crouched in the corner of the room. God, he missed her talking to him. Michael still slept; his face turned to the wall. The boy's breathing was good and regular now. That should make Alena happy. He glanced over at her.

She set the candle on a plate and struck a match, then dropped a metal tray on the floor in the clear space in front of the television.

He jumped to his feet. What was she doing?

Setting the lit candle on the floor, she sat before it, legs folded. She took a deep breath and let it out.

He shuffled a few steps toward her. Well, she had told the shrink she spent time in some kind of Buddhist commune. Was she meditating?

She dug into her handbag and pulled out a slip of paper.

He twisted around and peered at the top of it, where "From the desk of John Henderson, MD" appeared in bold black script. He backed away. The prescription?

"Okay," she said, looking around the room.

What!

"I'm taking a big chance here." She clutched the prescription against her chest and scrunched her eyes. "Joe?" She took in a deep breath and held it.

His form shivered. He struggled to speak, but only staccato grunts slipped out.

Alena deflated. She pressed her knuckles against her eyes, then pulled them away and stared at the prescription, still clutched in her hands. "Shit!" Her head dropped. "I must be crazy after all. What am I gonna do?"

"Alena?" He could vocalize, but the sound was rusty and harsh.

Her head shot up and her eyes rounded. "What!" She half stood, half crouched. "F-F-F-Fuck!"

He slowed the vibration of his particles and whispered, "God bless it, woman. Watch your mouth!"

"Omigod, omigod. Yeah, okay. Deb says that, too. I've been trying to find alternatives, you know?

Words that aren't cussing, but I can still express...God, Joe." She cleared her throat. "It's you, isn't it?" Her hands rumpled the prescription. "You're *real*."

"Yes." She was speaking to him again. Talking to him! He hadn't realized how, well, *lonely*, it was, doing what he did. "Damn, I never thought..."

"What?"

"Ah. Nothing." Warmth in his arm drew his attention to his side. Bursts of golden and buttery glowing sparks flashed from his right arm, all the way to his hand. "I'm here, Alena." He raised his hand and tracked the glittering embers flaring from his fingers. He'd better calm down, or Alena would see this. He glanced at her. She still sat there. "Alena?"

She jumped, but smoothed the crumpled prescription and froze in the half crouch she'd settled into. "Yeah?"

"Why didn't you tell the shrink you could hear me?" The glow from his hand was fading in violet strands. He cradled the arm next to his chest. It tingled. The colors were all gone in seconds, but his arm still prickled.

"So you *were* there." She turned her head and tipped it toward him. "I thought I heard you, but the doctor didn't."

"Yeah, well, other people..." How could he explain it? "I mean, I'm glad you didn't tell him, that is..." Damn, he was making a mess of this. "I'd like to know why you didn't tell him."

Her face crumpled. One hand waved. "He might have taken Michael away." She looked down and swallowed. "Away from me." She hugged her middle, cradled her elbows in her hands. "Someone still might take Michael away, if I say I'm hearing voices." Her tongue darted out and moistened her lower lip. "Sorry. Hearing a *Joe*."

Jeez. "Lena..." He ran his hands through his etheric hair and strode to the door, just as he would if he were a man. "Do you want me to go away?" He reached for the door handle, then halted and rolled his hands into fists. Door handles were no longer necessary. He could slip right through it, couldn't he? But the vibrational extensions that were his feet seemed stuck to the floor.

"No. Wait." She stretched her hand toward where he had just sat. "I mean, I didn't tell him about the mistake I made either, Joe. I didn't tell him I almost overdosed." Her hand first groped and then dropped to her knee. "Puh-please don't go." How is it she knew where he had sat? "Joe, work with me here." Tears spiked her lashes. "Okay?"

His midsection ached. He moved to her side and squatted. "Alena, stop crying." The ache grew. "I beg you."

Unshed tears shone from her eyes. "I am not crying!" She blinked once, hard, and fat droplets streaked down her face. "Damn!" She lifted her robe and rubbed at her face. "I'm not crying, see? It's just, I don't know. Maybe my eyes are irritated, by, by, uh, by the candle smoke."

"Whatever you say."

"I'm not crying; I'm not. But why?"

"What?"

She ran the back of her hand across her cheeks. "Why would you ask me to stop crying?"

Why indeed? "It..." He floated up and turned around, then around again. "Hurts." And it did. "It hurts me." Her tears and the sorrow filling her eyes spread a thick layer of grief across him.

"Oh." She stared at the prescription again, then leaned forward and held the tattered slip of paper over the candle flame until it caught. It kindled in her hands and dropped onto the metal tray.

He lunged forward and reached over to put it

out, but it flared and curled into gray ash. "Alena?" He moved right next to her. "Why did you do this?"

"Well—" She gestured toward the metal tray. "I don't want to take anything, see?" She looked around the room. "Any drug that would prevent me from hearing you. But I have a problem here. If I really am crazy, well, I'm endangering Michael." Her head turned toward Michael's bed. "I'm not crazy. I'm *not.*" A weak laugh sputtered past her lips. "Crazy people say that, don't they?" She shook her head. "And that's just the first problem."

"You're not crazy."

"Well. If you went away, that would solve the first problem, but—" She gave a quick nod and looked directly into the space where he sat. "—the other problem is..." She drew in a breath and straightened. "I don't think I want you to go away."

"You don't." His arm tingled again.

"You see, it's like this." She shifted her legs and rose up on her knees. "You helped me, I mean, with Michael, and—" Her brows lifted. "—you just told me that my tears hurt you." She looked into her lap. "How could you be bad? Anyway, I couldn't possibly have come up with something like this." Her head shook and she raised her hands. "I mean, if I were crazy, I'd think you were Jesus, or God, not some guy named Joe, right?"

"Uh." The grunt rasped out of him. He rose to his feet, just like a man, and moved back. "Right." His mouth was hanging open. When did that happen? His tongue was dry. Hell, he didn't even have a real mouth, let alone a tongue. *This body is as real as the one you left behind.* "Can I have some water?" He was parched. *Your form is simply subject to different laws.* "Please?" How could he be thirsty? Christ. He'd worry about this later. Right now he needed a drink.

A smile traveled from her eyes to her mouth, but

she raised her hand to her lips and swallowed before she replied. "Yeah, sure." She peered into the space where he stood. "Be my guest." A thin stream of giggles bubbled out. "There is m-milk in the fridge." She leaned back on her heels. "Or cherry cola."

"Water is fine." He glided into the kitchen and stuck his head under the faucet, drawing some water out. Drops trickled down his mouth; he caught them with the back of his hand and looked at her. She was still on the floor glancing all around the room. Now that she was talking to him again, he didn't want to do anything that would frighten her away. Her hair, even as short as it was, made a black-fire frame for her face. He leaned against the door. What should he do now? He couldn't tell Ram she talked to him.

"It was you who saved me, when I took too much Zamatrex, wasn't it?"

He stood poised in the kitchen doorway. "I was there. You did most of the work, though. Sorry I had to make you throw up." Candlelight made a golden nimbus that played over the planes of her face and deepened the green of her eyes. It reminded him of something.

"No problem." Her lips twisted. "I was doing that a lot anyway because of the migraines." She cleared her throat. "I haven't really thanked you yet."

"Hmmm?" He entered the room and sat down in front of her. She looked right at him. The steady flame of the candle trickled across her face in a dance of light and shadow. "Caravaggio!"

"Huh?"

"The light on your face; it reminds me of an Italian artist." He remembered the slick paper turning under his fingers, the painting of the Virgin Mary, illuminated by the light of a single flame.

A quick grin crinkled her eyes. "A painting? Now I know I'm not crazy. I would never have a Voice, sorry, a *Joe* tell me I reminded him of a painting!"

She lowered her voice and looked back at Michael. "Carra-who-zio?"

"Caravaggio. He painted pictures of people with a single point of light shining on them." God, how long had it been since he had looked at those paintings and fell in love with...Well, he was just a boy when he saw that painting, and Alena, with her rumpled, partly spiked black-fire hair, was as modern as any Gen-X punk on the street. Why had he thought of Caravaggio just now?

"Did he paint women standing in front of windows?"

"That was Vermeer." He couldn't take his eyes away from her face. "Different country." A single point of light. A candle illuminating the face of the Virgin Mary. He sighed. By Caravaggio.

She looked down. "I guess I don't know much about that." Her shoulders twitched. "Anyway, I never thanked you for saving my life." She looked up and said with that rare, solemn grace of hers, "Thanks."

"You're welcome." Even her skin glowed. Like that daughter of Ingrid Bergman. Isabella. The shining cap of hair, the full curve of her mouth beckoned.

"Where are you?" She clasped her hands together. "I mean, like, I can't even see you. Now. No shadow, no nothing."

"I'm right here." He blew air molecules gently into her face.

"Oh!" She caught her breath. "You're here?" She reached out. Her hand passed through his throat. "In front of me?"

He fell back and rubbed at his neck. Always hated it when that happened. Felt like he'd been punched whenever someone brushed against him or walked through him. "Y-yeah."

She made a fist and drew her hand to her face.

It was shaking. "I guess you must be." Her hand opened. The palm was slick with sweat. "I feel this electric tingle. I always feel that when you're near." She fixed a stare in his direction. "Why can't I see you for real?" A nervous laugh rattled in her throat. "I mean, I could before." She wiped her palm against her robe. "That was you in front of the bank too, right?"

"That was me." Happy, he was happy. If he could carry a tune, he would sing. But oh, man, was he ever nervous. His legs quaked, toes kept wiggling. "But you're not supposed to see me." And what was this about toes, anyway? He didn't really have toes.

"Why not?"

"It just, well, um." How could he tell her he had made a mistake in letting her see him without sounding like a complete idiot? "It's not done." Oh, man, now *that* was priceless.

A line creased her brow, but all she said was, "Can I ask you a question?" She looked down now, hands kneading her thighs. "I mean, you won't be pissed, uh, insulted—" She looked back up. "—will you?"

"Ah, no." How could she insult him? "Shoot."

She drew in a deep breath. "Who are you? I mean—" She looked down. "*What* are you?"

"Alena." How the hell could he tell her? He reached out and touched her face, then drew his hand back and smelled his fingers. What was she wearing? He caught a hint of jasmine and roses. "I'm, um, kind of a guide." Smell? How could he smell without a nose?

A line creased her forehead. "A guide."

"Well, I'm Indian." That was still true, wasn't it?

"A Hindu Master?" She leaned forward. "Like Swami Ananda? When I saw you, you had dark skin, kind of."

"No, not that kind of Indian. I'm Native

American."

"A shaman?" She nodded, but scooted back a little. "A spirit guide?" Her voice trembled.

Oh, for the love of God. "Well, I'm not exactly, that is..." Not alive. He looked at her face, caressed in the glow of the candle. He sure as hell felt more alive than he had in the forty years since his death. Would she spook if he told her the truth? "I'm not at liberty to say."

A line between her brows deepened. "I've gotta tell you, Joe." She inched farther back. "I don't know what to think about this spirit guide thing." A gulp visibly shook her throat. "I mean, are you dead?" She shivered.

"Uh." What could he say? "I can't tell you more. There are rules, you see."

"Rules."

"Yeah. The other, er, shamans I work with, well, we don't want people to know what we do."

"Oh." She nodded, her face relaxing. "Like at the commune. Those Tibetan Masters can do just about anything. Once I saw Master Wang appear right in front of a bunch of us, but he was still in Tibet and we were in New Mexico. It was really cool." Then she frowned again. "Hey! You're not with me all the time, are you?"

"Huh?"

"I mean." Was that a blush spreading across her face? "You know, in the bath and places like that." Her eyes narrowed. "Can you see me?"

"Yes."

"Describe what I'm wearing."

"Um, it looks like a bathrobe."

She startled and drew the robe closer.

"Alena, we have rules about privacy, too." He would never watch her bathe, though he'd been tempted. "I'd never be where you didn't want me to be."

She frowned. "Don't you have to work or something?" Her fingers played with the belt of her robe. "I mean, there's work in the ashram, or wherever you are, isn't there?"

"This is my main work." Perfectly true. And now her face was shining. Oh, boy. He'd gone and done it.

"How long will you be with me?"

"As long as you need me." Another truth. But it was painted upon a lie. Alena's eyes glowed, but a cold spot grew inside him, right where his stomach would be if he were alive.

And that was it, wasn't it?

He'd let her think he was alive. A shaman working with a group of shamans. Healers, helping people, long distance.

Alive, not dead.

Chapter Ten

"Joe, how's this?" She held the rattan-framed mirror up and glanced behind her. Until Joe spoke, she couldn't be certain where he stood. But she knew he was there. "Joe?" When Joe was around, he filled the room somehow. The air had a slippery shimmer to it. If she glanced to the side, then quickly away and back again, she could almost see him, glimpse a filmy shoulder or fall of dark hair. A breeze swelled the lace panel she'd tacked over her bedroom window and brought the scent of summer: acacia and citrus. She bent back until her neck muscles screamed. Frickin' hell! "Joe!" It wouldn't be good to squish her neck discs again. She set the mirror down.

She wished she could just see Joe. His disembodied voice sometimes gave her the creeps. But he hadn't fully appeared to her since the time she had seen him in front of the bank. Why wouldn't the other shamans let him appear to her again? What would be the harm in that?

Well, people at the commune told her that Master Wang sometimes appeared to them in times of great need. Like she told Joe, Master Wang even had appeared to them when he was in Tibet and they were in New Mexico, but only when they really, truly needed him. She sighed and pushed her hair back. She'd started to let it grow and it was long enough now to get in her way. She wasn't all that needy anymore, was she? It would be better to be grateful that she could still hear Joe, happy that he still came to visit her. But where the hell was he now?

She drew in a breath and looked around the room. Joe had a way of standing that laid claim to the space around him. Even when she couldn't exactly see him, she often knew where he was standing. There was a thickness, a transparent density to any space where he stood. But until he decided to speak, she couldn't be sure. And he wasn't speaking now.

She looked at her hands. "Dang it." The cherry nail polish she'd just put on last night had chipped. "See, Joe? You had me paint my nails last night and now I chipped them holding this mirror up for so long." She listened, but Joe didn't speak.

"Okay, be that way. I'll just put this up later." She pulled her hair back and fought the grin that always seemed to crinkle her eyes whenever she surveyed her new apartment. The rent ate half her paycheck, but it was worth it. Two bedrooms, hardwood floors, floor to ceiling windows. From a corner of her bedroom, if she stood on her toes, she could see the bay. Her apartment was close enough to the park for Michael to hear the ice cream truck when it trundled up the street. She leaned down, peered into the mirror and stuck out her lower lip.

"All right, Alena, cut it out!" The rich baritone drifted from the door behind her. "You're beautiful." An amused tremor shook his voice. "Lift the mirror again. I'll tell you when it's straight."

"Hmmmph." She hefted the mirror and shifted it until the wire across the back caught on the screw in the wall. "Come on now, Joe." Her arms started to burn. "This is fu…it's heavy."

"A little to the right—there!" The voice emerged just over her left shoulder. "Perfect."

She stood back. A shimmer of electric pulses cascaded down her left arm. "Yow!" She edged to the right. "Sorry. Didn't know you were so close."

"That's okay." Joe's voice was farther away. "I'm used to it."

"I don't see how you could." She glanced around her. Besides her bed, the room was bare. "Get used to it, I mean." She needed furniture. Well, rattan was cheap. She could get a couple of chairs and make cushions for them. Maybe get a chest of drawers from a yard sale. "Does it hurt your real body when I bump into you?" She turned and looked at the translucent swirl standing right by the door.

"Real body?"

"You know, your physical body." She leaned over and retrieved a half-full can of cherry cola sitting beside the bed. "Where you are with the other shamans." She waved her hand toward the window.

"You can't hurt me."

"I'm glad to hear it," she laughed. "Then I don't have to worry about where I walk." She took a sip of the cherry cola. "Hey—could you come to visit me sometime?" Her head swiveled. "For real?" Not a sound. "In your body?" The room was silent except for the gentle hiss of carbonation in the drink she held. The air was free of the crystalline sparkle that always seemed to accompany Joe.

"Hell." Slipped off again. He'd taken to doing that lately. She was hoping that he'd give her his last name. Maybe even a phone number. But whenever she asked, he went all cagey and silent. Then he disappeared.

A jangling trill startled her. The can of cherry cola lurched and sloshed drops over her hand.

"Mommmmm!" Michael bellowed from his room. "The phone."

"All right, all right." She strode into the living room and grabbed the receiver. "Yeah."

"Hi, kiddo. It's me." Deb's voice came over the wire, underscored by the echoing murmur of voices. Lots of voices. An ocean of voices.

But not the voice she wanted to hear.

"Hey, Deb." She leaned against the wall. "Where are you?"

"The Harmonic Vision conference." Deb paused and the voices swelled, followed by the sound of hundreds of hands clapping. "Right over in San Francisco. Thought I'd give you a call."

"Is it a good conference?" Hey—New Age stuff. Deb knew all about, well, weird things. She twisted the receiver cord in her fingers. Maybe Deb could tell her about the shamans Joe spoke of. Deb might even know where they lived.

"It was great. I did the tarot booth." Deb paused. "Can I speak to Michael?"

"Sure thing. Hey, Michael?" Michael sidled into the room. "Here you go, sport." She handed the receiver to him. "It's Auntie Deb."

He took it and breathed heavily into the mouthpiece. "Don't hang up after you're through—I want to talk to her."

How much should she tell Deb? She stared at Michael, who kept nodding through his one-syllable statements. She couldn't tell Deb that Joe had come to her. Too much of a risk. Deb was pretty far out there, but her concern over Michael's welfare might prompt her to talk to Child Protection Services. Maybe they would have her committed, or at the very least, take Michael away. She bit into her lower lip. She wasn't sure Deb would really do that. But even if Deb couldn't have her hospitalized, it would strain the relationship. Deb was her best friend. How could she ask her about a phantom shaman or whatever Joe was?

Michael offered the receiver. She grabbed it and took a deep breath.

"Hi again, Deb."

"Why is it that Michael's so talkative when I see him and like a Neanderthal on the phone?"

"All little kids are like that."

"How do you know?"

"I just do—look, Deb, I want to talk to you about something."

"Sure thing."

"I have this, ah, friend who has had some pretty weird experiences."

"Like what?"

"Um, she hears a voice." She waited, but Deb was silent. Murmurs of the Harmonic Vision crowd drifted across the wires. "When there's no one around, she hears this voice talking to her." She alternated between straightening the cord and curling it around her index finger.

"What does the voice tell her?"

"Just things. Like a regular conversation."

"Does it tell her to do things she wouldn't normally do, like stealing or hurting someone? Maybe taking drugs or drinking a lot?"

The sound of paper rustling tickled her ear. "No. Nothing like that. What are you doing?"

"Just looking through the conference program. Did she tell you what it says to her?" More rustling. "I need some specifics."

"He helps her."

"He."

"She says it sounds like a guy."

"And what exactly does this guy say?"

"He cheers her up, you know, encourages her."

"Hmmm."

"He makes jokes sometimes."

"Uh huh."

"He tells her to paint her nails."

"He *what*?"

"Never mind that," she sighed. "He says he's a shaman, that he works with a group of shamans."

"Alena."

"Yeah?"

"Has your friend seen a therapist?"

Hell. "Yes."

"And what does the therapist say?"

"She, ah, didn't tell him about the voice."

"You mean there's more?"

She stifled a sigh. "There's a shadow."

"A what?"

"A shadow." The receiver cord bit into her fingers. "She thought she was crazy at first, like she was seeing things. But he really helps her, you know." She swallowed. "He does."

"Wait a minute, Alena." The sound of a door closing muffled the crowd noises. Silence hummed over the wire now. She started rubbing her shirttail between the touch-tone numbers, wiping the dust there. Deb's voice rumbled in her ear. "Alena, I've never heard of anything like this. Angels, yes, and ghosts who are spirit guides. But that's usually a relative who comes to help for a brief time and then leaves. Does she recognize the voice? Could it be a relative who passed on?"

"No, he's not anyone she knew."

"I don't know, Alena. Maybe she should talk to John Gray Wolf. He knows more about shamans than I do." Her voice dwindled, then sharpened. "Hey—is the voice with her all the time?"

"Mostly."

"Did it first appear during a crisis?"

She jumped and the receiver slipped from her hand; she grabbed it before it hit the wall. "Yes! I mean, yeah, it did."

"There you go! I'll bet it's her higher self, you know, her inner voice."

"But it's a guy, you know, and she's a girl."

"Her Animus."

"Er..."

"Never mind, it's Carl Jung. I'll tell you about it sometime. We all have female and male traits in us."

The humming voices returned. Deb must have opened the door again. “Have her read *Man and His Symbols*. She’ll love it. It’s just an inner voice, maybe scary to her, but I doubt that she is crazy.”

“That’s what I thought, too.” So she wasn’t crazy after all. But why did the notion that Joe was just a piece of her hurt? Like she’d lost a best friend. It was a good thing if he was just her “higher self.” Wasn’t it?

“Well, that’s my take on it. Want to have her call me? I’d like to talk to her about it. And she definitely should talk to John Gray Wolf.”

“Uh, okay, Deb.” Her finger hovered over the receiver cradle. “Can you give me John Gray Wolf’s number?” She swallowed again. “I can pass it on to her.”

“I’d rather talk to her first before I refer her.”

Dang it! “Sure.”

“And Lena…”

“Yeah?” Her hands sweated, palms slimy and cold.

“Try to convince her to see a psychologist again. She should tell her doctor about this voice. It could be nothing, but…”

“But what?” She had almost shouted into the phone. Better cool it. “What, Deb?”

“It *could* mean she needs help. Heavy duty help.”

“But if it’s her inner voice?”

“That’s what I think it is, but she really should see a specialist. And tell her to give me a call.”

“Okay. Thanks. Talk to you later.” She set the receiver into its cradle right after Deb hung up and placed her forehead against the wall.

“Ah, shi…shoot.” Back where she started. She couldn’t go to a therapist again. No way. She moved away from the wall and paced the length of the room, stopping at the windows. How could she explain all this to a psychiatrist? The little bit she told Dr. Henderson got her a prescription. The next professional she talked to might put her in a straitjacket. Even the cab company thought she was bonkers when she called them to ask who had picked her and Michael up at four in the morning and driven them to the hospital. They had shown no record of *any* of their drivers taking a fare to Mercy Hospital that night.

What should she do about Joe? Trouble was, she liked being with him. It was magical, like having a best friend at your side all the time. But that was weird, too. He never intruded, yet whenever she spoke to him he answered, no matter what hour of the day or night. Except when he took off, like he did just now. The rest of the time he was always there. Didn't he ever sleep? And why wouldn't he tell her where he lived?

She chewed on her thumb and stared across the street where a mother was striding along the sidewalk toward the park, holding the hand of a little blonde girl. A man trailed after the woman, a younger child on his shoulders, tiny legs hanging on either side of his neck.

A family.

She rubbed her eyes. "God, I want a cigarette." Whenever she saw families together this happened. She got nicotine fits and her eyes hurt. Hell, nobody knew what went on in families. She knew that better than anyone. Maybe the guy beat his wife. Or maybe they weren't even related at all and the toddler the guy held on his shoulders wasn't the woman's child. She leaned against the window. They sure looked like a family. The man caught up with the woman and smiled down at her.

Not for me. Nope. Not for Alena Morgan. She'd already had her chance at family and look where it had got her. Well, life had handed her David a really raw deal. She leaned against the window. "It's just the roll of the dice."

Deb thought Joe might be her own inner voice. What if she was making it all up somehow? Maybe the booze and Zamatrex had fried her brain circuits and an invisible friend named Joe had been the result. And why did that bother her so much? Why did just the thought that Joe might not be real twist her guts into a hard knot?

"Mom?"

She made a half turn. "Hey, Michael." Michael slipped under her arm and leaned. "What's up?"

And there was this, too. Joe had stopped speaking to her when others were around. Ever since she took Michael to the ER, he went silent when she was in public. He was mute when Michael was with her. Wouldn't her inner voice be there all the time? Especially when she was with Michael? Weren't inner voices there to guide people? She chewed on her lip. Well, she'd asked him to stop speaking to her around other people. But if it was just her inner voice the result would be the same, wouldn't it? Her inner voice would just be obeying a command her, her, uh, *outer* voice had given it? What does all this mean?

"God, this is scanless." It was making her dizzy! Anyway, Deb knew what she was talking about. If Deb was worried, well, there was something to worry about.

"What's for dinner?" Michael lifted his face to hers. She hugged him close.

"I don't know, sweetie." She lumbered toward the kitchen with Michael hugging her left hip. "We'll have to take a look and choose."

Chapter Eleven

The office was silent. He perched on the window. Alena sat slumped in front of her computer, just staring into her lap, where a large book rested. He glanced out the window. The day was a fine one, full of sun and the crisp breezes of early fall. Alena usually took her lunch outside, but the brown paper bag holding her ham sandwich and apple still sat on the desk, unopened. Everyone else from her office was outside, enjoying the sun before the rains of winter started. Why was she still sitting in front of her computer? She'd turned it off. He leaned toward her, careful to keep his form from touching and startling her. She looked pale. Was she getting sick?

Ever since that day last week when she asked him to come to her in his physical body, she had seemed to crumble. What was up? It wasn't as if anything new had happened. Michael was okay. Her friend Deb was fine. What could be wrong?

The only difference was that he'd fled whenever she asked his full name or where he lived, where his "ashram" was. He didn't know what else to do. She had freaked at the mere thought that he might be dead. How could he tell her the truth?

Alena inhaled and let her breath out in a long sigh. Her fingers worried at a piece of lint clinging to her black skirt. She lifted her hand to her mouth and started to chew on her thumbnail. "Dang it." She pulled her thumb out of mouth and frowned at it. "Gotta stop that." Her hand dropped back to her lap and she stared at the book. But she didn't touch the bag that held her lunch.

Joe sighed. *Oh, what a tangled web we weave.* Or as his grandfather used to say, *False words come back to bite.* They sure do. Well, Grandfather also said *Niksápa hántans ecánu kte. If you are wise you will do it.* Grandfather was right about that too.

How could he tell her it was impossible for him to come to her in a body? Last night, after she'd gotten into bed he asked her what was the matter, but she had just snorted and turned her face to the wall. Wouldn't say a word to him all week.

Éya, this had to stop. He had to fix this now. "Hey, Alena? Check this out!" He leaned hard against the other chair in the room, a worn green padded vinyl chair with wheels, and it skidded across the floor. Whoa! He was getting pretty good at affecting dense matter. He turned to Alena.

She startled and sat up. "Stop that."

"Why?" He toyed with the chair, swiveling it back and forth. Took a lot of concentration, but it was getting easier.

She reached out and held it still. "You're a delusion."

Oh, yeah? "Who told you that?" He was certain she hadn't gone back to the doctor.

She let go of the chair and put her hands over her eyes. "Deb." The air seemed to go out of her. "She thinks you're just a piece of me. A good piece, my higher self, you know? But just a bit of me. It's all in this book by Carl Jung." She reached for her lunch and pulled her sandwich out. "You're an animus. She said that's what you are...or I am seriously wacko."

"A piece of you?" He settled into the chair and couldn't resist swiveling it again. "How did she figure that?"

She looked at the chair and swallowed. "Well, it's either that or I'm crazy, Joe." A shudder shook her hands and the sandwich dropped into her lap. "A delusion would mean I'm nuts." She retrieved the sandwich and took a single, defiant bite. "I'd rather think you are just a piece of me. My higher self or something, like this book says." She placed it on the shelf.

"You'd rather think that?" Why did this make him angry? It was the perfect solution, his way to fade into the background, go back to Ram, and ask for another case.

"I guess." She ran her finger along the edge of her keyboard. "I don't know."

"So, Alena tell me your animus is the one doing this." He twirled the chair all the way around. "Can a delusion do this?" He puffed out and blew a sheet of the paper on her desk onto the floor. "Or this?" He grabbed the lamp and shook it.

"Stop!" She squeezed her eyes shut. "Don't you see? You won't tell me where you live, won't tell me who you're working with." Her eyes blinked open and she pointed straight at him. "You won't even tell me your full name." She stuffed the sandwich in her mouth and mumbled through it. "What am I to think?" Her hand grabbed a pen and she wrote furiously on her desk calendar. "How do I know any of this is real? I'm going to tell Deb everything, and I mean *everything* and see what she says."

"So you haven't really told her?"

"I told her what was happening."

"And?"

"I told her it was happening to a friend, okay? Now bug off. Go do some meditating or something. I'm calling Deb in the morning."

Joe could almost hear his grandfather laughing. Okay. Nothing else he could do. Give her the truth. Break even more rules. Ram hadn't told Joe not to give out his name, but hell, if he wasn't supposed to interfere how would this even come up?

"Look, tell Deb...well, my name is Joe Littlehawk." Alena's hand slowed. "I was born in

Pine Ridge, South Dakota." She pushed back from the desk. "My mother's name is Mary, my dad was, well, he was Joe, too." What else could he tell her? "I have a sister." She reached for a stack of papers. "Her name is Samantha." He drew air molecules in and blew the papers on top across her desk. "I call her Sammie." The papers fluttered to the floor.

"Great!" She grinned and threw her hands up into the air, leaving the papers where they fell. "All right." She pulled her chair over to the computer and flicked a switch. The screen sparked, then filled with tiny file folders set against a blue background. "We're cookin' now."

"Cooking?"

"I'll look for you on the Internet. I'll bet your ashram is there. I mean, everyone's got a website, right?" Her fingers moved over the keyboard. "What's the URL?"

"I don't know." Ram didn't say anything about a URL, though Joe wouldn't put it past the angels to have a site on the internet. Hell, maybe they were all over it.

"Okay, then. Where do you live?" She looked up, hands poised.

"Ah, I'm not exactly, that is..." Damn. Wasn't it enough that he had given her his full name? No, he had to come clean. Just not yet. "Can you ask something else?" He would tell her later, after she was more used to him. Maybe if she found his family on the Internet that would be enough.

She pushed a hand through her hair and sighed. "Very well." Her fingers drummed on the side of the chair. "How about this? Where were you before you came to me?"

"Well..." He wasn't supposed to discuss the other people he helped, even to other angels or sacred guardians and this rule he would *not* break. What could he tell her? "Vietnam." That was true. In a way. “I was in Vietnam.”

“Really?” She looked up. Light from the desk lamp flared and her eyes went neon. “What were you doing there?”

“Fighting.” He leaned toward her and caught a whiff of sandalwood and jasmine. Damn. This weird sense of smell was growing stronger.

“I see.” She tucked her chin and typed the word “Vietnam” across a small box in the center of the screen.

The picture on the screen shuddered; then a long list appeared, each line starting with the word “Vietnam.” He stared at the pulsing blue lines on the white screen while Alena pulled at the mouse.

“Joe.” She stopped and pulled her hands back. “Were you, are you missing?” She gulped. “I mean, are you still in Vietnam?”

“In a manner of speaking.” He guessed they sent his body back home, what was left of it, anyway. But he went directly from his death to cruising with Ram. He had no idea if it was his body in the coffin his mom put in the ground.

“Oh, God, Joe.” She seemed to be looking for something, peering intently at the screen. “Here.” She pushed on the ovoid box until it clicked. “The Vietnam POW and MIA lists.”

“Wait!” He wasn’t missing in action.

Too late. The screen sparked and darkened. White letters appeared. She nodded. “I can enter your name here and we’ll know once and for all if your story is true.” The corners of her mouth thinned. “Or if I’m just nuts.” Her shoulders lifted in a shrug. “Here goes.” Her fingers flew over the keyboard. His name materialized on the screen. She grabbed the mouse again and raced it across the pad. “Damn mouse needs cleaning.” She picked it up, blew hard into the little ball underneath, and thumped it on the pad again.

How could he find the right place? The place that would tell her he was real? A place that wouldn't tell her he was dead. He had scanned the first list that appeared, but nothing looked right. Many of the lines were in Vietnamese. Others had "Veteran" in the title, but they looked more like self-help organizations, places saying they dealt with problems from chemicals like Agent Orange and something called PTS.

She pushed the arrow to a square button marked "Search," then pressed hard on the mouse.

He stared at the screen. She wouldn't find him there. How could he get her to go back to the list of web sites? Maybe he could get hold of the mouse. He watched her fingers wrangle the contraption in a smooth slide over the pad. Yeah. He could do that, too. Only he'd have to get it away from her first.

A line puckered her forehead. She rotated the mouse again. "Oh, look." Her finger stabbed at the screen. Her shoulders drooped. "Damn!"

Littlehawk, Joseph. No Name Found. New Search?

She leaned over the board. "Well." Her forehead rested against the screen. "Now we know, don't we?" She clicked on "Back" and the line of blue titles appeared again. "Now I know."

Hell on a stick! "Alena, I wasn't a POW." He tugged at the cord that attached the mouse to the keyboard. "I wasn't MIA."

"Cut it out." She leaned back and jiggled the mouse. The cursor arrow did a wild dance. "God." She pressed her fingers against her eyelids. "What the hell am I doing?" Her hand dropped into her lap. "I just proved you're not real. Yet here I am talking to you again." She straightened, her spine forming a rigid line all the way to her jaw. "Though if you were real, you'd be what, sixty or so?" She covered her face with her hands.

"Alena." He reached out and traced a line from her wrist to her elbow. "What's up?"

"I just wanted you to be real, Joe. I wanted, oh, I don't know." Her head shook from side to side. "I wanted you to come to me, to find me." She pulled her hands away from her face. "I wanted you here. Real. So we could, I don't know, go to lunch or something. Be friends." She snorted. "Stupid, huh?"

Hell. He shouldn't have done it. "I am your friend, Alena." He shouldn't have let her think he was alive. Her shoulder was warm beneath his hand. He gave a little squeeze.

"Dang it!" She shivered. "I'm still talking to you. Well, maybe talking to me." She shook her head. "Well, maybe…" She grabbed the mouse and slid it over the pad. "Double dang!" Her breath hissed out her teeth. "This whole thing is making me dizzy again." She leaned forward, her eyes tracking the cursor. "I'm out of here."

He laid his hand over hers. She startled. The hair on her arm stood on end. "Hold on, Alena." She had to find him; he had to make her see he was real. "Not missing in action," he whispered. Christ! What was it they called out when you bought it? How could he forget this? He could almost hear the throbbing whine of the choppers, taste the blazing wall of superheated air, the furnace that was Vietnam. He pushed hard on her hand. They gave the name, the rank, the company, the unit…"Kilo India!" Killed in action.

She jumped. "What?"

"KIA." There! He wrested the mouse from her and spun it around. The cursor sped all the way down the blue titles, all the way to the line he wanted. The cursor hovered there, while he fought for control, for the burst of intent that would depress the clicker, that would show her…

He didn't have to. She glanced at the screen.

“Oh my God.” Her mouth tightened. She swallowed and put her hand over his on the mouse. He watched her fingers melt through his hand, felt the tension in her muscles as she depressed the clicker.

Chapter Twelve

It was called the Wall. The Vietnam Veterans Memorial.

She sat staring at the monitor. A jet black background spread across the top and bled all the way down the screen. Statues of soldiers stood underneath the title. Lines of a sorrowful poem unfurled to the right. And a blank, stark white box blinked the word "Name" down at the bottom.

Of course. Her arms seized. She could barely move them. A ghost. She turned her head and peered through air that trembled on her left. Joe was dead. Her lids closed as she jerked her head back toward the screen. Did she really want to know this? If Joe was real, then she wasn't crazy, right? Michael wouldn't have a crazy mom. If Joe wasn't real, she was back where she started. But if he was real, then he was dead.

Stuck. She was stuck. There were no such things as ghosts. Telepathy and visions like Master Wang she could almost deal with, from what she had seen in the commune. But a dead guy? If Joe was dead, why had *he* had come to her; why hadn't her David come to her when she needed him so much?

Her head dropped and her body jerked down toward the screen. "God." She shook from the crown of her head to her toes. "God help me. Please."

"Alena."

There he was again. The hot prickle worked its way up her spine. "Move back, Joe." A ghost. "You're too close." She couldn't accept this. If she accepted this, then everything, everything she'd ever believed was false. All her life she'd thought that life after death was bogus, that you lived your life and you died and it didn't mean much of anything, except to live it the best way you could.

Oh, there was a sort of order in the universe, but she thought God was the result of all living things on the planet. Psychic stuff like the things they practiced in the commune was all the result of the living brains of the people practicing it. Kind of like the "Force" in *Star Wars*. There was no life after death. "There can't be, there can't be." But she had to know.

Well, she'd better get it over with. Her hand shook so much she mistyped the name, turning "Littlehawk" into "Kottlejak." She massaged her palm and breathed. "This is for Michael." She had to know, didn't she? "And for me, too."

She typed in the name again, clicked on the "search" button and sat gazing at the screen while the computer churned.

The details were in black. Against a gray background.

JOSEPH LITTLEHAWK JR.
Sgt. - Marines - Enlisted
Age: 24
Race: Native American
Sex: Male
Date of Birth: March 3, 1944
From: Pine Ridge, South Dakota
Religion: Catholic
Marital Status: Single
Length of service 2 years
His tour began on January 4, 1966
Casualty was on January 10, 1968
In QUANG TIN, SOUTH VIETNAM
Hostile, GROUND CASUALTY

Her eyes stopped tracking. Hot tears made briny streaks down her face and dropped onto her arms. "Damn!" She swiped at her face and clasped her hands together when she saw them still shaking. The edges of her nails pressed dents into her palms. She stared at the final entries.

MULTIPLE FRAGMENTATION WOUNDS
Body was recovered

A little puff burst close to her ear. Was he laughing? "Body recovered?" Joe scoffed. "Well, what was left of it."

"How dare you!" She shot back from the terminal. "How dare you make little of this, this…" She couldn't seem to get the words out. The bare facts on the screen just kept stealing her breath. "God, Joe." Her face felt raw. "You were only twenty-four."

"Lena—c'mon."

"Oh my God. My God." The screen flickered in front of her. "You're real." The universe was one great big hole, just waiting to swallow her. "You are real." If ghosts were real, then David…why hadn't it been David who had come to help her? God, what if her parents came back to haunt her!

"Yeah!" He sounded triumphant. "That's what I've been telling you."

"Go away."

"What!"

"I can't deal with this." She stood on legs that wanted to crumble beneath her. "Not right now." The air thickened beside her. "No!" She glanced away. "Don't show yourself." Her breath hitched. "You said you cared about me."

"I do."

"Then you must go away, Joe." She wrapped her arms around her waist. "I can't deal with you right now." It didn't help. Cold shudders traveled from her neck all the way down her back.

The room fell quiet. A fluorescent panel above her desk hummed. The computer added its own electronic whine. "Joe?" The air to her left shivered.

"Are you sure?" His voice was barely there, nothing more than a husky whisper.

Was she? "Yes." She needed time. "I have to think this through." She stared into the pulsing currents of air.

The second hand on the clock over her desk made three full sweeps around. "If you ever need me." A long sigh rattled the papers on her desk. "Just say my name." Air now sucked at her face. Her ears closed against the pressure, then popped.

She was alone in the room. The screen still blinked at her. She pushed the print button. While paper whispered out of the printer, she pulled the file menu down and pushed "Exit."

Alone.

****

She pushed the door open with her toe and stumbled into her apartment. Books filled the wire cart the doctor had ordered her to get in order to save her neck from strain. The books on top fell off, making thumps all the way to the couch. Michael bounded past her, straight to the television. "No! Michael." She caught his arm. "Clean your room first."

His lower lip jutted out. "But it's Saturday morning. I want cartoons!"

"At least pick up your toys first." She retrieved the books, one by one, stacking them on the table. *Haunted Houses of California. Appearances of the Dead. Ghostly Matters. Haunted People.* She glanced up. Michael was sidling toward the television. "Room." She jerked her thumb toward his door. "Take your library book with you." He gave her one last mutinous glare then trudged with a heavy tread all the way to his room. "I'll come in later to read with you," she called after him and looked down at the table.

The library had scads of books on ghosts. She'd picked as many as she could carry off the shelves, along with two on demonic possession. The scarlet cover of the one in her hand showed a black skull face. *Tales of the Dead.* She sat cross-legged on the couch. When she'd tromped up to the check-out counter at the downtown public library, she was afraid the clerk would question her choice of books. Or at least give her a weird look. But he'd simply stamped her books and waved to the next in line. Well, this was Berkeley, after all. Or, as Deb liked to call it, "Berzerkeley."

"Ouija boards and automatic writing," she mumbled, thumbing through the chapter headings and sighing. Nothing there seemed to even remotely describe what she had experienced. No dead marines over six feet tall with eyes that reached right inside you…

"Dang it, I have to stop thinking like that!" She was looking for guidance here, not cute guys. Pages flipped over in an accordion rhythm. "Helpers!" The word jumped right off the page. She settled back and started to read.

****

"Mom?"

She looked up and blinked, glancing around the room in surprise. Night pressed against the windows. The living room was completely dark except for the small circle of her reading lamp. It had been just after eleven in the morning when she had started reading.

Michael stood clutching his stuffed dolphin. "I'm hungry, Mom."

She jumped off the couch and swore when her

legs were stabbed by about a thousand needles born of blocked circulation. "Damn!" Michael hadn't even had any lunch. She stared in shock at the blank television screen. "Didn't you want to watch TV?"

He stood slumped, watching her warily. "You said I had to clean my room first."

"Right." She sped into the kitchen and grabbed a can of *Space City* ravioli. "How about some ravioli, champ?" She turned when he didn't answer. His eyes brimmed with tears.

"Michael, what's wrong?" She dumped the ravioli in a pan and set the stove on medium.

"I cleaned my room."

"Why didn't you come and tell me?"

"I did."

Fuck. She didn't remember him coming in. "What did I say?"

One tear spilled. He didn't even wipe it away. "You said go away."

"What!"

"You made mean voices."

"Oh, Michael." She dropped to her knees and drew him into her arms. His little body was stiff and unyielding at first, but bowed into her embrace. "I'm sorry." She remembered now. She'd been deep into a section on angel guides. That was no excuse. Oh, she'd snapped at Michael before. But to get so lost in what she was doing that she forgot to feed him lunch, that was, that was...well, it was irresponsible. *And so like my own mom.* "You must be real hungry."

The ravioli bubbled. She stood and took a wooden spoon off a hook by the stove.

"You were nicer when Joe was here."

The air fled her lungs. Her hand froze until the bubbling pasta splashed a burning blob of sauce on her knuckles. She changed hands and stirred, sucking on the burned knuckles. "What did you say?"

"You weren't so mean when Joe was here." Michael still stood clutching his dolphin. "I want Joe to come back." His thumb went in his mouth, but he pulled it away and hid his hand behind his back. "He told me bedtime stories."

She stirred slowly now and watched her shaking fingers lower the gas jet under the pan. "Michael…What kinds of stories?"

A tiny frown creased the space between his brows. "One story was about Coyote. Another time he told me one about Antelope."

"Animal stories?" Why hadn't Joe told her this? Oh, God, Michael was seeing him. Joe talked to Michael, too.

Michael snorted and gave her his best *oh, brother* look. "They're spirits, Mom." He seemed to loosen. His hand came back to his front and he held up two fingers, one at a time. "Coyote's tricky, but he teaches a lot. And I like Sister Antelope. She's nice." The dolphin dangled from his other hand now. "I'm hungry."

"Huh?" She jumped, then gave the gas burner control a quick twist all the way off. "Yeah." She scooped the ravioli into a bowl and dropped a fork in it. "Michael?" She whirled around and filled a glass with milk, set it down to the right of his bowl.

He settled into the worn vinyl kitchen chair at their small table and stuck a wad of ravioli in his mouth. "Mmmmph?"

"Is Joe a real person?"

He chewed and squinted. "I can hear him." His fork captured a ravioli shaped like a space ship and he stuffed it into his mouth.

"Can you see him?"

"Nope." He talked through his full mouth, but she didn't say anything. This was not the time to teach manners. If Joe was talking to Michael, too, wasn't that dangerous? "Well." He swallowed and reached for his milk. "I can see him if I close my eyes." He squeezed his eyes shut, hugging the glass of milk to his chest.

"What does he look like?"

"He's big like a daddy." He frowned and opened his eyes. "A daddy with long hair like Timmy's dad."

She hugged her elbows and shivered. Michael's friend Timmy had a father who had long dark hair. She had to resolve this. "Have you seen Joe since last week?"

Michael shook his head. His lower lip gave a little tremble. "He came to say he was going away." Tears stood out in his eyes. "I want him to tell me stories again."

"Did he say why he went away?"

"No." He sniffed, and pulled the front of his T-shirt up to wipe his eyes. "You said Daddy went away, too." He looked up, eyes still teary. "Are you going away?"

She lifted him from his chair and held him close. "No, Michael."

"I want Joe."

What should she do? "We'll see, Michael." She pressed kisses against his hair. "I'll see what I can do."

****

"Joe?" Her throat was sore and the name came out in a pathetic croak. "Joe, come back please." She'd been saying his name and pleading with him to return for the past hour, but the living room remained silent. So silent she could hear Michael breathing in his room, even with the door half closed. She coughed, then sneezed and pressed a tissue against her nose.

Fuck it. "This is completely scanless." If Joe wouldn't come back, she'd have to tell Michael he was just an imaginary friend. Kids had imaginary friends. She slumped down on the couch. Michael would understand; she'd make sure of that. But her gut clutched at the thought of never seeing...Scratch that. Never *hearing* Joe again. She should turn off the lights and go to bed. Tomorrow was a work day. She couldn't stay up all night calling for a ghost who didn't seem to want to come. Leaning to the right, she reached for the lamp switch.

Air next to the lamp trembled. The wall behind it rippled.

She jumped off the couch, poised to run, crumpling the tissue in her hand. "You came back!" She backed away when the column of translucent swirls came closer. "You won't try to take me over, will you?" The air tasted of copper. She ran her tongue around her teeth and dabbed her lips, then stared at the scarlet flower spreading on her tissue.

"Alena." Joe's voice was close. "What have you been reading?" The shimmering air stopped next to the low table where the books sprawled. "What's this? Possession?" Something between a sigh and a breeze floated toward her. "We don't do anything like that."

"How could I know?" She bit back a growl. "Joe, you've been talking to Michael!"

"Yeah." The pages of the book on top rustled open. "He had a nightmare a while back." The book fell closed with a snap. "You were beat, so I helped him with it."

"Why didn't you tell me?"

"I'm sorry, Alena." The middle of the couch sank, as if a person had just sat there. "I was afraid you'd freak out." Another heavy gust, then his voice sharpened. "It was wrong. I should've told you."

"I couldn't find you in here." She gestured to the books.

"I wouldn't be in these books."

"How do you know?"

"Alena. I work with an angel." He paused. "He

told me this."

"So what are you?" She slid toward him. "An angel?"

A short burst of mirth made the lamp quiver. "No. I'm a Sacred Guardian."

"What's that?"

"We're dead people who are helpers."

She grabbed a book on the edge of the table. "Here." Flipped through the pages. "It says helpers are ghosts who are relatives or friends who have passed on." She sniffed. "Joe, I don't know you." Her voice shook. "I couldn't have known you. I was born in 1981."

"I just know what I was told, Alena. Sacred Guardians help people."

"Okay." Maybe she could ask Deb about Sacred Guardians. Surely there must be something on them. "Michael wants you to come back."

A long silence spread out over the apartment. It swallowed the tiny sounds of floorboards settling; it even stole the beat of her heart.

"Michael wants me?" The air shuddered. She could almost see him. "How about you?"

She perched on the arm of the couch. "I've always wanted you around, Joe." Her shoulders hitched. "I'm just scared."

"I'll help you. You don't need to be scared." The swirl of air leaned toward her. "I'd never hurt you or Michael. You've got to know that."

"Well." She dabbed at her mouth again and the tissue came away all crimson. "I don't want anything floating around." Just how badly did she bite her lip? "And don't scare Michael." She held the tissue tight against her mouth and counted to ten.

"I promise."

"Good." She swallowed. "So you'll stay?"

His voice warmed. "As long as I can." A prickling current settled on her shoulder. "I promise."

Chapter Thirteen

She'd asked him to help her sleep. She was more and more tired during the day now and blamed it on not getting enough sleep, so she asked for his help.

He didn't mind. Not really. Each night he lay next to her in the bed, drew her close and matched her breathing, slowing his own until she followed his breath and lapsed into the deep and slow breathing of sleep. But sleeping next to her was getting pretty uncomfortable.

Trouble was; she wiggled. It was just her bottom, and she stopped wiggling once she settled into a spooning position with her behind placed firmly against his groin. But that little wiggle never failed to start something, something he'd never experienced as a Sacred Guardian, not even when Ram had assigned him to watch over Gloria Welton, up and coming actress with a 36C bust and legs that went on forever.

It was a tingle in the groin, almost an itch. The damnedest thing, really. He just didn't know what to make of it. And each night he positioned his form next to her, his whole groin got hot and ached for hours. If he didn't know better, he'd suspect he was becoming aroused. But that was impossible.

Wasn't it?

He let himself stroke Alena's hair and she murmured in her sleep, muttered something that sounded like "redwoods." Burrowed in closer to his groin. Wiggled.

He leaped away. Holy Mother of God! His loins were on fire. Alena half turned and mumbled again, but didn't wake. He stood at the side of the bed, hand poised over his groin. Did he really want to know this? Damn, he had to know. The ache now resonated throughout his form in a widening ripple. He placed his hand on his loins. What the hell? His fingers traced the massive swelling. This was not just an erection. It was a throbbing hardness that demanded his full attention.

"*Éya, wan ká wan*!" Well, what do you know? A ghost with an erection? Jesus, Joseph, and Mary! What should he do now? He glanced down at Alena. She had snuggled all the way over on the side he usually occupied. If she went any farther she'd fall right off the bed. He'd better stick something behind her so she wouldn't tumble off. He darted into the living room and grabbed one of the large couch pillows. When he slipped back into the bedroom, she was curled up like a baby, a tiny frown between her brows and one hand jammed under her ribs. The oversize T-shirt she wore to bed strained against her, outlining her breasts and belly.

He groaned. Just looking at Alena made his situation worse. Seeing her like this made him itch to cup her delicious breasts in his hands. And the soft little pouch, that small, swelling curve to her belly left over from giving birth to Michael drew him. He wanted to skim his hand across it and make a slow and careful glide all the way to...His hand froze over her stomach. He gasped and fell back. When had he reached for her? He didn't remember extending his hand.

Oh, man. He had to get out of there. Fast.

He shoved the couch pillow behind her back and shot up through the ceiling, barreling past three floors of sleeping tenants until he blasted out of the roof. Got to cool down. He kept climbing up to the clouds and burst above them into the silver and sapphire sky. Floating on his back, he peeked downward, surveying the damage. Yep, still there. What if it didn't go down? Hell, Ramael never said anything about *this*.

Damn, think, Joe, think! It wasn't like he could take a cold shower. What else would cool him down? He drifted toward the Oakland Airport and watched the planes circle and leisurely dip down toward the bay. Almost looked like they were going to hit the water, but they always touched down right at the edge where the runway met the bay. He used to spend a lot of time up here, watching planes land. And now this seemed to help his, er, problem. Concentrating on the planes had cooled him down. A bit.

What did he do when he was alive? Jesus, he never thought he'd have this particular situation again. Okay, okay, when he was a teenager and he wanted to put the ice on his arousal he used to do times tables. Worked like a charm back then. He put his hands behind his head and drifted on his back. "One times one is one. Two times two is four. Four times four..."

"What are you doing?"

The dry voice of Ram catapulted him upright. "Uh, just hanging out." He was afraid to look down. "Taking a break." What if the angel noticed? And why hadn't he felt Ram before the angel arrived? He's always known when Ram was around, right from the moment he died. He grasped his right wrist with his left hand and held his hands poised over his groin, going for a casual stance. Right. *GQ* for Sacred Guardians.

Ram just looked at his face. The angel's eyebrow didn't even give the usual amused twitch.

"I need you to go to JJ."

"Sure thing." *Hécetu*! This would get him away from Ram fast. He couldn't think of anything better to cool him down than a dose of his nephew's problems. Unless JJ was having woman trouble. But Ram wouldn't send him to JJ if a fight with his girlfriend was all that was happening to the kid.

He looked up and faltered. Ram's face was even more like stone than usual. But something in the angel's eyes sorrowed. "Anything else, boss?"

"Just go to JJ."

He reached for his nephew's essence and yanked.

****

And found himself hurtling down US 18 just outside the rez at eighty miles an hour, right above JJ.

Oh, boy. Just what he needed: midnight in South Dakota, in a dark, freezing rain. He looked down. The kid was on a Harley, not the bike he'd had parked outside the bar. Looked more like JJ's own bike. Old. Not vintage, but in good condition. Kid was really moving.

So what was the deal? Why had Ramael sent him here?

JJ was a good driver when he wasn't drunk. The kid had great reflexes and he certainly didn't look drunk right now. Looked angry, though, really pissed. But except for speeding, he wasn't being reckless. This section of US 18 was flat out, a great place for letting your engine roar, feeling the wind and rain pelt your face. Matter of fact, it was getting hard for him to see. Well, JJ had goggles on but he—

Goddammit! He reached up and wiped his eyes, slicking back his hair. What had happened to Ramael's shield? He was soaked through and that rain was damn cold. Cold? Since when could a ghost feel cold? Just how and when had he gone solid? He glanced down at JJ. "Ram, why the hell did you send me here?" he muttered, spitting sleet out of his mouth. "Nothing's happening."

JJ's head jerked up. "Wha?" He looked right into

Joe's eyes.

Damnation! He made the motion to elevate but couldn't go any higher than a few inches. What the hell was this? He'd never had any trouble lifting before. Maybe he was stuck in JJ's slipstream; usually all he could do was hover, float, and do a particle sluice, but right now he was wailing along at a breakneck pace, and in a solid form to boot.

He glanced up ahead for a place to dive into so he could hide. The pavement glowered back at him from half a mile ahead. "Shit!" Black ice pooled in at least six spots. "Watch out, JJ!"

JJ had slowed but he was still looking up at him, not at the road. He'd be upon the black ice soon.

"Holy hell, JJ, look at the goddamn road." Three hulking pickup trucks loomed at the side of the road up ahead, where some clapboard truck stop promised all-you-could-eat ribs on Thursday. If JJ didn't look down soon, he'd plow right into the trucks. "Look at the fucking road, JJ!"

The kid finally looked down. His front tire hit the edge of the first pool of black ice and his bike spun sideways in an out-of-control skid.

No time to even think about it. He dropped to the road, grabbed the rear tire, and pulled. Pulled with everything he had, as the pavement scraped and chopped away at his solid form. Pieces of him sheared right off, his legs disintegrated just below the knees, and a huge chunk of his shoulder tore off, but he held on, guiding the skid toward a patch of snow just beyond the trucks. Wouldn't be great, but a hell of a lot softer landing than hitting a bunch of two-ton trucks.

He let go just as the bike struck the snow bank. JJ tumbled over the handlebars into the snow, rolling three times before he stopped. The bike bucked and twisted, then came to a rest on its side. A thin line of smoke and the bite of gasoline hung over the road.

He looked up as people poured out of the truck stop and peered over to where JJ stood looking at his bike, cussing a blue streak. Oh, man. Kid was okay, JJ was okay. But he had to get out of there fast. He was way too solid. If anyone could see him, well, see what was left of him, that is, there'd be hell to pay.

In the end, all he could do was roll. Didn't have any legs and his left shoulder was shredded. He used his right arm and the stump of his left hand and rolled until he was dizzy, rolled right off the highway and over the embankment on the opposite side of the truck stop. Kept rolling until he rested among a copse of tangled brush.

Damn, he was tired. He'd never been this tired, not even when he was alive and on patrol in 'Nam. "Ramael?" His voice crackled. "I can't fly, Ramael." Now, what were those words to bring the angel to him? "Screw this. *U Wanto*! Get your tight ass over here, Big Wing." Aw, he was too tired to think. Maybe he could just sleep, you know, rest. Like you're supposed to when you're dead. "Can the dead die?" This seemed really funny to him, but it hurt to laugh.

Hurt? How could he hurt? He glanced down. No blood, but a whole lot of his form had sheared off. "Christ!" He shouldn't be able to feel but some kind of nerve endings were screaming at him.

Yeah, he hurt, all right. At least he hadn't entirely felt the bomb that exploded him in 1968, but he sure as hell felt *this*.

"Dammit, Ramael," he whispered. "Help me. I need you." The lids fell over his eyes and blackness took him.

****

"Joseph."

"Not now, Ma." He stretched a little and wound his arms around his waist. "Just a few more minutes." He yawned through the last few words.

"Joseph."

He blinked. "What the?" He floated on his side over the short grasses on top of Mount Tamalpais, looking down a hundred-foot drop toward the ocean. "What happened?"

"You interfered."

"Huh?" He sat up and tested his form, running his hands up and down his side from his toes to his head. Everything seemed to still be there. "But my legs were gone." Other big chunks of him, too.

"You were a mess." Ram reached toward him, offering a hand. He took it and bobbed upright.

"Hey, I feel great now." He lifted and spread his arms. "What did you do?"

"I think the real question is what did *you* do?"

"It was my fault."

Ram just stood there, arms crossed.

"JJ's spinout." He stretched his hands toward the sky and looked in amazement at his fingers. They'd all been down to stumps when he last saw them. "He saw me flying above him." Well, his body—or whatever you would call this form—was back to normal now. "I went solid."

Or nearly normal. His groin still held a slight ache.

Ram nodded. "You interfered."

"What was I supposed to do?" He flung his hands out. His shoulders felt a little wobbly. "Let him die?"

"We don't interfere."

Oh, great. "Then what is all this for? How the hell do you expect me to help someone?"

"You didn't have a problem with the people in the hospital."

"But they were old and sick. Some of them needed to die. They were begging to die." If the angel went on and on about how he couldn't interfere...Jeez, he *wished* he had his hunter's knife. He went to smack his left palm with his fist, but it traveled right on through. Shoot. Well, never mind. If he could hold a knife he'd make sure to get a few of those waving wing filaments before the angel could blink. Serve him right.

"Yet you didn't kill them." Ram grabbed him with the angel's laser stare. "Those who you thought needed to die."

"Of course not!" He snorted, looking away. "It wasn't their time." Why did Ram always have to make him feel he'd done something wrong?

"It wasn't their time," the angel repeated.

Christ. "It was JJ's time?" He drifted back.

Ram just looked at him.

"Aw, *damn*! What would that do to my sister? JJ is her only child." He dragged his hand back through his etheric hair until it crackled. "Why didn't you tell me?"

"I shouldn't have had to."

He hugged his form and looked out at the breakers. "Does this mean JJ will have to die soon?" Ram was right. He should have known. But JJ was too close, too goddamn close. JJ was his only nephew. Even though JJ could be a hell-raiser, he loved the kid. He didn't have the distance needed to see what God intended.

"Not right away, no." Ram seemed to soften. His form took a blurry-edged glow all around it. "The others have changed their minds about this. We won't have you help JJ cross when it is his time."

"I see. What about the Alena Morgan case?" Ram controlled the assignments. At least, the angel seemed to have the power to tell him what to do. "Am I finished there? She seems to be doing okay."

Right. Alena was just an assignment. Just a case. Yeah. Sure she was. His form oscillated and spread almost to the shore hundreds of feet below.

He pulled his form back together in an instant and coalesced just in time to hear Ram's answer.

"No."

"What?" He whipped around. The angel wasn't looking at him. Ram gazed at some kids who were scrambling up the trail.

"We want you to go back to Alena." The angel backed up and pinned him with a glance. "For now."

The yelps and giggles of the kids climbing up the trail settled someplace inside him, someplace special. Someplace warm.

"Am I free to go?"

The angel nodded.

He took off, did three spins and a half gainer through the mist. "Here I come, Alena and Michael." He burst through a series of puffy cumulus clouds and dove toward Berkeley. "I'll be there soon." And careful, oh, man, was he ever going to be careful. He wouldn't get too close. He wouldn't let her see him.

But if Ram thought for one moment that he would let anything happen to Alena, well, the angel had another think coming. If it came down to a fight, then so be it.

The itch between his shoulders became unbearable. Must be something left over from when he lost big chunks of his form while he was helping JJ. He slid through a series of swells just off the Berkeley Marina to allow the water molecules to soothe the burning.

Damn, he hoped he could hold it together enough to stay with Alena and Michael. He could do this job, and do it right. He just knew he could.

He knew it.

Chapter Fourteen

Michael sat in his room, playing with the Game Boy Deb had given him for his birthday. His laughter and the inane music of the game floated into the kitchen. The apartment filled up with the tangerine glow of a California sunset. Three windows stood wide open. A warm spell for mid-December.

She'd gone out with Michael that afternoon and picked out a little Christmas tree from the lot just down the street, one she could carry home in her wire basket. It stood in the corner of her living room, twinkling with lights and bristling with cut paper ornaments. She touched one of the paper stars and smiled. This was the first time since David died that she'd been able to afford a Christmas tree.

She rummaged through her cupboards and hummed "Take All of Me." The staff party at Living Light had been cool. Really cool. She wasn't sure if they would accept her, with her pierced nose, the studs in her ears, the tattoos and all, but they were friendly. It was weird how working in a normal job made her hands steady—the shakes and insomnia had pretty much stopped when she started working—but it had been so long since she'd been in the company of adults, she almost hadn't known what to say to people. What do you say when your whole experience of life had been looking after a couple of drug addicts?

David hadn't minded Alena's past. He'd admired what he called "Alena's guts." She snorted. It had taken guts all right, and a whole lot of jiving.

After David died, her life had centered on Michael. She'd taken her boy to the playground to play with the kids of all the other moms, grandmoms, and even an au pair or two who frequented the Regent Street playground. Along with her battle with pain, the sum total of her time for the past two years had been spit up and colic, then skinned knees and the redwood splinter that stuck under Michael's toe and required a trip to the ER to have it removed before the foot got infected. Her days were filled with smiles and Uncle Fart, bedtime stories and oat cereal that somehow always got spilled and crunched under her feet even when she thought she'd gotten all of it. She smiled. What the hell did she know of adults?

She pushed cans of peas and corn around, looking for something that would be good for a Sunday evening with Michael. Settling on homemade spaghetti, Michael's favorite, she pulled a package of vermicelli and a can of tomato paste out of the cupboard and grabbed mushrooms, garlic, onions, and sausage out of the refrigerator.

God, she was sleepy, though. A nap sounded like a good idea. She glanced at the clock. Maybe after dinner. The party tired her out more than she thought it would.

At the party, some of the guys had even flirted with her. Just flirted. That was amazing. Before David, she had only known guys who assumed she would put out, go to bed on the first encounter. She'd never even thought of anyone flirting with her after David died.

Her throat clogged. She bowed her head and let the ache of his loss whip through her heart and allowed a tear to streak down her cheek, but dashed it away. Before Joe, she hadn't ever cried. She couldn't remember crying when she was little, though she must have. Michael cried so easily. He had his father's tender heart. David had loved her. She knew this.

She set the vermicelli aside, filled a pan with water, and added a dash of olive oil to keep the pasta from sticking and going all gummy. Good thing Deb was teaching her how to cook real food, not just "open a can and slap it in the pan" like her parents had done. She turned the burner on and watched the water ripple; the oil caught light from the kitchen ceiling fixture and glistened. When he was alive, David liked to cook.

David was a good man, despite his trouble with money. She'd been married to a good man, at least. That was something. Many of the women at work had been involved in really bad marriages. Nearly half of them were divorced. "Who knows what would have happened to us?" If David had lived, the money problems would have surfaced eventually. What would she have done? She'd like to think she would have stuck with him, for better or worse, but things could get dicey. "And I sure know that." She smiled again as the water began to gurgle. "But sometimes you get a real miracle."

Like Joe Littlehawk, her old, dead guy. God bless him. He looked young, but he was really her parents' age. He liked all the songs from the fifties and sixties. She hated that boomer stuff, but if Joe liked the songs, well, maybe she should listen to them again. After all, he'd saved her life. A quick glance around the kitchen told her she was alone. The air was clear and there was no electric shimmer.

She leaned against the counter and sliced the mushrooms. Last month he'd been gone for several days and when he came back, he didn't say much. She peeled the onion's skin off and walked over to throw it in the compost bin under the sink. Joe wouldn't say why he'd gone quiet. Not that he was a chatterbox before, but he used to joke around. Now it was like he was always holding his breath. If a ghost could do that. She sliced the onion and set another pan on a vacant burner, then started the sausages sizzling in a skillet.

A brush across her arm warned her. The hair on her neck moved, as if someone had kissed her there. She looked up and across the kitchen to the corner where the counter met the refrigerator. The air in front of it wavered, like heat rising off pavement.

Joe.

She waited for him to speak as the sausages hissed in the pan. After several minutes of silence, she turned back to the pan, flipped the sausages over and lowered the burner to simmer.

She still hadn't asked Deb about Sacred Guardians and her search on the topic at the public library had come up empty, but everything Joe had told her about Sacred Guardians sounded like they were junior angels. Maybe he felt he'd gotten too personal. She nibbled at her lip. He wouldn't even lie next to her anymore. Well, that was probably against the Sacred Guardian code or something. Felt awfully good when he'd lain by her side, though. She missed it. Missed him talking to her too. And that was really funny, because she'd been so upset about him talking to her. About feeling like she was crazy. She grabbed the vermicelli and laughed.

"What's so funny?"

"This is weird." She dumped vermicelli into the now boiling water, leaping back from the spatters. "I used to hate it when you talked to me."

"And now?"

"I like it." She spilled the sliced onions and mushrooms into the other pan. "I mean, I like it that you don't talk to me when I'm around other people. That gets confusing, and people might think…"

"That you're crazy."

"Right."

"But otherwise?"

"I like it." She shook her head. "I've never asked you something I'd like to know, but I'm a little, you know, afraid to ask."

"Why not just ask it?"

"I may feel a little weird about the answer."

"I won't tell you when you or anyone close to you will die."

"Oh, I wouldn't ask that." She paused and tried to stifle a yawn. "At least, I don't think I would." The yawn won, and it was a real jaw cracker. "God, I'm sorry, Joe. I don't know why I'm so tired."

"You should go rest up."

"Dinner won't get made unless I do it."

"Sorry I can't help with that."

"So am I." The water bubbled, the onions and mushrooms simmered, the sausages browned. "But hey, I'm glad you're here."

"You were going to ask me something."

"What's it like—" She took a breath. "—being dead?"

The air swirled, but he didn't speak.

"Hey. If you don't want to answer, well, that's okay."

"Ah, no, it's not that." The shimmer settled into a wavy tube. "It's just...nobody ever asked me that before."

"You're kidding. How could they not ask you that? I mean, you are dead, right?"

"I am."

"Then why hasn't any of your, um, cases, you called them?" She glanced at the waving tube of air.

"Yes. Cases."

"Well, why haven't they? I mean, if you're talking to a dead person, you'd want to know, um, what was like, wouldn't you?"

"I would."

"Look, I get the feeling you don't want to talk

about this. It's okay."

"It's not that."

"What, then?"

"Nobody ever talked to me before." Each word dragged out, as if he were reluctant to speak.

"No shit!" She caught the spoon that flipped right out of her hand and tumbled to the counter. "Oops. Sorry. I mean, no shoot? No, that doesn't make any sense. I need a new expression." She stood holding the spoon.

"How about 'damn'?"

She managed to stir the onions. "Is 'damn' allowed?"

"Alena, c'mon."

"Okay, okay. Um, well, why hasn't anyone talked to you?" She swallowed. "That is, you mean I'm the only one?" The thought sent a little tingle through her chest that settled midway between her belly and her thighs.

"People usually don't hear me." The shimmering air leaned against the refrigerator. He didn't say anything for another few minutes.

The vermicelli bubbled. "Is it me? Is there something weird about me, that I can hear you?"

"No." His voice came from right above her ear.

She shivered. "No?"

"Something special."

"About me?" The electric prickle that meant he was very near danced up and down her back. "You've got to be kidding."

"Not about something like this."

"God." She looked down at her hands and saw them shaking. "I don't know what to say." She was just a punk daughter of a couple of hippie drug addicts. How could she be special?

"Just take it in some." His voice came from further away. "You asked me what it was like."

"What?" She shook her head. "Oh, yeah. Right.

What is it like? To die. To be dead."

"At first, I didn't know I'd bought it. I mean, I didn't remember anything." His voice was low and sad.

"But that's good, isn't it? You wouldn't want to remember being, um, exploded."

"Yeah, I guess so. I just wanted to know, well, I wanted to know the score."

"How did you scope it out?" She glanced at the vermicelli. It needed a little more time. "Did you just float around, or were your relatives there to help you?"

The tube of air swirled. "Been reading again, huh?"

"*Past Lives*."

"Oh. That's one I haven't seen."

"Can you read?"

"Well. Uh. I can't hold a book in my hands, now, can I? Not for very long, anyway. Sometimes I read with the people who are my, ah, cases."

"They turn the pages for you?"

"Something like that."

The silence in the kitchen now had warmth to it, the comfort of companionship. "So how did you figure things out? About being dead, I mean. And what is it like? I want to know."

"Because of David?"

She startled. "I dunno. I guess so. But I was just thinking what if I had actually died that night?"

"You didn't."

"You saved me."

"Yeah."

She wanted to touch him, to touch him like a friend, touch his arm or his hand. She reached toward the swirl of sparkling air but he moved away.

"There was someone there when I died." The translucent air glided past the refrigerator. "And about being dead; it's weird sometimes, but it's also kind of amazing." He spoke slowly, as if he were measuring each word.

"How is it weird being dead?" She leaned against the counter. It must be uncomfortable when she touched him, that's all. He never really said, but he did move away. Too bad...She liked to touch. Her parents were haphazard and sometimes cruel when they were coming down from speed or coke, but they always touched her when they were around. Little pats on the head, a brush down the arm, a hug. She did that with her friends, and with David and Michael. It was hard to be this close to someone she...cared about, and to never see him, never touch. "Stop it, Alena," she muttered. It wasn't good, longing for things that weren't for her.

"Huh?"

"Nothing." *Just don't go there, girl.* "I mean, is it weird when people touch you? Does it hurt?"

"I don't mind so much. It's just strange. People walk right through me sometimes. It makes me dizzy."

"God. Dead and still feeling dizzy," she laughed.

"Well, yeah, I guess you could say that."

"How do you get around?"

"Different ways. Sometimes I just float or hover. Kind of. Other times I think about where I want to be. Sometimes I walk."

"Like you walk beside me when I take Michael to the park." She turned. "I can feel you there beside me, Joe." Her cheeks felt warm. "It feels, I guess, so natural, like you're a friend walking beside me."

"Yes." One word only, but several registers of warmth.

She shivered again and busied herself with turning the sausages. The scent of hot fat and basil rose in a cloud. "What else do you do? I mean, what's amazing about being dead?"

"I can help people." He was closer, she could tell.

The prickle dusted her left arm. "I can fly." His last words were breathed against her neck.

"What about David?" She could barely get the words out. He was so close the hair on her arms swayed. It tickled, but she didn't want him to go away. "Why can't I talk to him?"

He sighed, the sound brushed past her ear and she suppressed another quiver. "I'm really not allowed to discuss that."

"Why not?" And why didn't it hurt more to hear this? Didn't she want to talk to David?

"Alena." His voice had gone low and husky. "He's passed on to another realm. Even I can't reach him."

"Does that mean he's in a good place? A place where he's okay?"

"Better than okay."

Her hands trembled. "How long did you say you'd be with me?" She curled her fingers and waited for his answer.

Silence broken only by the gurgle and slosh of boiling pasta stretched for several minutes. The prickle no longer ran down her spine. She pulled the colander off its hook, dropped it in the sink, and poured the vermicelli into it.

"Until you no longer need me." His voice came from across the room now.

She grabbed a can of tomato paste and jammed the opener down on the lid. "Oh." She sucked at paste that had slopped onto her fingers. "Guess I'll have to do something so I'll need you a good long time."

"Don't even joke about that, Alena."

"Hey!" She whirled around. "I didn't mean I would be so stupid again." She couldn't even tell where he was now. "Seriously." Had he left again? "I hardly ever have to take Zamatrex anymore." She turned around. "Joe?"

"I'm still here."

She ran her hand across her forehead. "I'm glad. Real glad you came into our lives. That's all." She rinsed the spoon and set it in the sink.

"So am I, Alena. So am I."

The whole kitchen had a glimmer to it. Something inside her glowed, something she didn't even know she had. She couldn't name it yet. But it was there.

Chapter Fifteen

"Why have you called me?"

Ram flew high above the ocean in full glory, streams of clouds slipping around the multicolor tentacle things that formed the angel's wings. He never got used to seeing them. They reminded him of squid. Right now, really fast squid.

In fact, it was getting hard to keep up with Ram. He finally pulled his arms to his side and led with his head, barreling past Ram and right into the angel's path.

"Watch it." Ram's eyes sparked as he halted. "I could have vaporized you."

"Can the dead die?"

The angel's wings vibrated in dissonant tones. "No."

"Good to hear it."

Ram moved in close. "But it would be most unpleasant."

"You are supposed to be guiding me, correct?"

"You are my assignment, yes."

"I have a question."

"Very well."

"It's about Alena."

"You're nearly done there, aren't you?"

"I'm not sure."

Ram's gaze sharpened. "She's not in pain again, is she?"

"No." He forced his form to keep level with the angel's face. Ram's wings had the angel lifting and descending on each beat. "But she seems to be tired all the time."

Ram lifted a brow. "She has a job and a child."

"This is more than what you'd expect from all the work she does."

"Has she seen a doctor yet?"

"She won't go."

"Why not?"

"She doesn't think there is a problem."

"You called on me for this?" Ram spun. "Make her see a doctor. Use your influence." The angel suddenly was not there, just not there at all, though his exit caused a funnel to form in the air, a twister that sucked him down into the unquiet sea. It plunged him nearly all the way to the shadowy beds of kelp floating far off Stinson Beach.

He came up sputtering, gathering his form together and shaking off long strands of glistening kelp. "Use your influence," he snorted. "Yessir, lieutenant, sir!" He rose to the stratosphere and pushed his limits, allowing the vacuum of space to suck the fish smell from his form.

****

Café Pisano was doing a brisk business. The Cal students were still around until finals were over, and the café seemed the favorite place for them to cram for their exams. Alena snagged the last table open upstairs when a couple of girls left it. "Sit," she told Deb. "I'll get us some coffee and pastries and be right back—you hold the table." She draped her coat over one of the chairs and made for the stairs.

"Cinnamon on the coffee!" Deb hollered.

She fought her way to the line at the counter. Coffee was her savior these days. At times it seemed just too much trouble to keep her eyes open. She looked over the array of pastries and muffins under glass near the counter. "Which one," she said under her breath.

"Deb will want a chocolate muffin," Joe told her. "Why don't you try the poppyseed?"

"Shh."

"Eh?" The man at the counter grinned at her. "We don't have any *shhh*."

"Sorry, I meant two large coffees, one chocolate muffin, and one poppyseed." She dug into her purse for the money. "Leave room for milk," she added as he filled the cups.

"I'll get you a tray." The man at the counter placed the coffees and muffins on a tray with napkins.

"Hey, thanks." She paid and took the tray over to the condiments. She measured out sugar and cinnamon for Deb, poured milk into both and carried the tray up the stairs. At the top she had to stop to catch her breath.

"You okay?"

"Sure, I just need to eat something," she whispered. "I also need you to go away for a bit, okay?"

"Why?"

"I need to talk to Deb in private." No one near seemed to notice she was talking to the air.

"Girl stuff?"

"Something like that."

"Okay, I'll leave you to it."

She waited a moment, but couldn't tell if he'd gone or if he was still hanging around. Well, she meant to have this conversation with Deb and she'd have it. She placed the tray on the table and eased herself into her chair. "I put enough cinnamon in it for you?"

"Mmmm." Deb eyed her. "You want to tell me what is going on?"

She gulped her coffee. "I need to ask you something."

"Go ahead."

"Do you really believe in ghosts?"

Deb sipped at her coffee. "You been going to

mediums or something?"

"I'm serious."

"It's not a matter of belief, Alena."

"Huh?"

"I've met a ghost or two." Deb shrugged. "There's been enough solid evidence to convince me." She bit into her muffin and chewed it.

"Wow." She sat back. "I knew you were into the whole new age stuff, but..."

"Is this about your friend?" Deb's crinkle-eyed smile beamed at her.

She took a good long swallow of her coffee. "Never could fool you, could I?"

"I wasn't sure, Lena." Deb put her elbows on the table. "So. Tell me about this ghost."

"I think he's more than a ghost."

"Hmmm."

"Maybe a junior angel."

"Never heard of a junior angel."

"Deb, c'mon." She nibbled at her poppyseed. "This is hard enough for me."

"Okay, then." Deb put her chin in her hand. "Why do you think this ghost is a junior angel?"

"Um." She squirmed. "He used to lie next to me at night. But he doesn't anymore."

Both Deb's brows lifted, but she remained silent.

"And I've been having these dreams..." Dang it, why was this so hard to say. Conversations around them were loud enough so they couldn't be heard, and nobody seemed interested in them.

"Sexual dreams." Deb nodded and winked.

Trust Deb to lay it out there. "Not really. That is, he is there in the dreams, but we, you know, we don't..."

"You don't have sex."

"Ri-i-ight." She looked around. No one seemed to notice.

"And so this is why you think the ghost is a

junior angel? Because the two of you don't have sex?"

"God, Deb." She waved her hand and leaned in. "Keep it down, please!"

"Tell me—" Deb leaned forward, too. "—what does the ghost have to say about all this? Is this the Sacred Guardian you've been asking me about?"

"Yeah."

"Alena, there isn't any book on Sacred Guardians, but it sounds to me like something I've heard of, the thing you said was troubling your 'friend.' It's a Native American path-working…what?" Deb startled when Alena nearly knocked the coffee over.

She gulped and looked down. "He's, that is, he *was* Sioux. Lakota."

"Well."

"Yes."

"So you are attracted to this, ah, fellow?"

"I'm not sure. I like him, I know that."

"Just what do you like about him?"

"He's strong." She took a moment to savor her muffin. "He's kind of prickly, though."

"In what way?"

"He'll get miffed over the most scanless things."

"Like what?"

She felt her cheeks go hot. "My swearing."

"Well, that's good, isn't it?"

"But."

"There is always a 'but,' isn't there?"

"He won't lie next to me anymore, and God, Deb—" She brushed at the moisture seeping from her eyes. "I used to sleep better when he, well, when he lay next to me. Now I hardly sleep at all."

"But you dream."

"There are some dreams, yeah."

"I'll look into this more, Alena, and I'll talk to John Gray Wolf, but I have to tell you, I'm concerned." Deb took hold of her hands.

"You think I'm crazy." She looked down at the hands holding hers, veined and lined, yet soft and strong at the same time.

"No!"

"You think I'm possessed."

"No, I don't." Deb laughed, but she shook her head. "Now that you've opened up about this, I will look into it some more. But I need to ask you some questions first."

"Okay." *Just don't ask the big question, Deb. And don't tell me he has to go away.*

"Do you socialize with other people?"

"Um, well, yeah." She looked down. "That is, as much as I can."

"What do you mean?"

"Work and taking care of Michael kind of wear me out."

"Alena, you're young. That should be a snap for you. Go get your blood checked." She took hold of her hand again and pinched the skin.

"Hey! Ow." She rubbed the pinched spot. "Why did you do that?"

"You look pale to me." Deb leaned back. "Your skin elasticity is a little off. It's probably just anemia, but please do this for me. Go and have it checked out, okay?"

"I will." She cleared her throat. "What else?"

Deb leaned in really close. "Have you had sex with him?"

"What!"

"Have you?"

"No!" She looked from side to side. "Jeez, Deb."

"Do you want to?"

She looked at the table and took a long swallow of her coffee. "If he were alive. Maybe." She shrugged. "But if he were alive, he'd be pretty much out of my age range."

"What, hundreds of years old?" Deb settled back

in her chair and chuckled.

"Nah, probably more like sixty-five or so."

Deb's eyes narrowed. "That's not dead very long, then."

"Nope, only, let's see, 1968...about forty years. Does it make a difference?"

Deb leaned in, her eyes widened. "You mean he told you exactly when?"

"Yeah. I brought his record, here." She unfolded the copy of Joe's record from the Vietnam Wall site.

Deb pulled out her reading glasses and scanned it. "Holy shit."

"You said the S word!"

"So sue me. Can I keep this?"

"Sure, I have other copies." She'd made ten, just to be sure she wouldn't forget. As if she would. Ever.

"I'll take this to John, but Lena, be careful."

"Careful of what?"

Deb shook her head, removing her glasses and nibbling on the end of one earpiece. "There's something to what you told me; it reminds me of some case I'd read about, but I just can't remember what it is."

"It's not a good something?"

"I don't know, but it may be. Not good, that is. Anyway, just be careful, okay? Go out with people when you can. Don't spend all your time with this, ah..."

"Dead guy."

"Is that what you call him?" At least the twinkle was back in Deb's eyes.

"No," she said, looking directly into Deb's eyes. "I don't." She reached behind for her coat and purse. "I call him Joe."

Chapter Sixteen

Lights on the tree blinked red and green. She flicked one that had gone out. Chili pepper lights; Michael had picked out lights that looked like chili peppers. All the presents were wrapped up underneath, waiting for Michael to tear them open in the morning.

She glanced at the clock. It was past eleven. No doubt Michael would be up before it got light. She'd best get to bed, but there was one more thing she wanted to do before she went to sleep. "Joe?"

"Yo."

"Ha. Ha. Very funny." She blinked at the tube of translucency hovering in the center of the room. "I've been meaning to ask you something."

"Shoot."

"Before you leave me..." Her voice quivered. "Ah..." She cleared her throat. "Dang, this is fricking hard."

"Just spit it out, Lena."

"Okay. Before you go away, for good, that is, can you, you know, find me a guy?" Now that would take a long time, wouldn't it? According to the women at work, really good guys were few and far between. "A good man, right? No shi...no creeps."

Tall, with long dark hair that moved like silk.

Dang it, she had to stop that! Anyway, she didn't really want Joe to find her someone; she just wanted him to have a reason to stick around. "No guys who will suck off me, uh, I mean, no freeloaders."

Fathomless brown eyes that tilted over a high

ridge of cheekbones.

She shook her head and grabbed the edge of the sofa. *Don't go there, don't go there.* "Someone who can pull his own weight."

A resonant voice that caressed and cherished.

This was ridiculous. "Anyway, someone good." Joe was off-limits. She glanced around the room. "Someone who likes children." It was empty. "Joe?"

No answer. Silence settled over her in a way it hadn't in weeks. "Joe?" Still nothing. "Where did you go?" Maybe she had chattered too much. When she asked too many questions, he would go silent for a while, but she could always tell he was still there. The air sparkled wherever he stood. The tiny sounds of another person's presence—the gentle brush when he leaned against the wall, the creak of the floor—all announced he was near. She had no idea how he managed this. Even the air moved differently around him.

She paced the floor, swinging her arms. No electric prickle. Just the blink of the chili pepper lights. She leaned against the couch and rubbed at her arms. When Joe was around, the air lived.

"Come on, now, Joe." She cleared her throat when her voice cracked. Took a deep breath. "Come back."

The air swirled and thickened next to the tree. "Yeah?"

"You went away again." Her voice trembled. She cleared her throat. "Was I beginning to bug you?"

"Pardon?"

"What is it—I'm not supposed to ask for your help in finding a guy? Is that against the rules?"

"Um." Another long pause had her holding her breath. Finally, the air shivered and he spoke. "I don't think so."

"Then what is it, Joe?" She stared hard at the tree. If she did that, looked away, then back again quickly, she could nearly see him. "What?" She wanted to see him, squinted, and just made out his form. He was looking down. Silken hair made a black sheet in front of his face.

"I'm not good at that sort of thing."

"I'm sorry." She reached out to pat his arm and stopped when her fingers entered the electric pulse of his body. "I won't ask again." She drew her hand back and rubbed her fingers. "I'll make it. I'll be okay. I will." She didn't even know why she asked. If it weren't for the dreams...dreams of Joe that left her shaking with need.

"Do you have anyone in mind?"

She started. Yes, his voice was definitely strained now. Clipped, too. Like the drill sergeant tone he'd taken when he'd ordered her around that time Michael got ill. "Yeah, I guess so." What had she done to piss him off?

"Who?"

"Dan Striker."

"Him?" Disbelief made the word three syllables.

"Why not him?" She ticked off her fingers. "He has a good job."

"He's a clerk, Alena."

"A good job." She raised another finger. "He's single."

"No woman would have him."

Her teeth ground. "He's easygoing."

"Lazy."

"He's heterosexual."

"And just how the hell do you know that?"

Count to ten. She held one last finger up. "He's mature and not in debt."

"He's forty."

She jammed her hands onto her hips. "You're sixty-five!" She glared at the thickening air twisting in front of her tree. "Dammit, Joe!"

"Lena." His voice dropped to a rumble. "He's not

good enough for you."

"All right, all right." She spread her arms and breathed deep. "Let's shelve this, okay?"

"Fine with me."

"Okay, I need to go to bed…" She stopped before turning out the light. "Oh, Joe. Wait! I almost forgot." She lifted a small package under the tree and offered it. "Merry Christmas." She looked down at the package and shrugged. "It's not much, but I thought you might like it."

The translucency seemed to condense and swirl.

"It's a present, Joe. For Christmas, okay?"

"A present."

"It's Christmas Eve, but hey, Michael will be front and center in the morning, so why not now?" She tossed a grin at the wavy air as it moved and hovered in the middle of the room. "It wasn't so easy to get it for you, since you're almost always with me."

"You got me a gift." His voice was flat, but it caught on the last word.

She stood, offering the package. "Oh yeah. Right." She coughed and pulled at the paper. "I forgot you can't open it."

"You got me a present."

"Well, yeah. Why not?" She freed the gift from its wrapping. "They're not expensive. I got them at Pegasus Books' used CD counter. You know; that place down by Peet's Coffee and Noah's Bagels." She held it out. "Can you, um, see them?"

"The best of…Jefferson Airplane?"

"Yup." She slipped another compact disk out from under it. "Jimi Hendrix, too."

"Alena." The tube glistened. "I don't know what to say."

"Just listen, okay? This is the music of your time, Joe. You told me you liked it." She slid the first CD in the player. "When Deb gave me her old CD player and amplifier last month I thought, well, this is something Joe can enjoy." The first notes filled the room, swirling and rich. "I got it when you went away for a while." She paused.

"Yes. I did."

She sighed. Guess he'd never tell her where he'd gone. "Anyway, this is classic boomer music." She swayed to the beat as the bass kicked in. Grace Slick's voice warbled. Guitars wove around the vocals. "I remember my folks playing this, stuff like this." Never thought she'd ever listen to it again. She'd avoided anything that reminded her of her childhood, but for Joe, well, she'd do it.

"I had a problem coming up with something to get you." She shrugged. "I figured at least you could hear music and maybe this would bring back some good memories." She clapped her hands. "Hey! Let's dance." She spun around and held out her hands. The roiling air that was Joe bent toward her. Her fingers shivered as the trickle of electric charge met them. She swayed and turned. He followed close beside her.

The music took over. It wasn't her kind of music, but she had to admit it was good to dance to, in a kind of free-form way. Joe was beside or behind her all the time. He never danced in front of her. Why was that? She shook her head. Just his nearness was enough. She felt him all around her, as if he'd taken her in his arms. Her hair stood at attention and the most curious, hot, achy swelling bloomed between her legs. She stumbled. "What?"

The song faded into an echo. Joe moved away.

God. That felt weird. Almost like she was aroused. *Super* aroused. Damn, she hadn't felt anything like that since, since… Well, she'd never felt anything like that!

"Alena?"

"Yes?" What the hell was that, anyway?

"What kind of music do you like best?"

"Um." Now, nobody had ever asked *her* that. "I'm a throwback." She knelt, the last pulse of arousal fading, leaving her damp and ashamed. "I mean, I like a lot of the current bands, you know, Radiohead and Mogwai. But my favorite music is real dinosaur."

"Dinosaur?"

"Yeah. Real oldie." She dug through the used CDs she'd bought. "My friends all thought I was nuts, but I didn't care. I like grunge rock like Nirvana and art rock like Sigur Ros, but my favorite is vintage." At least she had jeans on. They wouldn't show the damp in her panties. Her hands shook as she slipped the CD into the player.

Anyway, what she'd just felt was impossible. Must be a delayed reaction to her accidental overdose. Like the post-traumatic stress she'd read about. Her body had just gone all goofy. She'd never in her life experienced that level of wanting, not even during puberty. It was nuts. She couldn't possibly want Joe. He was like, like, um, a father or a brother. Yeah. A cute father or brother, but man, she was truly damned if she let herself go there. Joe was almost like an angel. Like a priest. She wasn't Catholic, but there were some boundaries even a punk like her wouldn't cross.

"Here." She punched the control that started the song. A long, sad clarinet dirge sprayed mournful notes. "Billie Holiday." The weary, uncompromising voice followed, promising someone she'd survive. No matter what, she'd survive. She bowed her head as the final notes ended.

"I wouldn't have expected that. Why Billie Holiday?"

"She had a rotten life, but she made something out of it. People do the damnedest things, don't they?" She swayed as the next track flowed out over the room. It was her favorite. “I love this one.”

“Alena.”

“Mmmm?” She hugged her arms around her and rocked from side to side.

“I’ll help you find someone.”

“What?” She swung around.

He’d faded now to a thin column of sparkling air.

“You don’t have to do that. I mean, really, Joe.”

“No, you need to be with someone.”

Someone alive. The thought hung in the air, so thick that she was sure he had spoken it, or she had.

“I’ll help you,” he said.

Chapter Seventeen

He couldn't help it. Just couldn't stop. He knew he shouldn't. Ram had told him not to do it.

No; it was worse than that. Ram had forbidden it.

The glow of the clock radio said it was midnight. He sat next to the bed. Alena tossed and turned, tangling her legs and arms in the sheets. He reached out and touched her hand. Her breathing slowed. The rich amber glow of the dream path oozed around her. It pulled at him, beckoning. Caught at him with its sticky, sweet promise.

Hiyá. Not this time. He drew back and clasped his hands in his lap, watching her rise from her body and slip into her dream. Watched until he couldn't look anymore.

The need to enter her dream hurt him with an ache he'd never known before. It was more than wanting. More than desire. It was like a drug, taunting him to partake. He looked away until the glow faded, then glanced back at her. She was dreaming; he could see that. Her eyes slowly tracked behind her lids.

He'd promised Ram he would stay out of her dreams. He fully intended to keep that promise. Every night he tried to do what the angel had commanded. But sometimes he couldn't help it. He needed her, needed to laugh with her, to have her see him.

Needed to touch her.

He'd entered her dreams by accident at first. It had happened when Ram let him come back, after he'd saved JJ. He didn't lie next to Alena anymore, couldn't risk it. But he also couldn't stand being far away from her, so he sat at her side that night. And every night after that.

It was raining when he'd first entered her dreams, a steady downpour that streaked the windows. She'd been restless, full of soft moans, bitten back. He'd reached out to soothe her. Or so he thought, so he told himself. His hand had stroked her forehead, traced her face, her eyes and eyebrows, her nose, and finally her mouth. He'd lingered on her mouth, stroking her lips until they parted. When he'd done this, Alena no longer moaned; her eyes had trembled behind her lids. As the dream path opened, he'd leaned in and touched her lips with his.

He hadn't even tried to avoid it, hadn't given a moment's thought to what he was doing. Once it started, once the honeyed road spread out before him, he had slid down it until he burst into her dream landscape.

After that, he'd continued to enter her dreams, telling himself this was all right.

Who the hell was he kidding?

He had promised not to touch. This was not a promise to Ram. The angel didn't know he had touched Alena.

He had promised himself.

He just could not keep that promise.

Problem was, other men touched her. After she'd given him the CDs, she started going out, first with a group of co-workers, and later with men from other departments at the college. Once she went out with a student who just couldn't keep his hands off her.

It drove him mad. He kept telling himself it was wrong to go into her dreams, and he'd stopped for a while, but when she went out with guys he couldn't help himself. Other men were touching her. He had to reclaim her. She was his woman. The only way he could claim her was to enter her dreams.

She hadn't gone out with any man for more than one date. If she had, he didn't know what he would do. Having to watch other men pawing at her was bad enough.

Well, they didn't exactly paw at her. In fact, only the student put his arms around her. The others did no more than hold her hand, or drape an arm over her shoulders.

Still, if she'd ever kissed one of them...he was sure he would kill the bastard.

But she hadn't, and after three weeks, she'd stopped going out. She told her friend Deb she was just too tired from demands at work and taking care of Michael. She'd sidestepped the promise to go to the doctor by saying she had to wait for an appointment slot to open, which was true, but it worried him anyway.

He told himself it was just as well, though. He'd promised to help her find a man, but none of the men around her were good enough. He told himself he needed to keep going into her dreams in order to understand her, so he could help her.

What utter bullshit.

He leaned against the wall and watched the soft rise and fall of Alena's chest. It was his own need that drew him into her dreams, his need that drove him to sit at her side, holding his hands together, wondering where she was, which dream landscape she had entered. "Where are you, Alena?"

His left hand extended and floated toward her. He drew it back. No. Tonight, he would be good.

A soft keening drew him forward again. She was huddled, hands covering her face, shaking. "Alena?" He pulled her hands away. She was still dreaming, but tears pooled at the corners of her eyes and spilled in tracks down her face.

What should he do? Wake her? He'd only

awakened her once, when Michael was sick. Maybe he should wake her now. He reached out and said, "Wake..." but his hand stopped just above her head and stuck there. A sparkling, syrupy glow spread from a place just between her eyes and flowed through his hand, all the way up his arm.

"Well, I'll be damned." Ram had always said he had to enter at the start of a dream. He'd never tried to enter at any other time. He thought it was impossible. He also thought it wasn't possible to enter someone's dream without the angel there to initiate the process, as Ram had done with JJ, and that turned out to be false as well.

The dream path, the sweet road to Alena's dream landscape was still there, dragging at him. He grasped his wrist and tugged his hand away.

What should he do? Alena still cried, shoulders quaking. She cried like she was lost. Or alone. He couldn't let her cry like this. She wasn't alone; he was with her. But if he woke her she might not remember her dream. She might not be able to tell him why she was crying.

If he entered her dream, he'd be able to see what was making her cry.

His form quivered. *Hécetu.* Okay. One more time. Just this once. After all, she needed him. He could help her. That's what he was here for, wasn't it? To watch. To teach. To learn.

A burning itch strafed his back. "For Christ's sake!" He floated to the corner of the door and attempted to slide against it, back and forth. "Not now, dammit!" The molecules in the door helped ease some of the burning, at least. "This just keeps happening." It had never happened before he started caring for Alena.

Well, it wasn't going to stop him.

He drifted to Alena's bed and reached out to touch her face.

The dream path grasped his hand, poured up his arm, his shoulder, and raced through his etheric form. He trembled at the liquid bliss traveling through his particles. The path enticed. The way opened.

The honeyed road to Alena's dream captured him whole and sucked him in.

****

He steadied and looked around. Redwoods and pine trees strained toward a milky sky. The ground below was padded with leaves and needles. A deep quiet swallowed his steps as he stumbled and fought the dizzy spin the dream path always brought. He searched left and right for Alena.

She stood in front a towering redwood, head bowed, whispering, "No suffering. No end to suffering." A gravestone leaned against the tree. "No death. No end to death."

"Alena?"

She startled. "What?" Her face was swollen with tears. "Oh, Joe." She rubbed at her eyes.

"It's me." He shuffled through the loam until he was standing beside her. "What's this?"

She gestured toward the stone. "His ashes are there." A single tear slid down her cheek.

Joe ducked away from her and peeked at the stone. David Morgan. 1962-2005.

"I didn't kill him."

"Huh?"

She was shaking. "It wasn't my fault."

He couldn't help it. Two steps and he had her in his arms. "I know, I know." He brushed at the tears trickling out of the corners of her eyes. Comforting her was okay, wasn't it?

She looked up at him. He turned his face away. "Can I see him? Can you bring him to me?"

"No."

"Can you come to where I am?" Her face looked

raw. "So we can be together?"

"Alena, you know I can't do that."

She choked and her bitter laugh split the silence. "Of course." She folded her arms and pivoted so she faced away from him. "You don't want me." Her shoulders hitched. "No one does."

"How do you figure that?"

She didn't answer for a long time. The landscape shifted and swirled in huge clots. Everything around him stretched thin and tore.

He stepped close to Alena and took her arm. God, he hated it when a dream shifted. It didn't bother the dreamer—they hardly noticed—but it was unsettling to him. He shut down his visual receptors. A final, immense tug rocked him. He stumbled and steadied, his hand still grasping Alena's arm.

A night-dark room with torn window shades formed around him. A man and a woman lay on a sagging bed, tangled in the aftermath of passion. Paisley India-print cloth draped and bunched, barely covering their naked limbs. He looked down. The arm he held now belonged to a little girl. She looked about four, or maybe was small for her age. Her eyes didn't look like little girl eyes as she stared at the man and woman with something between rage and adoration.

The air was filled with the scent of marijuana and semen. A tiny bed stood in the corner of the room. A rudimentary kitchen with a free-standing sink and a shelf with a hot plate hid behind another India-print spread hanging from the ceiling. The opposite wall held a door that stood cracked open. A toilet and grimy shower stall stood beyond the door.

"They didn't care."

He jumped. The couple on the couch remained inert. He looked down at the little Alena. She nodded toward the people on the couch. "My mom and dad didn't care." She jerked her arm out of his grasp. "So why should you?"

"What did they do to you?" He'd been lucky. His dad worked hard and his mom always let him and his sister know how much she loved them. Didn't say the words much, but she showed it in other ways. Like the care she always took in packing special treats in their lunches when they went out digging potatoes or fishing with his dad. The way she brushed his hair in the morning until he grew too old and too embarrassed for this show of affection.

Little Alena shook her head, eyes clouded with confusion. "It wasn't any one thing. My dad hit me once in a while, when he was crashing. But they didn't love me. I know that." She drew in her breath. "How could they love me?" Her toe made a careful circle on the moth-eaten fake Persian carpet. "I'm evil."

"No child is born evil." Ram had told him this. "Not one." It was the best bit of information he'd ever gotten from the angel.

She snorted. "What do *you* know?" Her head shook from side to side. She tucked her thumb in her mouth and her eyes were now the eyes of a child. Her other hand clutched at her little ear.

"Why do you think you're evil?"

"I must be. I was never good enough. My mama told me." She was crying again. "She told me a lot."

"She told you that you were evil?" The apartment was a mess, but there was nothing there that spoke of an obsession with the devil. And now that he looked he could see curious, sweet little touches: a row of shells lined up on the windowsill; pale ribbons woven into a small tapestry that hung over the tiny bed in the corner; a painting of a rainbow on the opposite wall. He reached for the essence of the parents and recoiled in surprise. He'd forgotten they were dead. He poked at the arm of the man. It gave a flaccid jiggle. He stepped back.

Alena's parents weren't here. This was just Alena's memory.

"Maybe she told you that because she didn't want you to watch her, ah, you know, with your dad." This was a guess, but not a bad one. The one-room apartment left no room for privacy. That in itself wasn't good.

But little Alena shook her head again. "They waited until I was asleep."

"Then what..."

"Don't you understand?" Her whole body shook now, sobs turning her words into bullets. "My mom told me this." Her voice cracked. "Over and over again, she told me the story of when I was born." She stared in fierce love and anger at the woman on the couch. "When the doctor held me up for her to see me, she said I looked deformed." Her voice broke again, and both hands covered her face. "It was my fault they took drugs. My fault. All my fault. She said so." She fell to her knees and heaved with tears. "Not even God wants me."

He strode to her and dropped to the floor, drawing her into his arms. She fought him, twisting away until her back was jammed against his chest. He held her fast, murmuring. "Alena, it's not true, not true." She was a rigid lump in his arms. "You're not deformed." He glanced at the woman on the couch. "And how can you be responsible for their addiction? Alena..." He shook her arm gently. "Addicts say all kinds of things so they don't have to quit. Anyway, she just said you looked deformed because she felt guilty." He wasn't sure how he knew this, but he did. "Who knows what drugs she did while she was expecting you?" Her body loosened. "She was just scared, that's all."

"Do you really think so?" Her whisper threaded all the way through his form.

"I know so." He pulled her even closer and she

let him this time. Her little dream heart tripped wildly.

"Then why won't you let me see David?"

"Alena, I can't. I would if I could." He sighed. "If you only knew how much I want to help you. How much I need to help you." His hands stroked her hair, one arm wound around her. "If you only knew."

"But I do know." Alena turned and looked at him, square in the eye. She was her full adult size now. "*That the sons of God saw the daughters of men, that they* were *fair...*" she whispered.

"What!"

A lightning bolt speared through the dream scene. "Alena!" He grabbed her and held tight. Alena's dream body disintegrated in pieces, as his etheric form had when he'd tried to save JJ. "Dammit, Alena don't wake up yet!" He hung on with all his might. "Tell me what you mean, Alena. What are you saying?"

Something buckled. His form unraveled. Still he held on. He'd never touched JJ when his nephew awakened. Ram had warned him not to do this. But he clutched Alena in his arms as the dream burst into fragments. Shattered and evaporated. Sent a savage current through him.

"Alena...please tell me!"

Chapter Eighteen

She woke slowly. God, what a dream she'd had. She moved back in her bed, snuggling under the covers. The long, warm length of a body seemed to heat her back. This couldn't be real, but she wanted it so much she kept her eyes closed. It was what she'd liked most about being with David, that warm body next to hers. Waking in the morning to have coffee and bagels. When she was expecting Michael, David often got up first and put ginger tea and crackers on the table beside the bed, to help with her morning sickness. She moved her legs. God, how long had it been since she was able to remember the good times with David? She moved again and seemed to bump against a form beside her in the bed.

Was she still dreaming? Her left eye creaked open. Buttery sunshine found its way through the lace of her curtains. Damn! She'd slept in! She should get up and make Michael breakfast before she had to leave for work.

No, wait. It was Saturday and Michael was at his friend Tim's house. Tim's mother had been inviting Michael to sleep over; she'd finally given in and let Michael stay with Tim just last night.

Wow! Oh, this was so cool! She could laze in her bed for hours if she wanted to, just being a slug. Tim's mother wouldn't be bringing Michael back until late this afternoon. She reached up and rubbed at her face. It was wet and her eyes felt hot. Tears? Well, she couldn't remember crying. She remembered some of her dream from last night. It had been by David's grave, and Joe had been there. But whatever part of the dream that had left her crying was gone.

Probably a dream of the accident. That usually made her cry in her sleep and left a cloud of sadness that hung over her for weeks afterward. But she didn't feel sad now. She had a whole day to do whatever she wanted. Deb had turned her on to some good books. She loved to read now, to disappear into another world for a time. Before, reading had been a chore, but over time she looked forward to reading stories to Michael every night. After that, she'd devoured everything she could find, from *Splatter Punks* and *The Body Farm* to *Old Bones* and *Crave.*

She'd gotten Anita Diamant's *The Red Tent* from the library last week, and made it to chapter six so far. The book was about Jacob from the Bible, but his daughter told the tale.

She made little circles with her big toe against the sheets and sighed. Jacob's daughter had a tough life, but then life was like that. The world knocked you down, and you had to get up again.

Now she wiggled her toes and laughed. The struggle was worth it for moments like these, little pearls of time that ran on a string of joy. She could read her book in peace, all curled up on the couch. Or maybe she could watch television. Something besides Michael's new favorites, re-runs of *Pokéman* and *Dragon Ball Z.* She grinned and stretched.

She came up hard against something behind her.

Whoa! She reached back. Her hand met smooth skin over sleek muscle and the expanse of a broad chest. Sure felt like she was awake, but dreams were tricky. Might as well test it. She gave her arm a hard pinch and yelped when her newly-grown nails dented her skin.

"Alena, calm down." A large, square hand came around her side and pressed on her chest. "Your heart is racing."

"No shit!" She exploded out of bed and tumbled to the floor. The blanket came with her and caught at her feet. She rolled onto her back and kicked it away, looking up at the bed.

"Hey!" A man lay on her bed. "Watch your mouth!" He scowled at her.

"Oh, my God." She swallowed. "Joe?" It was Joe. Had to be. He looked the same as the man she had seen in her bathroom, in front of the bank, in glimpses in her kitchen. But this was no thickening of the air, no floating shadow. He lay large as life on his side under the sheet, leaning on his right arm. Long dark hair fell across his left eye. He shook his head and the hair shimmered back over his shoulder.

"Huh?" His eyes widened. "You can see me!" He looked down. "Goddamn. I did it again. Well." He lifted his head. "I'm here. For now, I'm here." He made a fist, then spread his fingers and smiled.

White. His teeth were blinding against his golden skin. "Joe." She could barely breathe, let alone whisper. The name seemed to disappear as soon as it left her lips.

"Alena, it's just me." He reached for her.

She scooted back in a rapid crab-walk on her bottom, all the way to the door and sat there, panting, out of breath.

"Don't be scared." His arm dropped on the bed with a thump. The glorious smile wavered and disappeared. "Do you want me to leave?"

"No! This just…it…God!" She lurched to her feet and sidled toward him. "It was you in my dreams, wasn't it?" She perched on the edge of the bed farthest from him. He just watched her, not moving. Her legs bunched, muscles twitched. She inched closer until she was right next to him.

"Yes." Was he blushing? "I'm sorry. I couldn't help it. If you want me to stop..."

"No!" If the dreams stopped she'd...well, she didn't want the dreams to stop. "But how can this happen?" She caught a lock of his hair. "How is this possible?" It fell through her fingers like fine silk. "You're so real."

"Alena!" His face went blank, but lights flared in the depths of his eyes. "You're right. We can touch!" He reached out slowly with his left hand. His finger traced a line from her temple to her chin.

She shivered and caught his hand. "You're solid!" Warm, too, and firm. How could that be? She lifted his hand to her cheek, placed it so it cupped her face. "Am I awake?" He held it there after she let it go, gently stroking her cheek. "Please tell me I'm awake." She looked into his face.

He went still. The broad slash of his mouth made a thin, tense line. He withdrew his hand and pulled back from her. "I shouldn't be here."

"Why not?"

"I've made a mistake." He flexed his hand and ran it back through his hair. "I'm not supposed to go solid."

"Go solid?"

"Something makes my form solid enough so people can see me." A frown creased the space between his brows. "But I've never been able to touch anyone before, not really." He shook his hair back again. "Not for long. Not like this." He stared down at his hand.

"A mistake."

He glanced up. "Yes."

"Does this mean you have to go away again?"

"Probably."

A weight pressed in on her heart. "Okay." The effort to sound casual squeezed her throat. She could barely speak. "Go, um, transparent, then." She waved her hand in what she hoped was an *okay with me* gesture. "Or whatever it is you do." No way would she make trouble for him. She'd pretend it was no big deal.

Like she didn't care. Like it was nothing to her. A pressure over her heart tightened and grew. She put her fist over it and stared at Joe.

"Right." He closed his eyes and trembled from head to foot.

She kept staring at him. If he was going to disappear again, she wanted to savor every inch of him, the strong planes of his face, the slash of his generous mouth, the golden glory of his skin.

She straightened. Skin. A lot of it, too. No shirt covered his chest. The sheet draped over him at the waist, but she'd bet he was naked under it. What did this mean? She'd never seen him in any other clothes than the jeans and T-shirt he always wore. Certainly, she'd never seen him without clothes. Now *that* she would remember.

He opened his eyes and gave a weary sigh. His legs shifted under the sheet and he looked over at her with a yearning so blazing it took her breath away.

She choked and turned it into a cough. "So when are you going to disappear?"

His mouth dropped open and eyes widened. "What!"

"I can still see you." She looked away. "A lot of you." Peeked back at him.

He lifted the sheet. "*Éya, wan ká wan*!" The sheet dropped and he dragged it up to his chin. "Ah." He looked away. "You wouldn't happen to have any jeans." Was that a blush tinting his cheeks? "Jeans in my size?"

"You're not going away?" She jiggled and a series of squeaky hiccups bubbled out of her mouth.

"Not right now." He paused, staring out the window. "At least, that's what it looks like." He glanced back. "You okay with this?"

"Sure." *Hic. Hic. Hic.* She shook her head. "I. Um. This-hic-happens sometimes." Pulling in a deep breath and holding it, she looked straight at him. The air just bled out of her. "Do you know what happened to you?" God. Joe was *here*. With her!

"No." A shake of his head stirred his hair.

She stood. "Hey! Hiccups are gone." She couldn't seem to stifle the silly grin plastered on her face as she shuffled through her top drawer, pulling out an oversize T-shirt she usually wore for a nightgown. "Here." She handed the shirt to him. Her hands shook. She couldn't make them go still any more than she could stop grinning.

He took the shirt. Their fingertips touched as he grasped it. A spark flared out from his fingers and streaked all the way up her arm and down to her toes, spinning a burning ache that settled between her legs. A swelling, bulging mass seemed to grow there.

He went pale, eyes stunned.

She snatched her hand away. "What was that?" It was what had happened before Christmas, when they had danced. She fought the urge to look down.

"You felt that?" His face was a study in white slashed with warm blush.

"I felt something." How could she tell him? She'd felt desire before, but this was something completely different. "I don't know what." She couldn't tell when it had happened before, but this felt more *defined*. It was like, for a moment, she'd felt *him*.

He busied himself with the shirt, pulling it over his head. "We'd better not touch again."

"Ah. Right." She clasped her hands to stop the trembling. "Well, then." She backed away from him, sliding her feet over the polished wooden floor. "I'll just go get you some jeans." The door caught her shoulder blade. "What size?"

He sat up but wouldn't meet her gaze. "Thirty-four waist." He shook his head. "I'm six foot one. Not sure what length."

"Sure. I imagine it's been a while since you, since you…I mean, that is…" She stuttered to a stop and rubbed her elbow. Her whole arm ached from slamming into the door. "Hey. Congratulate me, Joe. I only cussed once." At least that won her a tiny smile that tugged the corners of his mouth. "Make yourself at home." She slid around the corner and beat it out of there.

****

Thank God for the Salvation Army store. She juggled her keys with her purse and the black plastic bag that held jeans and underwear. She refused to think of dressing Joe in just jeans and a T-shirt. The very thought of him naked under the jeans sent all sorts of hot little aches running up and down her thighs. "Dang it!" The keys slipped out of her hand and made a jangling plunge to the floor.

Number 326 behind her opened and Lily Aguilar stuck her head out. "Oh." She looked blankly at Alena. "It's you."

"Hey, Lil." She grabbed her keys and flipped through them for the apartment key. She looked over at Lily. The woman just stood there, staring at her. "What's up?"

"I thought you were the guy, you know…" She waved her hand at Alena's door. "The one staying at your place."

"Ah, yeah?" The keys slid through her fingers again. Her head jerked up. "Say what!"

"Hey, I don't want to butt in, you know." Lily raised her hands and leaned against her door. "But could you maybe introduce me?"

"Introduce you." She scooped up the keys and let

them dangle from her hand.

"He's major hot." Lily shivered.

"Hot." She glared at Lily. Joe never seemed to want other people to see him. How the hell had Lily known he was there? Her hand clutched the keys. An itch to shove them into Lily's gut left her weak.

"Oh, he's your boyfriend? Sorry!" Lily backed behind her door. Disappointment painted a gray pallor over her face. "See you around." The door shut.

"That's right; you go after him and I'll eat your face!" She stepped back, her mouth hanging open. What had happened? Lily wasn't bad. She was a good neighbor and great with Michael. "Wait!" She stepped over to Lily's door, hand lifted, but stopped in mid-knock and rocked back on her heels. This was stupid. She was behaving like a teenage girl. Joe was like, well, a junior angel, no matter what Deb said. He wasn't her boyfriend. How could he be?

She turned around. This time the right key showed itself, slipped smoothly into the lock and the door opened. Joe stood on the other side. The T-shirt she'd given him stretched over his chest. He pulled at an old terry cloth robe that hardly made it around his waist.

She blanched. "Joe?"

"Alena, I'm sorry." He raised his hands, then looked down and grabbed at the edges of the robe, pulling it tight. "The T-shirt wasn't long enough to cover, you know."

"No problem." She pushed past him and dropped the bag onto the couch. "I told you to make yourself at home, right?" She glanced back as he shuffled away, tugging on the robe. "But I bet that old thing isn't real comfortable." The robe was huge on her; that's why she'd bought it. She loved the way the sleeves slipped over her knuckles, the way she could bury herself in its folds. But it barely covered Joe.

"No, it's fine, just fine." He seemed distracted, kept pulling his hand through his hair. "The woman from across the hall knocked on the door. I thought it was you, so I opened it." He sat down on the chair opposite to the couch.

"You mean you can't just see through the door?"

"I can't." The springs of the old chair creaked. "Not now."

She glanced over. He held a packet of Marlboros in his hand. The latest issue of *American Steel* sat beside him.

"I found these in your dresser." He lifted the Marlboros. "Didn't know you smoked. And you like motorcycles?"

"I don't smoke. But yeah, I like bikes." She walked over and took them from his hand. "Oh. Do you smoke?"

"Not for the past forty years." A small smile curved his mouth.

"Right." She tossed them on top of the television. "I stopped smoking when I was expecting Michael."

"Then why keep these around?"

She looked away. "Are you cold? Do you need a sweater?"

"Why, Alena?"

She picked at a callus on the side of her palm. Her elbow still ached. Must need a damn wrist brace or something to protect her while she used the computer. "I don't really know, okay?" She shook her wrist and looked at him. "They remind me I beat something. I licked a nicotine habit."

He reached out to her with his left hand.

She leaned over.

He started and drew his hand back, but she grazed his fingertips.

"Dang it, I forgot we can't do this." She let her hand drop.

"*Ksapa*, Lena." He put his hand on his thigh. "I

wish I could take your hand in mine." He opened the cover of the motorcycle magazine and looked at an ad for leather jeans. "You'd look good in these."

She sniffed, cleared her throat, and backed away. "My dad had a Honda 250 when I was little. Not much of a bike, but he used to take me on rides."

"What happened to it?"

"He sold it for drugs." She strode over to the couch. "Hey, what does *ksapa* mean?"

"Means you're wise. Not like me." He huddled forward, pulling at the robe, looking so miserable she had to do something.

She picked up the plastic bag and took out the jeans. "Here you go." She tossed them at him. "Underwear, too."

"Thanks." His face was set in tight lines, like a man before a firing squad.

"Are you left-handed?"

He flexed that hand and looked up at her. "Yeah. Does that mean something? Did you read something about left-handed ghosts who suddenly become solid and need the living people they watch over to shop for them?" His attempt at a smile was painful to see.

She sank onto the couch. "Joe, this is serious, isn't it?" When Joe had said the word "watch" his eyes had gone nearly transparent, a red-gold light glowing from them.

He nodded. "I think so." His hands smoothed the jeans. "Yes."

"Joe, your eyes just got all weird."

"How so?"

"They glowed red."

"Um. Sorry. Did it scare you?"

"No. Well, maybe a little." Her chest felt tight, but after a few breaths, it eased. "What will happen?" He could barely look at her now.

"I need to tell someone, get help."

"This angel you work for."

"Yes." He opened the bag containing the underwear and turned toward the windows. "He's not going to like this."

"Will you be sent to hell?"

"No." He gave a little smile, a real one this time. "They don't do that."

"What then?"

"I'll have to go away for good."

"Why?"

He drew in a deep breath, like a real person. Breathing. "I lied to him." Hefting the jeans and underwear in one hand, he stood. "Can I change in your bedroom?"

"Sure thing." She caught the edge of his sleeve as he passed her. "But Joe."

He startled, stopping dead in his tracks. "Yeah?"

"Once you're finished, you gotta tell me some things."

He didn't say anything, wouldn't look at her. He opened the bedroom door. He turned as he closed it, looking down. "We'll talk." The door shut.

****

What the hell did ghosts eat, anyway? She poured water into the glass canister, spooned ground Colombian into the filter of the coffee pot, and turned it on. It chugged and gasped as the fragrance of fresh coffee scented the air. She glanced at the clock. Eleven-thirty in the morning. No wonder she felt so hollow and worn out. Joe must be, well, starved, maybe. She grabbed eggs, onions, and mushrooms out of the refrigerator and sprayed a skillet with canola oil. She had no idea if he could eat, but hey, she'd make breakfast.

Chopping and slicing took her mind away from what had happened. She'd do anything right now to avoid thinking about what might happen to him. "God, this is scanless. He's a good man." The knife slashed furiously through the onion. “He saved my fricking life. That’s got to be worth something.”

Joe was here, *here*. Somehow, he was real. He was here on earth. In her apartment. Solid. Alive. With her. She set the chopped onions aside, speeded up her hand even more, and mushrooms fell in thin slices on her cutting board. At least, he seemed alive.

It made her giddy to think about it. What the hell had happened?

Why couldn’t he stay?

She stopped for a moment, staring at the mound of onions and mushrooms. Wasn’t it a miracle? Maybe God had decided Joe could come back. She wiped her hands on the kitchen towel. “Smells good.”

She whirled around. “Don’t do that.” Air wheezed out of her lungs. “You’re silent as, as…”

“An Indian?” He tempered the words with a grin. “A ghost?”

“I’m sorry.” She dumped onions and mushrooms in the skillet to brown. “I’m freaking out. I didn’t mean to say that.” She glanced to the side where he sat at her small kitchen table. “Can you eat?”

“I don’t think so.”

“This is new to you, isn’t it?”

“Damn straight.”

“So what happens now?” She cracked three eggs and stirred them into the onions and mushrooms.

“I’ve been calling the angel, the one I work with.” His face was impassive, voice bland. “He hasn’t answered.” But his fingers drummed on the table. “Yet.”

“What did you do wrong?” She folded the eggs, mushrooms, and onions together and slid the omelet onto a plate. She looked right at him. “What was the lie?”

He didn’t speak, just watched her as she poured the coffee and set both plate and cup on the table.

She dug a fork into the omelet. “Well?”

"You." He looked her right in the eye now. "I lied about you."

The eggs had no taste. She pushed her chair back and gulped her coffee, then jumped and patted her lips with a napkin when she burned her tongue.

"About you and about me." He looked at his hands now, set on the table in front of him. "I told Ram…I told the angel you still needed me."

"But I didn't?" The hell she didn't.

"You didn't." He drew in a breath. "You haven't needed me since you got your job. Maybe even before that."

"That was a long time ago. Wouldn't the angel have made you go away already if that were true?" The caffeine jolted her. She picked up the cup and made her hands clasp it in a firm grip. "I need this." She took another sip and let it slide down her throat. Before Joe's help, life was crushing her. Didn't how he helped her count for something?

"It was wrong for me to say you needed me when you didn't."

"Why?" What criteria did the angel use? Could she use the same argument to keep Joe here with her?

He shrugged. "It was a lie."

"Why did you lie?" There must be something in this she could use. Something to convince the angel that Joe should stay.

He leaned back, looked at the walls, the ceiling, the floor. Finally, he raised his hands. "I didn't know at first."

"But you know now."

He gave her that look again, half yearning and half despair. "Yes."

Lost, he looked so lost sitting there. She pushed the plate and cup aside and reached for his hand. Her hand stopped just over his knuckles. "Joe." She had to do something. Something radical.

He stared down at her hand. "Not a good idea," he whispered.

Blood pounded in her head. Her hands shook.

Something drastic.

"Oh, yeah?" God, she hoped she was right.

He looked up, startled again.

"You're in my territory, now, soldier." Her hand descended upon his.

The pulse of wanting took her by surprise, rushing through her, deep inside. It made her weak and quivery and strong at the same time. She looked up and found him staring at her. His hand turned. He laced his fingers with hers. Desire rose from her own center, a sweet ache pushing out to her limbs. She could only manage a breathy sigh. "Joe?"

He leaned forward and caught her mouth with his.

The kiss went on forever. He plundered her, laid claim to her mouth, her lips. The rapid swelling didn't shock her this time. This was her Joe she was feeling. She didn't know how. She didn't care. He took the kiss deeper and moaned against her lips. She pulled away for the time it took a butterfly's wings to beat. "Do you feel me, too, Joe?" Her belly was melting; she wanted him inside her so badly she shook all over. "Do you?"

His answer was something between a growl and a nod as he caught her mouth again.

She tugged at his shoulders and stumbled to her feet, never breaking his hold on her, staggering away from the table. He joined her, dragging her close to him. Her hands found his chest and stroked. The breath caught in her throat when her thumbs brushed across his flat nipples. She felt that stroke in her own, swollen nipples, all the way to the hot space between her legs, while he gave a desperate groan and grasped the front of her jeans.

And oh, God, did he want her! She could feel all

of him yearn, from the aching heat in his groin to the pounding hurt in his fingertips. The snap on her jeans gave way and the zipper slid all the way down.

And so did she, all the way to the braided rug on the floor. Joe followed, dragging his shirt over his head and tossing it aside. She helped him peel her jeans and underwear off. He reached for his own zipper, but she got there before him, zipping it down in a frenzy. If he didn't take her now, *now!* she would explode.

He wasn't wearing the underwear.

Every part of her quivered and dissolved. She tore his jeans off and he kicked them away.

Now he was in control. He held her down and suckled at her breasts until she screamed. Hot, driving need speared her; some of it was from him, from how badly he wanted her. "Is this what you feel, Joe? Is this you or is this me?" It was her own need, too, her need to have him inside her. Was he feeling this from her? Did he know?

"Is it only one way?" she managed to pant. "Can you feel me, too?"

His answer came in bursts of air all over her left breast.

"Joe." She was trembling all over now. "You're *laughing*? No fair!"

He used his tongue on the tip of her aching nipple. He grunted and licked some more.

She grasped his shaft and squeezed. He growled and flipped her until she was underneath him.

"Goddammit, Joe," she whimpered, over and over. "Take me!" She wound her legs around his hips.

"I can feel you, Lena." He entered her, driving all the way in. "God! How I can feel you!"

She was so close, so goddamn close, that she yelled with the first spasms of her fulfillment, but climbed back to a peak with him, shivering and screaming as he found his own release with a rough bellow.

The room spun and steadied. Her heart thudded in a wild gallop. Or was that his heart? Did he truly have a heart? She didn't know anymore, and didn't care. He lay upon her, panting, then lifted up on his arms and looked into her face, astonishment widening his eyes. His mouth opened to speak but she stilled his words with her fingers.

"No way!" she said. "You're *staying*."

Chapter Nineteen

For a moment, he couldn't remember his name. Tiny lights fractured and bled at the periphery of his sight. He looked down at Alena. Her eyes were nearly closed. The skin of her face glowed.

God would strike him dead.

No. He was already dead. God would strike Alena dead.

Hiyá! Fat chance! He'd pulverize anyone who came near her. Especially Ram. He didn't know just how, but somehow, he'd protect her.

She still covered his lips with her fingers. He hung over her, fighting to slow his breathing, astonished that he could breathe. Before, even when he went solid, he only moved air molecules around with his entire form, centering on his mouth. Now it almost felt like he had real lungs.

Alena smiled a slow, Sophia Loren smile that sent a jolt all the way through him. His body responded, heart racing and loins aching.

Wait a minute. Body? "My God, Alena," he whispered against her fingers.

"Glad I have that effect on you." Her cat-swallowing-canary grin brought out faint dimples.

He eased away, rolled onto his back, and looked up at the ceiling. His body felt real. He seemed to have a heart that beat, lungs that drew in air…and all the rest of him seemed to work, too. In fact, it worked real good. So good that the afterglow of spent ardor lapped over his limbs and left him pleasantly weak. "What the hell happened?"

"Um. It's called sex." Her voice was dry, but her

eyes twinkled.

"But how could I..." He held up his hands. "Make love to you?"

She stretched her arms toward the ceiling. "Beautifully. Completely. Perfectly."

"Come on." He ran his hands through his hair and fought the stirring down below. "This wasn't supposed to happen." If he didn't get some clothes on her, it was going to happen all over again.

"Why not?" That grin was back. "I'm glad it did. Aren't you?" She stretched again, then propped herself up on her elbows. "Whoa!" Her right arm gave way. She blinked several times. "Guess I got up too fast."

He sat up and took her arm. "Here, I'll help."

"Wait." She swallowed. "I'm real dizzy, Joe." Her head dangled. "Just give me a minute, okay?"

"Sure." What was this? Damn. The skin on her face was almost translucent; her skull showed through for a second. He squinted at her and saw that she was only pale, but the image remained.

"Can you see what time it is?" she whispered.

He glanced over at the clock. "Just about twelve-thirty."

"Good." Her eyes opened but remained unfocused. "I need your help, Joe. Don't think I can make it to the bedroom by myself." She gave a huge yawn. "Guess I'll need a nap before Michael gets home." She reached for his hand and stumbled to her feet, wrapping her arm around his waist and leaning against him. "Some date I am, huh?" A wobbly smile peeked through the hair hanging in front of her face.

"You're the only date I've ever wanted." He tucked her under his arm. "But I can't say I'm glad I have *this* effect on you." Her skin was icy. Her knees kept buckling.

"What did you say?" She stopped and peered up at him.

"I don't want you telling all your girlfriends I put you to sleep."

"No, no." She staggered to the left and tucked her head under his chin. "Before that."

"You know what I said."

"Say it again."

He sighed. "Alena Morgan." He held her close and lowered her with him as he kneeled. "Will you marry me?"

She didn't reply for a long moment. Then she looked up at him, full in the face. "Yeah, Joe. I will."

He laughed. "I don't have a ring for you yet." He lifted her and set her on her feet.

"I'll wait for it." Alena smiled, but her jaw creaked when she suddenly yawned. "It's not your fault I got so sleepy," she mumbled. "I'm just tired. Deb thinks I'm anemic." Her foot caught on the hooked throw rug and she went down.

He swept her up in his arms again and carried her into the bedroom, bumping the door open with his knee until it slammed into the wall. She flinched.

"Sorry. Not used to this." He carried her over to the bed. "I'd just pass through doors before."

"Don't know your own strength, eh?" Even her voice wobbled.

"You don't know the half of it." He tucked her under the sheets, piling blankets and quilt up around her face. "Hey—I'll join you." He lifted the edge of the blanket. His body seemed to have some heat to it. Maybe he could warm her up.

She opened one eye. "Mmmmm. Come here." Her hand beckoned with a weak curling of fingers. "I'll be fine in a minute." A shadow of her previous grin flashed. "Then we can have an instant replay."

"Maybe later." He didn't know what was causing her fatigue. Better keep his distance for a while, until he could ask Ram what had happened, why she got so depleted right after... "Aw, damn," he breathed. He tucked the blanket back in. Maybe it had nothing to do with him. She hadn't eaten. When you don't eat, you feel faint, don't you?

"You're no fun." Her eyes fluttered closed. "Can you pick up our clothes?" Another yawn stretched her jaw. "I'd do it myself, but…"

"Yeah, sure." He leaned over and kissed her cheek. At least she seemed to be warming under the covers. She wasn't as pale.

Maybe it was really as she said; she was simply tired. Maybe he could get in bed with her. He looked down.

She was sound asleep, legs drawn up, face mashed into the pillow. So still, she was so still. The quilt barely rose with her breath.

No—as much as he'd like to climb in beside her, until he knew what was causing her fatigue he'd put some distance between them. But he'd have to stay close enough to help, in case she got worse. Hell, he was so solid he could even take her to the hospital if she needed it.

He trotted into the kitchen and skidded to a stop. Alena's cup had overturned and coffee dripped onto the linoleum in a widening puddle. When had that happened? He bent and grabbed the clothes they'd tossed onto the floor, piling them in his arms. Alena's blouse was a disaster. Somehow he'd managed to rip all the buttons off. He scooped them up and laid them on top of her blouse, carrying it along with her jeans and underwear and depositing all of it on the laundry hamper in the bathroom. The buttons quivered, but then lay still. He'd have to deal with those later. Better get dressed now in case Michael got home early from Tim's house.

He busied himself with climbing into the jeans Alena had bought for him and shrugging into the T-shirt. Anything to avoid thinking about what would happen next. Like getting his ass whipped. Or maybe being hauled before the tribunal the angel had mentioned a couple of times. He stood up, glanced in the mirror, and froze.

His face stared back at him. "*Apã*!" Christ, he could see himself. He turned his head to the right and then to the left. After forty years, he could actually see his reflection. He made a face and leaned against the sink. Before, he couldn't see his reflection in mirrors or windows, even when he went solid. Ram had told him to be real careful when he let people see him. They could freak out if they saw he had no reflection. He snorted. Like a vampire. But was this body alive?

The thought grabbed him by the throat. He and Alena growing old together. A couple of kids. Grandchildren. Seeing Michael graduate from high school and college. He and Alena. *Óhinniyan.* Always. With each other, every day.

A life.

His shoulders twitched. This was weird. He'd never missed life before. Not with any of the people he'd helped. Well, by the time he was called in, most of the people he'd been assigned to help had been in pretty bad shape. He usually got to see only the shadow side of life, tears and pain instead of laughter. His life had been cut short, but he'd never missed it.

Until now. He leaned forward and stared into the mirror. Until Alena.

He backed away from the sink and glanced at his hands. Sure looked like he was alive. Veins bulged when he made a fist. That had never happened before. At least, not since he died.

Time to test it out. He strode into the living room. Up until now, all he'd done was call for Ram to come to him. "Let's see how far this goes."

Going solid was new for him, but whenever he went solid it was hard to see through walls, so the fact that he couldn't see through things now didn't tell him much. Walking through walls was difficult when he went solid, too, so the fact that he couldn't seem to do that now didn't say anything either. Truth was, even when he could go through, he didn't so much walk through as he oozed through. So how to test this?

When he was solid, flying over JJ, he was able to lift a bit. Not much, but a little. If he could lift, this body wasn't alive. Ram always told him beings in dense matter couldn't lift. Well, if you were a great master yogi who'd trained for years, or if you were Jesus or maybe a saint you could. But hey, Joe wasn't a yogi and he certainly wasn't a saint. He rocked back on his feet. Had to know for sure.

Okay. He stood stock still in the middle of the living room floor and closed his eyes. The tenants in 426 above dropped something heavy. The thump startled him and jolted his concentration. He balled his hands into fists, ground his teeth, and thought real hard. Pieces of his form shook in time with the swell of his thought. "Please," he whispered, "make my feet stay on the ground."

The air around him hummed. Azure light flared behind his lids. He opened his eyes.

Five inches. He hovered a good five inches above the floor.

"God." Well, that was that. He was still dead. Guess it wasn't right for him to have a life, anyway. After all, how could he ever visit his mother and sister? He wouldn't ever be able to see them. His mom and Sammie had moved on. He was still stuck at twenty-four. Not to mention the fact that it would scare the crap out of them to see him again. To them, he was dead. Long dead.

The light surrounding him shifted to dandelion gold, signaling readiness for him to go from solid to the higher vibration that would allow him to collapse his particles and travel. "Well, I'll be..." Why was this happening now? Earlier he couldn't shift out of solid at all. If he surrendered to the light now, he could go to Ram and find out what the hell happened.

Right. And be taken off the case. Reprimanded. Or worse than that, reassigned and not allowed to even check in on Alena.

He shook his head and floated down until he rested on the floor again. Not yet. He wouldn't leave Alena alone. Not now. Not after what they'd done. The light swirled and dissipated. He'd have to face Ram later. He'd own up to all he'd done and face the music. But for now he couldn't leave. He had to make sure she was okay. If Ram wanted to see him, the Big Wing would just have to come to him.

He padded back into the bedroom. Alena was still asleep. He pulled her robe off the back of the door and put it beside her on the bed, held the back of his hand against her forehead. Cool to the touch, but not clammy. "*Wacín yewákye...*" Yeah, he hoped all right, hoped Alena was simply tired, and this wasn't another surprise Ram hadn't told him about, hoped he could have more moments with her. Hoped she would be all right when he had to leave.

He would have to leave. He was certain of this. "Alena. I'm sorry. So sorry."

He settled down next to the bed and watched the slight movement of the quilt as air filled her lungs and departed. This is what he was supposed to do, wasn't it? Watch.

A tingle worked its way through his form, starting around his heart and traveling to his limbs, licking at his fingertips. Why did the word "watch" freak him? He shook himself and leaned against the window behind him. He'd watched people for over forty years.

But he'd done more than watch this time. A hell

of a lot more. Why hadn't Ram warned him? Goddamn tight-ass Big Wing probably had never fallen in love.

Well, to be fair, the angel had given him the rules. He wasn't to touch. If the angel had given him the reason he shouldn't touch, would it have made a difference?

He looked at Alena again. She was on her side, one arm flung out, the other resting on her hip. Her deep auburn hair spilled in a tangle on the pillow. She'd let it grow out from the punk spikes when he'd first seen her. Her mouth was slightly open, full lower lip trembling with her breath. A stubborn line drew her arched brows together. Dreaming again. He bet wherever she was, she was digging her heels in, refusing to bend.

Damn, but she was the most irritating woman he'd ever known. Near drove him crazy when she ignored his help for so long and wouldn't accept any help from her friend Deb. Yet a graceful strength suffused her. Steel spun through her, somehow. No matter what, the things life had thrown at her didn't break her. Even pain hadn't broken her.

Her own stubborn heart broke her. And she still didn't see that.

No. His work here wasn't done yet. He needed to be with her.

He shifted so he could look out over the street below. Even if Ram had told him what would happen if he got too involved with a case, it wouldn't have mattered. It was too late months ago. He'd fallen, and fallen hard. But if he'd thought even for a minute that he would hurt her, he'd have asked to be given another assignment.

He leaned to the side and pounded his fist against the windowsill. God, he could still feel her, the delicious, opening ache that had welcomed him into her body. Even facing away, he could still taste the salty musk of her arousal, the dewy promise that blossomed. He groaned and rubbed his face hard.

"Joe?"

He jumped. "Alena!" She was sitting up, knees drawn to her chin. "How are you feeling?"

A smile skidded across her face. She reached out. "Why don't you come and see?"

"I don't think…" Even as he denied her, his hand lifted to meet her fingers.

The melting ache was there again; it flowed out from her fingertips. Lights of amber and turquoise swirled up his arm. "Alena, we shouldn't."

"Why?" She withdrew her hand and looked down. "Oh." The quilt shifted as she moved back. "It's not right. A sin."

"What the hell are you saying?"

She curled her legs to the side and leaned against the wall behind the bed. "Sorry—that came out wrong." Her arms barricaded her chest. "What I meant was that I seduced you." Her head dropped and hair swung in front of her face.

"And?"

"You're a Sacred Guardian." She gave a long sigh but still didn't look up. "I don't know what that means, but I figure you're maybe a kind of priest."

He snorted. "A priest!"

"Well, like a priest or something. I don't know." Her finger clutched and released the quilt bunched over her chest. "I just wanted, I wanted…" She shook her head.

"I wanted too."

"What?" She looked up, eyes wide. "What did you say?"

He reached out and caressed her face. "I was saying that I wanted you, too. You didn't seduce me."

Her twenty-carat smile shone out. "Well. Hot damn!" She took his hand. "Let me take care of that now."

****

The lace curtain rippled in the breeze that trickled in through cracks in the casement. He focused on the window frame and frowned. Just a little warped. He'd have to see if he could plane it so it didn't let the wind enter. Alena stirred and snuggled closer to him. He drew the blankets and quilt up around her. Her skin was still cold as ice, even though the night was warm. It worried the hell out of him.

Michael hadn't noticed anything wrong with Alena when Tim's mother dropped him off. Her shadowed eyes and slow speech didn't frighten her son. When Michael had seen him, the boy had stopped dead just outside the door. His eyes had gone all round; his lower lip had quivered. Then the boy had run straight into his arms. He'd squeezed his eyes tight and ruffled the kid's hair. It wouldn't do to have the boy see him cry. He wanted to leave Michael good memories of their time together. Michael didn't even ask how he'd somehow gotten a body, how he'd just shown up like this. Well, kids were like that. All the younger kids on the rez before he left for 'Nam had watched while his grandad placed his spirit bag around his neck, pronouncing him safe from any bullets that may come his way. The kids really believed it. He could see it in their eyes.

A gust of wind rattled the window and puffed at the curtain. Maybe the kids had it right. It hadn't been a bullet that had killed him. But if he'd survived would he and Alena have met? If they'd met would she even give him the time of day? He'd be sixty-five and she was what, twenty-five?

He pulled Alena closer and watched the lace tremble. Time. How long did he have? Sometimes Ram left him alone for months. He ran his hand down Alena's side and was rewarded with a tiny, dimpling smile before her dream snatched her away.

He couldn't feel the dream path anymore, but that was okay. He didn't have to go into her dreams to touch her now. He rolled onto his back and stared up at spots on the ceiling. Gotta paint that. Maybe he'd have time to do it.

Easing out of the bed, he paced from one side of the room to the other, avoiding boards that creaked. His body had weight; it had mass. People could see him. They accepted him as real. Tim's mother hadn't batted an eyelash when she saw him. She'd merely smiled, reached out, and introduced herself. Alena had kept trying to get him to eat the pizza she'd ordered. He'd gotten as far as raising a slice to his mouth but had to put it down. Knew it was impossible.

He leaned against the closed door and sighed. He didn't miss eating, but he sure wished he could sleep. He'd never missed sleeping since he'd died. But he missed it now. The hours crawled by and he was left feeling a little punchy, like when he was alive and on an extended patrol. He kept thinking he was seeing things, like the light that seeped through the crack between Alena's bedroom door and the frame.

He straightened and frowned, running his finger down the crack to the knob. A golden light seeped through the space between the door and the frame making his finger glow red-orange. Must have left the living room light on. Or maybe Michael had gotten up—but no, if he were awake, the boy would have come in to Alena.

He sighed again and held the door handle. Michael must know he was sleeping with Alena. He could see something in the boy's solemn eyes when he'd tucked him into bed. Not censure, nor even surprise. But what?

He lifted his head. Relief. That's what he'd seen

in Michael's eyes. Michael must be glad his mom had a special friend. Poor kid had never known his father, had never known any father.

What would happen when he had to leave?

He shook his shoulders and opened the door. Better turn the light off. It was going on three in the morning. Alena was careful with her money; leaving a light on would cost her. He stopped at the edge of the hallway that led to the living room. Something about the light bothered him. Not the brightness, nor the flickering, but the color. It was all colors, not like light from a lamp. He hesitated, one foot in the bedroom and the other in the hallway. Maybe he should just go back to bed.

Screw that. He was a marine. Why the hell was he lingering here? Whatever was there, he would confront it. It was time he did. He pulled himself up straight and strode into the living room.

There were three of them. Their massive light-wings lay tight against their sides, yet still filled the room. Two of them were strangers. The middle one was Ram.

And man oh man, that angel was *pissed.*

Chapter Twenty

A wasp buzzed, hummed, and twisted. It flailed at her until she pulled the pillow around her head, covering her ears. No good. The zzzzzz sliced right through the layers of cotton and polyester filling.

"Damn thing!" She reached out and hit the button of her buzzing alarm. Have to get ready for church. She groped behind her for Joe. Her hand fell on empty sheets. Cold sheets. Frigid sheets.

Damn, but she was freezing. She sat up shivering and pulled the covers back, pushing her feet into the fluffy cotton slippers next to the bed. It wasn't even cold. The temperature had risen to over seventy degrees yesterday—typical of spring in Berkeley—but she just couldn't seem to get warm. She was already bundled up in thermal underwear, jeans, and socks. How could she still be cold? Last night Joe had laughed when he saw her bedtime ensemble. But somehow his laughter hadn't reached his eyes. She'd wondered what that meant, but was too damn tired to ask.

She shrugged into an old cardigan and lurched to her feet, holding on to the side of the bed for balance when the room tilted and swung, just like the mirrors in a fun house. "Just what I need." Maybe she should add iron to her diet. She hadn't eaten much yesterday. Have to eat something. Then she'd feel stronger. Warmer, too. Or maybe she could have Joe go to the vitamin store down the block and get some iron supplements. She smiled as the world steadied. Yeah, that's what she would ask him to do.

But where the hell was Joe? And why was the

bedroom door open? She was certain she had shut it last night. Not that they did anything that warranted a shut door last night. She'd conked out the minute her head hit the pillow.

Joe must be up already. She shuffled toward the door, but had to stop and lean against the frame. Couldn't stop shivering. And walking to her bedroom door had knocked the stuffing right out of her. She had to grab on to the doorknob and pant. What the hell was wrong with her? She'd gone without eating before. "This is stupid." She drew in a breath and let go of the door.

Her knees gave way. She slid to the floor. "Joe?" Was that her voice? That weak little squeak? "I need help." She concentrated on breathing, just taking air in and letting it out. "Joe?" The apartment was silent. Well, Joe had lost his powers, hadn't he? She'd just have to find him. She pitched into the hallway and crawled toward the living room. "Joe?"

She had to stop halfway there, only a few feet from her bedroom door, and pant. Now this was really scaring her. Dammit, she was taking in as much air as she could. It just wasn't doing any good. Her legs started to tremble. She pressed her cheek against her outstretched arm and stared at dust bunnies quivering in the corner of the hallway where it met the entrance to the living room. Must have missed those when she last vacuumed. She'd have to make sure she did that corner next time.

She rolled over onto her side facing the living room, and a deep groan slipped out. Fricking hell! Here she was, collapsed on the floor, barely able to move, and she was worried about a little dust? She gave a gurgling laugh, but the sound of her raspy, wheezing voice made her heart skip. Her head canted to the side. She blinked and squinted.

A crumpled bundle of what looked like clothes lay in a heap on the floor at the entrance to the living room. Dark blue. She inched forward and grabbed the edge of it, pulling it to her. Jeans? But the house had been clean last night when they all went to bed. Were the jeans Michael's? He used to drop his clothes around the house. Hadn't done that in a long time, though. She held them in front of her face. Thirty-four waist. What the hell were Joe's jeans doing on the living room floor?

The effort to read the label sapped her. Her heart stuttered unevenly and raced. She sagged onto the discarded jeans and tried to steady her breathing. This was not good, not good. But what the hell was wrong? She'd been fine yesterday morning before…

No. Her illness couldn't have anything to do with Joe. She must have a bad case of the flu. That's all. She'd get someone to take here to the doctor, though. Joe could do that. He was so strong he could carry her to the fricking bus stop.

Maybe Joe was in the bathroom. She rolled to the other side. Maybe he wanted to take a shower? The thought tickled her, but she was afraid to laugh. She inched down the hallway. The walls bowed and started to wobble. How would she ever make it there? She closed her eyes and collapsed, resting her left cheek against the cool wooden floor. Had to get him to come to her.

She focused all her will, took a slow breath, but the name that spilled from her lips wasn't Joe's.

"Michael!"

"Mom?" The sound of his little feet hitting the floor and his scramble to the hallway shook her and forced her eyes to pop open.

"It's okay, baby." Damn. He hated it when she called him baby. "I mean, Michael." She couldn't seem to get enough air. "Mommy just needs some help." The edges of her vision glowed maroon. What did that mean? Michael's face swam into focus. "You know when we watched that old ambulance show with Captain Kirk in it?" Now gray spots flowed in front of her eyes, forming a checkerboard.

"Where's Joe?" His eyes were dark with fear.

She shook her head and sighed. "I don't know."

"I'll go find him." He leaped to his feet.

"No, honey." She grabbed at his arm. "It's just you and me." The effort to grab and hold on to him cost her, for a moment she couldn't see anything at all. Light slowly returned, and with it, Michael's scared face. She wasn't sure how she knew that Joe was gone, but she was certain this was true. It hurt, but she'd have to think about it later. Right now she needed to think about Michael, and get some help.

She had to close her eyes again. "I need you to call."

"Like *Rescue 911*." His arm trembled.

"Yes, just like the TV show. Call 9-1-1 and tell them to come right away. Give them our address." She had drilled Michael for months so he could recite his full name, her name, their phone number and address, in case he got lost when on an outing with preschool. Her hand slipped from his arm. She hoped he'd still remember it. His feet pounded into the kitchen now. But his voice sounded so far away. She could barely hear him. It was like listening to someone at the end of a tunnel, distorted and metallic. Her heart lumbered, slipped and rattled. A dull gloom beckoned. Maybe she could sleep, just rest a bit. That would be okay, wouldn't it?

Her eyes blinked open. Michael. She needed to make sure he was all right first. Had to stay awake until the ambulance got here. She rolled her head to the side. How long did it take for the paramedics to arrive after you'd called them? She had no idea. Her list of emergency contacts was posted right by the phone. If she passed out, the paramedics would see it and call Deb, wouldn't they? She knew Deb would take Michael if anything happened to her, but she wasn't going to give up without a fight. She opened her eyes wide and practiced deep abdominal breathing, taking air in all the way to her toes. The walls around her appeared again. "Good."

Now where was Michael? Had he gotten through? "Michael?" She needed to tell him to call Deb's house, just in case.

Without warning, everything dimmed. The gray checkerboard that had bled across her vision roared back, covering the hallway, the floor, the ceiling. She held her hand in front of her eyes but couldn't see it. A fevered shriek trilled somewhere.

She sank screaming into the dark.

Chapter Twenty-One

Ram looked right into him. The other two flanked Ram, one on each side. The sun dipped over the ocean. The angels were all poised above a bank of deep violet and gray clouds. He faced them.

One of the angels looked Asian, Korean maybe, all tilted eyes, gold-tipped skin, and flat nose. He'd introduced himself as Tamael. His brilliant green and bronze light-wings caught the light of the setting sun and glowed, like verdant hills topped by storm clouds, backlit by a single beam of the sun.

Tamael's face held no expression at all. But the one on Ram's right, Azael, looked almost friendly. More at ease, anyway. And he was black, with light-wings the shade of Guinness stout; they were warm, brown-gold, and sparkling. *Well, I'll be damned. Affirmative action for angels? Who would have thought?*

For one, dizzying moment, he saw himself standing there before the three angels, aeons ago, being called to task for something he'd done.

No. That wasn't right. It was something they'd all done. But how could that be?

Ah, man. This was weird. Shoot, he didn't need this *Twilight Zone* stuff. He shook himself and concentrated on Ram's toes. That didn't help. Even the angel's feet were tense and angry, all the ethereal tendons visible and flexing.

"You touched Alena, didn't you?"

What could he say? Better get it all out. "I didn't just touch her."

Ram glowered. Tamael and Azael frowned. They

all hung there in the air, drilling him with their stares.

He squirmed. All the cruel or thoughtless things he'd ever done danced right in front of him, like the time he'd dumped cold ashes all over his mom's best beadwork and blamed his sister Sammie for what he'd done. The time he shot a BB gun at an old dog and injured the poor hound's eye. The time he sneaked a drink—well, more than a drink—of the sacramental wine. All the times he roared down the highway, plastered, not even giving a thought about which person he would hurt if he caused an accident.

The time he first stared a Viet Cong soldier straight in the eyes and pulled the trigger.

All these moments rushed toward him and buzzed around his face. He pushed on his ears until they popped. "Goddammit. I thought I was supposed to get the life review right after I died, not now." He looked up. They weren't laughing.

"You're killing Alena." This was Tamael. His voice hummed in a low, tuning fork vibration, rattling Joe's teeth. "Every time you enter dense matter enough to have sex with her, to be with her, you kill her."

"So? I'll s-stop." As he forced the words from his mouth, the world slipped. It just fell out from under him like the swift descent of an elevator. But he hadn't moved. No one had. The three angels still floated on the air before him. Damn! Weirder and weirder.

Ram shook his head. His light-wings rippled and his eyes glowed green, shot with streaks of red. "You can't stop." The angel looked down at the clouds billowing below them. "Once something like this has started, it's impossible to end it. Even if you could stop the physical relationship, every time you're near her, you'll still steal her energy, bit by bit."

How the hell could Big Wing know that? "How?"

He leaned toward the angel. "And why would I do that?"

"You want her to see you."

"So what?" He glanced at the other angels. The two were looking at Ram. "What does that have to do with killing her?"

"In order for you to appear to her, you have to siphon her energy."

"Then I won't appear to her."

"It's not that easy."

It was hard to meet Ram's gaze. The angel now had switched to that heavenly compassion thing, dripping from his head to the tips of his light-wings.

It irritated the hell out of him. "Don't patronize me." He floated back and watched the other two angels from the corner of his eye. If he ran now, how long would it take them to catch him? "Just tell me what I can do." Probably just the blink of an eye. He curled his fists. "If she's dying, it's my fault."

"I can tell that Jos...Joe wants to set things right." Azael folded his arms and frowned at Ram. "You'll have to tell him, Ramael."

He blinked. Dissension among the ranks? Could he use this? He glanced at Tamael. No help there. The angel was doing that eyes-closed statue thing. Holy hell. "Yes. Let me make it right. Whatever it takes." Why did this all seem so goddamn familiar? Like he was reading from a tired old script.

"Whatever it takes?"

"Just say the word."

The three angels looked at each other. "You'll have to tell him everything, Ramael."

Who said that? He thought it was Tamael this time. "Huh?" And Ram had the strangest expression. The angel looked chastened, almost, well, *hunted.*

But mad as hell.

What in blazes was going on here? None of them would look at him now. Ram gestured to the others.

"We need to confer. For now, you must stay here."

They disappeared. Completely. As Ram had disappeared days ago. Only this time, there was no tornado left in the wake of their disappearance.

He floated, his mouth hanging open. They hadn't even bothered to spread their light-wings. They just were there, and then they weren't. He looked down at the swirl of bad weather just below his feet and fought a queasy clutching. Ram had always tried to look as if he were physical, like his body was more than just strands of light, so Joe wouldn't freak out. Well, it looked like that was all over now.

What next? Hell, if they were going to take their time, he'd go back to Alena and see if she was okay. Maybe he hadn't drained her too much already. He prepared for his dive into the lower atmosphere, but when he tried to descend, he spun around in place like a bead on a string.

"Whoa!" He managed to straighten. "How did they do this?" He was stuck in place. But maybe, just maybe he could get around it by collapsing his particles. "Better try it, but not too far." If he aimed at any old place, he might get even farther from Alena and would not be able to home in on her essence. "Here goes." He knotted his etheric fists and thought really hard about the swirling tip of lavender and gunmetal clouds just below him.

With the swift descent of a powerful elevator, he arrived at his destination.

"Aiyiyiyiyiyiyi!" He whooped. Okay, now to go to Alena.

Have to hide from her, though. Could he pull in the mantle of heaven to cloak his form? He searched around for the sparkle of a seam between the etheric and dense matter.

There, a glint to his left. Had to be at least three feet away, though. He was still stuck in the glue the angels had placed in this immediate area. He thought really hard about going to the glint. He scrunched his eyes closed and concentrated.

"Okay, now!" He opened his eyes. Hadn't moved an inch.

Damn, it must be too close for a particle collapse. Hey! Maybe he could reach it. It was only three feet away. Could he do this? He stretched his arms and reached, leaned over until he was nearly horizontal. His fingertip grazed the edge. Got it!

Now. How the hell could he open it? Ram had always done it with his hands, and he'd always assumed it took an angel to rip it open.

What if that wasn't true? The notion stunned him. He ran his forefinger along the juncture between the worlds and shivered as the song of God trembled through him. He tugged harder. The rift bulged and spilled light in hues impossible to name.

He leaned way over, bent until he couldn't go any farther, taking the vent he'd made and squeezing. The mantle squirted out in a stream toward his open mouth. He sucked it in until his eyes pulsed. When he couldn't hold any more, he straightened and pushed it out in a flow all over his form, then into his hands. As the rip sealed, he splashed the bit he'd poured into his hands over his face and head, and glanced down at his arms. Well, they looked a bit more transparent. At least he guessed they did. And he felt less like a man and more like a dead guy.

It would have to do. Now to jet out of here. He called a picture of Alena's face, her essence, into his mind and got ready to travel. He thought so hard that his form rolled up into a ball. He let go, arms flung outward in a gentle spin. He opened one eye.

Nothing had happened.

He was stuck in place. His head could move. He could move his arms. He could lean and bend and float. But that was it. He'd reached the limit of the prison they'd made.

"Holy hell!"

****

She glared at the nurse as the woman fussed with the IV. Two needles sprouting clear tubes dug into her arms. Another tube puffed oxygen into her nose. "Where's. My. Boy?" Dang it, every word was such an effort. She drew in a breath to say more but the nurse forestalled her.

"Your son is fine." The woman's voice was muffled and distorted by the sterile suit she wore. It was white, like everything else in the room. The clear faceplate of the suit reflected her pale face and the dangling IV bags. "Don't worry." The nurse gave her arm a clumsy pat with her gloved hand and turned away.

"But!" She drew in a breath. "What's."

The woman was already squeaking her way across the linoleum floor to the pressurized door.

"Wrong." Before she could draw another breath, the nurse had punched in the key code and let herself out. The door closed with a hiss. "With me."

Nobody would tell her anything. She'd awakened in the ambulance, but after they took a blood sample and analyzed it, they had quarantined everyone who had touched her. They wouldn't tell her where Michael was. What if he was scared? He needed his mom. And as for Joe, well, wasn't that just like a man. Get laid, and then cut out when things got rough.

"Oh, Joe." No. No. No. Joe wasn't like that. Dammit. How long had it taken him to even stay next to her in the bed? He was always a gentleman, a real gentleman. She shook her head. At least she could move her head now. Couldn't even blink just a few hours ago. That was something, wasn't it? But what was wrong? And why wasn't Joe here?

Maybe he finally got in touch with the angels he'd talked about. He'd said they wouldn't punish him. She hoped that was true. *God, if you're listening, please don't hurt Joe.* What had happened between them wasn't Joe's fault. Not at all. It was her mistake, all that time wanting him, hungering to touch, to take him inside her. She'd even lied to herself about how much she wanted him. Pretending hadn't helped. It just had made her want him more.

Joe had warned her. He had. She hadn't listened. If there was any blame, she'd take it. But damn it all, she wanted to see him. Even if only for a moment. She could tell him, she never told him, well, the L word. *Face it, Morgan, you were a goner the minute he showed up in your bathroom, pounding your back until you puked.* Love. Honor. She'd never trusted these things; they were never real in her world, except with David. When David died, her world fell apart.

Joe brought her back to life in more ways than she could ever imagine. "Dang it, Joe." There, she didn't say it, didn't say the F word. He'd changed that about her, too. "Come back. Please." Just for a moment.

At least she could breathe a little easier now and say more words. Even complete sentences. "But I want Joe." If Joe were here, maybe he could go see Michael and tell her boy it was going to be okay. Everything would be okay. Of course, if Joe had been there in her apartment, he'd be in isolation now, too. Her lungs shook in a gurgling laugh. Just think how scared the doctors would be if they tried to take a blood sample from him!

Maybe his body was real. Maybe he'd crossed over to earth completely. But if that were the case, why couldn't he eat? She'd tried to tempt him last night with pizza. He didn't eat any. Said he couldn't.

Well, she was here and she was alone again.

She'd use her own resources to deal with this. He'd taught her that much. She was a survivor. Always had been. She would figure this out and work on getting better on her own. Her friends could help, and when she was well, she would do what she could to help them. If she could find him, if he came back, that would be more than a miracle. But if Joe was gone, truly gone, she would deal with it.

She'd make him proud. Wherever he was, she would send prayers and all the love she had inside her to him.

"I'm here, Joe," she breathed. "I'm here for you."

Chapter Twenty-Two

The gibbous moon bulged in a sky of deep sapphire. Clouds had all blown away to bless the area with a clear night. Didn't often happen here. Fog usually moved in and blotted out the stars.

He sighed. Must be going on eight or nine o'clock. Alena would be wondering where he was.

Well, he was worried sick about Alena. What had happened to her? She probably thought he'd skipped out. It was late afternoon when Ram and the others left him imprisoned here. They'd taken him away from Alena last night. What was taking so long? The hours seemed to crawl.

Now, this was weird. He'd never had a sense of the passing of time since he died, even though he'd been close to dense matter the entire forty-plus years. Must be an effect of the descent. Next time he'd have to calibrate...

He clutched at his middle as the world fell out from under him again, just as it had when he'd faced Tamael, Azael, and Ram. "What the hell was that?" He gulped and looked down. The soft, flannel-like grasses of the rolling hills still lay below him. He hadn't moved. He ran his hands down his body—no—form. His *form*. Gotta get used to that again. Everything seemed to still be there.

Damn, it was just like someone else had zipped into his mind for a moment and used it. But it still felt like him thinking. Strangest thing.

He looked up into the gleaming silvery emerald of Ram's eyes. Tamael and Azael floated behind the golden-haired angel.

"Christ!" He flung his arms out and backpedaled against the force that held him in place. "Ram, you've got to stop doing that!"

Ram just looked at him. "Doing what?"

He rubbed his shoulders. "Sneaking up on me. Use your damn wings, for Christ's sake! I'm not used to this." He straightened and looked at the three angels, one by one. "So what's the verdict?"

Tamael answered, "We will tell you what we are, first."

So what? "I already know what you are." If only he could back away from them. They were too close. It was making him jumpy. His back itched and burned again. He swung his arms around; the itchy part in his back buckled and then settled.

Azael shook his head. "Trust me, Joe. You need to hear this." He raised a brow at Ram.

Big Wing folded his arms. "We're known as the N'Aarta, the Watchers."

A feeling tone, a musical tone, a designation.

"Huh?" Where the hell did that other voice come from? And what was it saying? Tones? He shifted his shoulders. There was that annoying itch again—just between his shoulder blades. He shook his arms but it didn't help now. The itch danced up and down his spine and settled in a spot he couldn't reach. Of course.

He lifted his hand up and rubbed behind his neck. Still no relief. "But you're angels, right?" Why didn't they forget this crap and just let him go?

"That's one designation we have." They all nodded.

"Been here since the Beginning," Azael said, cracking a smile.

"Uh." Designation? Didn't some voice just...Was he going all psychic now? Maybe reading their minds?

Nah. Must have been that Tamael murmuring

something. "Ah, okay. Whatever you say." He shrugged. Tamael was scary, sort of like Bruce Lee and Toshiro Mifune in their most daunting roles. "Angels. You're angels." Well, maybe things would be okay. "So what's up?"

Watchers or whatever the N-word meant were angels and angels worked for the Big Guy, right? His mom had always said God wouldn't do him any harm. He glanced at Ram. The angel was glowering again. He sure hoped his mama was right.

"We need to show you something before we continue this conversation." Ram extended his arm in a long reach.

Now they all hurtled forward, like they were on the Extreme ride at Seaside Park. He swallowed and staggered. "What the?"

He was standing in a hospital room, complete with khaki plaster walls. "For God's sake, Ram, you know I hate hospitals." He stepped back and bumped into Azael. "Sorry, man." Something lay under a white sheet on the bed in front of Joe. He looked closer.

Not something, *somebody*. Tubes glistened all around the body and snaked upward to intravenous bags. A monitor blinked green with each beat of the patient's heart. Another monitor displayed a straight line that moved across the screen in a continuous streak.

Jesus! "Alena?"

Azael spoke again. "No." The angel seized him by the arm and led him over to the bed.

It took a moment to recognize the patient. "Hell, JJ." He bent and looked at his nephew's face. "He did it. The kid goddamn did it." After all the lessons and sweat he'd poured into JJ. He glanced up at the screen showing the faintly jiggling line next to the straight line. "Is he still here? In his body?"

Ram shook his head. "Your nephew has already

gone."

"Not to the hot place, I hope."

"No."

"Well, you told me this would happen, didn't you?"

Ram folded his arms and sighed. "You have a choice to make."

"I figured you brought me here for a reason."

"You can finish the life he threw away."

"Or?"

"Or you can spend the rest of Alena's life imprisoned."

Well, hey! Alena must be okay. "Ah. Why should I be imprisoned?"

Ram's nostrils pinched. Looked like the angel was getting ready to sneeze. Or maybe slug him. He shuffled back until he bumped against the IV pole.

The glistening bags swung; tubes leading into the bags hit the metal pole. Ram reached out and stilled the bags. "This is partly why. You shouldn't be able to make these things move simply by walking into them. You're dead, Joe. What you and Alena did…" The angel looked down. "I know you didn't mean to, but you've disrupted the balance between the worlds. It has to be set right."

"And if I refuse both choices?" There must be something else. Think. He had to think.

"You don't want to go there, brother," Azael murmured.

"Will I be able to remember all of this?" That might work. He could go to Alena. Of course, he'd have to convince her he was really Joe Littlehawk. "I mean, when I'm in JJ's body?" He swallowed. Jumping into his nephew's body—damn! What would it be like to inhabit someone else's body, take on that person's life? He backed up. It felt…forbidden. And familiar. The room tilted. He reached for the railing at the edge of the bed and steadied himself. This was happening a lot these days. What the hell was going on?

"No."

"What?"

"You can't take memory with you."

Damn those rules. Scratch that, then. He stepped back from JJ. "Sorry, kid." It all boiled down to one form of prison or another. He turned to the other three, but Tamael and Azael were both glaring at Ram. "What's up?"

Azael nudged Ram. "It's time, Ramael."

Ram stiffened. "They want me to tell you who you are." Each word was surrendered unwillingly through his glistening teeth.

"What the hell do you mean?" He glanced at the three. "I'm Joe."

Ram looked him right in the eye. "You were Joe." He lifted his hand. "But before that, you were…well, you." The angel closed his eyes, but he just looked tired now, not like a statue. "You've always been one of us." The silver-rimmed, pine-green eyes opened; the iron hand rested on his shoulder. "You simply forgot." Ram stepped back.

Azael nodded. "Spread your wings, Josael."

Air stretched tight all around him, alive and gliding against his form. He reached out and clutched at Azael's arm. Each syllable of the name tore through him. "Jos." He fell to his knees. "A." Skin on his back rippled in a violent itching, searing bulge. "Elllll."

The tips emerged first, sherry shot through with red gold. Soft, yet impenetrable, his light-wings flowed out and spread, crowding the room. He glanced at the others. Their light-wings draped close to their forms. He wondered how to fold his, and with that thought, the wheels of his mind ground, flashes of his life as Joe Littlehawk spiraled in an outward spinning wheel.

Spun out and away.

He raised his head. "Well, I'll be damned." His light-wings still darted around, but the filaments started to obey him, all moving gracefully together, closer to his side.

"All of us were damned, Josael." Azael nodded. "Welcome back, brother."

"Hey there, Zaz." He grinned. "I'm back." He drew his light-wings in close to his form, the way the others had theirs. "It's good to be back," he said and, using the oldest language, added, "*Ecron Iad.*"

"Praise God," Tamael agreed.

He lifted his head and looked at his brothers. "Well, here we are." He couldn't remember everything yet, but he knew the ancient jest. "So who is watching the Watchers?"

"You mean Who, don't you?" Azael shook his head and chuckled. "And we are the Watchers."

"This banter is wasteful." Ramael's hands pushed him toward the bed.

He merely looked at Ramael. "Take your hands off me, Ramael." He stared at the golden-winged angel until the hands dropped away.

"Ramael, leave him alone. This situation is your fault, too." Azael stepped forward. "Go and finish what you started, Josael. Make something of your nephew's life." Azael placed a friendly hand on his back. "Soothe your sister's grief. It's your duty."

He scanned the three. They were all staring at him. He couldn't outrun them; he knew that. Tamael's gift was speed. No one could outrun the green-winged angel. He couldn't bargain, either. Azael looked easygoing but he was a Forever Judge. Anytime the dark-winged Azael incarnated, he took up the judicial robes—from the crook and flail of Maat in Upper Egypt to the Supreme Court of the United States.

And Ramael, well, old Ram had an axe to grind.

He rested his gaze on Ramael. It was always this way, always had been this way. *Born from the same Breath of God.* Closer than brothers. The N'Aarta, from the ancient language. The name they used to describe themselves. Others had called them many things. Sons of God. Nephillim. The Watchers. The Fallen Angels.

But they were family. Kin. Brothers. And yet more than that. *A feeling tone.*

Ramael's tone. Grief. Fear. Envy. "Goddammit, Ramael, it must have tickled you this past forty-one years," he murmured, moving away from Azael's hand.

"What?" Ramael's face was blank.

The prig was pretending to not know what he meant. "All that time you had me on a string, forgetting who I was."

"It happens, Josael." Ramael's form started to fracture. "You know we have to let you remember on your own." Ramael reassembled his form, but the edges vibrated.

"Not if it takes more than a turning around this star, we don't." He moved until he was nose to nose with Ramael. "You enjoyed it." He glared right into Ramael's eyes. "Didn't you?"

"That's beside the point. It's time, Josael." Ramael gestured toward JJ

"We're brothers, Ram." He moved away from the hospital bed. "I'm not less than you."

"Yes, we are later-wave N'Aarta."

"What do you mean? Why later?"

"The first wave of N'Aarta all incarnated and served Yeshua."

He looked down. "But we fell together." There was still more to remember. Something he needed to remember. But what?

"So?" Ramael huffed.

"We've all been here for aeons, right?"

Tamael answered; his voice hummed through the room. “We look after the children of God who were born on a different heavenly breath. The Morekala. They call us angels, and they call themselves humans. Since we fell, we must stay here and serve our chosen penance.” His hand sketched a graceful gesture that left traces of light in the air.

“Ah. It’s beginning to make sense.” He allowed his light-wings to lift and touch the walls.

Ramael frowned. “Why do you need tutoring?” His light-wings expanded. “You’ve already made the transformation.”

“Humor me.” Maybe he could buy some time. There had to be some way he could escape. *Think, Josael, think*!

Ramael looked at Azael. “Must I?”

“Why not?” Azael shrugged. “You caused this.”

Ramael looked away. His form shivered, but he spoke. “This world of dense matter was made for the Morekala, human spirits who chose to take the journey into dense matter. The Morekala all cut themselves off from the Eternal in order to grow, and in growing, to give more to the One.” Ramael paused and glared at him. “This is *their* world. We are not to interfere.”

Azael stepped forward, taking Ramael’s arm. “We all interfered, Ramael. It’s why we remain and take incarnation from time to time.”

Ramael shook off Azael’s hand. “We are *N’Aarta*. We are here to nurture the growth of the Morekala, to give assistance where we are allowed to, and comfort when we *cannot* intervene.” His eyes sparked.

Damn. Three against one. He could not fight them. Their powers were…*wait*. His light-wings quivered. He couldn’t fight, outrun them, or bargain. But there was one thing he could do. It was *his* special gift, his alone. He backed away from Ramael and smiled at all three of them, flashing his heavenly teeth, as Ramael had often done.

Tamael, whose gift was speed.

Ramael, whose gift was beauty.

Azael, whose gift was judgment.

And Josael.

Who could bend time.

He folded his arms across his chest. His light-wings extended farther, testing the space around him for the turning, the place where dense matter collided with the Eternal. The net that held the world of dense matter in place had many such junctures. It was these places that Ramael used to extract the mantle of heaven. He chuckled. Ramael had no idea of the other uses for these spots. He'd kept this to himself after…well, after they had fought, so very long ago.

"You knew this would happen when you assigned me to Alena. *My* Alena."

"I hoped it wouldn't." Ramael wouldn't look at him. "Think of it as a test."

"There is no such thing as a Sacred Guardian." The tips of his wings kept darting around the space inside the room, seeking the spot he needed to find.

"I had to improvise when it was obvious you didn't remember."

"So you say." There had to be a juncture here. He just needed to find it. The Song of God always bled through. *A musical tone.* Combination E Flat and B minor, sometimes just B minor. Where? *A feeling tone, a musical tone, a designation, designation…*A location! He nearly whooped as he would have when he was Joe Littlehawk. *Methkala*! He remembered. The fourth key. *A location.*

"The Eternal has judged and you must do as you are bid." Ramael lifted his head and looked down his nose. "I was merely His servant."

"You liked stringing me along, Ramael. Admit it." He squinted at the mesh of dense matter superimposed on the space all around them, on the walls and floor.

"I won't fight you, Josael."

Oh yes you will. He pivoted a degree and lifted the tips of his light-wings, humming the tones in a hushed voice, seeking the answering cry from the collision point. Had to be here somewhere. He looked at the three. *We'll have this out, but not now.* Not with three against one. He had to find Alena, to see for himself that she was alive and well. It would be just like the other three N'Aarta to push him into JJ's body and leave him there for the lifetime he was supposed to have. Then when he dropped the dense matter body at death, his brothers would say, "Oops. Sorry. Alena Morgan got married years ago." He couldn't even wait until she died to see her.

Alena was Morekala, a human spirit. Once the Morekala died, they went to a place where the N'Aarta could not go, a place for other teachings that would prepare them for the journey back into dense matter. He twitched his left light-wing filaments, still seeking the turning.

Lessons. It was always about lessons.

Well, he was sick to death of lessons.

He glanced around the room again. Tamael's eyes were closed; his attention focused on receiving from the One. Ramael was so caught in his grief over giving in to his envy and jealousy, Josael could even shout the tones and Ramael wouldn't know what he was doing. Azael, though, was a different case entirely. That old Zaz was a problem. The black N'Aarta leaned forward, his gaze spearing Josael.

Had to be now or never. *Sorry, Eternal Lord. I will do your bidding, but I need one more moment with her. Please.*

He stretched his wings to their limits. There!

Near the far corner of the ceiling. *Thank you, Lord*! He breathed the tones into the rift and glanced back. Ramael was grinding his etheric teeth again. His brother always did that when he felt guilty. "Ramael?"

Ramael jumped. "What!"

"You always were a piss-poor jerk." The tips of his wings entered the rift. "And Alena has always been *mine*."

Ramael's fury exploded, his wings tangling with the other N'Aarta in the room. "You *thalka*! Come here! I'll take you apart."

He beamed another grin at all of them. "Catch me if you can."

The rift split. Air now thickened and churned. He leaped into the Gateway. The trembling splendor of forever bled into the space in back of him, blinding the three N'Aarta he left behind.

The gateway sealed.

Chapter Twenty-Three

She turned her head in slow increments until she could see the window. Sunlight struggled through slits in the ivory blinds. The monitor on her right chirped. *Beep beep beep*. Marking off the beats of her heart. She let her head roll back on the pillow and counted the beeps. How many beats did a heart make anyway? Hundreds of thousands? Millions? Enough to encompass a lifetime. She never did pay much attention in high school biology.

Joe didn't get many heartbeats. Twenty-four years worth. He was twenty-four fricking years old when he died. How many beats was that? She let her breath bubble out and strained to move her right hand. The nurses' button was beside her index finger. They'd placed it there so she could summon someone. Her hand trembled, and her finger shook. She relaxed all the muscles. No way could she summon the strength to push one little button.

This sucked. Maybe she could practice talking. Well, what came out of her mouth was more like croaking, but the doctors had encouraged her to try. She opened her mouth and drew in a quivering breath. "Jsssssss." Nothing came out but a high whine like a hand-held fan, the tiny kind with batteries.

Fricking hell. Just couldn't clear her throat. Everything else seemed okay. Well, kind of okay. She could see and could turn her head from side to side, but her legs and arms sat like lead pipes on the sheets. That was bad enough, but saliva and stuff she didn't even want to name clogged her throat.

Breathing through it was a real trip. She had to take brief, gulping breaths. Coughing sometimes helped, but it scared the crap out of her. Every time she coughed, she couldn't breathe at all for a few seconds and her heart galloped.

Now she knew what Michael went through during one of his bouts with asthma. Her poor, sweet baby. She wished to God that she could see him. But he'd be scared to see her. All she could do was lie there and hiss. They even put in a catheter to collect her urine. Because she couldn't speak clearly, she couldn't tell the nurses what was wrong. And her hands were no use at all. So she couldn't write messages.

At least she was finally out of isolation. Three weeks ago they said that whatever she had was not contagious. And they had a diagnosis. Well, a "diagnostic impression." Something had taken most of the iron from her blood. Just sucked it right out. And she seemed to have picked up a nasty case of pneumonia along the way. They'd pumped her full of iron and antibiotics and in a couple of days she'd been able to sit up. But after that, she'd sunken down again. A relapse, they said. She wasn't getting better as fast as they'd liked.

Thank God, Michael was okay. Deb had come to get the boy last week. Deb would keep Michael until she recovered.

If she recovered.

No! She couldn't think that way. She had to get out of here, get on with her life. With her life, goddammit! If Joe had taught her anything, it was that she had something to offer. She had to get better, for Michael, for Deb, hell, even for Professor Potts. The sweet, spindly old man had sent her flowers.

She glanced over at the table on the far wall at the riot of indigo, lemon, and red snapdragons stuck in a glass retort. She could just see him picking them from Living Light's garden. The nurses had to find a container for them, and finally stuck them in a glass retort from the lab. *Dear Alena,* Pott's note said. *Please come back soon. My manuscript needs you.* She chuckled, gasped, burbled, choked, and finally caught her wind. In. Out. In. Out. Swallow. Inhale. Exhale.

Live.

She would get better. For Michael, for Deb, for the people at work, for herself. For Joe.

But Joe was gone. And she would never love another man.

It had been three weeks. Longer than any other time he'd gone away. Damn, she wished she knew where he was. The first few days, when she'd started getting better, she'd sat glued to the television, searching all the channels for a story that would lead her to him: *Naked man found wandering Telegraph Avenue,* or even, *Do you know this man? John Doe DOA at Mercy General.* His jeans...those were the only clothes he had on, dammit! And they were left in a crumpled pile on her living room floor. Where the hell was he?

Oh no! Not hell, please, not that. She turned her head again and her gummy hair stuck to her cheek, all hot and prickly. Why wouldn't they at least wash her hair? She couldn't do it herself but would it be so much to ask for someone to wash it? Looked like a piece of crap. Ah, she hated this. *Stop whining, Alena Morgan. You stop it NOW!*

She glanced at the white-faced wall clock with the sweeping red second hand. It was nearly time for them to come in and check on her progress. She'd better keep practicing her attempts at speech. She opened her mouth and croaked, "Joe." Hey! That sounded almost like her old voice. Her breath slipped out with his name and she coughed until sparks floated all around her field of vision. She held her breath until the cough sputtered out. Held her breath and listened, as she always did.

Beep. Beep. Beep. The quick squeak of rubber-soled shoes on linoleum sounded just outside her door. The muted roar of traffic hummed beyond her window. Faint voices chattered somewhere down the corridor. Must be early yet. A clicking rattled somewhere in the room, maybe water pipes.

Okay, okay. No Joe. She'd had her miracle. It was over now. Finished. He was probably on another case. She *hoped* he was on another case, not punished for what they had done.

Joe had said they don't do that. He'd not lied to her, though he said he had lied to the angels. And all for her. Tears spilled now, filling her ears and plastering her dirty hair to her cheeks. Goddammit, what a wimp she was! So what if she wanted it all? Joe beside her every night, warm and solid. Waking up next to him. Walking with him. Seeing him with Michael. Joe being there *with* them. At Michael's birthdays, knee scrapes, first bicycle, hell, high school graduation, wedding...Shit shit shit...He would be pissed off at all the foul language, but at least she wasn't saying it aloud.

Her breath rattled again. She gave a few, quick exhalations and coughed up a bit of gunk. She swallowed and lay there choking as the monitor *beep beep beeped*, the cars outside droned, a horn sounded once, sharply, and the clicking of water pipes turned into a clinking melody.

Huh? She turned her head, seeking the source of the tune. The IV pole swayed; its bag quivered. Metal clips holding the clear tubes in place did a wind chime dance.

Beepbeepbeepbeepbeepbeep.

She stared at the pole. Air thickened and sparkled. *Oh, Christ.* "Joe." Her croak was stronger this time. And she didn't cough.

"Alena." The voice was deep. And there was something silvery about it. Bells. Temple gongs, something like that.

"Is it you?" God—her voice was back. She could talk!

"It's me."

"Where were you?" Her throat caught and she retreated into a series of gagging coughs. A tumbler with a glass tube in it floated over to her mouth.

"Here."

She leaned up a bit and sipped, fell back against the pillow. "Better put that glass back. You don't want the nurses to see."

"I'm sorry, Alena." The tumbler floated to the table. "I've been around here for over a week."

His voice *was* different. It was deeper and, well, wider than before. *Tibetan bells.* That's it! The vibration from Tibetan bells on a CD Deb had played for her, a tone that always gave her the same gut-grabbing shiver, a tune that caught and held the base of her spine.

"Over a week?" Her voice was different, too. Stronger. "Why the fu...why didn't you say something?"

"I was trying to stay in the background."

All those nights when she wept? When she wondered if she would be joining him in death? All right. Enough of this. "Forget it." She fixed a stare into the column of air at her bedside. That seemed bigger, too. And deeper. "Are you okay? I mean, they didn't give you a bunch of shi...didn't punish you, did they?"

"No." The side of her bed dented. "Alena, I can't stay. I can see that now."

"See what."

"Your illness. It's my fault. I can see that now."

"Wha?"

"I can't go into that. We don't have much time."

"Why not?"

"I need you to trust me on this, Alena."

Beepbeepbeepbeep.

"Trust you." A great big lump wedged between her throat and her gut. "Michael is okay. He's with Deb." She couldn't seem to swallow it down.

"I know. Look, Alena, I need for you to do something for me."

Tears puddled in her hair. "What, what." She shook her head to make the stream of sadness slip away. "You know I'd do anything."

"Promise me you'll go see my family. In South Dakota."

"Um. Might take a while." She attempted a smile. "I'm kind of tied up here."

"You'll get better really fast once I'm gone. I'm shielding you now so you can talk, but..."

Gone. "Why do you have to go again?"

"Alena, you have to listen." The tubing and metal clips rattled again.

"Okay, okay. What do you want, Joe?"

"Just go see my family. And, well, if you meet someone there, or you meet a guy...anyway, I want you to memorize some things to say."

"What the hell are you talking about?" Her heart tripped and fluttered in her throat. "You're leaving, right?"

"I need you to pay attention, Alena."

"All right, all right, all right. Whatever." She stared at the wall. "Uh, I have to memorize something? You mean like lines in a play?"

"Yes, like lines." The room quieted. Air at the side of her bed still sparkled, but Joe was silent. Her chest tightened. This was it. Just this column of air and the voice in her head. Like it was at first. *Alpha and Omega.* Damn. Where had she heard that before? Sounded like some Bible thing. She'd have to ask Maddy.

"If a guy asks you where you are from, could you tell him this city?"

"You mean Berkeley?"

"Yes. And could you tell me something about Berkeley, something about the city?"

"You mean like the Marina, Fourth Street Bar and Grill, Live Oak Park..."

"No. Something from the old days, from Joe's, er, from my time."

"Oh, you mean like free speech, power to the people, People's Park, that boomer crap?"

"Hey, that's great. That's fine. And do you remember when we danced?"

"Never will forget." She turned her head. "What's the point?"

"Just trust me on this."

"Joe." She gulped. "I don't want you to go."

"Do this for me."

"For you." It was all she had left. This request. "Right." He'd never asked for anything before. "But this is scanless, you know that, right?"

The bed quivered. "It's bogus," he chuckled.

"Right. I'm listening."

"Okay. Here it is." The column of air shimmered and slid across to the end of the bed. "He says, 'where you from' and you say..."

"Berkeley." This was stupid.

"And he'll say free speech, power to the people, People's Park..."

"Huh?" What was this? A fricking joke?

"And the day we danced."

"To Jefferson Airplane, right?"

"And we listened to Billie Holiday."

"I remember."

"That's it."

"Joe." Her voice was tight. At least she could get some words out. But it was getting to be more of an effort. “What is this all about?”

“I have to go, Alena.”

“I get that.”

“I want to leave you with something.”

“Frickin’ lines in a play.”

“Just promise me you’ll say them.”

“Okay, yeah, sure.” Her throat was getting clogged again. “But Joe?”

“Yes.”

“Can you, I mean, would you...” She swallowed.

“Alena?”

“Let me see you again, Joe. Please. Just one more time.” She had to see him.

“Very well.” The voice dropped even deeper and filled the room. Air billowed at the end of her bed. “One more time.”

His face appeared first. She strained to see. It was Joe, and yet it wasn’t. It was Joe as if Michelangelo had carved him, the high proud brow, hawk nose, broad mouth. Stern and remote, and yet still Joe. His body followed, shoulders and chest, long arms and large hands.

Beep. Beep. Beep. Beepbeep. Beep. Beepbeep.

She opened her mouth to take in more air, but kept her eyes open wide.

His belly, groin, and legs filled in. She squinted. Something heavy extended from his back, branched out across his shoulders, and flowed down to his toes. “What...” She blinked her eyes. They must be too dry. She wasn’t seeing right.

“It’s me, Alena.” He extended his hand and touched her foot. An electric pulse skittered up her leg. Her vision cleared.

“What, what?” She blinked. “Holy shit!”

Wings, it was wings that sprouted from his back. Huge wings. Massive wings. Wings that sparkled and were filled with red-gold light. He lifted his head and the wings snaked out, engulfing the room, taking up all the space, from the monitor on the left wall to the door on the right.

"And Alena?"

"Wha?" She couldn't be seeing this. It goddamn couldn't be true.

"Watch your mouth."

"So sue me!"

He laughed, bent, and started to dissolve, bit by bit. "*Ecron Iad*, Alena." Only his face showed now. "Farewell." His face blinked out. "I love you."

Beepbeepbeepbeepbeepbeep.

"I love you too, Joe." She shivered. "But damn you! You left before I could tell you. Joe, please hear me. Just let me know you heard."

The monitor beeped, the traffic outside hummed, her exhalations whispered, but besides these, it was silent in the room.

Chapter Twenty-Four

The others still searched.

He knew this. He sensed their questing beacons. It was only a matter of time before they found him by homing in on the essence he had dampened, the etheric signature of his N'Aarta nature.

He stood in the mourning quiet of the hospital room. The sister from his lifetime as Joe sat four feet away, next to her son. She had her hospital uniform on, a thin green cotton lab coat with her name badge over the pocket.

How long did he have? A few hours, maybe even a day? They would find him and they would force him into JJ's body or another body if he fought them. Eventually, they would prevail.

And it was right that they prevail. He'd broken the Law. N'Aarta cannot blend with Morekala. They are completely separate beings, born on different breaths of the One. It disturbed the web of Creation when N'Aarta, in their true form, merged with Morekala. It was unfair to the Morekala, too. The N'Aarta were closer to the One and had, well, abilities when they were in their eternal forms. Aeons ago, all of them—Tamael, Azael, Ramael, and Josael—had broken this Law. Doing this made them Watchers. It would take aeons more for them to make restitution to the One.

The One never punished. The first wave of N'Aarta who came to this place set the penalty and applied it to themselves and all N'Aarta who transgressed. Loving Alena was not wrong. It was wrong for him to have stayed with her, even though the signs of what he was doing to her were so evident. His ignorance was no excuse. He'd been given the rules, and it was he who was in his eternal form. He knew better and must pay the price.

But being forced, being pushed to do *anything*—he hated that like hell. Always had. Well, it would be hell indeed, shoved inside a dense matter body with no memory of who he was. In his lifetime as Joe Littlehawk, he hadn't had a choice. All the N'Aarta took a turn in dense matter from time to time, sipping forgetfulness at the banks of Lethe, in order to understand what humans, the Morekala, had to endure. Every piece of his life as Joe Littlehawk had led up to the single moment he'd been born for, that moment when he stepped on the mine and saved the lives of all his men. That one moment.

And now he had to perform a "shrink-to-fit" and take over Joe's nephew's life. The life of a kid he used to terrorize with dreams so the bozo would shape up.

He started to laugh, but stifled it. He was not entirely sure Sammie would not hear. Dampening his essence kept him so busy he feared he might even go solid, and with his wings filling the room, that would probably cause Sammie to pass out.

Or maybe not. She sat next to her son's bed, her face an impassive mask. Oh, the left eye twitched every now and then, but that was the only thing that gave her away, that opened a window onto the well of grief inside her.

He hoped he had some time. Perhaps he could help Sammie, give her some peace, tell her that death is not the end. If only he knew how long he had before the others came for him.

Of course, he could truly give her the solace she needed. All he had to do was agree to enter JJ's body. He looked at the still form under the sheets. It would be a long time before he could do anything in that body. The cerebral cortex was pretty much jellied; that would take some heavy fixing. The right leg was shattered. Lots of time in rehab.

He stepped back from the bed. Even if he could bring memory to that body, how could he contact Alena? He'd be dependent on Sammie for a long time. How could he expect Alena to deal with that?

It was entirely his fault that Alena had forgotten about the dose of Zamatrex she'd taken in the morning and had ended up taking an overdose. He'd been watching her for six months and not once had she ever made such a mistake. Deep down, he knew she'd never endanger herself that way, leaving her son to deal with the grief of losing his mother. He may not have been conscious of this knowledge, but the fact that her action didn't make much sense, that he kept coming back to this fact again and again, should have warned him. Thing was, he wanted her, as he had so many years ago, when he first fell. In his love for her, he pulled her energy, drained her so much that she couldn't think clearly, and she made a near-fatal mistake, something she wouldn't have done if someone else had been assigned to watch her.

The others were right. He needed to bite the bullet and learn the lesson the One had wanted him to learn. *Though who can say what the One's intentions are?* Often millennia passed before he realized he had learned something he was intended to learn.

He'd bought himself a little bit of time to think, though, being here. JJ's hospital room was a good place to hide. The others would expect him to be with Alena, or at least nearby.

He scanned the monitors. All the vitals were good, though a respirator breathed for JJ. The heart beat strongly, too. Yet JJ was no longer there.

Sammie entwined her fingers with her son's.

"They say there is no higher brain activity, Mother."

He glanced at Mary Littlehawk, the mother from his previous lifetime. She sat at the end of the bed, sewing something, picking at it with that silent single-minded focus he remembered from when he was Joe. She'd been so quiet he had forgotten she was here, too. What was that she was sewing? He moved closer. A medicine pouch? It looked like one. Indigo beads circled the top of the worn leather. A single peregrine feather pinioned the opening of the bag. Looked familiar.

"They want me to sign the forms."

"Not yet." Mary Littlehawk continued to sit at her station, face implacable, veined hands repairing the medicine pouch.

Forms? What forms? He turned and stared at Sammie. He had to shield himself more, throw up a barrier to hide from the thick grief that seethed underneath Sammie's still face and trickled through to grab at him. God, he wished he could help her.

JJ's body lay there, breathing in and breathing out, respirator hissing and clicking with each breath.

Forms. Oh. Yes. Of course. The doctors wanted JJ's organs.

Should he allow this to happen? He'd come back to the hospital room in part to hide from the others. But he'd also come to decide what to do.

He could take no memory with him when he entered JJ's body. Even though the others hadn't fully explained why, he knew this now. Entering and repairing the damage to the brain that had catapulted JJ from his dense matter form would take every bit of his attention. If the body were in better shape, he could keep his N'Aarta memory, could walk into the dense matter form and take over JJ's life as his true self, as Josael. He could do some wonderful things that way, and there was nothing that said he could not marry Alena when they were both in dense matter forms. But all of his power must go into reconstructing JJ's damaged brain. This was certain. He knew what it would take.

He'd done this before, at the time of Yeshua, in service to the first wave N'Aarta. He'd been a full angel then, able to ascend to the heavenly realms, not yet fallen. But at that time his entry into a body had been brief; he'd quickly given way to the Morekala spirit who'd inhabited the body he'd repaired. At that time, he'd worked in tandem with Yeshua.

And Lazarus had risen from his shroud.

But this...He would have to forget both his time as Joe and his true self. He didn't want to do that.

No, it was more than that.

He *hated* having to do this.

There would be no way he could remember his time with Alena.

He'd have to depend on Alena and on the lines he'd given her. This was risky. What if she just wrote him off? What if she went on her way and found a man who would give her more children? A man who was not a "walk-in," not a fallen angel who had to take over a dead man's life. Someone who was not a wayward ass of a man working in a motorcycle shop. Worse still, what if she came to him and he never made the connection, never remembered. That would really hurt her. She might begin to doubt herself, to doubt the miracle, to question her sanity.

Alena deserved better.

"Who are you to decide that?"

He started. Mary Littlehawk glowered at him. At *him*! Had he gone solid? He backed away and lowered his gaze, just as he had done when his mother had caught him lying or shooting BBs at Round Crow's old dog.

He glanced back up and met the steady glare of Mary Littlehawk's eyes. But Sammie didn't see him.

And he was Josael, third wave N'Aarta. Not one of the Primes, but a true fallen angel, nonetheless. How had he slipped; how had he fallen right back into the persona of Joe? How had the mere admonishment of Joe's mother called forth that response: shame and the desire to please?

"I'm his mother." Sammie stood and disentangled her hand from JJ's. The hand dropped onto the bed with a muted thud.

Ah. Mary Littlehawk must not be talking to him after all. But she still glared at him like she saw him.

A single tear made a shiny path down Sammie's cheek.

"Aw, Sammie-Sparrow." He reached for Joe's sister, but pulled his hand away. Didn't want to freak her out. And he surprised himself again. He'd stopped calling her by her Lakota name when they were children and had been sent to different schools.

Now Sparrow stood, back straight, as Mary—no—as *Blue Jay*, her mother, taught her. Taught him. Taught both of them.

"Well, I'll be." *Thy will, not mine, be done, Oh Lord.* Was it pride that had brought him to this place, this moment?

Blue Jay nodded her head at her daughter Sparrow. "It's your decision." She held the medicine pouch close to her chest. "Life is not meant to be easy."

"I will go and tell them." Sparrow leaned down and kissed the cool cheek of her errant son.

He looked down at JJ. This body was probably better than another Ramael might force him into. Might as well step in and save Sammie some tears. Though he'd be coming back as part Joe and part Josael. Part JJ, too, since it was JJ's body and there would be some memory tracks in his brain. God, what a mess that would be. Could he even remember how to do this? He seemed to be still caught in time, not the eternal present. It seemed so long ago when he'd last walked into a dense matter body, rather than being born into one.

"Remember who you are."

He jumped. Sparrow had left. "What the..." He reached with what essence he had left to touch Blue Jay. A jumble of images tumbled into him. He saw George—no—Short Arrow, Joe's father, and Sparrow as a young girl, daring Joe to climb the monument. The coffin of White Eagle, his own coffin, American flag draped over it, Blue Jay standing beside it as the Honor Guard removed the flag with precision, folding and handing it to her.

He had been White Eagle, son of Short Arrow and Blue Jay. Brother of Sparrow.

He slid away as Blue Jay leaned over the breathing body of her dead grandson. She hummed the song of death and rebirth. *Life is not meant to be easy.* The medicine pouch lay tucked in her hand as she brushed JJ's face with the peregrine feather. The edges of the bag were charred. It was darker than he remembered it to be.

Fire of God! It was Joe Littlehawk's medicine bag, the one he wore all the time, the one Quick Bear had given him after his Manhood Hunt. How the hell had it survived the blast in Vietnam?

Blue Jay rose, standing with her shoulders back. "Do what you were meant to do."

"For the love of..." It didn't matter to whom she spoke. He knew what he must do.

Coils of his form spiraled from his middle. He had to thrust forth his essence, the strands of pure Light that made up his Being. *First the heart.* He moved without motion. Circled without spinning. *The Universe is empty. The Universe is full.* Full and empty all at once, his Light form plunged through the layers of molecules, penetrated and raced through blood and bone, muscle and sinew, soft tissue.

He finally reached the web of synapses, neurons, and cells crushed by the massive swelling of JJ's brain. Push, push, push. Down to the atoms. He could rebuild from there. Swirling. All his immortal essence poured into this dense space. Cells responding to his force.

He recoiled. Pain! *Alena!* Everywhere. *Father, help me!* Neon pulses of blue-edged blinding white. Too much, too much. His essence shifted and sought to escape the agony that clutched him.

"No. It must be done." *Life is not meant to be easy. Get the job done, soldier*! He slammed his eternal form into the body, sent his essence deep into the electrons, protons, nuclei. Twisted some, bent others, smoothed the rest. Opened the eyes.

The EEG spiked. But the heart galloped and stuttered. Was it too much? Should he have waited for Ramael and the others to help him? He was able to look out of the eyes he'd opened.

But was that really a peregrine falcon sitting on his chest, its black eye fixed on his face? It seemed to have the weight of an elephant. The tube down his throat strangled his cry.

The EKG fluttered in time with his heart.

Chapter Twenty-Five

"Mom."

She startled. The box of Cinnamon Life slipped from her hands and crashed to the floor, popping open and spilling little squares of sugar-laced oats over her feet. "Oh, well." She bent and retrieved the box, brushing Life cereal off her toes and crunching the remains into the wood of the floor. "Here, Michael." She shook undamaged cereal into his bowl.

"Do I go to preschool today?"

"No, it's Saturday." She stood poised to pour milk. "Mommy is taking you to Timmy's house." She reached out and gave a little push on his nose with her index finger.

Michael bounced up and down, his spoon held high. "Timmy, Timmy, Timmy."

"Quiet down!" She leaned toward Michael. "Auntie Deb is still asleep."

"Did I hear a little boy shouting?" Deb shuffled into the kitchen.

"Auntie, Auntie, Auntie." The spoon went flying across the kitchen and smacked into the refrigerator.

"Simmer down, sport." Deb retrieved the spoon, dumped it in the sink, and pulled another one out. "Here." She gave Michael the clean spoon. Her feet did a crunch, crunch across the floor on her way from the sink to the table. "Ah. Good! You're not so compulsive about immediate cleaning anymore, I see. We can vacuum this later, but Alena, we do have to make sure you get a new sofa bed." She grunted as she sat opposite Michael. "I can't sleep another night on that one."

"Oh, shoot! Deb, I forgot how bad it was." She pulled up a chair and placed a cup brimming with Peet's coffee in front of her friend. "You can have my bed—it's much better." She looked closely at Deb. The older woman seemed pretty happy. She hoped Deb stayed happy after her friend heard what she had to say.

"How long am I staying?" Deb picked up the cup and held it under her nose. "Mmmm. Maybe a long time if you serve me coffee like this." She scrunched her eyes. "Okay, kid. You invited me here but wouldn't say why. What's up? I heard you go out at—" She glanced over at the clock. "—five thirty in the morning. It's Saturday, Alena. People sleep in on Saturdays, and you just got out of the hospital last month. Why out so early?"

"Mom goes to Mass," Michael chirped through a slurry of oats and milk in his mouth.

"No talking with food in your mouth, little guy." She picked up his napkin and wiped his mouth. "I'm sorry I woke you, Deb. It's just that they hold the early Mass at 6:00 AM, and I always try to make that one." She bent and scratched her ankle. "Later on, there are some people who, well, they don't like the way I look, and they're always telling me how I should dress." Her own coffee tasted like heaven; she sipped and savored the moment it gave her to conjure the nerve to ask Deb for a favor again. "Anyway, it takes about half an hour to walk over there to St. Joseph's." Damn, she wished she hadn't given up smoking. A cigarette right now would be perfect. After she got out of the hospital and came back to her life without Joe, she'd broken down and smoked several, outside on the patio. She only had one Marlboro in the pack now. Better stuff it under her underwear so she wouldn't get tempted.

"Mom-I'm-done." Michael ran the words together in a rush. "Can I go now?"

"Sure." She picked up his bowl and placed it in the sink, running water and rinsing it. "Go to your room and get your backpack. Put your pajamas and Chuckie in it."

"Yippeeee!" He shot up and skipped into his room.

"Deb, I…"

"Wait a minute, Alena." Deb held up her hand. "They don't like how you look?"

"Um, yeah. The tattoo and sh…stuff."

Deb stuck her tongue out. "Screw 'em."

She sank into her chair, dumbfounded. "Deb, you said another S word."

"So I can't swear just like anyone else?"

"Well, sure, but I never heard you swear when you were taking care of us."

"I have to be *really* provoked."

"Hey!" She gave Deb a little punch on the arm. "You like me, huh?"

"You're just figuring this out now?" Deb's eyebrow rose to her hairline as she took a sip of her coffee.

"Well, it's a cool church. They have the Mass in Latin." She stood and rustled through a pile of mail, magazines, and library books by the front door. "Here." She handed a worn volume to Deb. "I'm learning Latin. That is—" She looked away from her friend's shocked face. "I'm trying to learn it. A lot of the Roman Catholic churches use English now for the Mass, but I like to hear it in Latin." She shrugged. "It sounds more, holy and sh…stuff like that." A community college catalogue fell from the sheaf of mail and magazines Alena held. "Oh—and I plan to take a class a semester starting next year." She thumbed through it. "Might even get a degree."

"Alena."

"What?" She looked over at her friend. Deb's eyes were wide.

"I want you to savor this moment." Deb sat back and stared at her. "I'm speechless." She sat for a long moment, mouth opening and closing, but no words came out. Finally, she said, "I never thought I'd see this. My Alena Morgan going to Mass."

Her cheeks got all hot. "I'm just trying this out."

"Well, I have to say I approve. I may not be Catholic, but Alena, sweetheart, you were my last holdout, the last person I still have contact with from my days working at the youth center. The last one I still worried about." She put her elbow on the table and placed her chin in her hand. "All the rest have found spouses, jobs, or their life purpose in one way or another. But you—" She gestured toward Alena's nose ring, studs, and the caduceus tattoo circling Alena's arm. "You were always my tough punkette who didn't believe in anything."

"What?" She sat back. Was Deb kidding? "I mean, *what*?" Had she really been that bad? She looked down at her hands. "Deb, you know I spent time in a commune. We did Buddhism and stuff there."

"I know. Lots of my kids came from communes or junkie parents. You had both. But when you were placed in the center, everyone was scared of you, Alena. You were so tough even the *guys* were scared."

"No way! You've got to be kidding."

Deb just looked at her.

She placed both her hands on the table and leaned forward. "I had to be like that to survive, Deb."

"I know that, sweetie." Deb patted her hand. "That's why I hoped you'd find something to center you." She took her coffee cup and just held it below her chin. "At first I thought David would do it, and I think he did when he was alive. Then I think Michael did, but you were slipping away." She shook her head. "I didn't know what to do. I tried to give you a chance to find yourself in any way I could, but I couldn't reach you."

"But you did reach me, Deb. You always did."

Deb's cheeks pinked, but all she said was, "Look, I know you always sneered at my New Age stuff. But I have been *dying* to ask this of you." Now Deb leaned forward and peered intently into her face. "Could I please meet your ghost?" She glanced around the kitchen. "Is he here, now?"

She froze. The tears that had soaked her pillow, her tissues at work, even her goddamn hands when nothing else was available, now rose and spilled.

"Alena!"

"It's o-okay." She grabbed a napkin and mopped her eyes. "It's just that, well..." She wiped her nose and let her breath out in a long sigh. "He's gone."

"When did he go?"

"Right before I got sick."

Deb leaned back. "Tell me."

"At first it was like I told you. I could hear him and he was in my dreams."

"But?"

"He became real, Deb." She took the older woman's hand. "Real enough to touch."

"And?"

She paused. Deb looked like she knew what was coming. "We made love."

"When was that?"

"The night before I got sick."

"And he's gone now?" Deb stared at Alena. "Gone for good?"

"Completely."

Deb relaxed in her chair. "Thank God."

"What?"

"Alena, sex with ghosts or beings from, well, the 'Other Side,' isn't good. And I know it may have seemed like he was solid and real, but..."

"Michael?" Alena called out.

Deb startled, nearly knocking over her cup. "What the?"

"Can we go now?" Michael bounced out of his room.

"Soon." She gestured to Deb. "Tell Auntie Deb about Joe."

"I'm not supposed to talk about..."

"It's okay with Auntie Deb, Michael."

"Yes." Deb pulled Michael onto her lap. "Tell Auntie Deb about Joe."

"He used to tell me stories, but I couldn't see him, only with my eyes closed." The words came out in a rush. "Then he was here when Timmy's mom took me back home. He was big like a daddy and had hair like Timmy's daddy."

"Brought you back home," Deb corrected. "Did Timmy's mom see Joe?"

Michael rolled his eyes. "Everybody could see Joe then. Timmy saw him, too."

"When did he go away?"

"I don't know."

"When did you last see him?"

"Before 9-1-1 came to the house. They had badges just like police and a bed thing..."

"Stretcher. Okay, Michael, back to your room. Auntie wants to talk to your mom."

"Awwww." He scowled and stomped all the way.

"Okay, Alena." Deb stopped and looked down at her coffee cup. "Now I have something to tell you."

"What?"

"Remember when I said I would look into this?"

"God, it seems so long ago."

"Only a few months." Deb toyed with her spoon. "You've read about possession and spirits who overshadow the living in order to experience the senses?"

"I read all that." She gripped her hands

together. "That's not what Joe is."

"I don't know, Alena. What you just said worries me. I have had experiences with ghosts and guides. They can be good, you know."

"Joe was good, Deb."

Deb raised her hand. "Hear me out."

"Okay, Deb."

"For him to be able to be seen by others and to, as you say, make love to you—" Deb waved her hand. "Well, I'm not saying I don't believe you. But in order to do that, Joe must have been pretty powerful. And that worries me."

She settled back and gazed at her friend, her mentor, her idol. "He *is* powerful, Deb." She beamed a smile.

Deb tilted her head. "What?"

"He's an angel. Joe is an angel. I saw his wings, Deb."

"Holy shit." Deb's eyes were wide and round.

"That's two S words in one day."

"Well, you provoked me." Deb clasped her hands; her voice trembled a little. "I hear a lot of people who say they've seen angels, Alena. And maybe they have." One shoulder lifted. "Who can say? But I know you, Alena. You never believed in anything. And yet here you are, going to Mass, talking about an angel. Wait." She dug into the bag beside her chair. "I brought this with me." The details of Joe's death looked stark and naked on the white page. "You have proof." She shook her head. "So I believe you."

"Good." She leaned toward Deb. "Because I have to ask something from you. You see, I made a promise to him, a promise I need your help to fulfill."

Chapter Twenty-Six

Light skidded across his face. Slick air with the faint tang of disinfectant and under it, the sweet-sour shroud of illness, pushed into his lungs.

Why was it so cold? Where were the choppers? What had happened to his men!

"Unh." Why did his lips feel so…thick?

He opened his eyes and stared up at a white ceiling speckled with tiny black holes. His mouth crackled when he moved his tongue and his teeth tasted like the inside of a dumpster. A hot ache ran all the way down his side to his left foot.

"What…" He lifted his right hand. Clear plastic tubes streamed down from surgical tape. "Happened?" How drunk had he been last night? No. Wait. Hadn't he been on patrol?

"You're awake!" A woman's face swam into view. "JJ."

He knew her. "Sis?" He stared at the furrow between her brows, the deep brown eyes. Worried eyes. Scratch that. Frantic eyes, shadowed by a light of wonderment. She took his hand and held it against her cheek. Tears sparkled and brimmed in those eyes.

"Aw, Sammie." He patted the dampness on her face. "Don't cry. S'all right."

A line formed between her brows. "What did you say?"

Shit. "Ma." What had he just called her? And that was his name, wasn't it? JJ? He blinked and the room whirled. Jesus, he hurt and thinking just made it worse. "Where am I?"

"You had an accident."

"Oh, man." A low groan rumbled out of his throat. "Was anyone else hurt?" He tried to sit, but stopped when the ache down his side shot blistering torment from his foot to his armpit.

His mother just looked at him. "They said you may not remember." Each word was painstakingly pronounced. As if she was speaking to a goddamn infant, for Christ's sake!

"Was anyone else hurt?" He was on his bike, wasn't he? He'd left the tavern alone on his bike, at least, he thought he had. "I mean, I didn't hit anyone, did I?"

"No."

"That's good." He rolled his head to the side and caught her blank stare. "That nobody else got hurt." Why did she look so bewildered? "How bad am I?"

She flinched, swung her head away, and talked to the floor. "You broke some ribs and shattered your left leg." When she raised her head, her mask was on. Her goddamn iron Indian woman face.

"Shit!" *Stow that comment, soldier.* "Sorry." Damn. What's with the soldier crap? Who said that? He glanced around the room, but only his mother was there with him. Sammie...Ma didn't like cussing. She looked at him like he was some kind of alien life form, but at least she didn't read him the book on swearing, how all your words come back to you, didn't trot out a story about his Uncle Joe-who-could-do-no-wrong.

She just stared at him.

"JJ—you all right?" She plucked at the tape fastening the IV to his hand. "I mean. Well. You're not yourself." She glanced up at the IV bag. "Never mind. Guess it's to be expected."

JJ—the name didn't seem to fit, but he accepted it, took it in. He was John Joseph Parker. Sure. Yeah. He let his hand slip, and his mother grabbed it, held it tight. "You mean besides breaking my leg and—" He swallowed. "Hey—what the fu...what happened to my bike?" The memories were there now: highway careening in an asphalt blur, the intersection, the pockmarked truck with at least seven drunk-as-crap Brule tribe teens hanging out the windows and over the sides of the open flatbed. Damn drunks ran the light! "Ma?" *When I get outta this bed, I'll ki...kil...* Aw, damn.

"That's more like you." She stood and stroked his forehead. "Your bike is totaled, JJ." Another puzzled frown creased her face. "But the cops said it wasn't your fault. You swerved to avoid a truck and slammed into the signal pole."

Totaled! "Well, I couldn't ride a bike with a busted leg, could I?" Of course it wasn't his fault! What the hell did she think he was? Goddammit! *Always in my face.* He coughed. It hurt. *Always.* Damn, he wanted a cigarette.

"You just concentrate on getting better."

"How long have I been here?" Had to be at least a week. He hurt, but not as bad as he should if it had just happened. Been through *that* before. Which leg was it then? Jesus. It hurt to think, too. So why think? He shrugged. And *that* hurt, too. Double damn.

She fussed over his sheets. "About three weeks."

"What?" He lurched forward. "When can I go home?"

She pushed him back. "Cut it out."

"Huh?" When his mother spoke, her face melted, oozed into another face; her golden skin turned pale with a dusting of freckles; the deep brown-black of her eyes brightened to a gray-green; the lower lip pushed out into a luscious curve. He squeezed his eyes shut. "Did I have a head injury?" Just what he needed. Another concussion. Hey! If it was bad enough maybe that bad-ass lieutenant would send him home. What was that guy's name? Ralph? Roy? Stallone? Secret Agent Patrick McGoohan? Who the hell was he?

"You had a bad one, JJ."

"Hoo, boy. Concussion. Yeah." *Secret Agent Guy, Secret Agent Dude. They took away the name. I'm not to blame, la la la la*...Huh?

"I want you to rest." Her hand patted his arm. She stood and walked to the door.

"Wait! Mom!" What was happening to him? *Okay, I am freaked out now.* Secret Agent Lieutenant Rambo? "What happened to my head?"

She paused at the door. "You were in a coma, JJ." Her hand grabbed at the frame. "It's a miracle that you survived."

He lay back against his pillow. "Coma."

"I have to go tell your father you're awake." But she didn't leave. She still gripped the door frame. "JJ?"

"Yeah, Mom." His dad. Oh, Christ, would he be pissed. They'd worked on the bike together and now it was toast.

"What's a 'lena'?"

****

The tavern looked the same. He pushed on the door and hobbled inside. The scent of stale beer and old cigarettes clung to the walls. A long, vinyl-covered bar the color and texture of worn leather shoes stretched across the back. He rubbed at his chin. What the hell was he doing here?

"Hey, Parker! My man." Travis Beekman rose from a stool on the far side and lumbered over to him. The only other patrons this morning, a guy snoring in the back booth and a couple of women over by the window, talking about the men in their lives, didn't even look over.

"Yo, Beekman." He looked at the red blotches that dotted Beekman's nose, creeping from his mouth to his sideburns.

"C'mon." Travis took his arm and tugged him toward the bar. "Drinks are on me."

"Thanks, Trav." He disentangled his arm from the meaty fingers that held his shirt. "I'll take a rain check, okay?" He half turned to leave.

Travis blinked. "Sure, buddy. Short *visit,* huh?" He waved his hand and stepped back. "Next time." He climbed up on the bar stool. "Give me another, Chuck. C'mon now. I can pay you tomorrow."

He sighed and turned back. His cane thumped as he swung his leg about and limped over to the bar. "How many has he had?"

Chuck shook his head. "More than enough."

He took Travis by the shoulder. "Why don't we go upstairs?"

"Hey." Chuck braced both his arms on the bar. "Why don't you take him home?"

"Sorry." He gently pushed Travis away from the bar. "Gotta get the car back to my mom."

Chuck huffed and nodded. "Okay for now. Take him upstairs."

"Hey, JJ." Travis brightened. "You holding?" He slid off the stool and staggered sideways. "Sure could use some coke. I can pay tomorrow."

"You know I'm not into that crap anymore, Trav." He propelled his friend toward the stairs. "I don't deal." The narrow stairwell bristled with pushpins attached to old calendars; the firemen of New York were most prominently displayed. Phone numbers scrawled across all of the pictures. At the top of the stairs, the words "Men Suck" blared in foot-high letters on the right side. He pushed the door open. Chuck's office at the top of the stairs held the overflow of his stock under lock and key, but it also had a couch for drunks to sleep it off. Chuck was pretty much a no-nonsense guy, but he had a wife with a tender heart. She'd insisted on the couch, and he blessed her for it. He guided Travis inside. Many nights he himself had slept off a bender on this very couch.

"You used to be into a lot." Travis hung his head. "What happened to you, man? We were brothers. *Kola* and all that Sioux shit."

"I flatlined, Trav." He dropped his hand when Travis lurched to face him. "Kinda does stuff to you when that happens."

"Bummer. Hey, they give you some of that drug when you crashed, that ketamine stuff? Your old lady still works at the hospital, don't she? I can get you good bread for ketamine. No lie."

He looked at his friend. Just looked at him, but Travis backed away.

"Okay, okay." Travis rubbed at his face. "Don't be lookin' at me with that warrior face, bro. Your eyes go all weird when you do that."

"Have a seat, Trav. Just rest for a while." He leaned on Chuck's desk and watched Travis plop down on the couch. The springs squeaked as Travis's head lolled to the side, and he drew his legs up on the couch.

"Wha' happened to you?" Travis closed his eyes. "Used to be fun." His mouth fell open. Spit dribbled through his day-old beard and fell to join the wine stains on his flannel shirt.

"I know, Travis." He pulled the tattered green afghan off the arm of the couch and draped it over his friend. "Sleep well, kola." Lieutenant Nguyen would have said Travis needed a connection to his *dharma*. According to the lieutenant, people were born to purify the mind, this is the work of life, the dharma. Only then could they step off the wheel and transmute dense matter into...He blinked and rubbed his face, real hard. "Damn. Gotta keep on track." Some kind of Asian stuff again. Flashes of jungle and laughing, almond-eyed children streaked past him. “Christ on a stick!” Some of the kids were missing limbs. He looked down at Travis. His friend was twitching but seemed to be dropping off to sleep.

He let out his breath in a sigh. The docs said all this crap he was experiencing—the music coming out of nowhere, the blinding spears of light, the scenes of tanks and Quonset huts, all of these came from his brain injury. “Must have been fricking serious.” He frowned. Now that was weird, too. He’d never in his life said the word “fricking.” Recently he found himself saying it a few times a day. Found himself saying “Dang it,” too, which was even weirder.

He touched Travis’s foot. His friend didn’t move. The sounds of sloppy, regular breathing filled the room. He turned and closed the door before he navigated down the stairs to Chuck’s Bar and Lounge.

“Beekman in the usual spot?” Chuck swiped a damp rag across the top of the bar.

“How long can he stay here?”

Chuck shrugged. “Times are bad, JJ. Lots of people lost their jobs. I ain’t making what I used to.”

“So how long can he stay here?” He looked at Chuck. The older man faced his stare and didn’t blink. “Okay. How much does he owe you?” He balanced on his cane and pulled out his wallet without looking away.

“Forty bucks.” Chuck blinked and broke away from his stare. The bartender looked down at his rag. “He’s been drunk all week.”

“So don’t serve him anymore.” He pulled two bills out. “Here’s thirty. How long can he stay here?”

Chuck slapped his hand down on the money. “Noon tomorrow.” He pointed at the door. “And that’s it. You come back and take him home tomorrow.”

“Don’t give him any more booze.” He put his

hand on the bar and rubbed at the grooves he and Travis had cut into it when they were both twenty-two. "I'll come and get him."

Chuck just turned away and shoved the money into the register.

He limped out of the bar, stopped, and gazed up and down the length of the avenue at tired, defeated storefronts. Crumpled newspaper circulars scattered when the wind dipped down and then whipped in his face. He pushed the hair back from his forehead. What had he ever seen in this place? He hobbled across the street to his mother's car and climbed inside. His hands rested on the steering wheel and he spread the fingers wide. Why did his hands look different? They were too narrow. It was spooky.

He shoved the key in the ignition and the engine rumbled to life. Sometimes when he looked in the mirror, he was startled, as if he expected to see another face there. Other things looked wrong, too. He didn't know how to work his compact disc player. He knew what it was, but the shimmering plastic circles confused him. Yet his mom's old turntable was no problem at all.

He pulled out of the parking space and roared away from the street of bars and pushers. Hell, his grandmother even had to teach him how to use the microwave. He shook his head as the streets slipped by until he reached Peachtree Lane and maneuvered the car into his mother's driveway. His doctor told him all this was normal, that his brain would recover slowly. Hell, as he told Trav, he'd even flatlined. Twice.

His mother trundled out the front door and stuck her head in the car window. "Hand over the keys, JJ." She grabbed them from him, then stepped back when he eased himself out of the seat. "You're late."

"Sorry, Ma." She worked early afternoons down

at the hospital in Gordon. He chuckled as she hugged him and gave a few discreet, slow sniffs of his breath. "I'm sober, Ma." He let his grin slide all over her. She gave that satisfied tip of her head she always did when he was good.

"See ya later." She jumped in and roared off in an explosion of blue exhaust.

He ran his hand across his chin. Have to change the oil soon. Maybe tomorrow, after he deposited Trav in his friend's apartment and visited Uncle Joe's grave. He hobbled to the front door and let the screen bang into his backside as he passed through, wincing at the sting of the aluminum against his bum leg. Maybe he could skip going to the cemetery. He lifted his hand in greeting to his grandmother and slumped over to the couch. "Grandmother, how is your day going?"

She patted the seat next to her and scooted over to make space for him. "C'mon, Joe." She held the remote out. "Find me something good." The cool plastic slipped into his hand. His grandmother watched as he found the plus and minus signs over "channel." She'd had to show him how to do that, too.

He flipped through the channels until he found the news. "I'm not Joe, Grandmother. I'm JJ." She had taken to calling him Joe after he got out of the hospital. He usually let it pass, but his mom got scared if Grandmother kept it up.

"Sure you are." She popped a slice of fried bread into her mouth and chewed. "Lunch is in the microwave."

"Thanks." He struggled to his feet.

Hi mom had covered the plate with thin, clear plastic wrap. "Crap." This stuff always melted a little and stuck to the sides. He peeled it off, placed a paper napkin over the plate to keep it from spattering and punched the buttons. As the light came on and waves zapped his fish and corn, he probed his memories, pushing slow and careful, ready to scuttle back to the here and now if something spooked him.

The bell beeped. He shook his head and slipped the plate out. So many things just didn't fit, but he was still healing. Healing took time.

He rubbed his eyes as he brought the food into the living room. "Grandmother, do you want my company while I eat my lunch?"

"Always loved your company, Joe."

"JJ, Grandmother." He settled on the couch beside her. "I'm JJ." He took a bite of the fish. "Good meal."

"Your sister knows how to cook."

He chewed his corn. Just leave it. If his grandmother wanted to think he was Joe, well, she was old. Old people got notions in their head and held onto them. "The corn is fresh." His eyes were tired. Travis's father would be peeved when he dropped his friend off at his apartment. He'd have to soothe Trav's dad, so he and his son didn't get into a fight. "Grandmother, is Dad at the station?" Maybe he wouldn't go to Uncle Joe's grave. He could rest after he brought Trav to the apartment.

"Yes. Standing Elk is at work." Mary Littlehawk patted his knee. Her fingers were gentle. Her hand never hurt his leg. "Things will be better," she said. "You'll see."

Chapter Twenty-Seven

A bouquet of lilies and iris sat propped against the stone. She picked at the crumpled lower petals and settled back on her knees in the grass. Tears still seeped from her swollen eyes and burned a salt track down her cheeks, finally dripping off her chin. She could barely focus on the inscription.

Well, this was it. He was really dead. Joe was totally gone from her life.

Screw it. I'm crying again. "Shit!" she choked. "Shit shit shit shit shit..." What did she expect? She pounded the ground and bent over the ache in her gut. "Why, why, why." Why did she always fall in love with someone who went away? "You're not even here to slag me for swearing. I can say whatever the hell I want to now." The words clogged her throat. She hacked and spit. "This is scanless." She wiped her lips and sat up straight, staring at the grave. "I'd give anything for you to yell at me, Joe. Please. Come here and tell me to stop swearing. Please!" She knuckled her right eye and listened to the whispered breeze that fluffed her hair.

That was all. No *Alena, watch your mouth.* No rich chuckle. No prickling touch to the back of her neck. Maybe this was why he'd made her promise to come to his home. To visit his grave and lay everything to rest.

Gone. Joe Littlehawk was really gone. *And lost forever.*

No. That was wrong. She rubbed at her face, sniffed, and dragged a cigarette out of her mirror-embroidered bag. "I've got a hippie bag, Joe." She laughed. "I'm carrying a fricking hippie bag I bought on the Avenue. Just for you." She ran the cigarette under her nose. Couldn't smell much, her sinuses were way too clogged from crying, but it helped. "For your memory." Joe was gone, but not lost. He was somewhere, somewhere good. If he taught her nothing else, he'd shown her miracles do happen.

But there were no guarantees. She put the filter end in her mouth and let the cigarette hang from her lips as she glanced up and down the line of graves.

Joseph Senior's grave lay to her right. A tiny American flag on a toothpick stood in jaunty salute at the base of Joe's grave.

Why couldn't she stop crying? She'd been here for hours, first holding the bouquet clutched in her hands, then cradled in her lap, while tears streamed from her eyes. When she finally laid the mangled flowers on his grave, the tears were still there. She had to stop. Her flight back to San Francisco was tomorrow. If she went to pick up Michael looking like this, he would be scared of her tear-swollen face, scared she was sick again. "And you—" She took the cigarette out of her mouth. "—have to go." The smell of the nicotine and the feel of the cigarette in her mouth soothed her. "But for now..." She popped it back in her mouth. "All right. All right. This is over, I am so out of here," she mumbled, shifting her weight to stand. "Damn." The cigarette fell into her lap and rolled to the damp ground. "Now I've wrecked my skirt, Joe." Laughter gurgled into a sob. "I got it at Delphia's." The teal cotton bore streaks of grass stains and wet blotches. "I wanted to look pretty for you." But Joe wasn't here. "Only for you."

Joe died more than forty years ago. He was finally at peace, no longer a ghost, or Sacred Guardian, or whatever stupid limbo he had fallen into. She had never understood what the hell a Sacred Guardian was anyway, but she was sure Joe was at rest now. An angel with strange wings, but he had to be an angel. That would have to do. All the bull he had babbled before he left her—about her favorite music, his special song, the dance they shared—that must have been a lure of some kind to draw her to his grave and have her let it go. She had tried the lines on men ever since Joe vanished, just like he asked her to, looking for someone who would say the right words. But none had.

Well, he *had* said she was to try them on guys in South Dakota, not California, right? And she had. As soon as she entered the airport. They'd all looked at her like she had some kind of disease.

Joe had a scanless sense of humor. How the hell could she have loved him?

Okay, she'd gone to Pine Ridge, as she had promised him. But his grave wasn't there. And his family was gone, too. The taxi service she took from the airport all the way to the town of Pine Ridge waited while she searched for the Littlehawk family. When she got back in the car, the cab driver told her there was a Catholic cemetery in Gordon, and took her there. She had marched up and down the plots all morning, her feet dragging and the flowers drooping, until her glance fell upon Joe's name.

She should just get up, but her legs didn't want to move. When she shifted her weight again, the pins and needles of blocked circulation started a fresh spate of tears. The electric prickle, Joe's signature. It wasn't Joe this time, it couldn't be, but she goddamn hoped all the same. "Joe?"

A shadow fell across his grave. She sucked in her breath. *Just what I need.* "Yeah?" *Some gonzo redneck.*

"What are you doing here?"

"Hey! I have a right..." She looked up. The words died on her lips.

Clean lines of muscled legs encased in torn jeans

towered over her. Higher up, a trim waist and tucked-in red flannel shirt, topped by the broad expanse of a male chest stopped her breath. Higher still, dark eyes slanted over cheekbones to die for. The air squeezed out of her throat. There were differences. This man had dimples, and a widow's peak. His hair was a black-brown, rather than Joe's midnight locks. And his hair was longer…on one side, that is. The other side was cropped in a buzz cut. But the wide mouth was the same. He leaned on a wooden cane and smiled down at her. "Maybe you do, kid." He stopped smiling when she turned her face up to him.

Oh, man! She looked like hell. The mirrors on her bag clicked as she dug into it for her compact. And her black nail polish was chipped again. God, she really looked like hell!

"You okay?"

She abandoned her search for her compact and struggled to her feet. "No." *What does it look like*? Her legs seemed to hold. "But I'll deal."

"You can't have known my Uncle Joe." He shifted the cane to his other hand and stared into her eyes. "You're just a kid."

His Uncle Joe? Joe's nephew? She wanted to speak. Words rattled around her head in a slippery current. She opened her mouth. "Twenty-seven," was all that came out. "I was twenty-seven on Tuesday." She couldn't tell him how she knew Joe. He'd think she was fricking nuts. "I'm no kid."

"Well, happy birthday." His face stilled and he leaned back.

She stuck her arms into her jacket and shrugged it on. He didn't leave, just stood there regarding her, thoughtful and silent. She looked up into his face again and tried not to flinch.

"So how did you know Uncle Joe?"

He wasn't going to let up, was he? "My

grandparents knew him." Thank God, she'd practiced this. "In Vietnam." She groped for her story. "They were Quakers." Well, that was kind of true—her parents were. For all of ten months. "They worked in an orphanage just outside Khe Sanh." And please don't ask the name of the orphanage. She hadn't gotten that far.

"Éya." He didn't back away, though his face was wary. "So you came to pay your respects? All that kind of stuff?"

"Something like that." She glanced at the grave of Joe Senior. "Is his mom still alive?" Joe had never said anything about her.

He followed her gaze, then gripped his cane until his knuckles were white. "Grandmother?" He gave a quick nod. "Yeah—she lives with us now." His left hand stretched toward her. "Sorry, I'm John Joseph Parker." He took her hand and held it firmly. "People call me JJ." His hand was clean, but the nails were stained underneath.

"Alena Morgan." Tears made a fresh wash across her eyes. His grip was so like Joe's that she shook. The ring in her nose jiggled and felt damp. She fought the urge to rub it with her sleeve.

"I never knew him." He had Joe's voice, too, dark and rich.

Not fair! "What?" He still held her hand. His grip was solid, but the fingers were restless. Like Joe's.

"My uncle." He looked down at his hand as if it didn't belong to him. "I was born the day he died." He let go, but pulled his hand back slowly.

"Samantha is your mom?" She cradled the hand he had just released. Little shivers danced from her palm out to her fingertips. Must be genetic. Maybe all Littlehawks would have this effect on her.

God, she wanted a cigarette.

"Yeah, that's right. Sammie." He looked down.

His toe scuffed at the grass. "Well, hell, since you have this connection, I mean your grandparents and all, why don't you come out and say hi to the rest of the family?" He glanced up at her. A lock of his silky hair fell across his left eye. He shook it back in one smooth motion.

She choked and stood gasping for air while he patted her back. This was ridiculous. Every time he did something like Joe, she freaked. She had to stop this. "Yeah, sure. I'd like to meet your family." If this John Parker still wanted her to meet them. "That is, um, I'd be honored." She must look demented, face all tear swollen, then hacking like a chain-smoker. She fingered the bulge the pack of Marlboros made in her bag. Maybe later. They were her security blanket. She felt like hell. A puff or two would be in order, wouldn't it?

"Great!" A wide grin brought the dimples out of hiding and he gestured to the right. "My car is this way." When she moved to join him, he added, "Where are you staying?" His dark eyes caught her from the side.

Where you from? She shook herself. He hadn't asked that. "Near Pine Ridge in a little place called Henry's Hotel." He matched her gait with his own hobbling lope. "I took a cab out here."

"I can take you back to your hotel after you meet the family." He opened the door of a white Chevy Impala and held it while she got in. "Grandmother said after Uncle Joe died, a bunch of his buddies in the marines came to visit." The engine purred as he pulled out onto the highway. "A few of them dropped in from time to time, but they stopped visiting years ago." He shook his hair back and glanced over at her. His nose was not as long as Joe's, but his eyes, the way he held his head, the little shake he gave to get the hair off his face—all of these were pure Joe.

Genetic. Had to be genetic. "Happens all the

time." She could barely breathe, let alone speak. "People get busy and full of their lives. No time."

"You said your grandparents knew him in 'Nam?"

"He used to visit the orphanage when he could." She'd never met her grandparents. Joe had told her about the orphanage. God would forgive this lie. She was sure of it. Maddy had told her God forgives. But how the hell could she handle this in confession? *Bless me Father for I have sinned. Well, I lied about my grandparents knowing a man I knew, only he was dead and I knew him after he was dead and...*She leaned her head against the car window and let the motion rattle the earrings climbing up her right ear. "After he died, they got major sad and came back home."

"It got to them, did it?" He shook his head. "That war." His mouth now made a grim line. "One of your parents must have lived in Vietnam, too, with your grandparents." He glanced at her. "Mom or dad?"

Her stomach clenched. She hadn't thought of this. "I don't remember my mom saying anything about being in Vietnam." This was true. "She was probably in college when they were there." Lie. Her mother was shooting up in the Haight Ashbury during the war.

"He stepped on a mine, you know." He gunned the engine and passed a lumbering truck. "A pressure mine."

"I heard that."

"Yeah—he sent all his men back to a safe distance before it blew. They told Grandmother that when they came to visit."

"He was a hero. An icon."

"Huh?"

"You know, like angels and sh...stuff. Your uncle Joe was. An icon, I mean."

His left brow edged up. "My mom would love

that." Then, before she could open her mouth to ask why, he nodded and said, "Here we are." He coasted into a driveway. A compact bungalow stood behind a neat lawn. "No pink flamingos on the lawn."

"What?"

"I mean, it's probably a little tame for a city girl like you." He swung out of his side and limped over to her door, opening it with a graceful sweep.

"I like flamingos." She stumbled. He caught her arm and steadied her. No words, just the same sober gallantry Joe always showed. She straightened her back and smiled up at him. "Your house is tight, JJ." At his blank stare, she amended, "It's good." He gave her his dimpled grin again and held her arm all the way to the door. No guy did that anymore. Not for her. Except Joe. Well, of course JJ was a gentleman. He was Joe's nephew, right?

The living room welcomed her with a large sofa and two overstuffed chairs. JJ flicked open the cinnamon drapes and early afternoon light flooded the room. The scent of potatoes and onions wafted toward her. A woman sat on the sofa holding a People magazine in her lap. Two thick silver braids fell to her waist. "Ah. Who is this?"

"Grandmother." JJ pulled her toward the old woman. "This is Alena Morgan. Alena, this is my grandmother, Mary Littlehawk." Mary offered her hand and peered into her face.

She pushed her hair back. Her hand came away sticky. Dang it. "How are you, Mrs. Littlehawk?" She took Mary's hand in her clean one and pumped it up and down. "Pleased to meet you."

"Alena's grandparents knew Uncle Joe."

"Did they?" Mary looked at her from eyes that bore the shape of Joe's.

She took a deep breath. Could she do this? It seemed so simple at home. "I always wanted to hear stories about Joseph Littlehawk." Well, yeah, she did want that. "They told me some, but I bugged them for more."

Mary nodded and gestured toward the mantel over the fireplace. "There he is."

"What!" She turned to the mantelpiece. *Goddamn*! Her hand went up to her mouth. Three pictures. One large portrait in a silver frame displayed a serious-looking, short-haired Joe dressed in his uniform. Another showed a younger Joe with hair down to his shoulders and eyes sparkling, side by side with a woman that must be Sammie; she looked like a female version of Joe. He was grinning and had his arm around her. The third was just Joe looking into the camera, head tipped and a one-sided smile.

Sobs crested and broke. Her knees buckled. JJ rushed toward her and broke her fall. "What the!" He placed her on the couch beside Mary and stood rubbing his hands against his jeans, looking like he'd rather be any other place in the world. "I don't know what's wrong with her, Grandmother."

"Leave her with me, Joe."

She started. She couldn't have heard that. Mary Littlehawk wrapped a blanket around her and held her close. "Get us some tea, Joe." Mary pointed toward the arched doorway to the back. JJ shifted from foot to foot and nodded.

"Call me if you need me, Grandmother." He padded out of the room.

Of course. First he finds her sobbing over his dead uncle's grave then she collapses in his living room. "I'm not bugga-bugga. Really, I'm not. I won't hurt anyone. Honest." Her voice came out weak and thin. "I'm not crazy."

"No one here would ever say you were."

Mary's arms were plump, her shoulder soft and warm. The old woman stroked Alena's hair.

"You've got black-fire hair, girl," she said. "It

means for you, life has been hard."

"Never thought my hair caused it." So nice to melt, to let go. So nice to let someone take care of her. "Is that a Lakota tale?"

"Nah. Just this old woman's view of things." Mary kept stroking her hair and crooned a song filled with soft vowels; each verse ended in something sounding like *heh heh heh.*

She closed her eyes and listened. At some point she heard English words. "I know I had something special," Mary crooned. "I know he was only mine for a time. When he went away, I knew it would be well. I knew everything would be as it should be."

Mary fell silent. A large clock on the mantle ticked. She started to drift. *Don't get too comfortable.* She had to go back tomorrow. Her head lifted. "How old was Joe in the picture with his sister?"

Mary squinted. "Seventeen and full of vinegar."

"Vinegar?" Laughter bubbled out from somewhere. "What was he like when he was little?" She touched her lips in surprise. Could she possibly be smiling?

"He's a good boy, our Joe." Mary patted her arm. "A real cutup, but good through and through."

He is? Our Joe? The Lakota tenses must be different. "Is his sister here now?" She really *was* smiling. Mary released her and she sat up, pushing her hair back and running her palms across puffy eyes.

"No." Mary leaned forward and placed her magazine on the low table in front of the couch. "My daughter went down to the garage to have lunch with JJ's dad."

"Did I hear my name?" JJ stood in the doorway, a mug of steaming tea held in each hand. He set them both on the table. "Feeling better?"

"Yes, thanks."

"Juniper and pine." Mary sniffed the steam.

"Good medicine." She stared at JJ "How's your leg today, Joe?"

Alena started again, but JJ only tilted his head. "Still kickin', Grandmother."

The tea was warm and fragrant, woodsy and green. She let it wash across her tongue and slide down her throat. Mary must call her grandson by his middle name, that's all it meant. Some people did that. JJ sat in an overstuffed chair facing her. He looked ready to bolt, though. Kept looking at her like she was diseased. Just like the other men here when she'd tried out Joe's "lines." *Oh well, so much for the gallantry.*

"I gotta get back to my hotel." She did feel better. The fog that had surrounded her lifted. The young man sitting across from her still looked a lot like Joe. But that was cool. She could deal with that. "I can call a cab."

"No way." He lumbered to his feet and grabbed the cane that rested next to his chair. "I'll take you back."

Mary smiled up at him placed a hand on her shoulder. "Good journey, Alena Morgan."

"Maybe I can come and see you again someday." She looked into eyes as ageless as the earth. *Like never.* She'd never be able to afford another trip like this. Hell, she could barely afford this one. It was rice and beans again for her and Michael for a while. But that was okay now. It wouldn't be forever. She would cope.

"You'll be back." A triple nod shook the old woman's braids.

Chapter Twenty-Eight

The South Dakota wind yowled, thrust strands of hair into her mouth, and made the long pale grasses growing on the low hills on either side Highway 18 all shimmery. She clawed at her hair and leaned away from the open window of JJ's Impala. But that just brought her in closer proximity to Mr. Ironface JJ Parker. The minute he'd agreed to take her back, he went all silent and cold. She twisted her hair into a loose braid and endured the wind's tug on the hoop earrings studding her right ear.

"Window's broke."

No shit, Sherlock. "Yeah, I got that." So what if he thought she looked like crap and could hardly wait to get rid of her? He'd brought her to Joe's mother. She could send the old woman cards at Christmas and her birthday.

"Have to fix it before the rainy season."

"Sure thing." She glanced at peach-edged clouds scudding across the sky. "Isn't a storm coming now?" She'd lived in California so long she'd forgotten how to read weather. Nothing but fog-bank summers and El Niño winters in Berkeley. Didn't they have tornadoes in the Dakotas?

"Nope." He didn't even look out the window.

"Great." She went back to studying the landscape. "Glad to hear it." She hadn't noticed anything on the taxi ride out to the cemetery. Well, not much to notice. Just wind-flattened grass as far as she could see. Splintery poles leaned together in a spiky crisscross along the edge of the highway, then morphed into something resembling a fence. Not much there.

Not much conversation, either. JJ just drove and did the don't-screw-with-me look with his hair flooding the right side of his face and the buzz cut feathering the left. His flat black glare skewered the road. And the dude wasn't at ease in his skin. Edgy one moment and frozen the next.

Bad boy, bad boy. She knew the type. Bad boys had fricking loved her. And, oh, how they'd loved her folks. It was drug heaven to them. They always stole her mom's stash. That was good; it had saved her from flushing it. But their bad-boy energy made demands she wasn't willing to meet. *Why don't you use, Lena? Your parents do.* Crap like that.

Even when her groin got all hot and throbbing from their thrusting tongues and the scrape of studded leather across her chest, she refused them access. Well, most times she did. Hell, she was no good; she knew this. But she also knew if she gave in and hung out with any one of them, things would never change for her. It was why she'd cut and run right after her folks died, had run all the way down the path that led her to Deb. That led her to David. That led her to Joe.

The wind kicked up, slapping her face with pollen and dust. Screw this. She put her back to the broken window and faced JJ.

He was just another bad boy. She could deal with bad boys.

JJ glanced in the rearview mirror and pressed down on the accelerator.

"Why did you stay in a hotel near the rez?"

"Huh? Oh." *Careful now.* "I wasn't sure where J—where Sergeant Littlehawk was buried." *Keep your story straight.*

He just snorted and turned her way. In the fading light, the last steps of sunset, the lines of his face etched a blues riff in the air. A dark indentation in his septum puckered when he snorted again. "Right."

What? She shifted in her seat and peered into his face. There it was, a hole flaring as he turned back to stare down the highway. Dude had his nose pierced too! She fought the urge to touch the ring dangling from her own nose. Why'd he have it pierced and then not wear a ring in it? Joe had always teased her about her tattoos and studs. He's said nothing about a nephew who was a punk, complete with piercings.

Wait a minute, Alena. She did not need this. The car hit a dip and she grabbed the dash to steady. She was supposed to go to this wasteland-hick-place and say goodbye. Not hello.

The road did a loop-the-loop and a forlorn tumble of low-slung buildings blossomed up ahead. A cracked Henry's Hotel sign fronted the pinky beige plaster and stucco two-story on the right.

"Here's the place." JJ swung the wheel in a smooth turn onto the circular drive. He backed into the closest space and shifted into park. The engine coughed, then stilled.

"Thanks for driving me." She stuck out her hand.

He looked at it. "You going back tomorrow?"

"Yeah." Her hand sagged.

He took it and held on. "What time?"

"Uh. Plane leaves at ten." His skin was warm.

"Morning or night?"

The nail of his ring finger was broken. She bent over it. Broke all the way to the nail bed. "Ouch!"

"Did I hurt you?" He pulled away.

"No." She pointed at his ring finger. "I mean, that must have hurt."

"Yeah, like a bitch."

"How'd you do it?" What was *she* doing? Her

eyelids felt like raw hamburger. And goddamn, but she was hungry. So why was she still sitting talking with Ironface?

"Caught it in the chain."

"Chain."

He stretched his gimp leg as far as the driver's seat would allow and dug his fingers into the thigh, massaging it. "Yeah. Dan's T120."

"Oh." She looked away from the long fingers kneading thigh muscle. "What! You have a Triumph Bonneville?" Goddammit. Bikes too?

His eyes glinted. "Belongs to my boss." He patted his jacket, dragged out a pack of Lucky Strikes and shook it at her. "Smoke?"

God, yes. "Thanks." She plucked one and held it under her nose.

"Not in the car." He swung out his side and limped around, opened her door.

"Why not?" Just the smell of tobacco jellied her legs.

"My s—mom's car."

"Ah." She stumbled out. He caught her arm.

"I'm okay." She leaned against the car, placed it in her mouth, and sucked at it. Not Marlboro, but it would do.

"You gonna eat it or smoke it?" Rasp of a match and taste of sulfur. She looked up. JJ held it out to her, hand cupped around the flame, against the wind.

"I'm trying to quit."

"Sure." He lit his own and drew a long drag.

"I just like to taste it."

"Yeah."

"It helps."

"Does it?"

She slipped the cigarette behind her ear. "Sometimes."

He stood there watching her, head tipped, hair

swirling.

"Well, thanks again." She straightened and inched toward her room.

"Wait."

"What?"

"You're hungry."

"How'd you know?"

"It figures."

"I'm okay." Maybe the vending machine had some Cheetos or stuff. "Bye."

"No."

"What!"

"I mean, let's have dinner."

"Where?"

"I know a place."

"Right."

He flicked the cigarette into the gravel and stomped on it. "It's called Joe's Joint."

Her heart did a twirl. "You're f—kidding."

"No." He opened the car door again and pointed. "Come on now. You're starved."

"Um."

"Throw in the T120."

"What!"

He took her arm and eased her into the seat. "You just get to sit on it, okay?"

"Okay, okay." Why not? Dinner couldn't hurt. And she'd dig having a bike between her legs once again. She looked down at her wrinkled and stained skirt. "Ah, I gotta change." Stood and backed toward her room.

"I'll wait."

"Be right back." Well, she was hungry. And a T120. Dang. How long had it been? She reached the door to her room, leaned for a moment against the flaking pink paint, and glanced at JJ. Dinner and a bike. That couldn't hurt. Could it?

****

This woman had one great butt. Just walking behind her up the tired gravel to Joe's Joint kicked his groin from idle to first gear. She had this tight, black jeans wiggle as she jammed past dust-covered cinder blocks and Dave's puke-tan '78 Chevy flatbed, up to the screened door leading into Joe's.

He lay on some extra speed. Damn this stiff leg. Made him feel like a goddamn wimp. But he made it to the door before Alena, reached over her shoulder, and opened it.

She turned. "Thanks." Her eyes were gray-green. One of her ears hadn't been pierced right. The lobe was torn.

She moved into the bar and stood to the side as he entered, waiting just long enough before moving toward the seats crowding the back of Joe's, like she'd wanted to pause instead of *had* to stop to wait for her crippled date to catch up.

Damn, he liked that. Last woman he'd dated had been in his face all the time. Too bad Alena was leaving tomorrow. There was something—some words—he wanted to say to her. Something that stuck in his throat every time she turned those slate-emerald eyes on him.

Razor eyes. Like she'd been chewed up, spit out, but left still standing.

Yeah. He liked that. But damn, he couldn't remember what he'd wanted to say to her. He placed his hand on the small of her back and guided her to the table he usually took when he came to Joe's.

She slipped into the seat with a little dip. The opening riff of Hendrix's *Purple Haze* licked his ears. He gave his head a shake. The jukebox was blaring Garth Brooks. Why was this goddamn boomer music in his head? First it was Jefferson Airplane. Over and over and over. God. At least Hendrix had some good licks. But damn, he hated hippies, the whole peace-love-happiness crap. Just a bunch of wasicun, white city people sucking it up to Indians because they thought living on the land was so great. He was just a kid when they'd come streaming onto the rez. Every one of them left when they saw how the Lakota really lived. Water-stained walls, dog crap, and no toilets. Getting plastered, all piling into trucks and cars, hollering and whooping, playing chicken, barreling right at any car they encountered on the road.

"Heyyyy, JJ Parker. How's it goin' now?"

"Hey, Beekman." He ducked his head and breathed. Travis reeked of piss-stained pants but not alcohol. Not yet, anyway.

"Some night, huh?"

He lowered himself in stages, leg jutting out, hip locked in place, down down down until he hit the seat. "Night's a good one, Trav." He slung his arm over the back of Alena's chair.

She looked at him. But she didn't object.

"I'm Travis." Beekman leaned toward Alena.

He shook his head. "Didn't give me time, bro." He fished in his shirt for a cigarette. "I'd have introduced ya." He tapped the pack until one popped out. When the hell had he started smoking Lucky Strikes? "This here is Alena." He usually smoked Camels.

Alena extended her hand. Small hand. Compact fingers. Black nails. Tattoo that was mostly hidden by her shirt he hadn't noticed before. He peered at it. Looked like snakes. Well.

"Hey, there, Travis." She took Trav's hand and gave it a brisk shake.

The Garth Brooks twang died, replaced by the scrape of chairs on the scored wooden floor, voices booming off the aluminum ceiling.

"Join you for a drink?"

"This is private, Trav." He shook another cigarette out and offered it.

Travis stuck it in his mouth and lurched back from the table. “Wasicun, brother?”

“*Hau.* So what?” He drew in the smoke and leaned back, arm still slung across the back of Alena’s chair. “Doesn’t your dad want you back soon?”

Alena grasped her hands together and shifted so his arm touched her back.

“Yeah. He does. I’ll be goin’. Just not like you, bro, to taste wasicun.” Travis backed away, one shoulder hunched in a shrug. “See ya around.” He stumbled over to the bar.

“He needs a hit.” Alena looked him square in the eye. No judgment, just a bald statement of fact.

“Don’t we all?”

“Right.” Her head slanted down as she studied the menu. Her hands were square and sturdy. But the curve of her neck where she’d thrust her hair back from her face, that was fragile. “What’s with the *washeshoo*?”

“Lakota jive.”

She glanced at him; her eyes narrowed, then went back to looking at the menu.

“The steaks are high.”

She looked up; her eyes flared. “What!” Port-rich dark hair slid back into place, hiding her neck. “Stakes?”

“High-country beef.” He signaled Ralph. “Best there is.”

Her lower lip trembled but smoothed when she looked down at the menu again. “I’m fine with steaks.” And just before she turned away from him, fear and yearning skated across her face.

Ah, now what was *that* all about? “Steaks it is.” He rubbed his gimp leg. “Drink?”

“Cherry cola.” She pushed the menu over the pitted surface of the table. Crumbs of cornbread and sugar shook out of the grooves.

"You've got to be kidding."

She looked him full in the face now. "I'll tell you when I'm kidding."

He held his hands up. "Truce!"

She leaned back in her chair; the legs squealed along the floor as she moved to face him. "Are we at war?"

He glanced at the cigarette in his hand. "Just figured you for a bourbon chick." Took it in his mouth and sucked in.

A laugh shook her. "Your usual type?" She retrieved the cigarette from behind her ear, ran it beneath her nose, and breathed. "Ah."

He sat forward. "Huh?" Crushed his smoldering Lucky Strike in the tin ashtray. "Say what?" Damn. If she wasn't going to smoke, he wouldn't either.

"Usual girl a bourbon chick?"

"Maybe." He looked at her, stilling his face and hands. He let his silence lengthen and bind her. Her eyes narrowed, but she didn't look away.

"You gonna give me your order or have me find you a room?"

"Ralph, my man." He kept his gaze on Alena and drilled down into those sometimes emerald, sometimes slate eyes. "Two porters, medium rare. Baked potatoes with everything. You know, chives and stuff. Stringy beans with salt pork. Coors for me and cherry co-cola for the lady. Cheesecake for dessert. Don't spare the raspberries."

"JJ, you jerk." Ralph grabbed the menus. "We don't have chives. And forget the cheese-raspberry cake." He turned to Alena and nodded. "Sorry about that."

"Chives?" He looked up. "I didn't order chives, did I?" He glanced at Alena. "Are you okay?"

Her pale skin now had a milk-wash, her dark-red stained lips vivid against her face. "How did you know?"

"Ah." Aw damn. He'd ordered for her. Women didn't like that. "I can call him back." He swiveled to tag Ralph, but she took his arm.

"No." Some of her color came back. *If you could call it that.* Cream-rose fingers lay on his burnt sienna arm. *No color, meet a man of color.* "You got it right."

****

The T120 thrummed beneath her bottom. She gunned it and tore around the jimson weed and rutted track inside the crisscross fence JJ had breached. God, she loved this. Wind tearing at the sloppy short braid she'd fashioned, soft weight of the purpling sky anchored by the horizon, crimson-tipped wheat—or maybe just grass for horse feed—rippling all around her. She threw her head back and whooped, shutting her eyes.

And hit a ridge in the track, wheels leaving the ground and spinning. She nearly flew over the handlebars, but jammed her feet back down and hit the seat, hard, jarring her teeth and rattling the helmet, eased the bike down and rolled it to where JJ stood. "Dang it, I'm sorry." She idled it down and turned it off.

"You did fine." He paced the length of the T120, took in the wheels, the chassis, the Bad Dog pipes. "She's good." His eyes did a rapid eye movement jiggle. Was he really checking out her butt? "I ride the bikes I restore in this field. Sometimes I get wailin' and the bike goes sailin'." He shrugged and stepped away while she swung her leg over and dismounted.

She dusted her hands off on her jeans and pulled the helmet off her head. "You ever go to Sturgis?"

He gave his best Ironface nod. "In the days."

The sky had a blue-purple wash to it now, with stars spilling a patchwork over her head and winking out at the horizon. Alena drew in a breath and let it out.

"Damn fine evening." JJ smiled.

"Fu—frickin' A." She stuck her hands in her back pockets and leaned back, popping the tension out of her spine.

"Huh?" He ran his hand over the bike seat. "Frickin'?"

She shook her head. "Trying not to swear." She picked a long blade of grass from her jacket, rolled it up, and pitched it into the field. "Bad habit; new job."

He just looked at her.

"I got a new job where it's not okay to cuss."

"Ah." He nodded.

"I go back tomorrow..."

"Do you know..."

She glanced over at him. "Spoke at the same time."

"Aren't we supposed to link little fingers?"

"Huh?"

"You know, and make a wish."

She pulled her hands out and extended her right hand, pinky finger straight out. "This some Lakota thing?"

"Catholic school girls did this." He reached for her finger with his own.

"Huh?" Her heart chugged, but settled. "You left-handed?"

"Yep." He grinned and dimples blossomed. "Make a wish now."

He is not Joe, he is not Joe. Handedness must be genetic. That's all. She linked fingers and wished real hard.

He let go first.

She looked down at the furled earth. "You were going to say something."

"So were you."

"I said my thing." A bottlecap nestled next to her boot. "What were you going to ask me?"

He looked out over the field.

The wind was kicking up again. Alena watched the long hair on one side of his head whip around.

"I have this poem rocking around in my head," he said.

"Poem?"

"Thought a city girl like you might know poetry and stuff like that."

"What are the words?"

"It's kind of a song." He hummed a slow, bluesy lament. "Something like, 'I know a place where there are trees and weird berries or something.' "

Now she was cold. Her hands shook. She grabbed one with the other and held on tight. "What?" she whispered.

"Well, it's sort of like that. Weird black and crimson stuff. Something. Something." He waved his hand. "Are you okay?"

"It's a song. 'Strange Fruit.' " She cleared her throat and sang the opening words. Her voice broke. "That it?" *Ask me, dammit! Ask me where I'm from.*

He just looked at her. "Yeah." Took her arm. "I need to get you back to your room, right?"

She nodded, looking at the ground.

"Well, I have to take my dad to Pine Ridge Village anyway, so I can have him follow us to your hotel in my mom's car." He mounted the T120 and patted the back. "Why don't I take you back to my house and we can get my dad? That way you'll have a nice long ride at night on this. I'll leave the bike at your hotel. Dad always catches a ride from the other elders to go home. In the morning, Mom can take me to your hotel, and I can pick up the bike." He paused. "This baby can really wail out on the highway." He ran his hands over the handlebars.

Breath puffed out from behind her clamped-down teeth. "Yeah. Sure." She stilled the quiver at the thought of the long ride on the bike, behind him. "A little complicated, I didn't get all of it, but good." She tossed her hair. "I'd love to have another ride."

"Let's go."

Chapter Twenty-Nine

"Aw, Christ!" He slammed his palm against the cracked steering wheel, swerved, and skidded over the shoulder of Highway 18; the wheels jumped and bucked over ripped pieces of someone's blown-out tire. He twitched the Impala back on the highway and gassed it. "She didn't even invite me in."

He didn't know what to do. The refrain from the Stones' "Satisfaction" kept bouncing around in his head. He punched the button to turn on the car radio and flipped it through stations from his mom's middle-of-the-road country to KRRO all the way from Sioux Falls. "Knew that Power Antenna was a good investment." Puddle of Mud's "She Hates Me" blared out of the speakers. "Now that's more like it."

He nodded his head and tapped the steering wheel to the beat of the song. Alena must like this stuff, too. She had a Radiohead decal on the small suitcase in her hotel room. He'd caught a glimpse of it before she shut the door. "Wish she'd invited me in." He wanted to talk to her, to find out where he'd met her before. He must have met her. He knew too damn much about her, but he couldn't remember how they had met.

He sucked air in through his teeth as a Lincoln cruised past him, doing ninety. "Can't keep up with you, bro, any more than I can remember how I know this girl." Must be all the bruised brain cells. The cortex had needed repair. He'd done all the necessary work, but it needed the final touch of, of…

"Christ!" God. Why couldn't he keep it together? He kept flying apart, like someone who'd been drawn and quartered. "It's an MC Escher world, man."

Huh? "Who's that?" He knew of Usher, but Escher? Goddamn scrambled brains.

Hell, all he knew was that somehow, somewhere, he'd met this woman, dammit! He didn't know how, but he *knew* Alena Morgan. Knew what she looked like when she stepped out of the shower. Knew there was a tiny mole shaped like a heart below her left breast.

Knew the feel of her beneath him. Knew the sound that ripped through her throat when she came.

"Damn!" The Impala shimmied. His calf seized. "This is nuts." The scar that ran up to his groin and bones that were barely knit beneath the skin seared his thigh with a bright fire. He swung the wheel to the right and allowed momentum to take him into the scrub. He took the gears from second to neutral and let the engine die.

"God." He needed air. The handle stuck. He wrenched it and the door fell open.

He sat spread-eagled, aching leg stuck out, foot on the ground. His other foot sat on the runner, propping his elbow as he sunk his head into his hand. "Damn." He really pushed it tonight, taking Alena back to her hotel on the bike. Bikes used hands more than feet, but it had taxed him anyway. Hell, Alena would be going back to her life tomorrow. He didn't need to bug out. She'd be gone and that would be it. "Except for the goddamn boomer music in my ears." And that was beginning to grow on him. The opening riff of Cream's "White Room" had his good foot pounding the floor of his mother's car. "Jack Bruce, man. Incredible voice."

A drink would be good about now. Full pitcher of Coors. God, even Ba-Moi-Ba "tiger pee" would taste good.

What?

He raised his head and groaned. What's with this Chinese crap again? Well, some kind of Asian stuff. Goddamn nuts. Right. He *was* nuts. Hell.

He leaned back, grabbed his bad leg, and yanked it into the car, closing the door and settling in the driver's seat. Better get back home. Mom was working the night shift at the hospital today, filling in for one of the nurses who went off to Vegas to get married. She'd be looking for her car about now. He'd already dropped his dad off at the Hall in Pine Ridge Village. Standing Elk was an elder and took his duties seriously.

He glanced at his watch. It was time to go. His leg still screamed a little, but he could drive. He touched the key in the ignition but drew his hand back. What the hell was happening to him? Why did he want to see Alena again? Why was it so hard to leave her presence? What was it about her? His heart had leaped when she'd said "fricking" tonight. First he found himself saying it when he hadn't even heard it before, then this woman, this beautiful woman he was certain he knew, only he didn't know just how, said it. "Why doesn't she just go ahead and say the F word? Or just say nothing at all. This is nuts." Alena was beautiful, in a waif-punk way, like that rock girl with the real white-blonde hair who always wore rhinestones on her forehead, Gwen something. A beautiful woman could always turn his head; that was no lie.

He'd had scores of girlfriends. Hell, there was one he could go see right now. Lily Elltree, a tall, black-haired, golden-skinned Cheyenne who was hot for Lakota men. He could have his mom drop him off at Lily's house. Mom would do that. Oh, her mouth would go all tight, but she would take him there. He got a lot of prime karma from almost dying. Time to milk it. Lil would have sex with him six ways from Sunday. Yeah. He could dig that. Be himself again.

He stretched his arms and ran his fingers through the long side of his hair until it stood in clumps. He rubbed at the buzz cut side, glad that it was growing out. It was time he got it together and made his hair all one length. People would take him more seriously, though Lil liked it this way. She'd be surprised to see him. He hadn't gone out with her since, well, since way before the accident. Truth was, he'd been so busy with the bike shop and then, after work, with being drunk, that he hadn't dated in a long while.

That's it. He'd go see Lil. He reached for the key again, but let his hand drop before he touched it.

"Damn." Who the hell was he kidding? All he could see was Alena's face, her direct eyes, fleeting smile, that tough-fragile toss of her head. The way she looked at him when she didn't think he noticed. A look somewhere between measuring and longing, something clinical and cold mixed with hot yearning and awe, something like shocked wonder. But what the hell was she looking for? A crippled Lakota loser whose skills were repairing bikes and making his women come so many times they begged him to never stop?

He rubbed the scar on his nose. Damn thing itched. What was he thinking when he had it pierced? Looked stupid. Like he was still a kid.

Alena would have no idea what he could do in bed. She'd avoided touching him. A little skittish, like a filly that wanted to be ridden but wasn't sure she wanted this particular jockey. But oh God, did he want to be between her thighs. Not just for one night. For thousands of nights. For a lifetime of nights. He didn't want her to go back to where she lived. Who knew what kind of men she would run into there? She was just a kid. He could protect her.

He could marry her.

"Aw, shit! No way." There hadn't been a woman

born who had a lock on him, who could tell him what to do and how to do it, like his mom did with his dad. Oh, his dad loved it. Ate it up. “Not me.” Nope. No woman would put a ring through his nose. “I already did that and I took the damn thing out,” he huffed in disgust.

Now, Alena Morgan. She might try it. Maybe it would be okay. She seemed as far off the grid as he was. Anyway, she needed someone to take care of her. That tough act was sham, he was sure. He could hold her all night long, wrap his light-wings around her. Keep her warm and safe.

“Wings? What the hell?” He slammed the dash board. “I am out of here.” He cranked the engine to life, pulled out of the scrub, wheels spinning for a split second and catching the pavement. Home. He’d go home. Too damn tired to figure this all out now. That must be what was wrong with his brain. He felt split into pieces, like he was on acid or something.

Hell, he’d see Alena Morgan again. He’d left Dave’s T120 locked up and on the alarm system, parked in front of Alena’s room. His dad would be catching a ride home from his comrade, Keya, as he always did on the nights he went to the Hall. Come 6:00 AM, JJ would be sitting outside, waiting for Alena. His mom would take him to Alena’s hotel after she got off work. He’d be taking Alena to the airport. How could she refuse another ride on the T120? She’d hugged him tight, all the way to her hotel. He’d seen her face as she rammed the bike around his makeshift track, the way her eyes lit up, softened, transformed. No, that wasn’t right. Her face had been goddamn transfigured, like it was when she looked at her little boy.

Damn, damn, damn. He hit the steering wheel again, then ran his fingers over its pocked surface and the three-inch crack in the plastic as the lights of Gordon bloomed from down the highway. Why did he think she had a kid? She hadn't mentioned one. "Christ." He pulled out a cigarette and searched his pockets for matches. Came up empty. "Screw it." He held the cigarette, tobacco end in his mouth and sucked on it. "Go home, John Joseph Parker. Go home."

****

He put the vinyl record on the turntable and placed the needle in the grooves of the first song. As the beginning notes bounced out, he lowered himself onto his bed and tapped his chest in time with the music.

"Old-time boomer music" he used to call it when his mom and dad would play the records. Actually, he called it something much worse and sneered all the while. What a piss-poor jerk he was. How could his parents stand him?

"Sergeant Pepper," he crooned. Never did have a voice for songs, but he liked to sing.

A tapping on the bottom of his door had him lurching forward and picking up the arm of the turntable. Paul McCartney's tremolo squeaked and disappeared.

"God, that smarts." His leg burned all the way up, from his lunge to his feet. "Unh." He opened the door. "Is the music too loud, Grandmother?"

Mary Littlehawk lifted her cane. "The music is fine, Joe." She lumbered into the room and stood, staring around her.

"Oh." He grabbed shirts, underwear, candy wrappers, packets of condoms, and old *Motorcycle* magazines off the only chair. "Here, Grandmother." He looked up, panting. "A chair for you."

"You were always a good son." Mary placed herself in the chair and leaned on her cane, looking at him.

"How is your leg doing?" She looked right into his eyes. "It hurting?"

"Aches a bit, but it's coming along." He settled on the side of his bed. "What can I do for you, Grandmother?"

"Something else aches a lot more."

Oh, brother. "Grandmother, *owakahnige sni yelo*."

Mary sniffed and gripped her cane. "No need to talk Lakota to me. I speak better English than you speak Lakota."

He counted to ten. "I don't understand, Grandmother." He hated it when she went all obscure, like she was using smoke-signals. Grandfather used to do that too. "I just don't understand what you mean."

"You will." She nodded. "You taking that girl to the airport?"

"How did you know that?" He hadn't told anyone yet, not even Alena.

"I saw the way you looked at her. And the way she looked at you." She cracked one of her rare smiles. "It's good to help out. People must stick together." She took her cane and tapped it on the floor beside his foot. "You'll be going back to work soon?"

"Next week." He held up a hand. "Just to do desk sh—stuff, like billing, not to work on the bikes."

"Ha!" She tapped the floor again. "I saw you go by with the girl on that motorcycle. You'll be back to your old self in no time."

"If you say so, Grandmother, then it is so." He tempered the formal statement with a shrug. Grandmother liked being treated like the elder she was, but she sometimes thought his real respect was a pretense.

"I'll miss your company, son." She huffed for a moment, puffing "heh heh heh heh."

"Do you need your heart medicine, Grandmother?" He started to rise to get it for her.

"Sit down, Joe." She gave a sly smile. "I don't need the heart medicine." Her voice cracked with laughter. "You do."

He pulled a tissue out of the box next to his bed and handed it to her.

She mopped at her eyes. "You are good for me, JJ."

Ah! She finally called him by his proper designation. "*Designation*? What the hell does that mean? She called me by my name, dammit, my *name*."

She didn't seem to hear him; she just kept wiping her eyes and chuckling.

"I'm glad to be good for you, Grandmother." This was true. His Grandmother always had a soft spot for him and had intervened many times when he would have been backhanded by Grandfather. People said his grandfather used to be a great leader, but the old man had soured after Uncle Joe died.

She wadded up the used tissue and cleared her throat. "What will you do with your life now?"

"Um." It had been years since anyone had asked him that. His parents had given up on him long ago. Not that they didn't care, they just couldn't understand why he hadn't gone to college or trade school. They didn't know why the feel of a bike was so important, no, so crucial to him; they didn't realize how he knew what was wrong with a car or bike—with *any* vehicle—just by touching it and listening to it. "I want my own shop."

His grandmother just nodded.

"Well, I'll be…" He'd barely even let himself think that, let alone say it aloud. "Grandmother, Dad taught me everything about cars, and Dan taught me all about bikes." Now here he was blabbing everything to his Grandmother. He looked down at his hands. They were knotted together. "I'll learn the business end of things while I heal. Dan said he'd teach me what it would take."

"You wouldn't be able to make a shop work around here." She paused and rubbed her lower lip. "Not enough population."

He unclenched his hands and rubbed them together. "I know, Grandmother. This town has Dan's shop for bikes and Dad's for cars. Anyway, I don't want to compete with them." As much as he loved his dad and respected Dan, well, they'd eat his dust if he opened his own place and really let himself cut loose.

"Where would you go?"

"I thought maybe closer to Sturgis, you know, the racing circuit." He shrugged. "I'm too old to race now and my body was too beat up in this last spill, but I can maintain and finesse bikes so they can win."

"Sturgis is close."

"Mom would like that."

"What about you?"

He sat back. "I, I don't know, Grandmother." He'd never really thought this out. "I guess I'd want to stay close."

"Everyplace is close nowadays. You can talk on the computer."

"I mean, like, real close, physically close to Mom and Dad, and to you." He waved his hand. "As you said, people have to stick together."

"Whole world can stick together these days, JJ."

Well, hot damn. She'd called him "JJ" again. He shook his head. This was weird. He was sort of getting used to her calling him "Joe."

"Heard of cell phones?"

"Huh?"

Mary tapped the floor yet again. "Pay attention." She peered at his face.

He went all still, as Grandfather had taught

him. Best way he knew to truly listen with every one of his senses. Scent, taste, sound, sight, touch—all these could tell him what he needed to know. Which animal was best for this? Panther could go still, no movement at all, until he attacked. There. He'd become Panther and listen, as Grandmother asked of him.

He drew up and gave his head a sideways jiggle. This was all screwed up. Something was wrong. His father didn't teach that and his grandfather had turned away from Lakota ways, embittered by the fact that Uncle Joe's medicine bag had not kept him safe. It was his great grandfather who taught such things.

Something was screwy here, all right. He had never known his great grandfather.

"Cell phones and airplanes, heard of them?"

"Of course, Grandmother." Dammit. He must have heard of how to be Panther from his mom. That had to be it. But why could he see the old guy waving a feather at him? He squeezed his eyes shut. *Think.* It wasn't his great grandfather waving the feather. He opened his eyes. "Grandmother. Did you do a sacred rite over me when I was in a coma?" He leaned forward. "Did you make good medicine so I would heal?"

She shifted her weight and stretched out to take his hand. "No matter who you are or where you are, we are family. *Tiospaye.*" She dropped his hand. "Now. What you gonna do about money?"

"Say what?" He swallowed. "Sorry, Grandmother." Guess she wasn't going to answer his question, but damn, he wanted to know why all this stuff kept churning in his head. "I have a little money from the accident settlement." He traced the scar on his leg. "They weren't insured, but our insurance paid some."

"Hmmph." His grandmother put both hands on

her cane. "When you are ready." Her face seemed to cave in for a moment. "I have some money from my son."

"Uncle Joe?"

She nodded. "He sent money home when he was over in Vietnam." She rocked back and forth. "I gave some of it to Sparrow when she married, as a wedding gift from White Eagle."

He shivered. He knew his uncle's Lakota name, but people rarely said it. Uncle Joe's grandfather had given him a powerful name. Some people said Uncle Joe's Lakota name got him killed. No one should have such a strong name. "That's good, Grandmother. I'm sure Mom and Dad appreciated it."

She nodded. "I invested the rest in some good stocks."

He tipped back his head and squinted at her. "What stocks?"

She pointed a finger at him and shook it. "I got that money out! Sold all the stocks before the market went bad." She shrugged. "The world spins and time does, too. People must know these things. Cycles of plenty and cycles of want. Like in the Bible your Grandfather used to read. The seven years of good harvest and the seven years of famine."

"This is a good thing, but what are you saying, Grandmother?" Okay, Grandmother, what was the lesson here? He leaned back on his hands to decrease the pressure on his leg.

She patted his good knee. "No matter who you are or where you go, we are tiospaye." She gave a solid nod and struggled to her feet. "We are family."

He eased up and gave her his hand.

"When you are ready, there will be money there to give you a start." She moved toward the door.

"What?" He missed a step.

She squeezed his hand. "You were always a good

boy. Just needed to find your footing."

What could he say? His head was spinning before, but now, it was gyrating. "Grandmother. I thank you." He stepped back and lowered his head in respect and gratitude. That was the strangest thing of all. He hadn't often done this, bowed to an elder. Most of his friends had blown off the whole Lakota life. Many of them were dead, from fast cars and booze, or a real sharp knife drawn across a major artery.

Mary stopped at the door. "Oh, JJ." She looked back at him. "That young girl who came here today, the one you are taking to the airport tomorrow."

"Yes, Grandmother?"

"Did she say where she is from?"

"Not to me."

"Get her address for me." She moved through the door and into the hall. "So I can write to her or send her a card. Ask her where she is from. Do this for me."

"I will, Grandmother." He'd write her request down so he didn't forget. God almighty. Money for his own shop. He'd better work real hard at learning how to keep books, how supplies were bought, the profit margin for keeping a place going. He ran his hand back through his hair and grinned. Life is not meant to be easy, as Grandmother always said, but damn, if it wasn't sweet sometimes. Real sweet.

Chapter Thirty

He was somewhere cold. It wasn't winter yet, but this cold bit him right in the butt. He wasn't sure what this place was, either. It wasn't exactly snow that surrounded him, but everything was white, searing white. He tried looking at his hands, like Travis said Don Juan—or was that Carlos Castenada—told his apprentices to do when they were dreaming, but when he put his hand out, his fingers were not only as blinding white as everything else was, they looked like bundles of light fibers.

Dreaming.

"Hey, I'm dreaming!" He moved to the left and to the right. "Hell." It didn't seem to matter which way he went; it all looked the same. "Might as well fly." He tried to flap his arms, but something behind him got in the way. When his elbow knocked into whatever it was, it hurt.

He stilled. It wasn't his elbow that hurt. He reached behind him and gingerly fingered what felt like firm skin covering something like cartilage. "Ouch!" There. That was what hurt. Not his arm, not his elbow or anything else on his body. It was the thing behind him. He'd smacked it and felt pain *in* it. Like it was part of him. "How is this attached?" He spun around. Whatever was attached to him spun, too, but slow, very slow.

"Oh, I get it." He chuckled. "More light fibers." The tips of whatever was attached to him swarmed in front of him for a moment and settled behind him again. "What a dream! Maybe I can make them move." He concentrated on the fibers, first individually, then as a group. He could make them wiggle in front of him, and retreat, but nothing else.

"Oh, well." He shrugged. A *huge* shrug. "What the hell!"

He shot up, all the way through some kind of eggshell he'd been inside. Up and out into the brilliant night sky above his mother's house. He looked up. Not many clouds, and what was there was all filmy and tattered. The sky was that rich, three-dimensional black of near midnight. Stars trumpeted at him: *Look at me*! He got all giddy just staring at them and looked down to escape becoming enthralled. Below him, the neighborhood spread out in a checkerboard of roads and houses.

"Well, I'll be damned." More effects of brain cell mush, no doubt. "Hey, maybe I can go see what Trav is up to." He circled Peachtree Lane and flew out over the highway until he got used to using the light fibers, then banked to the right and sped to downtown Destiny, South Dakota. "Yeehaw!"

People stood in clumps outside Chuck's bar. Lily Elltree was there talking to her brother Carl. He hovered above them. Lily was some piece of work; he had to admit that. She was a lovely woman with long legs she knew how to use. He dipped down closer and could see her as if he really was there, in Destiny, ten feet above her.

They didn't notice him. Just kept talking. Carl smoked his Marlboro Lights. Been smoking those since their dad died of lung cancer. Lily wasn't smoking anything now, but he knew she favored weed. The hair on her arms was as black as the long hair streaming from her head. She had a haughty way of looking at a guy, head tipped back so she looked down her nose. He happened to know she did that because she couldn't wear contacts and refused to wear glasses. The only way she could focus was to tip her head back.

At one time he thought of settling down with her, but she was way too restless. Right now, he felt a deep fondness for her, warmth for all the people, Breeds, Bloods, Blacks, Asians, Latino, or Wasicun, who stood under him this radiant night. His heart swelled. "Look at all those Morekala living their lives." If only they knew how precious they all were. If only Yeshua would come forth from the Himalayas into the open, and let them know they need not fear. Yeshua never left. He would be here until the end. Alpha and Omega.

"Goddamn!" He lurched and executed a spin cycle, whirling all the way over to the other side of the street, snagging a street light to stop his trajectory before he hit Dorothy's Laundry.

"Christ." He hadn't done any Ecstasy in years. "Maybe it's true that it fries your brain cells." Just what he needed: fried brain on top of mush brain. "What the hell is going on?" It hadn't felt like the warm, empathic high he'd gotten from Ecstasy. This had felt deeper, more real, somehow. "Real?" He extended his hand again, and now it looked, well, like a hand. Some kind of a hand. He gulped and lifted it closer. It looked like a hand, all right. The hand of a statue, rock-hard. He let it drop to his side and glanced back at the people in front of Chuck's.

He had no idea if this was real or not. It seemed real, but how could it be real if he had these light-fiber...wings? "Yeah. Light-wings." At least he had something to call them.

"Who are you?"

He turned. "Man, this dream had me going there for a while; nobody talking to me and all. Hau, kola."

"Who are you?" Travis stood in front of him, blinking, eyes rounded and wide, but blinking.

"Hey, Trav." He moved toward his friend but halted when Travis dropped to the ground in a crouch and scuttled away from him. "What are you doing, man?" He pointed at his chest. "It's me. JJ. Remember? We're friends."

Travis came up against the side of Dorothy's Laundry. Light still poured out the window and the neon sign across it winked *Open till midnight—Clean your duds at Dot's, git your suds at Chuck's.* People folded laundry on the long tangerine tables inside. The door opened and warm air puffed out, hitting the colder air outside and condensing into streams of white.

"Stay away." Trav shook.

"I won't come any closer."

"You coming to get me?"

"Why would I do that, Trav?"

Travis blanched. Tears gathered in the corners of his eyes and hung there. "You mean I'm going to hell?"

"What?" Aw, damn. "No, Trav, it's me, JJ. Christ, this is just a dream, dude."

"No. My friend JJ is alive." Travis pulled himself up. "You tell me he's still alive." He advanced, swinging a bottle of Jack Daniels, three-quarters full.

"Okay, okay." He glanced behind him. People were beginning to look over. "Damn, is this one of those dreams where I try to escape and it feels like my feet are stuck in mud?"

"JJ is alive." The tears seeped down Travis's face now. He stood sobbing, the bottle sliding down in his grip.

People across the street went back to their conversations. Lily still glanced over, though.

Why did this feel so familiar? "Travis. JJ is alive. You're alive. Everything's gonna be okay." He moved forward slowly.

"You promise?"

"It will be hard, Travis. But it will be okay." He

tugged the bottle out of Travis' hand. "You're just going to sleep now."

"Sleep is good."

"How much have you had to drink tonight?" He eyed the bottle. It was missing only a couple of glasses worth. From this bottle, at any rate.

"Just this." Travis pointed at the Jack Daniels.

"Good. Now come with me."

"Where we going?"

"I'm going to take you home, Travis."

"To heaven?"

He sighed. "No. To your dad." He grabbed at Travis as his friend stumbled and gathered him up in his arms. "Get ready for this, Trav."

He shot up into the sky, Travis held tight in his arms. After an initial stiffening, Travis held still, eyes tightly closed. JJ coasted to the apartment complex where Travis shared a two-bedroom with his dad.

"Okay, Trav." He entered through Travis's bedroom window, left open most nights so Travis could come back anytime he pleased. "Now the deal is this." Travis just looked at him, eyes so wide the whites showed all around. "You will go to sleep, and when you wake up, you will check yourself into rehab, got that?"

Travis just nodded.

"It won't be easy, but you'll be successful. And, and…" He paused. "You'll become a counselor there. Yeah, you will, and you'll help a lot of people in the tribes overcome alcohol. It'll be hard, but life was not meant to be easy."

Travis looked at him.

"You got that, Trav?"

"I'll sleep and wake up and go to rehab, and it will be hard, but I'll beat it, and I'll help others beat it."

"Oh, brother." He guided his friend to the tossed

and ripe bed. "Hey, and Trav, you'll wash your sheets."

"Wash sheets."

"Go to sleep now, Trav."

Travis climbed onto his bed and soon was snoring.

He stood a moment, looking down at his friend. They'd grown up together, gone to high school together, and become raging drunks together. The only reason Travis didn't have a job and was still a raging drunk was he had a father who beat the crap out of him, while JJ had a mother and father who loved him, however he bewildered them. "There but for the grace of God." Hell. Who knew what this was all about? Maybe he should head on home. "Gotta wake up early to go get Alena."

He launched into the sky and circled, looking at the rolling expanse of the prairie. "Looks amazing up here." Hawk's eye view. *A peregrine is a little hawk.* Littlehawk was the English name the wasicun had given Uncle Joe's family in the 1880s when they did the census of the tribes. The head of the family's Lakota name, Wambli, was Eagle, but the government didn't like an Indian to be named "Eagle," so the family became "Littlehawk."

"But I'm a Parker, not a Littlehawk. My dad was mixed, with some white ancestors way back in the Revolutionary War days." His wing tips trembled.

"Why did Alena come to see Uncle Joe's grave?" It didn't make sense. He was sure she was telling the truth that she came here to see Joe's family. He just didn't believe the "why" of it.

His aimless flying had taken him out over the rez. Some dogs ran out, low to the ground, and barked at him. "Woof, woof," he barked back, but stopped when they yipped and tore holes in the earth in their desperation to get away from him. "I'm not supposed to be seen, I guess." And that felt familiar, too.

He stretched his arms up and made a long left turn, looking down past his armpit.

A mist green sign blinked "Henry's Hotel." Fake adobe pink walls enclosed ten units. The T120 stood locked up at the end of the row of rooms. Right in front of Alena's room.

He alighted. Should he go in and see her? He didn't want to spook her like he had done to the dogs. Maybe she wouldn't see him. He paced, light-wings dragging. "Ouch. Dammit." He swirled the filaments around in front of his feet and reached down to pick burrs off them. "Gotta try to remember *this* dream."

"Is this a dream? Am I dreaming?"

He looked up.

"Want some help?" Alena stooped, and carefully plucked burrs and foxtails out of the shimmering coils that made up his light-wings. She got them out like she'd been doing this all her life. "There."

"Uh." He'd just stood there watching while she did all the work. "Good job. Thanks."

She picked a filament up and stroked it.

Yow! He felt the gentle pressure of her fingers all through him.

"You get used to picking ticks, splinters, and burrs when you have a little boy."

"How is Michael doing?" He still vibrated in time with the caress of her hands.

"He's great, Joe. He misses you." She looked up at him. "I miss you." Tears made her eyes all shiny.

Hell's bells. *Just go with it, JJ.* "This is why you came here? To visit Joe's grave because…?"

She looked back down. "You know why I'm here."

He took her shoulders in his hands and pulled her in front of him. "Humor me." The minute he touched her, he started to shake. The very air around him vibrated.

"You told me to come here, Joe."

"I did."

"Well, I'm here." She tipped her head, reached up and cupped his face in her hands. "To tell you that I love you."

"I know you do."

She shook her head and smiled. "I needed to say it." She nodded and continued, "Your turn."

"I've loved you since I first came to this world, Alena Morgan." He was shaking so hard he feared he'd fly apart. "I've watched you through all your incarnations. You were the one I, I..."

Alena stood there in front of him, strong and straight.

"You were the one I loved back when I first came to this plane of existence. You were the Being I left heaven for."

"How could you think you left heaven? God is everywhere." She caressed his face again. Her touch shivered all the way through him to the tips of his light-wings. "I'm glad they let you come to me this last time. Even if it's only in a dream."

"But I'm here, Alena." He wanted to tell her everything, how he'd taken JJ's body, what she needed to do to unlock him, bring him back to himself, but all he could manage was, "My name is Josael, Alena. I'm N'Aarta." He had to show her what he'd left. The mantle of heaven. The Song of Adoration. She had to understand how important she was to him.

"Of course you are." Alena stood on her toes and touched her lips to his.

He lifted her and opened to her kiss. It was like before, he felt her; he could *feel* her. The melting, moist ache between her legs drove him mad. He broke off the kiss. "Alena, I want to show you something before, well, before I won't be able to show it to you anymore." He was having difficulty speaking. The thrumming heat from his massive erection told him *make love to her now, you idiot—what are you waiting for?*

"One times one is one, two times two is four." He took a long, deep breath. "Do you trust me?"

"Josael, don't be a fool." Something eternal sparked in the depths of her gray-green eyes. "Take me for a ride." She wrapped her arms around his neck and gave a little hop, twining her legs around his hips, just below his light-wings.

He gave a giant shrug. His wings spread to their full length.

They shot up into the star-encrusted, deep sapphire midnight sky.

Chapter Thirty-One

She sure didn't have much to pack.

Her Delphia dress was pretty much ruined, but she rolled it up and stuffed it in with her brush, shampoo, map of South Dakota, and book. She stood a moment, riffling through the pages of the paperback. "Cool. I'll read this in the airport and on the plane." She'd picked it up from the library and could hardly put it down once she started reading it. The title was *Beast*. Cool name for a book.

She slipped her plane ticket in the inner pocket of her favorite black leather jacket. The book fit neatly in her pack, but she had to jam her hair dryer in.

There. Ready to go. She flipped the short braid she'd made of her hair over her shoulder and set her bag on the bed.

Time to call a taxi and hope it didn't cost more to return to the airport than it did to come here. She reached for the phone.

Three solid knocks on her door had her backing away. "Dang it. I already paid my bill and checked out." What did they want? She hadn't made any long-distance calls, just local. "Please don't delay me," she whispered. Her plane left in four hours, but it would take a cab time to get to her hotel and time to drive to the airport. Not to mention the time it would take to go through the security check. She went to the door and eased it open, but left the safety chain on.

"Yeah?" Early morning sun slanted into her eyes. A tall man stood there. Back-lit by the sun, he was only a shadow. A shadow with pools of black for eyes. She swallowed and squinted. The face came into view.

It was Ironface Parker.

She slipped the chain and stepped out. "Hi." He looked less dangerous in the sunlight. Sunglasses hid his eyes, but his smile made him more, well, approachable. "What's up?"

"Breakfast."

"No time."

"At the airport." He stepped back and gestured toward the gleaming T120 standing behind him. "Take you there."

She gazed at the poetry of metal and leather that sat waiting for her to climb on board. Ironface just stood there. Did she really want more time with him? She'd had the most incredible, erotic dream last night. And Joe was in it. All she could remember was that they'd said their goodbyes while making love in the sky.

"Um." Just thinking about it made her all shaky. She looked back at her room. "I was just going to call a cab." The dream had left her empty and shaking. No doubt being with Ironface yesterday had prompted it. She'd not had a dream of Joe since he went away. But last night in the dream, she'd told Joe she loved him, and he'd heard her. Even though it was just a dream, she felt he'd truly heard her.

That would have to do.

JJ reached out and took her hand. "No need." He drew her to the motorcycle. "I'm here, Alena."

"What?" Her heart flipped. Hadn't Joe said that?

"I said I was here to take you to the airport, and that's what I'll do." He looked at his watch. "Time's a wastin'."

Oh. She looked at the bike, but studied JJ from the corner of her eye. He seemed less jumpy today. If she rode with him, she'd save a whopping ninety dollars in cab fare. A slow smile curved her lips. She'd get breakfast, too. Even if it they went Dutch she'd be able to splurge on some dark roast coffee. "Can we go by Wounded Knee?"

He went still. "It's a little bit of a detour, but sure. Why not?"

She looked over at him and smiled. "Just let me get my bag."

****

The hills all around were coated with long grass turning ochre. "We've been having a drought." JJ kicked at a reddish-brown rock by his foot and fingered the unlit cigarette in his hand. "Hills are usually still green this time of year."

"Where were they massacred?"

"Did Uncle Joe tell you about this?"

"What are you talking about? I wasn't alive when Joe died. My grandparents told me." She turned away and moved toward a ravine near where they'd stopped. If JJ asked more questions, what would she say? This was a bad idea. She'd better work on her story. "Ouch." A pebble had lodged in her shoe and she balanced on one foot to remove it. As she shook the shoe out, she squinted at a sign just ten feet away. "Oh."

"I guess X marks the spot." JJ nodded at the sign. It proclaimed that more than two hundred Lakota men, women, and children had been killed there in 1890. "Just how well did your grandparents know Uncle Joe?"

"Well enough, I guess." She put her shoe back on. "Wow. Look at the time! Thanks for bringing me here, JJ."

He was silent and unmoving for a moment. "Sure." He gestured back toward where they'd left the bike. "Too bad you aren't staying longer."

She'd stayed entirely too long. Long enough for

him to question her knowledge of Joe. "Yeah. Maybe I can come back sometime next year."

"Oh, yeah?" He swung onto the bike and gave her a hand to mount up behind him. "In that case, come in the spring. The Badlands are prettier then. Lots of flowers and grass."

"I'd love to see it."

"We're going right by it. You must have come past it on your way down to your hotel." He caught the kickstand with his heel, putting it up, and toed the bike away from the soft ground. "It's along a long stretch of Route 40."

"I came in at night." She was glad he couldn't see her face when she told this lie. She'd come to Pine Ridge in full daylight. At that time, she didn't care if the Grand Canyon was outside her window. She didn't care. Getting to Joe, where she thought Joe might be; that had been her goal.

"Well." He shifted and looked back at her, his smile blinding. "Enjoy the ride, then.

****

The engine rumbled underneath her; the great stretch of what JJ had called The Badlands flowed past. She rested her cheek against his warm back and looked out at stacked ridges of the buttes and pinnacles of buff, gold, cinnamon, and rose. When she looked up, she saw hawks catching the updrafts, wingtip feathers spreading in their long, spiral glide. Once she thought she caught sight of an eagle.

She'd seen none of this when she rode in the cab from Rapid City to Pine Ridge. What a goddamn shame. It was bleak, breathtaking, and dangerous. "Fricking beautiful. What would it look like from up there?"

Terrifying, and wonderful.

She stiffened.

"Huh?" he yelled over the engine's roar.

"Nothing," she yelled back. It was crazy. For a

moment there, she was sure she knew exactly what it would look like above the Badlands. Her flight to Rapid City hadn't taken her over them. Yet she knew what they looked like from a thousand feet, with a knowledge that was bone deep. Like her time with Joe, this was another mystery that most likely wouldn't be solved. It didn't merit closer examination. She'd just never know.

She set her head against JJ's back, watched the miles go by, and thought of what to say if he asked more questions.

****

The café bustled. It was close enough to the airport that it shook each time a plane took off. Weathered wood formed the walls and big plate glass windows showed a crowd that had to be near to capacity. It was just eight AM and it looked like every parking place was taken. They rolled up on the bike and sneaked it into a space next to a police car. She jumped off. "Want me to run in and see if there are any tables left?"

"Nah." JJ yanked off his helmet, but took his time getting off the bike.

"Hey, take it easy there! Let me set her up." She grabbed the bike when he almost toppled it. "You bring your cane?" She reset the kickstand and grabbed his arm to steady him.

JJ's face was a study in pain. "My bad. I left it at home."

"Here, lean on me." She took his weight as he limped to the door. "Lucky we're so close."

His effort to grin wasn't pretty. "Dirk always parks here. I park next to him."

How would he get back home? It had taken two hours to get here. "Officer Dirk, huh? He a friend of yours?" She let him get the door but continued to take a lot of his weight.

"Nope. Busted me a couple of times when I was

a kid." He nodded at the woman in charge of taking names for the waiting list. "Morning, Doris."

Doris looked her up and down before she said, "JJ Parker, you fool, you shouldn't be walking without your cane. Come on, now." She snatched two menus from the slot next to her station and took JJ's other arm.

"Doris, I can manage."

"Sure, JJ." Doris ignored his efforts to slide out of her grasp and kept maneuvering him toward a window seat.

"I can take care of him, honey." Doris's short blonde hair swung as she tugged JJ away from Alena's hands.

"Yeah, whatever." She relinquished her hold and took her seat, studying Doris as the woman fussed over JJ, helping him into his seat and dimpling at him. The woman was definitely milk-fed. Doris had the kind of peaches and cream complexion you saw in the Midwest.

She sighed and opened her menu, laying it out on the table. "I'll have the huevos rancheros and a cappuccino."

Doris stopped her chattering at JJ, mid-sentence. "What?" Her blue eyes rounded as she stared at the ring in Alena's nostril.

Keep looking, honey. She shook her hair back from her eyes, making sure all the hoops in her ears jingled and held the menu out to Doris with her tattooed arm prominent. "Huevos rancheros. Cappuccino with all the trimmings." She smiled widely, so the nose ring wiggled.

"Uh. Yeah." Doris pulled out an order form and scribbled on it. "But we don't have cappuccinos, here, sweetie, just coffee."

"Then make it coffee with cream, sugar, and cinnamon." She turned to JJ before Doris could speak. "What did you say you wanted, babe?"

His face had lost its pallor. "Same thing as the lady is having, Doris. Bring the coffee now." He looked up at the pink-cheeked Doris. "Please?" He smiled.

Doris grabbed the menus. "JJ, you fool, we don't have cinnamon for coffee." She dimpled. "Sorry, dear. JJ is such a tease. This is South Dakota, not New York City."

Alena buffed her black-polished nails. "Whatever."

Doris wheeled around and marched back to the front desk, handing the order to a waitress and talking intently to the woman, all the while glancing over at JJ.

"Think I'll get poison with my rancheros?"

"You're something else, Alena Morgan." He nodded toward Doris. "I've known her and her family for years. She's a good kid, just a little eager to get married."

"I'm sorry. I just hate it when people call me *sweetie* and get all condescending." She looked out the window.

"That happen a lot for you?"

"Not so much now, but growing up it did." She thanked the waitress who delivered the coffee and creamer. "Did it happen for you?"

"Are you kidding? I'm Lakota."

"Sorry again."

"Stop that."

"What?"

"Saying sorry when there's nothing to be sorry about." He leaned forward, a frown forming between his brows.

God! Just like Joe. She started to rise to go to the restroom, but JJ's bad leg was straight out under the table, his foot resting right next to her chair.

"Now I want you to tell me the truth." His hands splayed on the table. "How do you know of my uncle

Joe?"

She looked to the side. "I..." His leg imprisoned her. She couldn't leave the table if he asked too many questions, for fear of bumping his leg and hurting him. She should have thought of that. Too focused on Ms. Doris.

"Okay." What did she have to lose? She would be flying out of here soon, never to return. She'd miss talking to Joe's mother, but that's life. "He came to me in a dream last year." There. Put that in your coffee and drink it, Ironface.

"How'd he manage that?"

Gotta hand it to him. He hadn't missed a beat. "I was in a bad spot. He helped me out. I think some angels were supervising him."

"Why didn't you tell Grandmother this?"

"Are you kidding?"

He just stirred his coffee and stared at her.

"Look. I promised Joe."

He fixed her with a blank stare.

"Well, I went to Joe's grave, see, and I cried until I looked like Rocky Balboa or Frankenstein, and you found me there and I thought, maybe I'm trespassing, and..."

He reached right over and took her hand. "Slow down."

She took a breath and let it out. "I just didn't want you to think I was a ghoul or something. Joe helped me, he really did. I just wanted to say thanks."

"Why didn't he stick around?" His fingers were restless. "I would have."

"It doesn't work that way." She pulled her hands away from his.

"How does it work?"

"Excuse me, sir." Two platters of huevos rancheros clanked in front of them.

"God, I'm starving, are you?" She took her fork

and dug in.

"You can eat." He took a bite, and when he finished chewing, he said, "But you have to keep talking to me."

"Hey, I know what you're thinking, because I would think that, too."

"That this sounds a little crazy?"

"That, too. But I would be worried that someone who'd said this to me would be wanting money." She stabbed some ham. "Hell, you still could think that. Even if I'm not asking for money now, I could later, right?" The scallions were perfect, the ham sublime, the eggs cooked to perfection, not too dry, not too runny. There weren't enough chilies, but you can't have everything. "Well, I'll be out of your lives soon. I promise I won't contact you." She lifted a shoulder briefly, and kept eating.

"Money." He chewed and cut some more of his omelet. "That's not something I would have thought of. And why would we pay you?" He gestured with his fork. "Just what would you be selling?"

"Oh, come on!" She put her utensils down. "It's the oldest scam known. Dude pretends to speak to the spirits of the dead." She raised her hands and hummed a few bars of the *Twilight Zone* theme. "Then, of course, he can deliver messages to the bereaved." The coffee was good and strong, went down smooth, but had a kick to it. "For a fee."

"I'm aware of that. But you didn't once say you were speaking to Uncle Joe, you haven't asked for any money, you were even reluctant to tell me all this, and the man has been dead for what, forty years?" He raised his brows and shoveled some eggs in his mouth.

"Forty-one." She nodded. "Yeah."

"So why would Grandmother or my mom pay you anything?" He shook his head. "I agree that they might have right after he bought it, but not now, over four decades later."

"Psychics are still trying to collect from the Houdini family."

He gave her the blank stare again.

"Before he died, Harry Houdini left a message with his family that was coded. Any psychic that could tell the family what was in the message could collect the money he'd set aside for that." She pushed the last scallions around on her plate. "He wanted to prove that life after death was real, to the people he left behind." Damn, the back of her eyes went all hot again. "Anyway, I read all this when I was trying to figure out what was happening when Joe first came to me." She blinked away the moisture, and yipped when JJ reached over and took her hand.

"This has been rough for you, hasn't it?" His thumbs stroked her knuckles.

She shivered and gave his hands a squeeze before she pulled away again. "Yeah." Her coffee was going cold. She drank it anyway. "But I wanted to thank him."

He swallowed. "Thank who?"

"Joe."

"You wanted to thank Joe."

"It sounds stupid, but there it is."

"Doesn't sound stupid. Different. Sounds different." He lifted his cup in the air. Doris bounded over with a pot. She poured coffee in his cup, ignoring Alena's. "Leave the pot, Doris?"

"You know I'm not supposed to, JJ."

"Please." His smile would make ice melt.

"Well, for you, Parker." Doris glanced over at Alena.

She smiled at Doris, showing a lot of teeth, and watched the woman stumble in her hurry to get away. "See how bad I am?" She held her cup as JJ filled it.

"I don't know about that. You just gave her a month's worth of tales she can tell her girlfriends about the city girl who came in with bad old JJ Parker." He tilted his head toward the front desk where Doris was surrounded by a pack of equally pale, fresh-from-high-school girls who hung on every word Doris said.

"Should I have charged?"

He wrapped his hands around the steaming coffee cup. "Maybe next time."

"Won't be a next time."

"Why not?"

She traced patterns in her napkin with her fork. "First, I can't afford it. Second, I can't stay away from my son very long. Third...what?" She looked over at him when he choked. When he just waved his hand, she continued, "Third, I accomplished what I needed to accomplish here."

He coughed and wiped his eyes with a napkin. "And that is?"

She shrugged. "I said goodbye."

"Why didn't you just say goodbye when he left you?"

"He left in a hurry."

"Why exactly did he leave?"

"Why do you need to know?"

He toyed with his knife. "He was my uncle." His face was wary again, as it had been when he first saw her at the cemetery with her eyes all swollen from crying over Joe's grave. "Humor me." He leaned back. "Please."

"I don't know why he left." She gave her head a triple shake. "That is, I have an idea, but I don't know for sure." No matter what Joe had told her, it was her fault he went away. She loved him and wanted him here, with her, when God had other plans for him. She looked over at JJ. "Hey. Are you taking this all as if it is real, as if you believe it happened to me?"

"Why shouldn't I?" He snorted when she raised one brow. "Didn't Joe tell you about our people? Our beliefs?"

"We didn't really talk about that."

"Now that's strange. Uncle Joe was big into the Manhood Hunt. He did all the ceremonies and dances, too. His grandfather gave him a tough name to handle, but it was a big deal name, not like mine."

The fork she handled tore through the napkin. She swallowed. "What name?" Why hadn't Joe ever told her this?

"He was White Eagle." He looked straight at her, focused and watchful.

"I didn't know that."

He shrugged. "Maybe he didn't mention it because you are, well..."

"White."

"You're not Lakota. If you were Cheyenne or even Apache, he may not have mentioned it, either."

"You don't believe that."

He spread his hands. "Did he tell you about the Ghost Dance?"

"I read about it."

"Before or after he went away?"

"Look, just say it if you think I'm making this up." She threw the fork down and started to rise. "Move your leg, please."

"Alena." He took her arm and tugged her gently. "We have another—" He glanced at his watch. "—two hours before you need to be at the gate." He nodded at the buildings across the street. "You could even walk from here."

She resisted his pressure and stood with her hands knotted. "I'm not crazy, JJ. Joe Littlehawk came to me. And you know what? He fucking saved my life." Her eyes were going all moist again. She rubbed them with her sleeve. "I don't care what anyone thinks anymore. What I experienced was real. God handed me a miracle." She stared down at his leg, still holding her hostage. "I won't stay here and have you throw shit all over it."

"Damn, woman." He laughed but didn't remove his hand from her arm. "Sit down." When she didn't respond, he said, "Please, Alena. I'm sorry you think I'm saying you're crazy or what you're telling me didn't happen."

She wavered, looking back at him.

"And you really need to watch your mouth, Alena." He smiled.

"What!" Her knees buckled.

"You told me you were trying to stop cussing."

"Oh." She looked down at his leg again. "Right."

"Alena, I believe you. For my people, everything has spirit. Why shouldn't my Uncle Joe come to help you in your time of need? It's what he was like. He helped people. Everyone always told me that. All my life."

"You sound bitter."

He looked down, then right back at her again. "I used to be, uh, not so much bitter, but disdainful." He rubbed her arm. "I don't feel like that now."

Little tingles cascaded to her elbow. She tried to pull away and her legs folded. She thumped down into her chair. He released her arm and she reached over to hold it. Must have bumped the elbow somehow. Hot pins and needles danced all over it.

"Uncle Joe was just a guy, Alena. He wasn't an icon or a saint. He did all sorts of crap when he was young. My mom told me about him."

"He didn't tell me he was a saint."

"So what did he say?"

"He was a Sacred Guardian."

He frowned. "Never heard of that."

"My friend Deb said it was a shamanic thing. Are you saying it's not Lakota?"

"Not that I know of, but don't go by me." He turned his head toward the front desk, where Doris kept taking names or showing people to tables. "I didn't go too much into our culture."

"Why not?"

"What's your ancestry?"

She sat back, the chair jarring her spine. "I, I don't really know." Her mom and dad never told her what they were and she'd been too busy trying to survive to ask about it. "My dad's last name was Jennings. I guess that's British. I never knew my mom's maiden name." She rubbed her elbow. "When I had to give a maiden name for her to banks or stuff, I just put N-O-Y-B, none of your business, you know?"

"That's really sad, Alena." He took and squeezed her hand, shifting his leg in stages. "But I rest my case." His breath puffed out as he started to stand.

"Do you want help?" She rose and stood ready.

"I think I can manage." He leaned on the table but his color was good. "You need to powder your nose?"

"No. I'm good to go." She slung her backpack over her shoulder. "We pay at the front desk?" She dug into her pockets.

He stopped her hand before she could pull money out. "Don't be like that, now." He winked at her and shook his hair back. "I can take care of you, little lady," he drawled.

"Oh, God." She positioned herself so he could lean on her. "Your John Wayne imitation sucks, JJ."

"Wasn't doing John Wayne." He hobbled with her to the register.

"Who then?"

He paid the bill, scratched his head. "I don't know. Lee Marvin, maybe."

"Get outta here." She poked his arm.

"Thought that's what we're doing."

Chapter Thirty-Two

It truly was a short ride to the airport from the café. JJ parked the bike in a spot near enough to her air carrier that he could limp through the doors beside her, but under his own speed.

Alena looked at him as she showed her driver's license and got her ticket and gate assignment. He was a real stand-up guy, this nephew of Joe. She liked him. He hadn't turned out to be a true bad boy.

"We've got a few minutes."

"Can we sit somewhere? I want to give this leg some more time before I get on the bike to go home."

"They don't let people without tickets go to the gate anymore. There are some chairs over there." She watched as he shuffled over beside her. "Will you be okay?"

"Say what?"

"Going back home, I mean."

"I'll be fine." He sat across from her, leg stuck out but not as stiffly as it had been at the café. "I was just wondering if *you'll* be okay going back home."

"Why wouldn't I?"

"Alena, anybody could see you were all torn up about Joe, at his grave, at my mom's house." He waved his hand. "I never knew the guy. It's been forty years since he died for Grandmother and my mom." He shifted and caught her gaze. "For you, it's fresh." He looked up at the ceiling, then back. "I mean you *just* lost him, didn't you?"

"Yes, JJ." Damn, now her eyes itched. "I just lost him." She knuckled them and sniffed.

"Have you ever had someone die on you before?" He frowned. "I'm sorry; you lost your husband, didn't you?"

"And my parents." What? She hadn't told him about David. "Crap, they're calling my flight, I gotta book."

He grabbed her hand. "Wait. I needed to ask you something." With his other hand, he pulled a torn piece of notepaper out of his pocket. "I need your address."

She stilled. "My what?"

"Where you from?"

She forgot to breathe. He heart stuttered and she drew in a lungful.

"You okay?" He still held her hand.

"Berkeley, I'm from Berkeley."

He gripped harder. His eyes went dark. "Free Speech."

"Power to the People."

"We danced once. You like...Billie Holiday? Is that for real? You like vintage jazz?"

"I like prog rock, too." She was shaking. Or was that him? The loudspeaker blared. She jumped and stared at him, a long, slow moment. "That's my last call."

He seemed to grow larger, to fill out, even though his body remained the same size.

She couldn't stop looking at him, at his eyes. "Joe?"

He laughed, the same laugh as Joe. "I forget. Who thought of these lines?"

"It was you." She swallowed past a lump in her throat the size of an elephant.

"Corny." He shook his head. "What was I thinking?"

"My plane. I have to get back to Michael." She glanced at the crowd streaming toward the security check line, but didn't move.

"Forget it. I'll get you another ticket for a later flight." He wasn't shaking. His hand was steady, rock steady, like that of a statue. He pulled her gently down to sit beside him, not across from him. "Alena. My God, Alena." He reached out and stroked her cheek. It was Joe's touch and she felt it move through her. "We did it." He grasped her face and stared into her eyes. "We really did it."

"I know." She put her hands over her mouth. "I know." She couldn't stop shaking. "What happened to JJ?" Tears spilled and she couldn't stop crying. "Where is he?"

"I don't know." He looked down and nodded. "Not a bad place." He held her hands, strong and firm. "I have to be JJ to the world, Alena. I've got enough of his memories to live his life."

"How did this happen, how did you do this?"

He smiled and rubbed her arms. "I didn't do it on my own."

"Who helped you?"

"I'm looking at her."

She swiped at her face so hard she scratched her cheek.

"Let the tears fall, Lena." He folded her in his arms. "Just let them fall." God, he was warm. It was just like when his form had heated her body in bed.

"I have to admit my mother helped. She wanted me to get your address."

"What? The lines?" She pulled at his shirt and wiped her face. "Those stupid lines?"

"I needed those lines, Alena." He looked off to the side. There was a stillness to him now, a presence that was pure Joe. But also something else. Something larger. "I had to find a way to fully incarnate." He put a gentle pressure on the space between her thumb and forefinger. "I've been a real mess. Part JJ's memories, part Joe, and part me."

"What do you mean? You're somebody else too?"

He pulled her in front of him and looked deep in her eyes. She felt the weight of his gaze all the way to her feet. "You remember the dream last night? Or do you just remember seeing me in the hospital when you were sick?"

"Oh my God." Now she was cold all over. "You had wings, Joe." She let her eyes trace his face. He looked different. His gaze was sharper and more commanding. His face was more chiseled. "What are you?"

"I'm not human, Alena." He looked sad now. "Can you deal with that?" He turned her hands over. "In this body, I'm mortal, but I'm not human. There are things I'll be called upon to do. I'll always support you and Michael, but I may have to go places, or people may come to me that I must help."

"I don't know what this means, Joe." She shivered. "But you know I'm yours, right?"

He laughed and pulled her hands up to his forehead. "Yes. I know." His voice was muffled, almost near tears, but when he lowered her hands his eyes were dry. "Even though you goofed."

"Did not!"

"You forgot the Airplane, Alena." He gestured around him. "We're even in an airport and you forgot them."

"You know I hate boomer bands, Joe."

"You'll have to call me by my nephew's name from now on, Alena."

"That will be hard." She wasn't shaking anymore. "Can you tell me your real name?"

He closed his eyes briefly, then nodded and opened them. "Later. They say…"

"They? Who are they?"

"They're the others, Alena. Others like me."

"You can hear them?"

"Like you used to hear me." He gripped her hands again. "It's something we do."

"Will I be able to hear them?"

"In time, probably."

"Well, then, JJ Parker. You'd better get me another ticket. I have to get back to Michael."

His smile broke out like sunrise. "We'll get back to Michael today."

She startled. "Won't you need to go back to your folks? And what about the bike?"

He laughed. "I'm over forty, Alena. They're used to me going my own way. Oh, I'll call them, but don't worry. The man who owns the bike shop will have someone come out to pick up the T120." He looked over at a flight monitor. "There's another flight in two hours. It's to San Francisco, though."

"We can take Bay Porter back home." She touched his face. "God, Joe."

He grabbed her hand and shut his eyes tight. "I know, Alena, I know." When he opened them, they were shiny with tears. "Don't worry about anything. I've got some money saved. And Mary Littlehawk promised to help me start my own shop."

"A bike shop! Oh man!" Alena jiggled in her seat. "But I have to call you JJ, right?" She was going to be pinching herself for years, to make sure she wasn't dreaming.

"Yes."

"Okay. So what is it, then?"

"What is what?"

"JJ's name. His Lakota name."

"It's Capa. Beaver."

"Eagle is bad, right?"

"Not bad at all, just powerful."

"What about Beaver? What does Beaver do?"

He took her left hand and ran his thumb over the third finger. "Beaver is industrious. Beaver works hard and provides for his family." He dipped his head and licked at her finger. "Beaver is very faithful."

She trembled. "Oh yeah? Listen, if any of JJ's old girlfriends or any new girls come for you, I'll..." She caught her breath. He'd taken her ring finger in his mouth.

"You'll what?"

"I'll eat their faces!"

He laughed. "Then I'll have to warn them off." He pulled her into his embrace. "Alena. Will you marry this gimp-legged, uneducated Indian?"

"If you'll have a woman who spent time in Juvie Hall, with tattoos, and piercings."

"Loved those women in prison movies." He hugged her, hard. "Sounds like the deal of the century."

He pulled back. They linked hands; he leaned forward, taking her mouth.

They melded, blended, and broke apart, placing their foreheads together.

"Oh, man, Joe, uh, I mean JJ," Alena panted, "We gotta get home. To bed."

His laughter rang out. The clerks at the ticket counter looked over and shook their heads.

"Plenty of time for that, Lena."

Alena linked her little finger with the little finger of his left hand. "Promise?"

He tugged until the fingers broke apart. "A lifetime, Lena," Josael said. "A lifetime."

Epilogue

The cemetery looked the same. The jaunty American flag at Joe Littlehawk's grave still stood at attention, the fresh indigo irises in Alena's arms echoed the flowers she'd brought last year.

But these flowers rested on her belly. And his wife's belly was huge.

The Medicine Man Standing Elk had brought to sing a ceremony of remembrance stood in front of the grave, softly murmuring and crooning his song. The scent of sage and piñon surrounded them. Josael blinked as particles from the sage dusted his eyes.

"Is that too much smudging?" Alena's friend Deb looked over at him with concern. "I'll have them put it out." She raised her hand to the Wiccans she'd brought from California.

He touched her arm. "It's fine for me."

"But Alena is seven months."

He put his arm around his wife. "You okay with the sage, babe?"

Alena raised her brows. "Say what?"

"Is the sage too much?"

"It's okay." She held the flowers close to her belly. Michael held her other hand but kept tugging away. "I think Michael's bored or something, though."

Mary Littlehawk smiled at Alena. "This little child in you will be strong."

Alena flushed. "I'm glad."

He turned to Mary. "Last time we were here, you said you had something for Alena."

Mary nodded, pushing her lower lip out. "I do."

She looked at him. “You.” She put Alena’s hand in his and waited until he twined his fingers with Alena’s. “Come on, Joe. Think I don’t know my own son?”

He blinked. “Mother. How long have you known?”

She nodded at the grave. “Long enough.” Her face sagged for a moment. “JJ was a good boy, but he got lost.” She patted his hand. “It is good that you are here to make Sparrow happy and to close the circle.”

“Mom, look over there.” Michael tugged at Alena’s elbow.

“You feeling okay, champ?”

“I said look. Look at the light man!”

“Shh. Shh. Honey, there’s no street lights here.”

“Look, look! Look, JJ, look!”

He glanced over to where Michael pointed. Joe Senior’s grave was there, the stone newly washed and polished, but besides the flowers around his plot and a flag, nothing was special about it.

“You need to be quiet until the ceremony is over.” Alena ruffled his hair.

“Look.” Michael’s voice filled with tears of frustration.

Mary took the little boy’s hand and pulled him away from his mother. “Which one do you see?” she whispered.

“Big wings.” Michael flung out his arms. “Like this.” He wiggled his fingers.

Josael startled, swiveled his head, and looked over at Joe Senior’s grave. “Ah.” He nodded and tipped his hand against his forehead in a salute. “Hello, Ramael,” he whispered.

“You see the pretty guy with wings?” Mary whispered to Michael.

“Big ones.”

Josael looked down at Alena’s boy. So Michael

could see Ramael. He glanced at Alena. Should he tell her? He looked back at Ramael. The N'Aarta inclined his head and stepped aside. A form edged with light moved up from behind and stood beside Ramael.

"Well, I'll be."

The spirit of his nephew JJ peered at him and brushed the side of his head, where the kid's etheric hair still flowed in a river. He nodded and ran his fingers through his own mop of hair, all one length and barely down over his collar.

The spirit of JJ shrugged, but made a thumbs up and pointed to Alena's belly. "Thanks, nephew." He relaxed, but the kid shook his head and drifted over until he was close to Alena. Josael put his arm around her and tugged her to him.

"What is it?" She leaned into him.

"Love you." He nuzzled her ear. She went back to watching the Medicine Man and the Wiccans.

The spirit of JJ stopped in front of Alena, but looked him up and down. "Glad you like my body. How's it hangin'…Dad?" He made a motion as if he were about to dive into Alena's belly.

"Ah, Christ!" he groaned. He leaned over to Alena and whispered. "When this is over, babe, well, we've got to talk."

Mary looked at him and grinned. "The wheel turns around and babies are born, the wheel turns again and people die, the wheel turns once more and people are born all over again." She leaned toward him, Michael resting his head on her hip. "What you gonna name this baby?"

He looked at the spirit of JJ again and sighed.

"Trouble, Grandmother," he said. "A whole lot of trouble."

A word about the author...

Carolina Montague lives in Northern California with her son, who is in college. She works at a major university. Her first novel, a paranormal medieval titled *Door in the Sky*, was published in 2000, and she recently sold the rights to her story "Angel Web" in *Words of the Witches*, originally published by Berkley Jove in 2002, through Tekno Books to Sony for promotion of Sony's new E-Reader. *Sacred Guardian*, a dark angel book, is her first book with The Wild Rose Press.

Visit Carolina at www.carolinamontague.com

Breinigsville, PA USA
29 August 2010
244491BV00004B/1/P

9 781601 547149